GW00493662

Palgrave Studies in the History of Subcultures and Popular Music

Series Editors

Keith Gildart
University of Wolverhampton, UK

Anna Gough-Yates
University of Roehampton, UK

Sian Lincoln
Liverpool John Moores University, UK

Bill Osgerby
London Metropolitan University, UK

Lucy Robinson
University of Sussex, UK

John Street
University of East Anglia, UK

Pete Webb
University of the West of England, UK

Matthew Worley
University of Reading, UK

From 1940s zoot-suiters and hepcats through 1950s rock 'n' rollers, beat-niks and Teddy boys; 1960s surfers, rude boys, mods, hippies and bikers; 1970s skinheads, soul boys, rastas, glam rockers, funksters and punks; on to the heavy metal, hip-hop, casual, goth, rave and clubber styles of the 1980s, 90s, noughties and beyond, distinctive blends of fashion and music have become a defining feature of the cultural landscape. The Subcultures Network series is international in scope and designed to explore the social and political implications of subcultural forms. Youth and subcultures will be located in their historical, socio-economic and cultural context; the motivations and meanings applied to the aesthetics, actions and manifesta-tions of youth and subculture will be assessed. The objective is to facilitate a genuinely cross-disciplinary and transnational outlet for a burgeoning area of academic study

More information about this series at
http://www.springer.com/series/14579

Hazel Marsh

Hugo Chávez, Alí Primera and Venezuela

The Politics of Music in Latin America

Hazel Marsh
School of Politics, Philosophy, Language
and Communication Studies
University of East Anglia
Norwich
United Kingdom

Palgrave Studies in the History of Subcultures and Popular Music
ISBN 978-1-137-57967-6   ISBN 978-1-137-57968-3   (eBook)
DOI 10.1057/978-1-137-57968-3

Library of Congress Control Number: 2016955553

Cover illustration: © Jesús Franquis

Printed on acid-free paper

This Palgrave Macmillan imprint is published by Springer Nature
The registered company is Macmillan Publishers Ltd.
The registered company address is: The Campus, 4 Crinan Street, London, N1 9XW,
United Kingdom

ACKNOWLEDGEMENTS

I would like to express my immense gratitude to Professor John Street and to Nick Caistor for their support and guidance over the years it took to produce this book. I would also like to thank the Society for Latin American Studies for funding my second research trip to Venezuela in 2008. I thank the many Venezuelans (several of whom must remain anonymous) in Caracas, Falcón and Lara, and at Radio Comunitaria 23 de Enero and Radio Comunitaria Guachirongo, who agreed to be interviewed and were so generous with their time. In particular, I thank Oscar Acosta, José Roberto Duque, Los Guaraguao, Charles Hardy, Sol Mussett, Alí Alejandro Primera, Florentino Primera, Juan Simón Primera, Sandino Primera, Ivan Padilla, Diego Silva, Lilia Vera, Gregorio Yépez and Sandra Zapata. In Barquisimeto, Lisa Sullivan not only provided hospitality, but she also gave freely of her time and introduced me to many interesting people. In Caracas, I thank Cesar Aponte, who first introduced me to Alí Primera's music, Mirian, for looking after me so well and for so many interesting conversations, José Miguel, for his assistance and companionship during my field work, Andrés Castillo and his family, for their warmth and generosity in making so much information about Alí accessible to me, and Lil Rodríguez, whose practical help during the final stages of writing this book was invaluable. Jesús Franquis very generously allowed me to use his original photographs, for which I thank him warmly.

I am grateful to the late Dr Jan Fairley, a much missed friend whose pioneering work on *Nueva Canción* has been hugely influential for many scholars of Latin American popular music and politics.

Dr Geoff Baker and Professor Julia Buxton offered tremendously useful advice and insights, for which I thank them wholeheartedly.

I would like to thank Peter Wilks for the invaluable support that enabled me to travel to Cuba and Venezuela in 2005 to begin research for this book, Dr Lucio Esposito for the very helpful comments he made on this work in September 2013, and professor Andy Wood, for his very useful feedback at the early stages of writing.

Dr Mike Robbins has not only offered helpful comments on my writing, but he has also been a tremendous support and source of encouragement and inspiration over the years. Thank you Mike. Sarah Bowey gave me some reviews of Alí Primera's concerts which were invaluable for the writing of this book, for which I thank her. My father John, an endless fountain of jokes and amusing anecdotes about life abroad, has always kept me smiling. Finally, without my mother Mavis, I would not have found the time to complete this work; I would like to thank her for her boundless energy in caring for my children with such love and devotion over so many weekends and school holidays.

I dedicate this book with love to my children, Johnny and Esme; their affectionate attitude of total irreverence towards my research has been and continues to be a joy, and always reminds me of life's priorities.

Contents

LIST OF FIGURES

CHAPTER 1

Introduction

POPULAR MUSIC AND POLITICS IN LATIN AMERICA

On 4 February 1992, a Venezuelan colonel called Hugo Chávez, together with other officers from a movement that had formed within the military, led an unsuccessful coup attempt against the country's repressive and deeply unpopular government. Given time on national television that evening to call for the surrender of all remaining rebel military and civilian factions, Chávez assumed full responsibility for the failed attempt and announced that, 'for now', the movement's objectives had not been met. Just over two years later, as he was released from prison on 26 March 1994 having served time for his role in the failed coup, Colonel Chávez was asked by a journalist if he had a message for the people of Venezuela. 'Yes', he announced, 'Let them listen to Alí Primera's songs!'. In December 1998, having formed a new political organisation and mounted a campaign rooted in these very songs, Hugo Chávez was elected president of Venezuela with 56 % of the vote, thus becoming the first head of state without links to the country's establishment parties in over 40 years.

This book is about the dynamic ways in which music and politics can intertwine in Latin America; it explores how a popular national music legacy enabled Chávez to link his political movement at a profound level with pre-existing patterns of grassroots activism and local revolutionary thought. It is about the significance of Alí Primera's music, and collective memories of that music, in Venezuelan political life, about how and

© The Editors (if applicable) and the Authors 2016
H. Marsh, *Hugo Chávez, Alí Primera and Venezuela*,
DOI 10.1057/978-1-137-57968-3_1

why Chávez linked his political movement to Alí's music, and about the ways in which this association affected the reception of Alí's legacy in the Chávez era.

Alí Primera (1942–1985) was a *cantautor*[1] who composed and performed from within the Latin American *Nueva Canción*[2] (New Song) movement. He characterised his songs as *Canción Necesaria* (Necessary Song),[3] and though he died some 14 years before the election of Chávez, Alí and his *Canción Necesaria* were audible and visible in numerous forms in Venezuela in the Chávez period: in murals depicting a bearded man with Afro hair and a guitar or a *cuatro*[4] in his hands; in lyrics painted on bridges and walls and quoted by Venezuelans in conversation and at meetings; in paintings, photographs and home-made figures placed in public and private spaces; in newspaper articles displayed in glass cases in the National Library in Caracas; at rallies and demonstrations in support of Chávez; at street stalls where bootleg CDs and DVDs were sold; on T-shirts and badges; at community radio stations; in students' and workers' organisations named for him; on the soundtrack of independent and state-sponsored films; on *'Aló Presidente*, the weekly state television programme in which Hugo Chávez often broke into song and discussed Alí's life and actions, and in political speeches, when Chávez regularly quoted Alí Primera's lyrics and discussed their significance at length. Moreover, Alí's *Canción Necesaria* was officially endorsed and actively promoted by the state. In February 2005, on the twentieth anniversary of Alí Primera's death, the Chávez government declared Alí's songs to be part of the country's cultural heritage and a 'precursor of Bolivarianism',[5] and the Ministry of Culture funded a number of documentaries and publications about Alí Primera and his music. For Venezuelans, and notably for Hugo Chávez himself, Alí Primera's songs apparently mattered a great deal. Even when he addressed a shocked nation with the news of his cancer in June 2011, Chávez quoted lyrics from one of Alí Primera's songs as he called for optimism:

> I urge you to go forward together, climbing new summits, 'for there are *semerucos*[6] over there on the hill and there's a beautiful song to be sung,' as the people's singer, our dear Alí Primera, still tells us from his eternity.[7]

Yet in spite of the surge in international academic and journalistic attention that Venezuela attracted after the election of Hugo Chávez in December 1998, the importance of Alí Primera's songs for the Venezuelan public and for the Chávez government has been almost entirely overlooked outside the country. If Alí Primera has been commented on at all, he has tended to be referred to only in passing as a 'folksinger' or a 'protest singer' whose songs happened to be sung by *Chavistas* when they gathered to demonstrate their support for the government. Chávez's frequent singing of these songs in speeches and on television seems to have been generally regarded as little more than an amusing or entertaining aside.

Music, however, is not mere entertainment; it embodies political values, memories and feelings, and it constitutes a realm within which political ideas and social identities are asserted, resisted, contested, negotiated and re-negotiated. In the twenty-first century, Alí Primera's popular music legacy, and collectively remembered stories about his life and death, were in a unique position to serve specific and significant political functions both for the Chávez government and for the Venezuelan public. Venezuela in the Chávez era thus offers a distinctive case study of the complex and dynamic processes that render popular music constitutive of political thought and actions.

THE *NUEVA CANCIÓN* MOVEMENT IN LATIN AMERICA

Nueva Canción 'constitutes perhaps the most widespread, organised, and deliberate challenge to corporate music industry manipulation by any artistic movement' (Manuel 1988: 72). The late ethnomusicologist Jan Fairley (2013: 120) has argued that the movement produced a body of popular music which remains 'emblematic' of the 1960s, 1970s and 1980s; the songs which *Nueva Canción* artists composed and performed became part of the social struggles they were tied to, yet these songs were not merely seen as *symbols* of those struggles. According to Fairley, the very act of engaging with the songs constituted a form of social and political activism in and of itself:

> To know the songs, to hear them, to personally distribute them by sending cassettes to others, to enthuse about them to friends, became a way of participating in the struggle for social change itself. Even though this might happen at a distance, it was an act of solidarity. (Fairley 2013: 122)

For Fairley (2013: 136), the 'pervasive influence and longevity' of *Nueva Canción* in the twenty-first century is in large part due to the fact that it was never created in 'protest' at all. Arguing that the term 'protest' obfuscated what was intended because it 'offered a narrow meaning of songs before they were ever heard and led to false assumptions about hortatory or dogmatic content', *Nueva Canción* musicians and audiences embraced a broad spectrum of political parties (Fairley 2013: 124–5). This rendered the movement 'an integral expression of the complex life experience of a generation of different individuals who networked together' (Fairley 2013: 136). It was the very breadth of experience and reality articulated in and through *Nueva Canción* that, according to Fairley, allowed the movement to become identified with a generation of young people looking for social, political and economic alternatives in Latin America in the 1960s–1980s. But brutal authoritarian regimes in the Southern Cone, combined with the Central American counterinsurgencies of the 1980s, appeared by the 1990s to have largely eradicated leftist movements in the region. Moreover, the fall of the Soviet Union and the subsequent isolation of Cuba together with the electoral demise of the Sandinistas in Nicaragua in 1990 'made any talk of a viable socialism appear hopelessly romantic' at the end of the twentieth century (Webber and Carr 2013: 2). On the threshold of the twenty-first century, many assumed that the fragmentation of the political left rendered *Nueva Canción* and its associated values and ideas no longer relevant in Latin America (Fairley 2000: 369).

However, collective memories of *Nueva Canción* have played an important role in the so-called 'pink tide', a marked turn to the left in early twenty-first century Latin American politics, and the elections of several leftist governments have rendered the movement relevant in new ways. In Venezuela, Alí Primera and his legacy of *Canción Necesaria* provided Chávez with significant cultural resources with which to construct a legitimate political persona that immediately resonated with and appealed to broad sectors of society. This book does not aim to evaluate the successes or failures of the Chávez government and its policies, though I accept the evidence that in the Chávez period previously excluded sectors of the population benefitted both materially and in terms of access to social services and levels of political inclusion which had not been possible for them before (Hawkins et al. 2011; López Maya and Lander 2011). What I do argue is that while these benefits may account for continued electoral support, they do not in themselves fully explain the Chávez government's ability to create what D. L. Raby (2006: 233) refers to as 'a mutually reinforcing partnership' through which many Venezuelans acquired a 'collective identity and were constituted as a political subject'. The processes of transformation generated by the Chávez government relied not only on the redistribution of economic and material services and resources, but also on cultural politics and an engagement in work which, at a symbolic level, aimed to redefine the concepts of citizenship, democracy and the nation (Smilde 2011: 21).

UNDERSTANDING THE APPEAL OF CHAVISMO[8]

Julia Buxton (2011: x) and Sujatha Fernandes (2010: 3–4) argue that the literature on Venezuela in the Chávez period is characterised by a polarisation between supporters and opponents of Hugo Chávez, with a tendency for both sides to adopt a 'top down' focus on 'high politics' which neglects to account for popular experiences of Bolivarianism. As Alejandro Velasco (2011) shows, scholars have tended to overlook the ways in which Bolivarianism grew out of and depended upon decades of political activism among underprivileged, marginalised and leftist intellectual sectors in Venezuela. Supporters have attributed Chávez's popularity to 'the fact that the government's policies have benefitted the vast majority of Venezuelans' (Wilpert 2013: 205–6). On the other hand, opponents of the Chávez government have predominantly viewed Chávez's repeated electoral successes as a form of demagoguery or clientelism (Buxton 2011: xvii), or as the result of 'a combination of demagoguery, populism, and the provision of reward and punishment' (Wilpert 2013: 205–6). The Western press has predominantly represented Chávez as a 'false Messiah' and 'a friend of religious extremists and leaders sponsoring terrorism', who ascended to power by 'helping and utilizing the poor' and through 'consistent manipulation' (Wilbur and Zhang 2014: 564). Private television in Venezuela (and by far the vast majority of the country's television is privately owned[9]) has overwhelmingly portrayed *Chavistas* in racist terms as hordes of 'monkeys' moved by base emotions and swayed by an authoritarian leader (Gottberg 2010, 2011). The academic literature could have done more justice to the agency of the masses; instead, opponents have propagated the idea that Chávez inherited a 'tabula rasa of organisations among the poor' which he subsequently set about moulding in his own interests (Buxton 2011: xix).

Scholars have noted that Hugo Chávez, by any standard and regardless of what one thinks of his politics, 'must be regarded as an exceptional communicator' (Smith 2010: 151), and that he demonstrated an 'uncanny ability to connect with poor Venezuelans, mainly because he strongly identifie[d] with them and they with him' (Wilpert 2013: 206). This ability to connect with the poor has been attributed to Chávez's personal charisma (Syliva and Danopoulos 2010: 67), his mixed-race origins (Cannon

2008: 734), his vernacular discourse (Smith 2010: 151), and his evoking of a 'sacred history' that placed traditionally marginalised groups at the centre of the nation (Michelutti 2013: 183). Zúquete (2008) argues that Chávez's verbal and nonverbal discourses played an essential role in the development of a 'missionary mode of politics' that was intended to provide underprivileged Venezuelans with a collective identity and a sense of active participation in national affairs. Identifying himself with 'the excluded, the downtrodden, and the poor', Chávez's rhetorical style emerged 'as a natural consequence of this "popular" dimension: his language [was] plainspoken, direct, and many times, particularly when addressing the perceived enemies of his project, crude' (Zúquete 2008: 99).

Richard Gott (2005: 91–116) details how Chávez connected with the poor by representing Bolivarianism as being based on three 'ideological roots'. These roots were drawn from and resurrected the thought and writings of Venezuelan protagonists from the nineteenth century who had been marginalised or cleansed of subversive associations under previous governments; the land reformist Ezequiel Zamora, the pedagogue Simón Rodríguez and the Liberator, Simón Bolívar. Chávez was able to reinterpret the lives and thought of these figures to provide a template for a new society in ways that were deeply meaningful for Venezuelans.

However, the literature on Venezuelan politics in the Chávez period has overlooked the central role that Alí Primera's *Canción Necesaria* played in constructing political discourses and in enabling Chávez to so profoundly connect with the poor and marginalised masses. This is arguably because international scholars unfamiliar with the *Nueva Canción* movement within which Alí Primera operated have failed to recognise the historical significance of these songs for the Venezuelan public, and the importance of shared collective memories of Alí's life and music as a form of grassroots activism which Chávez was able to tap into via his references to Alí Primera.

POPULAR MUSIC AND COLLECTIVE MEMORY: A DYNAMIC APPROACH

In *Music and Social Movements: Mobilizing Traditions in the Twentieth Century*, Ron Eyerman and Andrew Jamison (1998) argue that music can act as a cultural resource which new social movements mobilise in order to appeal not only to cognitive faculties but also to emotive sensibilities. Approaching music traditions neither as inherently conservative nor as barriers to innovation or change, but as a means to connect a selected or 'usable' past with the present, Eyerman and Jamison (1998: 29) contend that when such connections are forged, existing cultural materials are melded into 'a new vision or idea of some kind' (ibid.: 38). For Eyerman and Jamison (1998: 38), social movements are central in the making and remaking of music traditions, with the ideas that motivate social-movement actors being mapped onto 'revived' traditions and articulated as much through new or re-interpreted music and songs as through 'formalised written texts' (ibid.: 42). However, Eyerman and Jamison fail to explain how and why specific songs are likely to be collectively remembered and, therefore, become available to function as cultural resources for new social movements to subsequently re-use. In locating agency predominantly with social movements as constructors of meaning, which is then mapped onto the music, Eyerman and Jamison neglect to account for the precise mechanisms that cause particular songs to remain in the collective memory while others appear to be forgotten.

To shed light on the ways in which some popular songs can be remembered and take on new meanings in temporal and political contexts other than those that originally produced them, I adopt a 'dynamic' approach to collective memory.[10] This approach conceives of memory as an ongoing process of negotiation located in 'the space between an imposed ideology and the possibility of an alternative way of understanding experience' (Radstone 2000: 18). The dynamic approach recognises the power of the present to shape (re)interpretations of the significance of the past, but also the power of the past to endure and to shape interpretations of present experiences and circumstances; it analyses the many ways in which people, both representatives of the state and members of civil society, commemorate and (re)construct the past within their communities via rituals, memorials, commemorations and artistic expression. Through representing the past to themselves and to others, social and political groups construct a sense of shared identity which makes sense of and gives meaning to both the past and the present. Thus rather than adopting a top-down focus on *Chavismo* as the dominant constructor of meaning which is then mapped onto Alí Primera's *Canción Necesaria*, I explore how these songs have been understood in changing temporal and political contexts; I examine how *Canción Necesaria* has dynamically remained in the collective memory at grassroots levels, and been used to make sense of and produce knowledge about political and temporal contexts other than those that originally produced the songs.

POPULISM AND POPULAR MUSIC IN LATIN AMERICA

Historically in Latin America, elite groups have been culturally aligned with Europe and, in the twentieth century, with the United States of America (USA) (Wade 2000). Consequently, as Raúl Romero (2001: 33) points out in his study of music and identity in the Peruvian Andes, political elites have usually shown little interest in representing other social classes, regions and cultures besides their own. As a result, state uses and co-optation of popular music in Latin America have usually been associated with populist or with revolutionary leftist governments.

Thomas Turino (2003: 170) points out that cultural and musical nationalism was not generally emphasised in the nineteenth and early twentieth centuries in Latin America, when Western art music constituted the main official music forms, because 'creating a unified population within the state's territory was not a primary criterion of the *nation*' (emphasis in original). It was the rise of populism, defined by Turino (2003: 181) as 'the attempt on the part of new leaderships to circumvent the power of regional oligarchies by tying the masses to a strengthened centralized state through concessions', which in the twentieth century led to new forms of cultural nationalism and state incorporation of the music of marginalised sectors.

The populist incorporation of regional music into national cultural styles was however, as Turino shows, generally a top-down process, which aimed to contain and control the meanings attached to those styles for the benefit of dominant elites. The process also involved constructing these genres as 'authentic' musics of 'the people' while simultaneously cleansing them of their original associations with black and otherwise 'undesirable' sectors of the population (Béhague 1994; Quintero-Rivera 1994; Shaw 1998). In his study of the personal life of the tango artist and film star Carlos Gardel and the *porteño*[11] psychology with which his persona and the lyrics he sang were imbued, Donald Castro (1998) argues that President Juan Perón's promotion of and identification with Gardel's legacy was intended to demonstrate to the masses that a poor and humble-born immigrant[12] could go from rags to riches. In this way, Castro argues, Perón used tango to tie the masses to his government's model of modernity through the promise of greater access to material wealth. The tango lyrics promoted by the government catalogued suffering, but offered no political solutions; salvation was to be found in the form of escape, alcohol, or praying to one's mother (Castro 1998: 76). Moreover, as María Susana Azzi (2002) shows, tango artists were required to belong to the Peronist party in order to secure professional employment in orchestras and bands. Castro (1998: 76) argues that the close identification of Perón with Gardel 'served the Peronista movement well into the 1970s as a vehicle for political adulation and popular support'.

Similarly, as anthropologist Hermano Vianna (1999) shows, the shifting of samba music from the margins to become a national style epitomising modern Brazilian identity was a top-down process through which the populist government of Getúlio Vargas (1930–1945) was able to exert control not only over the lyrical content of samba compositions, thereby officially cleansing the genre of its celebration of the scoundrel or *malandro* lifestyle and its association with black slave descendants, but also over the organisation of the pre-Lenten carnival with which the genre was associated.

Castro and Vianna both argue that the incorporation of tango and samba into nationally representative styles provided populist governments in Argentina and Brazil with effective vehicles for social and political control of the populations of their countries and for the consolidation of modern national identities. As such, they approach the popular musics they study as 'invented traditions', which Eric Hobsbawm and Terence Ranger (1983) conceive of as constructs resulting from nineteenth-century European governments manipulating the past in order to create an illusion of shared identity and common history for communities in the process of being incorporated into a larger society. Castro and Vianna contend that tango and samba were officially constructed as national symbols in order to promote governmental models of progress and modernity and to tie heterogeneous groups contained within the country's borders to this model.

REVOLUTIONARY GOVERNMENTS AND POPULAR MUSIC IN LATIN AMERICA

In the latter half of the twentieth century, revolutionary leftist governments in Latin America frequently incorporated local musics into nationally supported styles. Their goals were aimed at raising the social status of those masses and harnessing and promoting their revolutionary potential in order to effect the transformation of society in favour of the formerly marginalised. In his studies of state involvement in popular music in Nicaragua during the Sandinista period, ethnomusicologist T. M. Scruggs (1998, 2002a, b) examines how cultural policy was used to attempt to raise the status of the musical forms of subaltern indigenous groups in order to recast national identity and to represent in cultural form the political break with the repressive and deeply unpopular regime of Anastasio Somoza. However, Scruggs (1998) shows that Sandinista attempts to empower indigenous musical traditions meant that those traditions were ascribed value on the terms of the dominant society rather than those of the subaltern groups themselves, and he concludes that cultural political action imposed from above ultimately fails to effect changes in social status if it does not recognise and address traditional Western-influenced conceptions of cultural worth. In her study of state support for the marimba folk dance in Sandinista Nicaragua, Katherine Borland (2002) reaches a similar conclusion, arguing that indigenous communities resisted the government's representation of 'the people's culture' because they had not been invited to participate on an equal footing in its official construction.

David Hesmondhalgh (2013: 165) points out that the incorporation of the music of subordinate groups into the state's power structures can indeed involve 'dubious projections' that 'misrepresent the agency' of the musicians involved. Nevertheless, Hesmondhalgh (2013: 164) argues, we should not dismiss all attempts to link music to national identity as regressive; the processes by which popular musics cross from the margins to become officially endorsed styles are, writes Hesmondhalgh (2013: 162), 'too complex to be interpreted either as a counter-hegemonic triumph or an appropriation of people's music by business and the state'. The official incorporation of previously maligned forms of popular culture in post-revolutionary Cuba highlights these complexities. Clive Kronenberg (2011) attributes the triumph and continuity of the Cuban revolution in large part to its success in linking political and cultural practice, and similarly Nicola Miller (2008) argues that culture has been a key element in the revolution's construction of an alternative model of modernity, distinct not only from the Western capitalist version but also from that promoted by the Soviet Union. However, relations between the state and artists in post-revolutionary Cuba have often been characterised by tensions and contradictions, which scholars have interpreted in different ways.

In her essay on the Cuban hip hop band Los Aldeanos, Nora Gámez Torres (2013: 12–13) argues that the Cuban state has deployed a variety of strategies to counteract critical music, the most important being censorship, policies of strong marginalisation and assimilation, or 'cultural appropriation' which she describes, borrowing from a study of rock music and counterculture in Russia, as being 'a process "whereby the cultural practices ... which threaten to disrupt the *status quo* ... are attended to and transformed through direct intervention by elites with the end of defusing their social transformative power"' (Cushman 1991: 19, cited in Gámez Torres 2013: 13). However, the extent to which Cuban state appropriation of critical cultural forms results in those forms losing their social transformative power is a disputed matter. Indeed, in contrast to Gámez Torres, Lauren Shaw (2008: 571) argues that Cuban musicians 'have had substantial success at finding ways to subvert institutional control while taking advantage of the support that is offered'. It is likely that many observers' assessments of the impact of state involvement in the cultural sphere in Cuba are influenced in large part by their political perspectives vis-à-vis the Castro government.

In his studies of hip hop in contemporary Cuba, ethnomusicologist Geoff Baker (2011a, b, 2012) argues that censorship is not a monolithic weapon of ideological control, but that artists engage dynamically with state structures and indeed that Los Aldeanos, far from being silenced by state policy, 'have built an international reputation on the idea that they are fighting censorship' while their work 'pours out' and they benefit from the professed suffering 'in terms of their cultural capital' (Baker 2011b: 32). In Cuba, Baker (2011a: 102) illustrates, state incorporation of hip hop does not automatically neutralise its capacity to convey critical ideas:

> the nationalisation of protest music has not entailed the purging of resistant elements, but instead the highlighting of facets that correlate to the ideology of what may be considered a protest state, since Cuba has institutionalised the notion of resistance

Baker (2011b: 12) argues that underground musicians in Cuba do not simply resist or capitulate, but that instead they continually test the limits; while critics of Castro's Cuba tend to see censorship 'everywhere', Baker (2011b: 3) shows how artists in fact face a complex mix of restrictions and openings regarding their work.

NUEVA CANCIÓN, COLLECTIVE MEMORY AND THE CHÁVEZ GOVERNMENT

Latin America is a region characterised by a shared history of slavery, colonialism, racism, class oppression, dictatorship and authoritarianism, resistance, imperialism and neo-colonialism. The persistence of economic and social injustice means that Latin Americans tend to remember the past in more conflicting ways than do inhabitants of the developed countries, which are more likely to be 'constructed unambiguously by history's winners' (Johnson 2004: xvi). In most of Latin America, no single group has emerged as 'history's winners', or achieved political or cultural hegemony for any significant length of time (García Canclini 1992: 17).

The music of marginalised populations in the region has at times been institutionalised by populist governments seeking to unify and link formerly disenfranchised groups to the nation-state in order to achieve or maintain mass support. However, these efforts have been implemented by state authorities in order to contain and control those marginalised groups and tie them to national modernist projects, and governments have tended to purge the music of any associations with resistance or with oppositional ideas (Manuel 1988; Plesch 2013; Turino 2003; Vianna 1999). Revolutionary leftist governments have also sought to incorporate the music of marginalised groups into state structures in order to raise the official status of lower class, indigenous, black and mixed-race populations and to construct national cultural identities standing in opposition to capitalist commercial values and to US influence. However, these efforts have tended to be top-down and have frequently excluded the very people the state sought to include by imposing middle-class definitions of cultural worth which subordinated and marginalised sectors failed to recognise as their own (Miller 2008; Moore 2006; Scruggs 2002a, b).

The literature on populist and on revolutionary leftist state uses of popular music in Latin America does not shed light on the precise motivations and mechanisms lying behind the Chávez government's official identification with *Canción Necesaria*; the Chávez government did not seek to purge Alí Primera's music of its associations with the poor, mixed-race masses, but instead highlighted and celebrated the resistant properties already associated with that music. Moreover, the Chávez government did not invent or impose from above the links between *Nueva Canción* and the interests of 'the people'; those links had already been forged by a generation of leftist *cantautores* in the 1960s–1980s.

The key to understanding why the Chávez government tapped into Alí Primera's music legacy in the twenty-first century lies in understanding how and why this particular body of song came to occupy a unique position within the Venezuelan collective memory in the late 1980s and early 1990s. It was this unique position, already acquired outside official state structures, which rendered Alí's *Canción Necesaria* of particular use to Chávez and his political movement at that time. I will, therefore, explore how Alí's popular songs acquired meaning and were used and understood within Venezuelan civil society *before* Chávez linked his political movement to them. I approach the Chávez government's promotion of Alí's legacy not as an 'invented tradition'; instead, I will adopt a dynamic approach to memory in order to elucidate the precise functions that the legacy of *Canción Necesaria* served for Chávez and his political movement, and what it was that the Chávez government aimed to achieve through officially supporting this particular body of song and linking itself to the qualities *already* associated with these songs outside state structures and within the collective memory. Finally, I will examine how the state institutionalisation of Alí's popular music legacy gave rise to competing and conflicting public uses of that music as Venezuelans asserted, defended or challenged the state's legitimacy as official 'interpreter' of the music's meaning and value.

STRUCTURE OF THE BOOK

Popular music has the enduring power to impact upon and shape political processes in dynamic and complex ways, long after its original composition. Early studies of music's direct relation to social problems and politics in the USA frequently tended to conceive of this engagement in somewhat narrow terms as being located predominantly in lyrical content circulated by protest singers in protest songs (Denisoff and Peterson 1972; Hampton 1986; Pratt 1990). However, as John Street (2006: 59) argues, the capacity for any musician or pop star to act politically is not simply 'a product of the cause they support or the earnestness with which they support it'; artists' claims to 'represent' audiences and causes have to be legitimated and authorised. This is a complex process in which genre, biography and 'moral capital' as well as commercial, political and creative factors all play a part (Street, ibid.).

Alí's music acquired importance for the Chávez government not only because of his lyrics and what *Canción Necesaria* represented at the time of its original composition and circulation in Venezuela in the 1970s and early 1980s, but also because of the dynamic ways in which Venezuelans collectively remembered and used this music after Alí's death. The first half of this book therefore examines Alí's music and its significance *before* the emergence of Hugo Chávez as a political figure, while the second half of the book focuses on Alí's music in the Chávez period.

Chapter 2 looks at the origins of the Latin American *Nueva Canción* movement in the 1960s, focusing on the social, political and economic factors that contributed to the shaping of the movement, and on the theories and aims that motivated movement practitioners' endeavours to use popular music as a tool for social and political transformation in favour of the masses. While the movement shares some concerns and characteristics with the Anglo-US folk revival of the 1950–1960s, *Nueva Canción* differs significantly from folk-based protest music as it is understood in Western Europe and the USA (Nandorfy 2003: 172). This is not only because folk music traditions in Latin America differ from those of Anglo-US regions, and nor is it only because the politico-economic conditions of Latin America differ from those of wealthier countries. In Latin America, *Nueva Canción* composers and performers have frequently faced far greater personal risk on account of their musical activities than have protest singers in more stable democracies in the Western world. Between the 1960s and the 1980s, when repressive military dictatorships and violent civil wars predominated in several Latin American countries, many artists were persecuted, threatened, imprisoned, exiled, tortured or even murdered by state authorities due to their involvement in *Nueva Canción* (Jara 1998; Márquez 1983; Seeger 2008: 72). Members of the public who owned *Nueva Canción* cassette tapes or LP albums were also subject to arrest, imprisonment, torture and 'disappearance' (Brister 1980; Cabezas 1977; Carrasco 1982). Following the 1973 military coup in Chile, master recordings were destroyed, albums, cassettes and songbooks were publicly burned, and *Nueva Canción* was severely repressed by military authorities (Morris 1986).

Nueva Canción was not characterised by a single musical style or genre; it was instead a musically heterogeneous movement associated with a leftist ideology and way of life (Shaw 2005: 41). It was not only the properties of the musical styles and lyrics that gave the movement meaning and legitimised it as a voice of leftist thought; the reactions of state authorities, the methods of dissemination, and the personal biographies of many of the artists who worked within the movement all contributed to the ways in which audiences understood the significance of *Nueva Canción*. Drawing on a number of studies and personal accounts of *Nueva Canción*, Chap. 2 examines the ideology and way of life associated with the movement, and how these influenced the production, dissemination and reception of *Nueva Canción* compositions in Latin America in the 1960s–1980s.

Chapter 3 looks at how Venezuelan social, racial and political circumstances, and particularly the unequal distribution of the country's massive oil wealth, shaped and influenced Alí Primera's political ideas, and also the ways in which Alí constructed a coherent narrative about his own origins and his motivations for composing and performing *Canción Necesaria* in the 1970s and early 1980s. Alí used this narrative to identify himself with the poor and the marginalised and to locate his music firmly within the *Nueva Canción* movement, as a means of bringing about social, cultural, political and economic transformation on behalf of the poor and the subordinated.

Alí Primera created what he called *Canción Necesaria* within the *Nueva Canción* movement in Venezuela, through which he himself said he aimed to raise awareness of the causes of social and economic injustices and to unite Venezuelans in a common struggle to transform society in the interests of the masses. Although he maintained strong links with leftist political parties throughout his life, Alí refused to allow his songs to represent any one of these in particular. Instead, he used his music to articulate an anti-racist, anti-capitalist and anti-imperialist critique of the social and economic impact of the oil industry on Venezuela, and he re-interpreted the Bolívar myth with the aim of uniting *el pueblo*[13] in a common struggle against social injustice and exploitation.

Alí Primera's contributions to the *Nueva Canción* movement are little known outside his native Venezuela; as yet, there has been no English language study of Alí Primera's work or of Venezuelan *Nueva Canción*. In Chap. 3, in order to provide the context for understanding specific references later made by Hugo Chávez to the themes and subjects of Alí's songs, I refer to the lyrics of key songs[14] composed by Alí, and briefly discuss how these songs critiqued Venezuelan society at the time and also constructed and disseminated a nationalistic revolutionary 'Bolivarian' ideology based on local symbols and concerns.

Chapter 4 draws on theories of collective memory and the posthumous transformation of meaning to study how and why Alí's songs in particular acquired new uses and functions in the decade after his death, and the ways in which collective memories of Alí's life and songs constituted a form of social action and a means of expressing political discontent in the late 1980s and early 1990s. In Latin America, a region characterised by social, economic, cultural, racial and political inequalities, competing groups tend to lay conflicting claims to symbols and heroes; among the marginalised and the oppressed in particular, there is a strong tendency to memorialise deceased men and women who are perceived to have struggled on behalf of 'the people' (Brunk and Fallaw 2006; Frazer 2006; Johnson 2004). Posthumously, such individuals can come to symbolise oppositional values and ideals in meaningful and profound ways, and thus in death contribute to the construction of group identity for the living (Pring-Mill 1990). This chapter explores the ways in which Alí Primera's compositions, and narratives about his life and conduct, were remembered in Venezuela in the late 1980s and early 1990s, and the functions that these memories served for those who shared them. I examine which features and qualities were 'forgotten' and which were highlighted in this process, and the values and ideals that Alí came to represent in the collective memory. This sheds light on the reasons why Alí's songs in particular were commemorated at a grassroots level and how they came to acquire new posthumous significance and functions for the Venezuelan public at that time.

Alí Primera's early death, and his own narratives about his motivations for composing within the *Nueva Canción* movement, added to the perceived significance of his songs in the collective memory and contributed to these songs being remembered and commemorated by the Venezuelan public in numerous ways after his death. That the songs were associated with general leftist values, rather than with the ideology of any single political party, allowed them to resonate with otherwise disparate social, political and ethnic groups. In rituals such as the *Marcha de los Claveles Rojos* (March of the Red Carnations), Venezuelans gathered (and continue to gather) on the anniversary of Alí's death each year to walk together from Alí's childhood home in the Paraguaná peninsula to his nearby tomb, collectively singing his songs along the way. I approach such commemorative practices as a form of what Peter Jan Margry and Cristina Sánchez-Carretero (2011) term 'grassroots memorialisation'. This form of memorialisation expresses not only grief for a deceased individual but also social discontent, therefore representing a form of social action (Margry and Sánchez-Carretero 2011: 2). It is important to note that between 1980 and 1996, poverty increased in Venezuela much more dramatically than elsewhere in Latin America, rising from 17 % to 65 % of the population (Wilpert 2013: 192). I argue in Chapter 4 that informal commemorations of Alí Primera and his songs, and leftist writers' and journalists' constructions of collective memories of Alí's life and death, played a significant role in the creation of new public spaces. These spaces, where Alí Primera's life and songs were commemorated and remembered collectively, united, channelled and articulated widespread but otherwise disparate forms of resistance and opposition to the hegemonic political order which was perceived to have led to such increases in poverty in the country at that time.

Chapter 5 examines how in the mid-1990s the then colonel Hugo Chávez connected with the public spaces created by grassroots commemorations of Alí's life and music in order to tie his new political movement with a cultural past, associated with resistance and opposition to the state, which was seen as despised and suppressed by the dominant political parties. Alí Primera's songs, and collective memories of Alí's life and death, provided cultural resources which Chávez mobilised in his political communication in order to construct a political persona and to represent his movement as a definitive break with the old regime.

When he first came to public attention with his unsuccessful but popularly supported coup attempt in 1992, the then colonel Hugo Chávez was a political unknown with links to none of the traditional political parties of Venezuela. For new political actors seeking to communicate with and appeal to the masses at such times, a version of the past which is defined in cultural terms can offer a powerful tool (Whisnant 1995: 190). However, since the culture of the immediate past is likely to appear 'inseparable' from the political and social order which the political actor seeks to replace, the past with which a connection is sought needs to be remote enough to predate the 'perversions and distortions of the old regime', or to have been despised and suppressed by that regime (Whisnant 1995: 190).

Chapter 5 examines how Alí Primera's *Canción Necesaria*, and collective memories of Alí's life and death, offered Chávez a means to communicate politically with the Venezuelan public. In the mid-1990s, Chávez made use of Alí's life and songs to create a political persona through which to connect with *el pueblo* in a profound way; narratives about Alí's life and songs allowed Chávez to represent himself and his political movement as a definitive break with the old order and as representative of the poor and the marginalised. I analyse Chávez's discourse with reference to Alí Primera in order to identify the themes that Chávez selectively highlighted and attached to his persona and his movement. I then offer a detailed case study of the ways in which Chávez talked about Alí Primera in a particular episode of *'Aló Presidente*.[15] This analysis illustrates the specific ways in which Alí's life and songs allowed Chávez to represent himself and his movement as connected to *el pueblo* and as a break with the old order.

Chapter 6 looks at how, by formalising and institutionalising collective memories of Alí Primera's life and songs, the Chávez government engaged in symbolic work aimed at communicating a fresh beginning characterised by the redefinition of citizenship, democracy and the nation in twenty-first century Venezuela. The Chávez government used cultural policy to connect with and raise the status of Alí Primera's legacy and, at a symbolic level, to connect with and raise the status of the poor and the marginalised, many of whom had commemorated Alí's life and songs at grassroots levels in the late 1980s and early 1990s.

At times of political and economic change, T. M. Scruggs (1998: 53) theorises, the cultural practices of subaltern groups can 'achieve an abrupt increase in symbolic power, a change in status which state cultural initiatives may both promote and utilize' in order to represent 'a significant break with the preceding order'. In order to study the extent to which the Chávez government can be seen to have used cultural policies to represent a break with the old order, I offer a brief survey of the themes that have traditionally characterised Venezuelan cultural policy, before contrasting this historical attitude with that of the Chávez government in the twenty-first century. I then analyse how changes in the concept of cultural heritage in particular during the Chávez period were used to place *el pueblo* and their cultural values, as they themselves defined them, at the centre of the nation.

I examine how Alí Primera's inclusion in official representations of Venezuela's cultural heritage was intended, at a symbolic level, to raise the status of subordinate sectors of society, and I briefly compare Bolivarian cultural policy with that of revolutionary Cuba and Sandinista Nicaragua in order to highlight continuities but also innovations in the Venezuelan case. To do this, I draw on the literature on Latin American cultural policy. I also draw on interviews I conducted in 2008 with former vice-minister of culture, Ivan Padilla, and with former president of FUNDARTE[16] (a state-funded cultural institute based in Caracas), Oscar Acosta. In addition, I analyse official documents and state-funded documentaries and publications about Alí Primera in order to identify the principal ways in which his significance was officially represented in the Chávez period.

Chapter 7 examines how state support for Alí Primera's *Canción Necesaria* gave rise to new uses and understandings of Alí's life and legacy in the Chávez period. The Chávez government's discourse about Alí Primera was not universally accepted or monolithically installed in Venezuela; while official references to Alí Primera's songs appealed to many Venezuelans, these references alienated many others. As writer Charles Hardy notes, Chávez's singing of Alí Primera's songs provoked 'love from some, and hatred from others'.[17]

The state's promotion of Alí's legacy gave rise to various contradictions, which I examine by focusing on examples of conflicting reactions to the government's recognition of Alí Primera's songs. I collected examples of these conflicting reactions via three methods; first, through semi-structured interviews with supporters and opponents of the Chávez government; second, through my observations as a participant observer during my field work in Venezuela, and third, through netnography,[18] whereby I collected non-elicited data from social media websites in which Venezuelans discussed the meaning and importance of Alí Primera's legacy. I approach these examples of public reactions as illustrative of how state involvement in Alí's legacy influenced the ways Venezuelans understood and used Alí's songs in the twenty-first century, and I argue that Venezuelans actively engaged with the Chávez government at a symbolic level by accepting, rejecting or negotiating the ways in which the state promoted Alí's legacy.

State involvement in the legacy of Alí Primera resulted in people no longer listening to and using Alí Primera's songs in the same ways as they had done before the election of Chávez. Political polarisation affected the apparent judgement of Alí's musical value and significance as a *cantautor*, and it led opponents and supporters of the Chávez government to use the songs as a symbolic political language with which to defend their competing and conflicting assessments of the government's worth. The songs were re-signified, re-interpreted and re-used in a variety of new ways; *Chavistas* often used them to express their support for the government, while some *anti-Chavistas* distanced themselves from the songs and others struggled to recuperate the songs and use them to express their resistance to the state. I argue that *Canción Necesaria*, and narratives about Alí's life and death, were interpreted and reinterpreted in new ways; Alí's *Nueva Canción* legacy created a new space where popular music acted as a resource that Venezuelans actively engaged with in order to assert, challenge or contest *Chavista* hegemony.

In my concluding chapter, I contend that Chávez sought to associate his government with Alí Primera's *Canción Necesaria*, and with collective memories of Alí's life and death, in order to link with and give official space to a history of grassroots political activism that previous governments had sought to suppress. At a symbolic level, this association was intended to represent the Chávez government as a break with the old order, and as bringing to fruition the goals of the *Nueva Canción* movement within which Alí Primera located his songs. My focus on the history of leftist political activism, which is collectively remembered and embodied in *Nueva Canción*, brings to light the agency of the Venezuelan masses, which much of the political literature fails to recognise.

Like many political phenomena in polarised regions such as Latin America, where profound social, cultural, racial and economic inequalities prevail, *Chavismo* generated both strong support and deep resistance from different social and political groups within the country. In 1979, Robert Pring-Mill observed that 'facts' are rarely verifiable in a region as polarised as Latin America; ideological and psychological factors combine to 'slant' the 'heightened versions of reality' which committed poetry and song present (Pring-Mill 1979: 18). Eye-witnesses edit and misremember what they see, and when stories are passed on by word of mouth, other alterations are introduced. However, Pring-Mill (1979: 19) argues that even versions which an opponent sees as 'downright lying' may not be a deliberate misrepresentation but simply a 'misconstruing', or indeed a valid 'alternative reading' of what the committed artist wanted to represent in their music; competing social and political groups have their own conflicting versions of past and present reality, and since the positions from which they view events and experiences are opposed, then each tends to dismiss the contrary version as deliberate distortion. In this book I do not aim to ascertain the 'authenticity' of any of the competing interpretations of Alí Primera's *Canción Necesaria* legacy, or to prove or disprove the veracity of the Chávez government's claims for Alí's influence and impact. Instead, I aim to examine how competing interpretations and collective memories of Alí's *Canción Necesaria* can elucidate the complex and dynamic mechanisms by which popular music and politics can become intertwined at a time of leftist transition, and the functions of popular music for the people engaging with it at such a time.

The legacy of the Latin American *Nueva Canción* movement endures, and the movement has continuing but newly acquired relevance and significance within a changed set of social and political circumstances in twenty-first-century Latin America. Conflicting political uses of Alí Primera's legacy in the Chávez period highlight the changing ways in which popular music can be collectively remembered and used in social, political and temporal contexts other than those that originally gave rise to it. In Venezuela in the Chávez period, a time of leftist social and political transition, state institutionalisation of *Canción Necesaria* was contested; while many supporters of the government saw official promotion of Alí's legacy as evidence of the state's recognition of their history, their struggles and their value, many opponents saw this process as a distortion of history and they sought to assert their own competing claims to the significance and meaning of the songs.

Popular music exists in dynamic relation to its audiences, and these audiences can actively (re)interpret that music and (re)use it in unforeseen and unpredictable ways; state institutionalisation of popular music at a time of leftist transition can cause that music to be remembered and used in new and conflicting ways, and these conflicting ways reflect, at a symbolic level, people's political attitudes in the present moment.

NOTES

1. Throughout the book, I use the Spanish term *cantautor* rather than the English 'singer-songwriter'. This is because the English term, in addition to being somewhat clumsy, does not carry the same political overtones as the Spanish term which, according to Pring-Mill (1990: 10), came to American Spanish in the 1960s from the Italian *cantautore*.

2. Though it is not the term used by all musicians whose music and activities link to the political struggles within their countries, the Spanish *Nueva Canción* is used as an 'all-embracing' term (Fairley 1984: 107) to designate a particular movement that brought music and politics together in the Southern Cone in the 1960s. I deal with this movement, and with issues surrounding its nomenclature, in Chap. 2.

3. In the sleeve notes to his LP *Canción mansa para un pueblo bravo* (1978), Alí wrote 'I believe in song ... *Canción Necesaria* ... It may not lead the battalions, but it will help to form them ... *Canción Necesaria* is the language of the people'. In this book I use the terms *Nueva Canción* and *Canción Necesaria* interchangeably to refer to Alí's songs. All translations from Spanish, unless otherwise stated, are my own.

4. Small four-stringed instrument, descended from the guitar, commonly used in Venezuelan folk music.
5. Bolivarianism, named for the Independence hero Simón Bolívar, is essentially anti-imperialist and committed to Latin American integration. See Gott (2005), Buxton (2005).
6. Cherry-like fruit native to Central America and humid tropical zones of South America. The *semeruco* bush can survive extended periods of drought, though it may not produce fruit until it rains. Alí Primera often used the *semeruco* in his songs and narrative as a symbol for stoicism and hope in the face of difficulties.
7. The song is 'Canción mansa para un pueblo bravo' ('A Humble Song for a Brave People'), from the LP of the same title (1978). The address was broadcast on *teleSUR* http://www.youtube.com/watch?v=mJt9pDO5DuQ&feature=results_main&playnext=1&list=PLFB F2DC01AADF8E06 (Last accessed 16 December 2012).
8. Between 1998 and 2012, Chávez won 14 of the 15 elections and referenda that his government held in what former US President Jimmy Carter has described as 'the best [electoral process] in the world'. https://www.youtube.com/watch?v=l9Dmt2_QioI&index=41&list=UUOpwE3m2KUdiFKSTSrmIC5g (Last accessed 8 January 2016).
9. See Weisbrot and Ruttenberg (2010).
10. I take collective memory to be 'The representation of the past, both that shared by a group and that which is collectively commemorated, that enacts and gives substance to the group's identity, its present conditions and its vision of the future' (Misztal 2000: 7).
11. The term *porteño* is commonly used in Latin America to refer to people from the port city of Buenos Aires.
12. Carlos Gardel (1890–1935), born Charles Romuald Gardes in Toulouse, France, emigrated with his French unmarried mother to Argentina in early 1893. In the first half of the twentieth century, Gardel's audiences were made up of the immigrant masses who have characterised Argentine history and whose support Perón sought to consolidate (Castro 1998: 63–78).
13. *El pueblo* translates into English as 'the people'. The Spanish term is ideologically loaded, however, in that it refers to the common people as opposed to wealthy and powerful elites. It is a term frequently used in Latin America to designate the proletarian and the peasant classes

who are exploited by the capitalist system (Obregón Múñoz 1996: 46).

14. Alí Primera composed over two hundred songs during his lifetime. It is beyond the scope of this book to analyse all of the lyrics and music of these songs. The songs I have selected to discuss in Chap. 3 are songs which I will return to in later chapters when I examine how Chávez and the Venezuelan public made use of Alí's music in the twenty-first century.

15. *'Aló Presidente* was a weekly television programme broadcast on state television and radio in which Chávez spoke directly with the public and addressed contemporary issues and topics (see Smith 2010). The mass media in Venezuela is concentrated into private companies such as the Cisneros group which depend on US corporations for programmes, technology and investment. Private media outlets have maintained an aggressively oppositional stance towards Hugo Chávez and his supporters (McCaughan 2004; Stoneman 2008).

16. *La Fundación para la Cultura y las Artes de la Alcaldía del Municipio Bolivariano Libertador.*

17. 'A Love (and Hate) Story, part 3'. www.vheadline.com/printer_news. asp?id=6956 (Last accessed 25 April 2005).

18. The term 'netnography' derives from combining the words 'Internet' and 'ethnography', and it refers to a relatively new research method defined as 'a technique for the cultural analysis of social media and online community data' (Kozinets et al. 2014: 262).

CHAPTER 2

Latin American *Nueva Canción*: The Leftist Revival of Folk Traditions

During the Chávez period, Alí Primera's songs were officially represented as the epitome of Bolivarian thought. However, these songs were not written for or about the Chávez government; Alí Primera had composed the songs, some decades earlier, from within the *Nueva Canción* movement. This movement brought together a generation of musicians who, like Alí, supported social and political change in their respective countries. Jan Fairley (2013: 119) argues that *Nueva Canción* was a loose network, based in many cases on personal friendships, which coalesced into a cultural movement characterised by:

> a music enmeshed within historical circumstances which included: the forging of revolutionary culture in Cuba; the coming together of political parties to form a coalition to elect the first ever socialist president through the ballot box in Chile; resistance to brutal Latin American dictatorships, which were established mainly in the 1960s and 1970s ... followed by the struggle for new democracies.

The movement, which began in the Southern Cone and from there spread throughout Latin America, was based on a new approach to the composition, performance and dissemination of music and song. *Nueva Canción* practitioners aimed to use music and song to bring revolutionary

© The Editors (if applicable) and the Authors 2016
H. Marsh, *Hugo Chávez, Alí Primera and Venezuela*,
DOI 10.1057/978-1-137-57968-3_2

ideas to the consciousness of the masses and thereby 'create a radical-
ized public'; they sought to 'refashion' popular culture by reviving and
re-interpreting local folk music forms to give expression to themes of '[n]
ationalism and anti-Americanism, and the related drive for economic,
political, and cultural independence' (Taffet 1997: 92–3).

By identifying his songs as *Nueva Canción*, Alí Primera linked his music
to the wider goals and ideologies of the movement while he also composed a body of song that addressed local circumstances and, in particular,
the impact of the oil industry on Venezuelan social, economic, cultural
and political life. It is partly because of their origins from within *Nueva
Canción* that Alí Primera's compositions were legitimated as representative of 'the people', and were subsequently to acquire specific uses for
Chávez in his political communication. *Nueva Canción* was a movement
through which a generation of committed young musicians and performers aimed to revive and renew local folk music forms in order to give voice
to 'the polemics of the leftist parties' in Latin America in the 1960s and
1970s (Taffet 1997: 94). This chapter explores the social, political and
economic factors that contributed to the emergence of *Nueva Canción* in
Latin America, and examines the ways in which artists composing and performing within this movement aimed to use popular music to transform
their societies.

NUEVA CANCIÓN AND LOCAL CIRCUMSTANCES

Robert Pring-Mill (2002: 10) argues that *Nueva Canción*, closely linked
to the specific period in Latin American history that immediately followed
the Cuban Revolution, needs to be examined as a product of the reality from which it emerged and which it sought to influence. While Latin
America shares some characteristics with other post-colonial regions characterised by 'underdevelopment', political instability, and economic and
cultural dependency, there are two significant conditions, specific to the
region, that *Nueva Canción* responded to and sought to influence. First,
Latin America is singularly and profoundly marked by its geographical
proximity to the USA. The Monroe Doctrine declared by the USA in
1823 was later used as a justification for repeated US intervention in Latin
America (Livingstone 2009: 9), and the region remains polarised between
those who welcome US involvement in its internal affairs, and those who
vehemently oppose what they view as self-interested interference (Scruggs
2004: 257, McPherson 2003). Second, beginning under the dictatorship

of General Pinochet in Chile post 1973, Latin America was the first region in the world to undergo neoliberal restructuring, and it was therefore 'one of the primary zones of expansion for capitalism in its transnational phase' (Reyes Matta 1988: 452). This economic model survived the transition to democracy, but subsequently, between 1980 and 2002, poverty rates increased from 40.5 % of the population to 44 %, rendering Latin America the most unequal part of the world with the top 10 % of the population earning 48 % of all income (Reygadas 2006: 122, cited in Webber and Carr 2013: 3).

Through their musical activities, *Nueva Canción* artists sought to participate 'in the struggles against rightist authoritarian regimes, economic inequity, and U.S. imperialism' (Austerlitz 1997: 109). However, participants in the movement aimed to do more than protest against social and economic injustices; *Nueva Canción* artists also aimed to create new popular national music forms based on local folk traditions (Party 2010: 674).

The term '*Nueva Canción*' was not widely used in Latin America until the *Primer Festival de la Nueva Canción Chilena* (First Festival of Chilean *Nueva Canción*) which took place at the *Universidad Católica de Chile* (Catholic University of Chile) in Santiago in 1969. Over a decade before this festival took place, the roots of what was at that time widely referred to as a 'protest song' movement were emerging in the Southern Cone, from where the movement spread throughout Latin America. The movement involved marrying local music styles to lyrics that expressed and commented on the daily reality of the marginalised *pueblos* of Latin America. The historic suppression of indigenous music forms endowed these folk music styles with associations of resistance to imperialism and elite political interests. Throughout the colonial period, ecclesiastical authorities had sought to eradicate indigenous and African musical forms, which they associated with 'primitive' peoples and 'backward' ways of life (Olsen 1980: 377; Tandt and Young 2004: 238–9). Following independence, official policy encouraged emigration from Northern Europe to 'whiten the race' (Wright 1990; Gott 2007). This policy signalled the continuation of colonial patterns of disparagement of the cultural forms associated with indigenous and African populations, an attitude that persists to the present day; as Nicaraguan *Nueva Canción cantautora* Katia Cardenal has said, in Latin America 'the local is never good enough'.[1] Faced with marginalisation and repression, the mere sight and sound of folk instruments and musical styles acquired a symbolic power in Latin America which was 'largely undiminished by changes of the twentieth century' (Pring-Mill 1987: 179).

Chilean ethnomusicologist Rodrigo Torres (1980: 5) argues that the two fundamental keys to understanding *Nueva Canción* are tradition and renewal. Evolving in urban settings,[2] *Nueva Canción* drew on predominantly rural folk traditions which resonated deeply with the Latin American public, but it also re-interpreted and re-signified those traditions to respond to and seek to influence local and transcontinental conditions in the second half of the twentieth century. *Nueva Canción* thus involved a new attitude towards music; the motivation was to create renewed national popular music styles that avoided commercial constraints and articulated what was perceived to be a more 'authentic' local and transcontinental identity.

ORIGINS OF *NUEVA CANCIÓN*

The Music Industry and 'Cultural Colonialism'

The early inspiration for the *Nueva Canción* movement can be traced to Chile, Argentina and Uruguay in the late 1950s. A major impulse at that time was the increasing influence of the recording industry, which was perceived to turn songs into commercial products, and the massive penetration of foreign (mainly Anglo-US) music, which threatened to stifle local production (Carrasco 1982: 601–2; Reyes Matta 1988: 454–5; Taffet, 1997: 94). Folk music provided an immediate resource with which to counteract the perceived threat of 'cultural colonialism' in the form of the mass media imposing 'a musical taste which resulted in everything being imported from the United States' (Cabezas 1977: 32) and acting as 'propaganda for the "American Way of Life"' (Jara 1998: 115). *Nueva Canción cantautor* Osvaldo Rodríguez (quoted in Bianchi and Bocaz 1978: 127) sees the movement as in part a response to the *engringamiento*, or the 'gringoisation', of Latin American popular music, a process which led many Chilean artists at that time to imitate the sounds of the Anglo-US pop music that dominated the mass media and to record their own versions of songs popularised by artists from the USA (Taffet 1997: 94).

The arrival of radio and cinema in the region in the 1930s had provided a massive boost to the diffusion and popularity of a first wave of early-twentieth-century Latin American music styles such as the Mexican *ranchera*, the Cuban *son* and the Argentine/Uruguayan *tango*. Radio and cinema however were also vehicles for the diffusion of foreign music which, according to Chilean *Nueva Canción* practitioner Eduardo Carrasco (1982: 602), 'occupied a central place' in the region by the 1950s and left little space for the diffusion of national forms. Joan Jara (1998: 79), the widow of Chilean *Nueva Canción cantautor* Víctor Jara, writes in her personal account of the *Nueva Canción* movement that in order to succeed in the music business Chilean singers were compelled to 'gringoise' their images. Therefore, in the 1950s artists such as Patricio Henriquez performed under the name of 'Pat Henry', Los Hermanos Carrasco called themselves 'The Carr Twins', and so on. This practice suggests that many Chilean artists saw music from the USA as 'superior' to local music, a stance that was perceived by the left to be 'analogous to accepting the U.S. domination of the local economy and of Chile's international position' (Taffet 1997: 94). With the mass media dominated by foreign music, as *Nueva Canción cantautor* Trabunche explains, the defence and affirmation of local folk styles, which carried a history of state repression, was readily invested with symbolic meaning. This defence and affirmation, 'a response to the cultural alienation that our peoples suffer due to imperialist penetration', was an attempt to construct and retain a local cultural identity independent of foreign encroachment and free of commercial constraints (Trabunche, quoted in Bianchi and Bocaz 1978: 128).

Argentina's Institutional Ruling and Renewed Interest in Folk Music

A further impulse for the development of *Nueva Canción* was an institutional ruling in Argentina. Here, the populist and nationalistic government of Juan Perón sought to protect popular culture, directing in the early 1950s that 50 % of all music played on radio and in dance halls should be of Argentine origin (Fairley 1984: 110). Although this ruling was never fully implemented, it created an increased demand for national music which in turn led to the formation of a number of folkloric groups whose music became popular in neighbouring Chile. Subsequently, in Chile Argentinean folk music provided 'the only massive alternative to the imported pop sung in English' and stimulated the emergence of a number of Chilean folk groups (Jara 1998: 80). Many of these new groups collected and performed folk songs and dances which they viewed as 'static, already petrified, to be investigated only in an anthropological way' and to

be preserved in what was deemed to be an 'authentic' manner; they performed folk 'for the comfortable middle classes' with 'patriotic or senti-
mental themes', 'dressed up, without the smell of poverty and revolution'
(Jara 1998: 78–80). In contrast, other groups and individuals in the early
1960s believed that folk could be contemporary and was capable of transformation as long as it remained linked to its roots (Jara 1998: 78). These
latter 'neo-folklorists' aimed to be more innovative and experimental; they
performed folk music, but also created new compositions 'firmly rooted
in folklore ... in both form and expression, [but] imbued with a spirit of
renewal', and which were intended both to represent and to address the
reality of the common peoples of Latin America (Carrasco 1982: 606). It
is from within this wave of neo-folk that the *Nueva Canción* movement
began to take shape as leftist musicians and performers turned to local folk
forms to construct a new folk-popular culture which would give expression to the left and offer 'the solution to the cultural invasion' (Taffet
1997: 94).

Violeta Parra and Atahualpa Yupanqui: Reviving and Reinterpreting Folk Music Traditions

The early work of the Argentine Atahualpa Yupanqui (1908–1992) and
the Chilean Violeta Parra (1917–1967) was seminal for the subsequent
shaping of *Nueva Canción* as a movement that recovered and reaffirmed
local cultural values and linked these with leftist political ideas. In Chile,
Parra, a Communist party member, spent the 1940s and 1950s in direct
contact with the sources of popular song, 'digging out folk music' which
she then performed in urban contexts (Torres 2002: 43). Yupanqui, an
ex-Communist party member, dedicated himself to defending the worth
of indigenous cultures. Indeed, Yupanqui, whose real name was Hector
Roberto Chavero, adopted an indigenous pseudonym as a political statement at a time when many other performers were anglicising their stage
names (Fairley 2000: 363). Atahualpa was the name of the last Inca king,
betrayed and murdered by the Spanish Conquistador Francisco Pizarro.
Yupanqui chose to adopt this Incan name in the 1940s after reading
Garcilaso de la Vega's seventeenth century chronicles (Galasso, cited in
Rios 2008: 155), a text that inspired many Latin American leftists at that
time with its depiction of 'the Incas as benevolent rulers over a realm in
which hunger and even poverty were unknown' (Davies 1995, 6–7, cited
in Rios 2008: 155). The folk music of the Andean region where the Inca

Empire had predominated 'occupied a prominent place in the imagining of ...[a] ...progressive Latin American community' and became linked with leftism and Pan-Latin Americanism in modernist-cosmopolitan circles (Rios 2008: 154).

Yupanqui was the first Latin American folkloric musician to win critical praise in Paris, earning the Gran Prix de L'Académie Charles Cros in 1950 for his Chant du Monde LP *Minero Soy* (I Am a Miner), and touring the country (and the Socialist Bloc) in the same year (Rios 2008: 155). Andean music was popular in Paris in the 1950s and early 1960s, but Latin American musicians working there at that time 'steered clear of politicized repertory' (Rios 2008: 153). Yupanqui and Parra were exceptions because they not only performed folk music that they had collected in rural areas of their countries, but they also composed original songs with music based on folk traditions and lyrics that denounced social injustices.

Parra alone collected over three thousand songs from various regions of Chile which, after months of searching for a radio station willing to give her performance space, she went on to present on a *Radio Chile* programme, *Canta Violeta Parra* (Violeta Parra Sings) with the support of radio announcer Ricardo García (Moreno 1986: 110). Until that time, Chilean folk music in the mass media had been limited to one type (the *cueca*, a couple dance in 6/8 metre) and restricted to national holidays. The 1956 release of Parra's first album, *El Folklore de Chile*, containing 17 songs she had learned through oral transmission in the Chilean countryside, demonstrated her 'intention to expand both the repertoire and function of Chilean folk music as presented via the mass media' (Moreno 1986: 111). Like Yupanqui, Parra also spent time in Paris, where she settled for one year in 1955. In 1962, she returned to Paris with her adult children, Ángel and Isabel, and lived in the city for three more years (Rios 2008: 153). According to musicologist Daniel Party, the Chilean folk music that Parra collected and disseminated became an important basis and resource for the *Nueva Canción* movement for two reasons:

> Nueva Canción owes Violeta Parra two of its defining features. First, as a performer and composer, Parra developed a pan-Latin American folk aesthetic. In her music she incorporated and hybridized traditional Chilean styles she collected in her travels at home as well as Andean and Afro-American styles she first heard in Paris ... Second, a sizeable portion of Parra's oeuvre was openly critical of the social inequality and the political regime of her time. (Party 2010: 673)

By recovering and disseminating previously disparaged folk forms and renewing folk traditions, Parra and Yupanqui created bridges that allowed traditional musical forms to pass into the age of mass media, from an older generation of rural popular singers to a new generation of urban youth growing up in the 1950s and 1960s (Fairley 1984: 110). Parra's work in collecting folk songs from rural areas in Chile helped to inculcate a sense of 'pride in a music that heretofore was considered backward and uncivilized' (Moreno 1986: 117). Moreover, in their own compositions, such as Parra's 'La carta' (The Letter) and Yupanqui's 'Preguntitas sobre Dios' (Little Questions about God), the *cantautores* drew on traditional folk music forms but added new lyrics that addressed contemporary events, celebrated the values of peasants, workers and urban migrants and denounced social injustices (Fairley 2000: 363). They thus 'opened a new way forward for the development of vernacular songs on the continent' (Carrasco 1982: 605) and influenced a new generation of young urban artists looking for alternative artistic models at that time. Parra and Yupanqui became models for a new generation of urban, leftist youth who, influenced in the early 1960s by the success of the Cuban revolution, were becoming 'conscious of the contradictions and conflicts inherent in their national situations' and beginning to recognise them as 'features of a larger phenomenon: underdevelopment and economic and cultural dependency' (Reyes Matta 1988: 452).

The Influence of Cuba

The Cuban Revolution was arguably the greatest single impulse for the consolidation of the *Nueva Canción* movement in Latin America (Pring-Mill 2002: 19). After the Cuban Revolution of 1959, the real possibility of constructing a new world and *un hombre nuevo* (a 'new man', the latter concept associated with the thought of Ernesto Che Guevara) circulated widely in Latin America (Antequera 2008: 39; Guerrero Pérez 2005: 22–3).

In Cuba in the 1960s, a generation of young composers began to draw on national *trova* folk music traditions to compose songs that reacted against 'banality and commercialism in song' (Benmayor 1981: 14). These new *trovadores* widely rejected political rhetoric in their songs but sought to draw on the experiences of ordinary, working people to convey a politically conscious message in an aesthetic manner (ibid.). While they had been too young to fight in the Sierra Maestra, these young composers had gone to the countryside to assist in literacy campaigns, joined cane-cutting brigades and worked on fishing boats or in other manual occupations. Generally without a classical musical education, they were inspired by their experiences in a revolutionary society and sought to convey this intellectual and emotional enthusiasm for the construction of a new man and a new world in their compositions (Benmayor 1981: 18). The young *trovador* Silvio Rodríguez, for example, titled one of his songs 'La era está pariendo un corazón' (The Era is Giving Birth to a Heart), and in another of his songs, 'Danos un corazón' (Give us a Heart) Rodríguez sang of 'new men, the creators of history, forgers of a new humanity'.

It was in Havana, Cuba, that the first *Encuentro Internacional de la Canción Protesta* (International Meeting of Protest Song) took place in 1967. At this meeting, *cantautores* from across the Americas and Spain met to discuss the role that music could play in the construction of a new world. The objectives of this meeting were sixfold:

1. To bring together creators, principally from Latin America, who would otherwise not meet one another
2. To work with Song of Social Content in a collective, analytical, political and social manner
3. To find points of contact between those starting out [as musicians and performers] in the new generation
4. To maintain and promote musical and poetic quality in Popular Song
5. To put into common usage a name for the song, but still maintain the local terms which belong to each country or region
6. To profile a new ethics and aesthetic for Protest Song (Kolectivo La Haine, cited in Guerrero Pérez 2005: 15).

On the significance of this meeting, Jan Fairley states that:

it was resolved that song should play an important role in the liberation struggles against North American imperialism and against colonialism, as it was agreed that song possessed enormous strength to break down barriers, such as those of illiteracy, and that in consequence it should be a weapon at the service of the people, not a consumer product used by capitalism to alienate them ... [singers] should work amongst their people, confronting problems within their societies. (Fairley, 1984: 107)

The movement took shape initially without institutional support. In Cuba, the *trovadores* themselves were responsible for building their popularity in an organic way, without the support of cultural policy; they had to 'fight against a cultural bureaucracy in order to be heard at all' (Moore 2006: 153). Castro himself acknowledged this in the mid-1970s when he remarked:

> Did we, the politicians, conceive of [the *Nueva Trova*] movement? Did we plan it? No! These things arise, like so many others, that none of us can even imagine'. (Díaz Pérez, 1994: 131, cited in Moore, 2006: 153)

The post-revolutionary Cuban state did not immediately support *nuevo trovadores*. This was because these young musicians were influenced not only by local folk traditions but also by European and US folk and rock musicians such as Bob Dylan and The Beatles, and because *Nueva Trova* fans and performers wore their hair long and dressed like hippies at a time when the revolutionary government was seeking to counteract US influence on Cuban culture (Saunders 2008: 162). Silvio Rodríguez was even banned from performing in the late 1960s because he publicly acknowledged the influence of The Beatles on his own music (Miller 2008: 680). However, the Cuban political establishment's suspicion of *Nueva Trova* was temporary; in the late 1960s, when Cuban officials recognised that young *trovadores* had become famous in Chile, Spain and Brazil, institutional supports began to recognise and formalise the movement in Cuba, and the state began to represent its *trovadores* as 'spokespersons of the revolutionary experience' (Moore 2006: 153). In the late 1960s and early 1970s, artists such as Silvio Rodríguez, Pablo Milanés and Noel Nicola began to work and perform with the general support of the *Instituto Cubano de Arte e Industria Cinematográfica* (ICAIC, Cuban Institute of Art and Cinematography), under the auspices of which in 1969 they formed the *Grupo de Experimentación Sonora* (Group of Experimental Sound) (Guerrero Pérez 2005: 24).

LA PEÑA DE LOS PARRA: A NEW PERFORMANCE STYLE

The idea that a new world was possible and that a new man was being born was subsequently 'picked up, reproduced and diffused in Latin American *Nueva Canción*' (Antequera 2008: 39). In the 1960s in Chile, *peñas* became important urban spaces for leftist intellectuals and *cantautores* to meet and exchange such ideas, and for the live dissemination of folk music and original folk-based compositions. The first of these *peñas*, *La Peña de los Parra*, was opened by the Parras in Santiago in 1965. It was based in an old house. Joan Jara writes:

> The idea was simple – to create an informal atmosphere, without the usual censorship and commercial trappings, where folksingers could come in their everyday clothes to sing and exchange songs and ideas, a sort of artists' co-operative where people could eat simple food and listen to Chilean and Latin American folk music. (Jara 1998: 81)

This *peña* initiated a new way of performing folk music to the public. Influenced by the atmosphere of the *boîtes de nuit* where they had performed in Paris, the Parras' aim in opening *La Peña de los Parra* was to demystify the artist as a privileged being and to remove the distance between performer and audience (Guerrero Pérez 2005: 64). The Parras had been 'deeply affected' musically by their experiences in Paris; Ángel recalled that he and his mother and sister 'returned from Paris playing music from Venezuela, Argentina, Bolivia, music from other countries' (Ángel Parra, cited in Rios 2008: 154). According to Ángel, his family's belief in the ideal of Latin American unity (in opposition to US imperialism) led them to combine 'the [Andean] *charango* with the [Venezuelan] *cuatro*, the *cuatro* with the [Argentine] *bombo*[3] ... the [Andean] panpipe, the [Mexican] *guitarrón*,[4] all mixed together', which was intended to re-signify these locally specific instruments to mean 'Latin America' (ibid.). Inspired by the Parras, other young leftist *cantautores* and groups such as Inti Illimani and Quilapayún started to use musical instruments from throughout Latin America. This new combination of folk instruments, which was popularised at *La Peña de los Parra*, became characteristic of the sound of Chilean *Nueva Canción* in the late 1960s and early 1970s. By composing original songs based on popular folk musical styles from other Latin American countries, these *cantautores* and groups, like the Parras, aimed symbolically to fulfil 'the dream of Latin American integration that neither political nor economic decisions' had yet achieved (Reyes Matta 1988: 451).

La Peña de los Parra spawned a chain of other *peñas* throughout Chile, starting in universities in the capital (Rodríguez, in Bianchi and Bocaz

1978: 127). At these *peñas* and at intermittent meetings, congresses and festivals, leftist intellectuals and *cantautores* interested in neo-folklore met informally to listen to one another's work and ideas and to discuss and theorise the role of popular culture in the transformation of society and the construction of a new world and a new man.

CONSOLIDATION OF THE MOVEMENT

Rejection of 'Protest' Label and Emphasis on Renewal of Traditional Forms

By the late 1960s, a new cultural movement had taken recognisable shape. This movement consisted of people who saw themselves as working together through music to articulate not just a national but a continental political struggle (Fairley 1984: 112).

There was much debate at this time around the subject of nomenclature. Various terms circulated, such as *Canción Social* (Social Song), *Canción Comprometida* (Committed Song), *Canción Propuesta* (Song of Proposal) and *Canción de Contenido Social* (Song of Social Content), all of which were used to refer to the movement (Guerrero Pérez 2005: 7). The term 'Protest Song' was widely rejected by Latin American musicians soon after the 1967 meeting in Havana. According to Chilean *cantautor* Patricio Manns, this was because of the term's perceived links with certain types of music popular in industrialised countries (Patricio Manns, quoted in Bianchi and Bocaz 1978: 119). Víctor Jara, the Chilean *cantautor* who was tortured and murdered by the Chilean military within a few days of the 1973 coup which brought the socialist government of Allende to an end, argued that:

> US imperialism understands very well the magic of communication through music and persists in filling our young people with all sorts of commercial tripe. With professional expertise they have taken certain measures: first, the commercialisation of so-called 'protest music'; second, the creation of 'idols' of protest music who obey the same rules and suffer from the same constraints as the other idols of the consumer music industry—they last a little while and then disappear. Meanwhile they are useful in neutralising the innate spirit of rebellion of young people. The term 'protest song' is no longer valid because it is ambiguous and has been misused. I prefer the term 'revolutionary song'. (Víctor Jara, quoted in Joan Jara, 1998: 117)

Nueva Canción cantautores saw themselves not only as protesting, but also as giving voice to the common people's hopes, struggles and feelings in Latin America; they saw the term 'protest' as too narrow to designate their musical work. The Uruguayan *cantautor* Daniel Viglietti claimed that his music was not *de protesta* (protest) but *de propuesta* (about proposing alternatives) (Pring-Mill 1987: 179). In different Latin American countries, the movement was referred to using locally adopted terms, such as *Nueva Trova* in Cuba, *Nuevo Cancionero* in Argentina, Uruguay and Paraguay and *Nueva Canción* in Chile. These different names were used by *cantautores* in various countries who saw commonalities in their artistic search for a form of musical expression identified with the Latin American struggle for liberation (Reyes Matta 1998: 459–60). Significantly, most of the terms adopted to refer to the movement shared the use of the word *nuevo/a* (new). This word, according to Chilean *cantautor* Eduardo Carrasco, emphasised the idea of renewal of old folk forms and of early-twentieth-century national styles, such as the *tango* and the *son*, which had been displaced in the mass media by foreign pop music, and which a new generation of leftist musicians consciously sought to link with:

> Of course, this music from the 1920s and 1930s ... did not end ... but it was becoming more and more limited in its influence, ... diffused predominantly amongst those social sectors closest to the land and most faithful to the past: peasants and workers. [*Nueva Canción*] ... is like a movement for the recuperation of national music. (Carrasco 1982: 14–15)

NUEVA CANCIÓN AS 'CULTURAL VOICE' OF THE LEFT

In Chile's 1970 presidential campaign, and following Salvador Allende's electoral victory, *Nueva Canción* was 'fully integrated into the left's political apparatus and assumed a semi-official status as a cultural voice' for Allende's *Unidad Popular* (UP, Popular Unity) coalition (Taffet 1997: 91). The leftist parties that formed this coalition 'could not agree on policy beyond destroying the power of the global over the local'; while the far left advocated the establishment of a socialist economic system and radical change in the political system, the more moderate left and the political centre did not find these ideas acceptable (ibid.). Thus issues with 'broad resonance' such as Anti-Americanism and nationalism became the supporting structure for a political platform for the UP coalition (Taffet 1997: 92).

Since this was something on which there was wide agreement, support for national forms with the aim of effecting a 'second independence' became a unifying force within the left and the UP socialist agenda was therefore 'lodged within an essentially nationalist framework' (1997: 91).

In the late 1960s and early 1970s, *Nueva Canción* gave voice to and disseminated this nationalist agenda as well as other leftist intellectual currents, which were becoming influential in Latin America. For example, in his composition 'Plegaria a un Labrador' (Prayer for a Worker), Víctor Jara subverted the Lord's Prayer to call on Latin American workers to 'stand up' and ask to be freed from 'he who dominates us in misery' and demand that 'thy will at last be done on earth'. These lyrics conveyed the ideas developed by Catholic Liberation Theologists at a conference held in Medellín, Colombia in 1968, and by the Peruvian Catholic priest Gustavo Gutiérrez in his 1971 text *Teología de la liberación* (published in English in 1974 as *A Theology of Liberation: History, Politics and Salvation*). This new interpretation of the Bible, influenced by Marxist thought, represented Christ as a revolutionary who identified with and sided with the poor and the exploited (Guerrero Pérez 2005: viii).

Other leftist texts which *Nueva Canción* was influenced by and to which the movement gave cultural voice in the early 1970s included publications that tackled what was viewed as the problem of cultural penetration. In his 1970 study *Pedagogia do oprimido* (*Pedagogy of the Oppressed*), Brazilian pedagogue Paulo Freire argued that the mass media alienated the poor from their own culture while simultaneously leading them to 'internalize the values of their oppressors' (Moreno 1986: 109). In *Para leer al Pato Donald* (1972, published in English in 1984 as *How to Read Donald Duck: Imperialist Ideology in Disney Comics*), the Chilean writer Ariel Dorfman and Belgian scholar Armand Matterlart argued that seemingly innocent Disney characters promoted US consumer values. The predominance of these foreign values, argued Dorfman and Matterlart, was leading to the erasure of indigenous and traditional ways of life. The resultant loss of 'cultural identity' facilitated and 'naturalised' US political and economic influence in Latin America, the region of the world that they viewed as the principal 'receptacle of cultural imperialism' (Armand Matterlart, interviewed by Hay 2013: 2). Víctor Jara expressed similar ideas about the dangers of US cultural imperialism in Latin America in his 1969 song 'Quién mató a Carmencita' (Who Killed Carmencita). In this song, Jara attributed the real life suicide of a Chilean teenager to her alienation from her own cultural roots and her desire to emulate foreign cultural models: 'the idols of the day ... dazzled her eyes' and 'poisoned' her mind while 'the traffickers of dreams ... get fat and profit from the young'.

In *Las venas abiertas de América Latina* (*The Open Veins of Latin America: Five Centuries of the Pillage of a Continent*), Uruguayan Eduardo Galeano argued in 1973 that Latin America was not an under-developed region due to a lack of natural resources or the deficiencies of its populations but rather because resources were extracted and used to finance the development of wealthy nations. Dependency theorists propagated the idea that Latin America's problems would not disappear with the modernisation that its governments were intent on constructing but that the region's impoverishment was due to its unequal integration into the world system, with the wealthy nations inhabiting the 'centre' while so-called under-developed nations remained on the 'periphery'. Leftist intellectuals applied these ideas to the musical realm, comparing musical traditions to raw resources which needed protection from relations of dependency. As a participant at a meeting of Latin American musicians held in Cuba in 1972 expressed it:

> As with other deeply rooted popular and nationalist expressions, but with particular emphasis on music for its importance as a link between us, the colonialist cultural penetration seeks to achieve not only the destruction of our own values and the imposition of those from without but also the extraction and distortion of the former in order to return them [now] reprocessed and value-added, for the service of this penetration. (Quoted in Zolov 1999: 226)

DISSEMINATION AND AUDIENCE RECEPTION

Nueva Canción, according to *cantautor* Eduardo Carrasco (1982, 14–15), emerged among the middle classes, student and university circles 'who, at that time, are those most influenced by foreign music. In this way, [*Nueva Canción*] is like a movement for the recuperation of national music'. *Nueva Canción* aimed to use native music styles to counteract the dominance of foreign music in the mass media and to communicate leftist thought in an aesthetic form; through the construction of a national music based on local traditions, *Nueva Canción* artists sought to express their reality and leftist ideas, and to make their audiences conscious of these.

Scholars do not agree in their evaluations of the degree of penetration of the movement and how audiences responded to it. *Nueva Canción* artists claimed to speak for *el pueblo*, but, Daniel Party argues, the majority of Chileans in the early 1970s preferred to listen to other styles of music:

> Between 1970 and 1973, government-supported record labels released numerous Nueva Canción albums, and Nueva Canción concerts were well attended by passionate fans. However, Nueva Canción was largely absent from radio broadcasts and fared poorly in terms of record sales. The vast majority of Chileans, including Allende supporters, preferred to dance to *cumbia* and emote to *baladistas* such as Camilo Sesto, Roberto Carlos, Mari Trini, and Buddy Richard. (Party 2010: 674)

According to Party (2010: 676–7), in Chile *Nueva Canción* was neither widely played on the radio nor purchased by the masses, and in the 1980s rock groups like Los Prisioneros were 'the most listened to … by Chileans of all political affiliations'.

In contrast, Chilean writer Fernando Reyes Matta (1988) argues that the *Nueva Canción* movement reached a high level of penetration and that it had a significant impact on large sectors of the population in Latin America. Reyes Matta (1988: 448–9) attributes the growth and acceptance of *Nueva Canción* amongst Latin American audiences to three factors. First, the movement had only a minor presence in the dominant media; it created its own systems of dissemination via the circulation of tapes, of records passed from hand to hand, of festivals and of artists' tours. *Nueva Canción* depended neither on the mass media nor on state support for its diffusion, and the very fact that *Nueva Canción* was largely absent from commercial channels of distribution legitimised it as a more 'authentic' form of musical expression that was independent of profit concerns. Second, the musical and lyrical symbols used by the *Nueva Canción* movement appealed to the popular sensibility in all Latin American countries; its proposals, both as a form of social and political commitment and as a perspective on the theme of love, were easily adapted in a 'permanent renationalization process'. *Nueva Canción* compositions, regardless of their country of origin, were recognised throughout Latin America as 'historically local and relevant' to ordinary people who recognised within them a set of shared interests. Third, the *Nueva Canción* movement generated its own independent dynamics and attained social significance through forging a close identification with proposals for 'truly democratic change' and a continued and reciprocal communication between *cantautores* and their public. With few formal structures, the movement developed a 'counter-strategy of dissemination' (Reyes Matta 1988: 448), diffusing music via live performance at *peñas*, political rallies, trade unions and factories and, with the establishment of the independent recording company DICAP (*Discoteca del Cantar Popular*) by the Communist Youth in Chile in 1968, via record sales.

Nueva Canción cantautores represented themselves as being motivated by ideological and not by commercial concerns. With the exception of the Parra siblings, very few of those who composed and performed *Nueva Canción* were professional musicians who earned a living from their artistic involvement (Rodríguez, quoted in Bianchi and Bocaz 1978: 145). This remained the case even when the government of Salvador Allende provided the movement with a tremendous boost that increased its diffusion; the importation of foreign records was banned (the result of the need to restrict the use of foreign currency as well as clear cultural policy) and Chilean records were sold at a fixed price (Fairley 1984: 113). The perceived distance between commercial concerns and the motivations of *Nueva Canción* practitioners was important for Latin American audiences; *Nueva Canción* created its own spaces and its own forms of dissemination outside formal state structures and commercial channels; it was, one Chilean essayist claimed, the product 'of a people, not of an industry', and, therefore, it was widely accepted and legitimised as expressive of *el pueblo* rather than elite interests (Godoy, quoted in Morris 1986: 133).

NUEVA CANCIÓN AND STATE REPRESSION

In post-revolutionary Cuba, Allende's Chile (1970–1973) and Sandinista Nicaragua (1979–1990) *Nueva Canción* received state recognition and support. In Nicaragua, the movement (known locally as *Volcanto*) played an active role in resistance to the Somoza family's dictatorship, and it became closely linked with the Sandinista government (Pring-Mill 1987; Scruggs 2002a, 2002b). After the Sandinista government lost the 1990 national elections to an openly US-supported coalition, the new rightist government in Nicaragua withdrew support from socially committed music in a strategy that was 'less one of active repression than a hope that volcanto would fade away into irrelevance and disappear' (Scruggs 2004: 261).

In contrast, state repression of *Nueva Canción* under the rightist dictatorship of Pinochet in Chile was extremely severe. *Nueva Canción cantautores* and groups had played an important role in the election campaign and presidency of Salvador Allende. Allende acknowledged this in his final speech[5] before his death in the rightist coup which brought an end to his government and initiated a 17-year period of military dictatorship headed by Augusto Pinochet. The movement's survival during this extended period of military dictatorship can be attributed in part to its independence from state structures. The junta's stated goal was to eradicate Marxism and to reverse the direction of Chile's economic and political development; unions were dissolved, political parties were banned, and most opportunities for groups to gather were severely restricted (Morris 1986: 122). Though the junta did not have a specific cultural policy, its actions had immense consequences in the cultural arena; in the first year of military rule, cultural activity virtually ceased in what became known as the *apagón cultural* (cultural blackout) (Morris 1986: 123). The military government sought to erase everything that in their eyes appeared to pose a threat to the political, social and economic model they proposed, and they applied strict censorship (Morris 1986: 123). Many *Nueva Canción* artists had supported Allende and the movement was closely identified with the *Unidad Popular* government. Since 'everything connected with the UP had to be wiped off the face of the earth' (Márquez 1983: 8), *Nueva Canción* artists 'topped the first death lists' (Brister 1980: 55). The folk instruments which had become associated with the movement were unofficially banned, records were burned, and *Nueva Canción* artists were blacklisted, imprisoned, tortured, forced into exile or murdered[6] (Morris 1986: 123).

In the mid-1970s, *Nueva Canción* was forced to adopt different forms in order to survive. A group of conservatory musicians created a group called Barroco Andino (Andean Baroque) and began to perform classical music on folk instruments at universities and churches. The military took no action against these performances, and gradually a renewed form of *Nueva Canción*, referred to as *Canto Nuevo*, began to emerge. *Canto Nuevo* was both the resurrection of *Nueva Canción* and a response to the changed situation (Morris 1986: 124). In order to circumvent censorship, lyrics had to be metaphorical and opaque. However, the use of folk instruments added political overtones (Morris 1986: 124). Numerous organisations were created to support the activities of this revived form of *Nueva Canción* during the dictatorship; in 1976 Radio Chilena began to devote airtime to it in a nightly programme, *Nuestro Canto* (Our Song), and in the same year the *Alerce* record company was founded in Santiago by disc jockey Ricardo García. In 1977 an independent concert promotion agency was formed, and at the University of Chile a number of artistic groups came together to organise what would later become the *Agrupación Cultural Universitaria* (University Cultural Association), the first independent student organisation since the coup (Morris 1986: 124–5). Thus while *Canto Nuevo* remained independent of state structures in Chile, the movement depended on some of the methods of dissemination of more commercial genres.

Canto Nuevo faced tremendous difficulties at the level of dissemination in the late 1970s and 1980s; in order to produce a concert in a public auditorium, the sponsor was required to solicit permission from the local police and submit a sample of song lyrics and a list of all performers. If permission was granted it was often not until shortly before the concert was scheduled to start, leaving producers, performers and the public in a state of uncertainty (Morris 1986: 125). In many instances, permission was denied or revoked at the last minute (ibid.). In spite of these difficulties, *Canto Nuevo* at this time allowed Chileans to invent another language, to 'say things without saying them' (Carrasco, cited in Morris 1986: 126). Under extremely restricted conditions, a communication code developed between musicians and the public, leaving to 'the songs and the applause what one would like to say with words' (member of *Nueva Canción* group Aquelarre, quoted in Morris 1986: 128). The continued existence of *Canto Nuevo* during the dictatorship, argues Morris (1986: 133), demonstrated the persistent need for an outlet for popular expression.

CONCLUSIONS

This chapter has examined the origins, features and goals of the *Nueva Canción* movement in Latin America, and what *Nueva Canción* practitioners sought to achieve through composing, performing and disseminating their music in new ways. Inspired by the success of the Cuban Revolution, and seeking to counter the perceived cultural colonialism of the USA and to influence conditions in their own countries, young urban leftists turned to local folk music forms and wrote lyrics that responded to and aimed to influence their societies in favour of the masses in the second half of the twentieth century. While protest formed part of their activities, they saw themselves as articulating the hopes and the everyday realities of subordinate peoples in their countries. The significance of *Nueva Canción* did not rest only within the lyrics or the properties of the music; *Nueva Canción* artists represented themselves as working for ideological and not for commercial reasons, and though they made some use of commercial channels of dissemination (such as recording albums and performing concerts) they sought to retain their independence from mainstream commercial popular music forms through performance style (adoption of everyday clothes or indigenous dress, refusal to adopt anglicised stage names), the establishment of independent record labels (such as DICAP), and an emphasis on direct contact with audiences in factories, trade unions, universities, *peñas* and so on. Identifying with the poor, the subordinate and the marginalised of the continent, they sought to distance themselves from 'show business' and the 'star' system. This attitude and approach to the composition, performance and dissemination of music contributed to the perceived significance of the movement in Latin America; *Nueva Canción* practitioners sought to remain linked to the grassroots, and they sought to articulate the values, aspirations and struggles of the masses they aimed to speak for.

Nueva Canción in Chile, Nicaragua and Cuba has attracted academic attention due to political events in these countries in the second half of the twentieth century. However, the *Nueva Canción* movement was not restricted to these three countries. The next chapter focuses on Alí Primera's work within the movement in Venezuela, and on what was perceived to single his music out from that of other *Nueva Canción* artists in the country.

NOTES

1. Personal communication from Cardenal, July 2002.
2. See Gilbert, 1998 and Green, 1997 on Latin American urbanisation. Rowe and Schelling write that industrialisation in Latin America has been 'insufficient to absorb the mass of poor peasants and rural labourers, leading to the "explosion" of cities and the co-existence of a wealthy minority ... and a large mass of under- and unemployed "traditional" migrants, living in shantytowns on the peripheries of the city' (1991: 50).
3. Drum traditionally made of a hollowed tree trunk and covered with cured skins of animals such as goats, cows or sheep.

4. Very large, deep bodied six-stringed bass descended from the guitar family.
5. Allende said in this speech that he addressed his final message to the workers, farmers, intellectuals, women, and to 'the youth, those who sang and gave us their joy and their spirit of struggle'.
6. See Jara, 1998 for an account of her personal experience of the UP years, the military coup and the subsequent murder of her husband, *Nueva Canción cantautor* Víctor Jara at the hands of the military.

CHAPTER 3

The Development of *Nueva Canción* in Venezuela: Alí Primera and *Canción Necesaria*

Latin American *Nueva Canción* originated in the Southern Cone in the early 1960s, and coalesced into movement of artists adopting local musical forms, socially committed lyrics and new performance styles in order to actively effect the social, economic and political transformation of their societies in favour of the lower-class, mixed race and marginalised masses. In Venezuela, severe political repression in the 1960s meant that as a movement of artists working together, *Nueva Canción* could not begin to take shape until the 1970s.

This chapter examines how Alí Primera contributed to Latin American *Nueva Canción* and its development in Venezuela, and what Alí himself expressed about his motivations and aims in operating within this movement. Alí's songs articulated a critique of Venezuelan conditions; the cultural, economic, political and environmental impact of the oil industry, the prevalence of racist patterns of thought, the cultural influence of the United States, and the way in which the dominant political system aligned the country with the interests of foreign capital instead of those of Venezuela's rural and urban masses. Alí used *Canción Necesaria* to comment on and articulate resistance to these conditions, and to construct an alternative set of national 'Bolivarian' values rooted in local symbols.

In Latin America, where European descended elites have traditionally monopolised political, cultural and economic power, the attitude

© The Editors (if applicable) and the Authors 2016
H. Marsh, *Hugo Chávez, Alí Primera and Venezuela*,
DOI 10.1057/978-1-137-57968-3_3

that inspired the *Nueva Canción* movement was almost by definition antagonistic to most governments in the region. In Venezuela, Alí Primera emphasised this idea when he wrote 'Of course our song is subversive! In this country, even a smile is! I am happy even though you [the government] do not give me permission!'.[1] Alí insisted that he did not compose and perform songs only to protest. Song was 'necessary', Alí said in an interview published in *Tiempo* on 16 July 1981, in order to preserve the memory and identity of *el pueblo*, and to fight for their liberation (cited in Castillo and Marroquí 2005: 40).

Alí's songs, as well as his narratives about his life and his motivations, were remembered and commemorated after his sudden death in 1985. Posthumously, *Canción Necesaria*—its significance augmented by Alí's narratives about his humble origins and his state persecution, and by new narratives about the *cantautor*'s early and sudden death—provided repertoires for the Venezuelan public to draw on in order to express their growing dissatisfaction with the prevailing political order in the late 1980s and early 1990s. The songs became cultural resources that large sectors of the population collectively remembered to construct a shared political identity.

In this chapter, I briefly describe the local conditions that Venezuelan *Nueva Canción* responded to and sought to influence, and how the oil industry shaped racial relations, political, cultural and economic life in Venezuela, and aligned the country with the USA. I then focus on Alí Primera's work within the movement and the factors that brought his music singular attention. In addition, I analyse Alí Primera's own narratives about his music and his motivations for working within *Nueva Canción* as reported in press interviews, open letters published in national newspapers and spoken interventions at music events. In these interviews, which were published in local and national newspapers throughout the *cantautor*'s lifetime, Alí Primera repeatedly referred to a number of themes, events and biographical experiences, which together form a coherent narrative about his life and music. This narrative starts with accounts of his rural childhood poverty and his student activism and politicisation at university, and encompasses accounts of his refusal to profit from his music, his solidarity with the poor and oppressed, his rebuttal of 'show business' spectacles on television, and the state persecution he claimed to be subjected to because of his musical activities.

In order to analyse Alí's life history as recounted in interviews, I adopt narrative analysis theory. This approach views narratives as related to experience, but not as transparent carriers of that experience (Lawler 2002: 242). My aim in adopting this approach is not to seek to access or recon-struct an 'authentic' biography of Alí. Instead, I examine how Alí Primera selected, reconstructed and interpreted his own life experiences in order to use episodes from his own biography to make meaning and attach social and political significance to his songs. Lawler (2002: 242) defines narrative as an account that contains transformation (change over time) and some kind of 'action' and characters, all of which are brought together in an overall 'plot' which connects the past with the present and the self to others and which thereby constructs a coherent sense of identity. Narratives are, there-fore, not studied as stories that carry facts or truths that are to be verified by the researcher, but as interpretive devices through which people represent themselves, both to themselves and to others (Lawler 2002: 242). It is the significance of the ways in which the person interprets facts and events that is of interest to the researcher, and not the 'truth' or 'accuracy' of these facts and events (Lawler 2002: 244). For Lawler (2002: 249–50), the narratives people tell help to create relatively coherent and stable identities; the self is understood as unfolding through particular episodes which both express and constitute that self. I use these concepts to analyse the sense of identity that Alí Primera constructed, and argue that the *cantautor*'s narratives were taken up by his allies and repeated, thereby adding to the perceived significance of his songs and the ways these songs were interpreted during his lifetime.

OIL AND ITS CULTURAL, POLITICAL AND RACIAL IMPACT

Before the election of Hugo Chávez in 1998, Venezuela received lim-ited attention from academics within any discipline. In the second half of the twentieth century, Venezuelans were seen by scholars as 'different' from the rest of Latin Americans because they had apparently succeeded in overcoming the socio-political turbulence endemic to the region at that time (López Maya and Lander 2005: 92). This perspective was reflected in the literature, which postulated the 'exceptionalism' of Venezuela within the Latin American context (ibid.). While authoritarian regimes and civil wars characterised many other countries in the region in the 1970s, oil wealth had a significant impact on Venezuela. Wealthy elites profited most from the sudden influx of petrodollars that accompanied the Organization of the Petroleum Exporting Countries (OPEC) boom of 1973–1983, but some of this wealth trickled down to other social strata. There was a gen-eral sense that the country was advancing and that opportunities for urban migrants and their children were expanding. Venezuela appeared to be an exception in Latin America; a stable and 'near perfect' democracy in a politically tumultuous region (Ellner 2005: 7).

In *The Enduring Legacy: Oil, Culture and Society in Venezuela*, Miguel Tinker Salas (2009) analyses in detail the impact of the oil industry on social, cultural and racial relations in Venezuela, arguing that oil created a false image of the nation that was premised only on the *illusion* of prosperity. Tinker Salas (2009: 206) illustrates how the oil export industry 'skewed social class alliances' by forging an important nexus between foreign interests and the Venezuelan middle and upper classes who 'depended on oil revenues to maintain their status', and argues that the values promulgated by foreign-owned oil companies influenced 'common-sense' beliefs about race, culture, progress and modernisation in profound and enduring ways.

Taking issue with the commonly held notion that before the discovery of oil Venezuela was 'backward' in its development, Tinker Salas (2009: 15) asserts that in fact Venezuela 'exhibited patterns of development commonly found throughout Latin America toward the end of the nineteenth century', and that the false notion of Venezuela's nineteenth-century backwardness 'is rooted in the idea that the discovery of oil was synonymous with progress and modernization'. Oil placed Venezuela in the US sphere of influence, economically, politically and culturally, and subsequently US cultural and racial values defined modernity for the Venezuelan middle class (Tinker Salas 2009: 144–5). The oil industry, writes Tinker Salas (2009: 171), led to the construction of a distinct model of political participation and a concept of citizenship that favoured its interests; intellectuals, academics and artists 'actively participated in formulating a national social and cultural project that identified the economic interests of the foreign oil companies with the welfare of the nation' (Tinker Salas 2009: 72), thus leading to a perceived loss of local cultural identity and the consolidation of consumer patterns based on those of the USA.

By the 1960s upwards of 25 % of the Venezuelan population lived on or near an oil camp (Tinker Salas 2009: 4), but access to the benefits of the industry were extremely limited. Tinker Salas (2009: 174) details how racial distinctions characterised the new urban reality in the oil camps; foreigners dominated the industry, while Venezuelan professionals and middle managers were predominantly white and the labourers 'represented a racial cross-section of the country'. Oil thus strengthened and reinforced racist ideas about social status; labourers were forced to endure harsh and frequently dangerous conditions of work, including a high prevalence of tropical diseases and risk of industrial accidents, but they were on the whole seen as 'expendable; if one complained or became ill, hundreds of others were ready to take his place' since no labour unions existed and no laws protected workers (Tinker Salas 2009: 75).

While socially and racially stratified relations privileged foreigners, the emerging Venezuelan middle class identified with foreign values and conceived of black migrant and local workers as 'backwards' and of oil as transforming the nation and its institutions for the better (Tinker Salas 2009: 78). The oil companies, with government backing, sought to 'civilise' Venezuela by 'de-ruralising' its population and instilling a new modern work ethic based on US values (Tinker Salas 2009: 95). This represented the continuation and the strengthening of traditional patterns of racist thought. In the nineteenth century, large-scale European migration was promoted for the 'improvement' or 'whitening' of the race (Herrera Salas 2007: 102). Afro-Venezuelans and indigenous peoples were viewed as the 'cause' of the country's social ills, and biological and anthropological theories supporting racial discrimination influenced government policy (ibid.). For political and intellectual elites at that time:

> the interpretation of the Venezuelan past ... [was] ... filtered through the lens of European racist theories. They arrived at an understanding that the violence and political instability that marred the bulk of the nation's history since independence owed to the inability of the multiracial and black masses to comprehend a democratic system of government. (Wright 1990: 75)

The ideology of *mestizaje* (miscegenation) represented the continuation of racism in social projects initiated by the dominant elites who had replaced the colonisers (Herrera Salas 2007: 103). This ideology purported racial equality, but it served to mask racial discrimination and the socio-economic situation of Afro-Venezuelan and indigenous groups by identifying the white European as the civilising agent and rendering African and indigenous groups and their history invisible (ibid.).

In addition to deepening and reinforcing racism, the environmental impact of the oil industry caused social disruption that affected entire communities. For example, one group of 'fathers and mothers of Cabimas' complained directly to the government that their towns, beaches and lakes were being polluted and that sacred land was being desecrated (Tinker Salas 2009: 85). Lack of access to clean water also became a constant complaint (Tinker Salas 2009: 88). However, the oil industry exercised increasing power in government decision making and could usually count on the state's backing for its actions (Tinker Salas 2009: 95).

The racial, social and economic inequalities that arose or were reinforced through unequal access to oil profits provided a new common ground for political action in twentieth-century Venezuela. Although 'exceptionalism' shaped predominant narratives at that time, Venezuela has a strong history of barrio[2] and grassroots activism, which emerged in opposition to the 'common-sense' ideas of modernity promulgated by the oil industry and backed by the government (Velasco 2011), and the apparent 'peace and harmony' of the 1970s were 'more an illusion than a reality' (López Maya and Lander 2005: 92). The country experienced acute social tension and important street mobilisations, though these did not until the late 1980s seriously undermine the legitimacy of the political system or the state structure that was established in 1958 (López Maya and Lander 2005: 92). The political system established in 1958 was characterised by exclusion; the centrist parties that formed the Pact of Punto Fijo did not allow the participation of the left, even though leftist union organisations and the Venezuelan Communist Party had played a key role in upholding the opposition movement during the 10-year period of military authoritarianism that immediately preceded the establishment of *Puntofijismo* (Buxton 2005: 335). After 1958, the two parties that formed the Pact, *Acción Democrática* (AD) and *Comité de Organización Política Electoral Independiente* (COPEI), worked together to exclude rivals from power and to share in the country's oil revenues, thus sustaining a vast clientelist and corporatist network of interests with which the Punto Fijo parties were affiliated (Buxton 2005: 334).

Puntofijismo did not challenge the basic model of production that allowed foreign companies to control the oil industry (Tinker Salas 2009: 206). The discourse of Venezuelan political leaders in the 1960s reflected US interests, leading a generation of leftist youth, influenced by the success of the Cuban model, to reject *Puntofijismo* (Isaac López, cited in Cañas 2007: 52). The Latin American left was tremendously affected by the triumph of the Cuban Revolution of 1959; the Cuban example led to a shift in the 'cultural repertoire' of collective action and 'redefined revolutionary possibilities', inspiring a wave of guerrilla movements (Wickham-Crowley 2001: 139). One of the strongest and most radical of these movements sprang up in Venezuela, where it coalesced around middle-class university students and teachers (Wickham-Crowley 2001: 141). The state response to the internal socialist threat inspired by the

Cuban revolutionary model was severe in Venezuela; during the 'violent decade' of the 1960s, the *Dirección General de Policía* (DIGEPOL, Venezuelan police agency created in 1958) kidnapped, tortured and disappeared thousands of people (Arzola Castellanos 2005; Bigott 2005: 90). The guerrilla activism of sectors of the Venezuelan left was used as justification to implement a 'pacification' plan aimed at the eradication of the perceived leftist threat under the 1969–1974 presidency of Rafael Caldera (Cañas 2007: 50). This severe state repression contributed to the rise of bitter divisions within the left and caused the Venezuelan Communist Party to splinter and weaken (Cañas 2007: 51). These were the local conditions within which the Venezuelan variant of *Nueva Canción* developed in the 1970s.

THE BEGINNINGS OF VENEZUELAN *NUEVA CANCIÓN*

Venezuelan essayist and writer Luis Britto García explains (cited in Martín 1998: 147–8) that during the 1960s in Venezuela, it was virtually impossible for leftist groups to hold large meetings of any kind since such groups were for the large part illegal. It was only in the early 1970s, with the revolutionary left severely weakened and the armed guerrilla struggle practically annihilated, that a new type of meeting centred on the recovery and celebration of local popular cultural forms started to take shape. Britto García (ibid.) argues that young Venezuelans had noticed 'those enormous marketing operations' that promoted 'rock and roll' at festivals such as Woodstock, but that young Venezuelans widely rejected pop and rock and roll as outlets for their own needs.

In Venezuela, young leftists viewed rock and pop as 'anti-system', but only as 'anti' the systems of the countries that produced them; these genres therefore were not widely accepted as cultural forms that could address local conditions in Venezuela (ibid.). Nevertheless, influences from other countries were significant at that time; immigration from overseas during and prior to the 1970s created 'intercultural bridges', bringing new ideas and musical forms to Venezuela which were subsequently available for leftist *cantautores* to draw on (Martín 1998: 22). In the 1950s, the military government of Pérez Jiménez had encouraged European immigration to Venezuela via a policy designed to 'whiten the race' in cultural and racial terms (Wright 1990: 123). This led to a massive influx of Italian and Spanish immigrants, who brought partisan and anti-Franco songs which took root in the new environment (Martín 1998: 24). In 1970, President

Caldera allowed a number of Venezuelan political exiles to return to the country and these leftists brought with them revolutionary ideas they had absorbed in Cuba and France (Martín 1998: 26). Furthermore, after 1973, Venezuela became the 'asylum of choice' for many Chilean and Argentinean *Nueva Canción* artists forced into exile (Guss 2000: 100).

In Venezuela in the 1970s, young people started to gather at mass meetings, but not to vent collective anger at government violence as they had done in the past; the idea now was to celebrate being together in 'a spirit of fraternity' and to recover and defend popular cultural values against the perceived onslaught of the foreign commercial forms that dominated the mass media and the recording industry (Britto García, cited in Martin 1998: 148). These young people had seen the 'pacification' of the armed struggle, a struggle through which they had failed to effect socio-political change, and the recuperation and protection of popular cultural forms offered them an alternative means of struggling for social and political transformation (Guss 2000: 99).

Most of the guerrillas were middle-class students from urban backgrounds, and their involvement with radical movements and their time in the countryside and mountains had offered them their first exposure to rural and peasant life (Guss 2000: 99). These young people, influenced by cultural and intellectual developments in Latin America, now turned to popular culture as a new means of uniting people in order to press for change. At a 3-day Congress against Dependency and Neo-Colonialism held in December 1970 in Cabimas, they outlined *El Nuevo Viraje* (The New Direction), arguing that it was time to move from armed struggle to cultural struggle (Guss 2000: 99). The idea was that in order to effect political and economic change, a 'cultural revolution' was needed; before Venezuelans could be ready to demand greater social, political and economic justice, they first needed to re-discover and re-value their cultural identity, and to recuperate and defend local cultural values in the face of a perceived 'cultural invasion' of commercial Western media and consumer products (Guss 2000: 98).

Jesús Cordero and José Guerra, members of the group Los Guaraguao, remember that there were many forums in Venezuela in the 1970s where young leftists gathered to discuss the role of popular culture in the revolutionary struggle.[3] Luis Suárez, a further member of Los Guaraguao, recalls how in the 1970s, committed singers' collectives in Venezuela aimed to 'create awareness and solidarity and recover historical memory' in a movement which they viewed as a key element in the liberation struggles of that period.[4] One of their activities, according to Suárez, was to organise music events which they called '*La Canción Solidaria por los Pueblos*' ('People's Songs of Solidarity'). At these events, Suárez recalls, *cantautores* were able to establish contact with 'several revolutionary struggles', such as those of the people of Nicaragua, El Salvador, Guatemala, Honduras and Puerto Rico, among others, and 'Venezuelan struggles such as the teachers' movement, the liberation of political prisoners, ecological struggles and so many others that I can no longer remember'.

Venezuelan *Nueva Canción cantautora* Lilia Vera remembers that in the early 1970s, she and other leftist *cantautores* and groups including Cecilia Todd, Grupo Ahora, Grupo Madera and Soledad Bravo, began to meet for the first time to exchange ideas and think about how they could use music to contribute to the leftist struggles of that period.[5] It was then that these young artists began to organise and perform at *Festivales por la Libertad* (Festivals for Freedom) and to use their folk based music to harness support for human rights committees and other local and international causes (Martín 1998: 73). By the early 1980s in Venezuela, *Nueva Canción* mass music events and festivals, organised by artists and the communities in which they worked at a grassroots level (i.e., without official support or funding) around 'base, community, religious, student, environmental [causes], committees created ... for the defence of human rights or in solidarity with other Central or South American countries', regularly attracted audiences of thirty thousand people or more and, for lack of alternative available venues, were usually held in sports stadiums (Martín 1998: 73).

At a time when political parties appeared to be losing touch with *el pueblo*, Martín (1998: 73) argues, *Nueva Canción* offered a channel for the expression of the hopes and discontents of the impoverished and politically powerless. It was a movement that was rooted in the popular culture of the masses not only at the levels of generation and distribution, but also consumption; marginalised and oppressed sectors 'identified' with *Nueva Canción* and granted its artists the role of spokespeople for their interests (Martín 1998: 13). Without official or commercial support or mediation, the links between artists and audiences created a space for the construction and circulation of an oppositional cultural movement of and for *el pueblo*; *Nueva Canción* acted as an intermediary between the state and the demands of civil society (Martín 1998: 71) and became a ubiquitous 'cultural referent' formulated and received as being 'committed to the possibility of a better future' (ibid.: 9–11). In 2008, two ex-guerrillas

I interviewed in Barquismeto, Venezuela, explained in their own words what Venezuelan *Nueva Canción* offered them when they were fighting and, later, imprisoned and tortured:

> it offered spiritual and moral accompaniment. [Alí's] song was an inspiration. It was a shelter, and it offered us faith and hope to continue fighting. Not only Alí but Gloria Martín, Mercedes Sosa, Soledad Bravo, Víctor Jara, Carlos Puebla.

Alí Primera was not involved in the first *Festivales por la Libertad* in the early 1970s, since he was in Europe studying between 1969 and 1973. However, as a student in Caracas in the late 1960s Alí Primera had already come to public attention composing and performing songs with overtly political aims. From 1973, when he returned to Venezuela from Europe, and up until his death in 1985, Alí Primera was arguably Venezuela's most active and prolific *Nueva Canción cantautor*.

'HUMANIDAD': ALÍ'S FIRST *NUEVA CANCIÓN* COMPOSITION

In an interview with Alí Primera published in *Espectáculos* on 25 November 1982, Mercedes Martínez wrote that Alí 'has been spokesperson for several generations embarked upon a revolutionary process' (cited in Castillo and Marroquí 2005: 36). Alí attributed his own revolutionary path to his personal experiences of hardship, injustice and state repression. Alí was born into rural poverty on 31 October 1942 and raised in the harsh and drought-ridden Paraguaná Peninsula. Before the discovery of oil, local livelihoods in Paraguaná had depended on fishing and agriculture (Tinker Salas 2009: 19–20). In his childhood, Alí witnessed the massive disruption of these rural ways of life in the wake of the establishment of the huge Amuay refinery and the Creole company's construction in 1952 of a 'modern city of the future', an *urbanización*, to be inhabited by fifteen thousand residents (Tinker Salas 2009: 200). The *urbanización* was based on a typical suburban middle-class neighbourhood in the USA, with parks, garages, lawns, a church, a modern supermarket, and so on, and it stood in 'stark contrast' to the adjoining traditional neighbourhoods (ibid.). In an interview he gave in 1982, Alí attributed his 'desire to fight for change' to having witnessed this social and economic disruption in his childhood (cited in Hernández Medina 1991: 143) (Fig. 3.1).

Fig. 3.1 View of Amuay oil refinery from outside Alí's childhood home, Paraguaná (Photograph courtesy of the author)

Alí's direct family did not benefit from oil wealth; before Alí was three years old, his father, a prison guard, was accidentally and fatally shot during a riot in the prison where he worked as a guard in Coro, and the family subsequently suffered severe financial hardship. According to Alí's widow, Sol Mussett, Alí's childhood was extremely difficult and his mother struggled to raise and educate him and his siblings.[6]

In 1961, aged almost 19, Alí migrated to Caracas from his family home in rural Paraguaná.[7] This move was made in order for Alí to have the opportunity to complete his secondary education, as there were few opportunities to study in Paraguaná. Alí's older brother Alfonso already lived in Caracas having completed his military service there, and having a family member in the capital facilitated Alí's move. Four years later in October 1965, Alí enrolled at the *Universidad Central de Venezuela* in Caracas (Central University of Venezuela, referred to by the acronym UCV) in order to study Chemistry. Alí's enrolment at the UCV coincided with the detention, torture and murder of teacher and Communist Alberto Lovera at the hands of the DIGEPOL state police under the presidency of Raúl Leoni (1964–1968).[8] Photographs of Lovera's mutilated cadaver were published in *El Nacional* newspaper, causing a tremendous impact on the Venezuelan public.

Government repression of the left, and of university staff and students, was severe at the time that Alí enrolled at the UCV. The UCV in the 1960s was a centre of radical student activism, and was frequently ransacked by the police. At the end of the decade, the university was closed down for two years by President Caldera in an attempt to eradicate the student movement, which had been one of the most active bodies calling for social and political change in the country (Martín 1998: 26). Alí was detained and tortured by the DIGEPOL police for over one month following a police raid on the UCV in 1967. Alí attributed the start of his political activism in music to this personal experience of state repression. Speaking to the press (*Cantaclaro*, a Communist Party publication) at the *Primer Festival del Nuevo Canto Latinoamericano* (First Festival of Latin American *Nuevo Canto*) in Mexico City in April 1982, Alí said:

> while I was being imprisoned, … I began to ask myself why we were being detained and why we were holding out and keeping our spirits up. I wrote a song called 'Humanidad' (Humanity). Since I didn't have any instruments, I used a cardboard box to try to accompany myself. But I realised that that song offered something different than a bolero could … it was the only song that I'd written differently from previous ones. (Alí Primera, *Cantaclaro* No. 15, reproduced in Castillo and Marroquí 2005: 13)

In interviews throughout his life, Alí Primera represented this experience—being held by the DIGEPOL police in a cell—as the event that caused him to turn from composing *boleros* and love songs to entertain his friends or to woo women, to thinking differently about music and the role it could play in the leftist struggle. Alí represented his song 'Humanidad' as his first politically motivated song, and as his first attempt to compose a song that aimed to influence or enhance people's awareness of social injustice:

The first time I realised the possibilities of song was when I was imprisoned by the Digepol; there I realised that song communicated ... something
more than mere diversion or a simple way of passing the time. I realised that
song could have an influence on ... man's character. With a song one could
express a response to [the question of] why we were prisoners, why we were
resisting. (Alí Primera interviewed by Gloria Martín 5 June 1984, cited in
Martín 1998: 100)

Alí thus presented this song, 'Humanidad', as a pivotal point, which
marked the beginning of his trajectory as a committed *cantautor*. The
reported experience of police brutality and its link with his first committed
song featured in a 'plot' of Alí's life which he repeated and consolidated
in interviews and which was subsequently accepted by his allies, who also
repeated and recycled this narrative about the origins of the Venezuelan
variant of *Nueva Canción*. Gloria Martín (1998: 27) emphasises this in
her study of Venezuelan *Nueva Canción*, in which she observes 'there are
those who affirm that the first reference to [*Nueva Canción*] in Venezuela
is the song "Humanidad", apparently written by Alí Primera while he was
being detained in the cells of the [DIGEPOL]'.

My aim here is not to ascertain the veracity of Alí's narrative, nor is it
to verify whether 'Humanidad' was actually composed in a DIGEPOL
police cell. My concern is to examine what Alí's narrative was intended to
achieve. Alí represented the experience of being imprisoned because of his
political activism as a transformative event; in his narrative, Alí turned to
musical composition and performance in direct response to state repression. Alí represented his composition as the outcome of a lived experience
of personal suffering at the hands of the political police. Thus Alí linked
his musical activism to direct personal experience of the government's
oppressive institutions; he constructed and represented himself as a *cantautor* whose art was born from suffering at the hands of a repressive state.

THE LATE 1960s AND ALÍ'S PARTICIPATION IN THE *CARGA SOBRE CARACAS*

Soon after his period of detention at the hands of the DIGEPOL police,
Alí Primera composed 'No basta rezar' (Prayers are not Enough), a
song influenced by Liberation Theology, and 'América Latina Obrera'
(Proletarian Latin America), which, together with 'Humanidad', he sang

during events organised by the Venezuelan Communist Party as part of the *Carga sobre Caracas* (Charge on Caracas). More than a decade later, at the *Primer Festival de Canto Nuevo Latinoamericano* (First Festival of Latin American *Canto Nuevo*) in Mexico City in April 1982, Alí described this *Carga* as an attempt to raise the spirits of the left at a time of defeat and demoralisation following the Punto Fijo system's 'pacification' strategies, and he said that his audiences' responses to his songs encouraged him to continue composing:

> during this *Carga sobre Caracas*, that lasted a month, we agitated by day and sang by night, like a travelling circus. People were hearing something new, and this sowed within me something forever; the liberating role that song can have when one proposes through it a respect for man. (Alí Primera, *Cantaclaro* No. 15, reproduced in Castillo and Marroquí 2005: 13)

In interviews, Alí Primera articulated his motives for composing and singing at that time. For example, in an interview published in *Kena* in June 1969 under the headline 'Alí Primera: The Voice of Protest in Venezuelan Song', Alí reported that he aimed to do more than agitate through his music. The interviewer, Livia Plana, makes a distinction between different types of protest music; she refers to the South African Mirian Makeba as one of the initiators of protest song, and asserts that while Joan Baez and Bob Dylan are also protest singers, their music has different motivations because, she claims, entrepreneurs converted their protest into a 'flourishing business'. Alí Primera agrees and distances himself from 'mainstream' protest music:

> Protesting should be something more than the expression of circumstantial non-conformity in the face of particular situations in life. My protest songs are a way of exteriorising my discomfort with the things I see and which, in all honesty, I can't find a reason for. [With my songs] I try to raise awareness in people. ... Most [protest] singers have been accepted well, but I think their type of protest, though rebellious, is still very conventional. (Alí Primera interviewed by Livia Plana in 1969, cited in Castillo and Marroquí 2005: 73)

Alí, at this early stage of his musical career, represents his songs as vehicles through which he seeks to make sense of the problems and injustices he sees around him in everyday life, and for which he can find no legitimate reason. He also clearly constructs himself as responding to local conditions and not to Anglo-US protest songs. In an interview with Mariam Nuñez published posthumously in the national newspaper *El Nacional* on 23 April 1985, Alí Primera claimed that his first songs were a response to his personal experiences of injustice:

> When I started as a singer I was totally unaware ... of the movement that many people throughout the world call protest song. I set out with the intention of speaking through song and making song a support for the struggle for life, for dignity, and ... for the battle for a profound change in our society. (Alí Primera, cited in Hernandez Medina 1991: 248)

'Casas de cartón': Alí and the Representation of Poverty as the 'Fruit of Capitalist Exploitation'

In his song lyrics and through his use of local folk music forms, Alí brought the local reality of marginalised masses to the foreground, and named and described this reality through a vernacular vocabulary which, he said in an interview in *Punto* in July 1974, 'ordinary people relate to' (Alí Primera, cited in Hernández Medina 1991: 64). In 'Casas de cartón' (Cardboard Houses), a song which Alí recorded in 1974 on the independently produced album *Alí Primera Volumen 2*, Alí portrays life in a local barrio. As in many of his songs, one of his verses is recited to a musical accompaniment. His guitar and *cuatro* accompaniment is simple in order to foreground the message of these spoken and sung lyrics. The lyrics create a strong visual and visceral impression of the impoverished masses living in the hills which surround Caracas; the self-constructed housing, built from whatever materials the poor can acquire, and from which residents must descend in order to reach the alienating chaos of the city in order to eke out a living; the hunger, squalor and hopelessness of the barrios; the monotony and despair of lives devoid of prospects; the ironic contrast between the conditions of human beings in the barrios struggling to survive despite a lack of resources, infrastructure and opportunities, and the lives of the *patrones'* dogs, who receive education and training so that they make good pets and do not damage the newspapers they carry to their owners. In this song, dogs can also be seen as symbols of the barrier between the rich and the poor; they are creatures trained and looked after to ensure that they guard the properties and wealth of the few, while their owners exploit the labour of the masses the dogs protect them from. It is a song which represents poverty 'as the fruit of exploitation' and which is credited with being 'the hymn of the new movement of song' in Venezuela and Central America (Guerrero Pérez 2005: 26).

In a letter he wrote and which was published in *Punto* on 13 March 1974, Alí claimed that 'Casas de cartón' was inspired by the 'sub-life' of the people who lived in barrios, whose situation Alí stated he was familiar with 'because I myself have lived in four barrios in Caracas' (cited in Hernández Medina 1991: 59). The lives of local poor and marginalised *pueblos* were frequently at the forefront of Alí's songs. In 'Ruperto', recorded in 1975 on the album *Adiós en dolor mayor*, Alí Primera bestows visibility upon the invisible masses; by naming his protagonist and telling his story, Ruperto becomes an archetype and a symbol of all barrio residents who, unable to survive on agriculture or fishing, and excluded from the benefits of oil wealth, have migrated to the city in search of a better life only to find themselves marginalised in modern urban Venezuela. The lyrics are steeped in local vernacular and idiomatic terms used specifically in Venezuelan Spanish, such as '*échale bolas*' and '*guillo*', a device which locates the songs firmly within common everyday Venezuelan reality.

For Ruperto, attempts to integrate into urban life and the capitalist system bring only exclusion, pain, suffering and the death of his youngest son. With the ironic juxtaposition of advertising slogans with images of misery, illness and death, in this song Alí represents the glossy images that Ruperto sees in the oil company's calendar as nothing more than a seductive but unattainable dream. For Ruperto, representative of the Venezuelan masses seeking a better future for themselves and their children in Caracas, attempts to achieve the exciting but widely unattainable urban lifestyles hinted at in advertising slogans such as 'it's easy to have a Mustang' bring only further misery.

In this song, Alí emphasises the social exclusion that the oil wealth of a few signifies for the anonymous masses represented by Ruperto. Ruperto's petty theft, committed out of desperation in order to pay for his son's funeral, is depicted as a justifiable act. In contrast the police, who are 'always efficient when it comes to the poor', are represented as acting only to protect the interests of the wealthy minority. Alí employs irony to make the startling claim that capitalism helped Ruperto to build his shack, only to add immediately afterwards that this help was not in the form of a dignified salary earned through secure and stable employment, as one might first imagine, but instead took the form of the waste products of consumer society; empty Pepsi-cola and Mobil Esso cans for walls, and a Ford company advertising billboard for a roof. The song ends with a direct and repeated call for Ruperto to fight, not only to bury the son who died while he sought to obtain medical attention, but to bury capitalism, a system which Alí unambiguously calls 'the cause of all the misfortunes/ that my people suffer'.

'YANKEE GO HOME': ALÍ AND THE DENUNCIATION OF FOREIGN EXPLOITATION OF VENEZUELA'S OIL

Alí's early compositions had come to the attention of state authorities in the late 1960s and posed Alí with the personal threat of further and more severe state repression. Therefore, in 1969, Alí sought and obtained a grant from the Venezuelan Communist Party to study oil technology in Romania. According to family members, Alí Primera left Venezuela at that time not so much because of a profound desire to study but in order to escape the personal danger that his compositions and his involvement with student activism and leftist politics had created for him. My concern here is not to access the 'true' reasons for Alí's decision to study in Europe at the end of the 1960s. There is no doubt that the government's 'pacification' programme led to serious abuses of human rights in Venezuela in the 1960s; numerous cases of political disappearances and assassinations have been documented (Arzola Castellanos 2005), as well as severe repression of students and academics (Martín 1998). Without denying that there was severe state repression under the Punto Fijo system, I accord with Geoff Baker's argument (2011b: 3) that the 'outlaw' image has 'considerable appeal to underground artists' and that reports of censorship and personal struggles for the sake of art heighten the perceived political significance of that art. Throughout his life, Alí denounced state attempts to censor and repress his music, and he reported several state attempts to intimidate him and his family in order to seek to prevent him from performing his songs. These narratives added to the significance of his artistic work as representative of the daily struggles of ordinary people. I do not aim to prove or disprove the content of Alí's narrative, but to examine how this narrative added to the public interpretation and function of his songs.

While in Europe, Alí travelled and came into contact with other Latin American leftists, which instilled in him a sense of 'continental solidarity'. Ultimately, Alí decided not to complete his studies but instead to dedicate himself increasingly to music, performing his compositions at 'Peace for Vietnam' events. In an interview with Edith Guzmán published in the national newspaper *El Nacional* on 17 February 1974, Alí claims that he was the first Latin American to record 'this type of song' in Germany, and that in order to support himself he chose to 'wash dishes and sing folk songs in little cafes' rather than seek commercial outlets for his music (cited in Hernández Medina 1991: 62). Alí continually emphasised that he was motivated by his leftist principles and political ideals, and that he did not see his song as a commercial product, insisting in a letter published in *Punto* on 13 March 1974 'I do not consider this type of song to be a means of personal profit', and claiming that his conscience led him to struggle 'with everything I can give in order to transform this inhumane society, the fundamental base and essence of which rests on the accumulation of wealth by a few on top of the poverty of the great majority' (Alí Primera, cited in Hernandez Medina 1991: 59). In his narrative, Alí constructed himself as a *cantautor* whose art was not 'tainted' by profit motives but instead stemmed from an authentic and selfless drive to sacrifice everything in order to contribute to the undermining of the capitalist order and its replacement with a more humane and inclusive social and political order.

These views led Alí to reject a potentially lucrative career in oil technology. In his 1974 interview with Edith Guzmán, Alí claims that after two years of studying oil technology he realised that this subject was 'incompatible' with his way of being (cited in Hernández Medina 1991: 61), and he wrote in a letter to his mother that he abandoned his studies because he did not want to be a part of the oil companies' 'exploitation' of his country (Hernández Medina 1991: 43). In an interview with Maira Martínez published in the Mexican newspaper *El Excelsior* on 10 April 1982, Alí Primera explained how he viewed the impact of oil both on his country and on his political consciousness; he attributed his early awareness of social and economic injustice to his childhood in the Paraguaná Peninsula where he experienced at first hand the social and racial inequalities created by the operations of the foreign owned Amuay oil refinery, and its negative impact on the environment. Alí grew up next to this refinery, part of the second largest oil refinery complex in the world. In his interview with Martínez, carried out while Alí was attending the *Primer Festival de Canto Nuevo* in Mexico City, Alí said:

> In the oil zone I had contact with the gringo and the worker. And there, in that refinery which belonged to a transnational company, through seeing the realities of exploitation, the desire to fight for change began to grow in me. (cited in Hernández Medina 1991: 143)

Thus Alí drew on selected elements of his past (his detention in 1967, his childhood in the midst of social and economic inequalities in the oil zone), in order to construct his songs as the end result of a sensibility and political consciousness born of his direct experience of injustice and the foreign exploitation of Venezuela's oil resources. Oil, Alí told Héctor Hidalgo Quero in an interview on 27 February 1985 (Hidalgo Quero 1998: 24), 'deformed' Venezuela's economy because it absorbed 'a small percentage of the economically active population' while poverty and unemployment increased for the masses, the environment was destroyed, and only a small minority of people (mainly foreigners) profited. In 'América Latina obrera' (Proletarian Latin America), recorded on the album *Lo Primero de Alí Primera* in 1973, Alí gave voice to leftist denunciations of US intervention and influence in Latin America's economic life, and called for Pan-Latin American unity and solidarity in the face of foreign exploitation of Latin America's natural resources. In this song, Alí makes use of the English language phrase 'Yankee go home' in an appropriation of the language of the foreign exploiters the song denounces. This appropriation of English words in the song lyrics is not intended to emulate foreign models, as many commercial singers sought to do in Latin America at that time by singing in English or by anglicising their names. Interestingly, in 1971 the Chilean Víctor Jara had experimented with rock/pop genres and recorded two songs[9] with local Chilean rock group Los Blops. Jara called this 'invading the cultural invasion', suggesting that this project offered a method to transform popular culture into revolutionary culture (Taffet 1997: 99). In 'America Latina obrera', Alí also seeks to 'invade the cultural invasion' by re-signifying the borrowing of English words; by using the English phrase 'Yankee go home', Alí calls on his audience not to emulate dominant foreign cultural models but instead to overthrow those models and unite in order to effect revolutionary change in Latin America.

In 'Black Power', recorded on Alí's first album *Vamos gente de mi tierra* (1969), Alí also uses English lyrics: 'Hurry up, black power .../ ... In a short time/you will win/you will walk/you will sing ... Angela Davis, George Jackson/Bobby Seat, Luther King' in order to express solidarity with the US civil rights movement. The oil industry had deepened racist patterns of thought in Venezuela, and Alí aimed to raise the status of Afro-Venezuelans through showing solidarity with the civil rights movement in the USA and by highlighting black contributions to Venezuela. In 'José Leonardo', recorded on the album *Canción para los valientes* in 1976, Alí celebrates the Afro-Venezuelan of the title who in 1795 led an armed revolt aimed at the abolition of slavery and taxes and who was hanged for these deeds. By invoking and emphasising black contributions to Venezuela's independence struggles, Alí sought to counteract dominant discourses that promulgated a *café con leche* ('coffee with milk') culture of supposed racial equality but which in fact masked a racist ideology which identified the white European as the 'civilising agent' (Herrera Salas 2007: 103).

Alí expressed his ideas about the negative social and economic impact of oil wealth on his country more fully in 'Ahora que el petróleo es nuestro' (Now that the Oil is Ours), which he recorded in 1978 on the album *Canción mansa para un pueblo bravo*. The song was composed as a reaction to the nationalisation of the Venezuelan oil industry under the *Acción Democrática* (AD) government of Carlos Andrés Pérez in 1976. In this song, Alí calls on the president to invest oil wealth in housing, health care and food for the country's poor, instead of allowing wealthy company owners to reap the profits for themselves. The musical accompaniment is based on local *cuatro* and percussion forms of instrumentation, and the lyrics are based on Venezuelan vernacular, idiomatic expressions (*tiene cuadrada la arepa*) and local foods (*pabellón, caraotas, carne mechada*). These vernacular references root the song within the linguistic and cultural traditions of the common Venezuelan people. The message is direct; it draws attention to the ironic contradiction posed by the existence of so much poverty in the midst of so much natural wealth. The song calls for the country's oil resources to be used to benefit *el pueblo* and not to perpetuate and maintain the luxury of the elite 'parasites' who live off the labour of the impoverished masses that are excluded from basic social services and affordable food staples.

ALÍ'S RETURN TO VENEZUELA AND HIS REFUSAL TO BE LABELLED 'ORANGE'

Alí Primera's return to Venezuela in 1973, after spending four years in Europe, was motivated by his desire to use his musical skills to harness support for the presidential campaign[10] of José Vicente Rangel, candidate for the newly formed *Movimiento al Socialismo* (Movement towards Socialism, referred to in Venezuela as MAS) which was established by a group which had broken away from the Venezuelan Communist Party. On 1 February 1973, Ernesto Braun wrote in *Punto* that Alí Primera had returned to Venezuela a few days previously and that the *cantautor* had stated 'My principal activity as a militant revolutionary will be to help those sectors who are committed to *el pueblo*' (cited in Hernández Medina 1991: 53), and on 14 May 1973 it was reported in *Punto* that MAS had celebrated its legalisation with a special presentation from Alí Primera, who accompanied Rangel during his election tour, and that 'as always happens in a presentation of the singer Alí Primera the participants joined in with his songs and at the same time called out slogans alluding to the socialist election campaign' (cited in Hernández Medina 1991: 54). Though such press articles represented Alí's songs as being closely linked to leftist party politics, Alí himself was at pains to point out in his 1974 interview with Edith Guzmán that he did not conceive of his music as the 'property' of any political party (cited in Hernández Medina 1991: 62). In 1984, Alí expressed this more fully in an interview with Gloria Martín, explaining that he had consciously sought to create a distance between his songs and party politics:

> Everyone who as a singer emerges ideologically linked with a party or a revolutionary line, has to fight to detach themselves from the dependence that ... arises between their cultural work and the party ... That happened to me ... [but] song that comes from a party does not reach where it should reach. I have ended up deciding that song comes essentially from *el pueblo* ... day to day, in any place. (cited in Martín 1998: 100)

According to Alí's oldest son from his marriage to Sol Mussett, Sandino Primera, Alí had always told Rangel, whose MAS party was represented by the colour orange, 'If you need my music I'm going to sing, but I don't want people to put an orange sticker on me'.[11] According to Sandino, 'my father didn't want anybody's colour'. Though Alí continued to support the MAS[12], in interviews he sought to link his songs not with a political party but with *el pueblo*.

In the early 1980s, Alí was instrumental in the establishment of a movement of 'popular bases' aimed at uniting leftist groups and organisations across party political lines. The *Comité por la Unidad del Pueblo* (Committee for the Unity of the People, CUP) set out a 24-point platform in which it called for an end to foreign domination, the 'true' nationalisation of the oil and steel industries, the universal right to health care and education, price control on basic services such as water and electricity, the right to strike, greater efforts to bring about full employment, agrarian reform, the protection of children's rights, the defence of national culture, respect for the rights of marginalised indigenous and black communities, investment in local technology, an end to state repression, torture, corruption, the 'creation of the political, ideological and organisational conditions which will advance the struggle towards socialism', for solidarity with leftist social struggles throughout the world, and for 'the Unity of the People' and their 'ideological strengthening' to work against the 'great exploiters; Imperialism and the Venezuelan Bourgeoisie' (Hernández Medina 1991: 84–97). In addition to this platform, the CUP had a three-point plan of action which involved targeting workers and corruption within trade unions, as well as barrios in order to press for basic services such as water and sewage, and universities in order to demand autonomy and defend against government control (ibid.). Such an extremely broad set of general leftist ideas was aimed at appealing to the masses in general and bringing them together to strengthen popular demands for greater social, racial, cultural and economic equality. Alí's songs became an important vehicle for the diffusion of CUP's platform:

> Why not unite?
> And fight as brothers
> For our suffering homeland,
> The homeland that we love
> ('Dispersos', [Dispersed], from the album *Lo primero de Alí Primera*, 1974).

Although Alí refused to tie his *Canción Necesaria* to a single political party, in December 1983 he stood for election as a congressman for the *Liga Socialista* (Socialist League) in Lara and Zulia. In a letter addressed to *el pueblo* published in *El Nacional* on 12 October 1983, Alí comments on this apparently paradoxical decision, claiming that other political parties have asked him to stand for election, and that his decision to represent the *Liga Socialista* 'does not lessen my recognition of, my gratitude for and my friendship towards those organisations as being at the vanguard in the search for the profound change that our society needs' (cited in Hernández Medina 1991: 206). Alí does not clarify his rationale for choosing to stand for the *Liga Socialista* rather than any of these other parties. Setting out his three main principles in the elections as being the defence of ecology, the development of popular culture independently of paternalistic state interventions and the defence of human rights, Alí emphasises the enduring importance of *Canción Necesaria* to him and insists that his election as a congressman would not detract from or diminish his musical activities:

> I will continue to carry out my activity as a singer with the same intensity ... I will go to Congress in order to set out the problems and demand solutions and fight so that laws are passed which benefit the country and not political parties ... I am not exchanging songs for votes; I ask you to give me another platform from which to fight. (Alí Primera, cited in Hernández Medina 1991: 207)

Alí Primera was not elected in 1983, and in subsequent interviews he appears to have referred to this experience very little if at all.

ALÍ'S IDENTIFICATION WITH *EL PUEBLO*

In his narrative Alí constructed himself as a humble person who knew at first hand the suffering of the poor masses; he frequently recounted his memories of his childhood experiences of rural poverty, the death of his father when he was only three years old and his subsequent efforts to support his mother and siblings through boxing and shining shoes in the street. When asked by Francisco Graterol Vargas in an interview for *Diario de los Andes* published on 13 August 1982, 'What does Alí Primera mean for Alí Primera?', the *cantautor* answered:

> Alí Primera is a man who identifies with the child bootblack, with the peasant, with the orphan, with the worker, with the revolutionary militant. Alí Primera is the man who, after getting to university following many sacrifices, at a certain moment in his life realised that song served for something more than entertainment and who thought that song could be a brother in the liberatory process of the Venezuelan people ... If some record of mine produces a profit beyond that which I need to survive, I have always been concerned to know how to share that money. Not like a gift or like philanthropy, but like what I consider to be the most beautiful attitude of human beings, which is the act of solidarity, which I have maintained since my childhood as a peasant. That is Alí Primera, with many mistakes and skills, but I have a vital commitment to *el pueblo* who each day teach me more, who are essential, and at the same time friends of the work I do. (Alí Primera, cited in Hernández Medina 1991: 156)

Alí thus represented himself as a person with first-hand experience of poverty, suffering and injustice, who identified with the poor and the revolutionary. He insisted that he did not sing to enrich himself, and that his music was nourished by the same people he aimed to represent. In an interview he gave in Nicaragua in 1982 while participating in a festival of solidarity for the Sandinista government, Alí told *El Nuevo Diario*:

> I am a man who cleaned shoes, who was orphaned at the age of three, who knew poverty in a sad rural area, sad not in the sense of the joy that there is naturally in the birds and the trees and the clean wind, but sad in the sense that poverty in some ways brings sadness. But as I shared bread a sense of solidarity was born in me, through seeing the peasant sowing with the hope that it would rain for the crops to grow ... my mother is a peasant and I am too, owing to my childhood in the countryside, to my formation in the countryside. (Alí Primera, cited in Hernández Medina 1991: 150)

Alí thus selected and lifted out elements from his life to create a narrative that constructed his personal experiences of bereavement, poverty, child labour, rural hardship, peasant life, drought and political repression as part of a life story which placed him in a unique position to feel a profound sense of solidarity with the rural poor, the marginalised urban masses and the economically and politically oppressed. Alí insisted that his songs emerged from this lived sense of solidarity, and not to express a party political ideology.

Public Narratives About Alí's 'Authenticity' and the Power of His Music

Alí's narrative was taken up and re-circulated during his lifetime by allies who, in press articles, represented Alí as a profoundly compassionate person whose identification with *el pueblo* was genuine. Alí was recognised as playing a crucial and founding role in the origins and development of Venezuelan *Nueva Canción*. The account of Venezuela's first *Nueva Canción* composition being produced by Alí in a DIGEPOL police cell while he was being detained because of his involvement in student activism formed part of a narrative that Alí's allies reiterated in interviews and press articles. For example, in *Patria Libre* Guillermo Morrell published an article about Alí's life and music entitled 'Yankys [sic] go home...', in which Morrell wrote 'in the cells of the sadly famous DIGEPOL [Alí] becomes aware that his song could be entertaining, and also make [people] think in order to construct the new society we dream of' (cited in Castillo and Marroquí 2005: 65). Alí is described by William Guzmán in *El Siglo*, Caracas, 20 May 1983, as 'the founder of the protest music movement in Venezuela' (cited in Castillo and Marroquí 2005: 41).

Alí's songs and performance at the *Carga sobre Caracas* and other events organised by the Venezuelan Communist Party while he was a university student were noted in the leftist press. On 14 November 1969, the *Nueva Voz Popular* reported that 'Alí Primera, a student in the Faculty of Sciences at the UCV, turned out to be an excellent composer of popular songs' (cited in Hernández Medina 1991: 48). The following year, in the Venezuelan Communist Party's weekly *Tribuna Popular*, it was claimed on 28 August 1969 that Alí Primera's songs made the audience 'vibrate' with emotion at an event organised by the Communist Party in a barrio in Caracas, while on 25 September 1969 the same weekly publication reported that Alí Primera had launched his first LP containing ten songs that:

> won him ovations in each of his presentations at the university where he is currently a science student, and at the events of the Communist Youth of which he is a member. 'Alí Primera sings to the peasant, to the people's soldier, to the worker, to the student, to the mother, to the farmer of the new life that is being forged in the world with the blood of *los pueblos*', says Héctor Mujica[13] at the presentation of the record. (reproduced in Hernández Medina 1991: 48–9)

The leftist press praised and supported Alí's songs and performances and reported an enthusiastic audience response in the late 1960s, thereby constructing Alí as a legitimate spokesperson for *el pueblo* and their interests. Journalists who interviewed Alí for local and national newspapers, or who wrote articles about Alí's forthcoming performances or albums, helped to legitimise Alí's role as 'the voice of the people' by introducing their articles in ways that invested the *cantautor* with profound significance and political authority:

> In Alí Primera we have the authentic and genuine representation of the Venezuelan people ... always with the truth on his lips, pouring forth songs for the unity of *el pueblo* ... [with] that fighting spirit. (Days Martínez, cited in Castillo and Marroquí 2005: 44)

> Alí Primera is a singer and a revolutionary militant ... With a figure of Alí Primera's stature, one has to do away with literary language and embrace a colloquial conversational style ... because he is a being who feels for his people so deeply that he is moved and speaks great truths, expressing without reservation what he feels and hopes for his [people]. (Alexander Contreras, cited in Castillo and Marroquí 2005: 45)

Alí's songs were accepted by sympathetic writers and journalists as representative of the daily struggles of the poor. In press articles, Alí's music was constructed as a resource that offered a 'new language' for the leftist struggle. In an article published in *Punto* on 28 August 1973, Ramón Rivasáez wrote:

> To speak of Alí is like opposing a whole order ... Alí has broken away from timid positions. He has erupted flat out on a search for a fresh language for the combat and for revolutionary struggle. Few artists like Alí have managed to maintain a clear commitment to a struggle which is starting to reformulate socialism and make of it a blueprint for infinite possibilities. To be socialist is not easy ... and that is reflected in the fact that new popular Latin American song like Alí's does not have access to the mass media. (cited in Hernandez Medina 1991: 56)

In such articles, writers and journalists helped to legitimise Alí as a person who, through his music, forged an authentic commitment with the poor and their struggles. Alí Primera's personal charisma during live performances was also emphasised in reviews of his music events throughout the 1970s and early 1980s. For example, Alí's 'mission' through song was described by Ramón Rivasáez in *Diario de Los Andes* in July 1981 as 'almost evangelical' (cited in Castillo and Marroquí 2005: 47). In an anonymous review of Alí's participation in one festival, Alí's appearance and political communication through song is described in almost religious terms:

> The bridges that he establishes between one song and the next, result in a notable political effect. One could say that he resembles a political orator. His speeches possess a certain mystical intonation; poverty and exploitation, the people's struggle, are treated like sacred themes which flow into songs of resounding momentum, as if each song could be a popular battle hymn. (anonymous, no date)

In a review of another music event, published on 9 August 1981 in *Los Andes*, Pedro Matheus wrote:

> The act was closed by the singer Alí Primera, who transmitted to the audience the energy of rebellion which he inserts into his songs. The popular singer of protest music remembered the heroic deeds of José Leonardo ...; he invoked the spirit of Alberto Lovera, and he conversed for a long time with [sic] the Liberator. The public followed his every step and the ovations were reiterated as Alí sang one after another of his songs. He spoke about himself and his confessions turned out to be political poetry declaimed without any kind of subterfuge. (cited in Castillo and Marroquí 2005: 20)

Furthermore, Alí's 'outlaw' status was highlighted by leftist journalists in the press, who referred to reports of state censorship of Alí's songs in order to support their own denunciations of governing authorities. Ramón Rivasáez wrote in *Punto* on 28 August 1973:

> Alí Primera is vetoed. Not a single TV channel or radio station would dare ... to transmit his clear and courageous denunciations of the current economic structures which maintain the rich in power. (quoted in Hernández Medina 1991: 56)

The leftist Venezuelan press published various dramatised public denunciations of reported repression of Alí's songs. For example, a poem published in *Punto* in 1973, entitled 'The Government doesn't Like the Songs of Alí Primera', describes an incident of state censorship of Primera's music thus:

> With guns in hand/...the police arrived/...[an] official announced/... 'I've been sent to collect the songs/that contain obscene phrases/because they offend the system/and incite to protest'. (Alejo Torres, quoted in Hernández Medina 1991: 55–6)

On 22 January 1975, Manuel Molina wrote an article in *Punto* entitled 'Alí Primera Affirms: Radio and TV Impresarios Want to Own our Thoughts'. In this article, Molina claims that disc jockey Napoleón Bravo had played Alí Primera's song 'José Leonardo' on his radio show. Molina reports that after Bravo played it, this was the song most requested by the public in telephone calls to the station. However, Molina writes that Bravo received an anonymous internal telephone call instructing him 'Look, don't play that song by Alí Primera'. In response, Molina writes that Alí Primera told him:

> ... the government is not a genuine representative of the people. No matter how nationalistic they want to look, they represent the dominant classes in Venezuela who see their interests endangered when *el pueblo* achieves a higher state of awareness. (cited in Hernández Medina 1991: 67–8)

It is not my aim to verify these narratives of censorship, but to examine their significance. Writing with reference to Cuban hip hop in the twenty-first century, Baker (2011b: 9) argues that censorship is 'an important trope in underground music', and that there is therefore 'an incentive to seize on every impediment as evidence of conspiracy'. It may be that media executives saw no profit potential in Alí's folk-based music. Interestingly, José Guerra and Jesús Cordero of the group Los Guaraguao recorded rock-pop versions of Alí's songs, most famously 'Casas de cartón', using electric guitars, electric bass and a drum kit. These albums were played on radio programmes, and Los Guaraguao also performed Alí's songs live on Venezuelan television.[14] According to Guerra and Cordero, the group did not encounter official attempts to prohibit these performances.[15] Whatever any impediments Alí faced in the dissemination of his music via the mass media may have been caused by, in his narrative Alí and his allies emphasised and denounced instances of censorship in order to heighten the subversive associations of Alí's songs. Alí and his allies made use of narratives about the prohibition of *Canción Necesaria* in order to construct it as 'underground' music. At the same time, Alí denounced the consumer values propagated by the mass media and represented himself as a *cantautor* who deliberately chose to shun the world of show business and commercial music in order to use his music not for personal gain but as a tool to raise consciousness amongst *el pueblo*.

ALÍ'S ESTABLISHMENT OF THE *CIGARRÓN* LABEL AND REJECTION OF WEALTH AND 'SHOW BUSINESS'

In 1973 Alí Primera, together with other *Nueva Canción cantautores*, established the recording cooperative, *Cigarrón*. This label disseminated Alí's music as well as that of other Venezuelan *Nueva Canción* groups and artists in a climate in which the local culture industries were dominated by imported rock and popular music (Britto García, quoted in Martín 1998:

147). Alí's work with this label has been characterised by one Venezuelan artist I interviewed in 2005 as evidence that he represented 'not just a song, [but] a conduct, a way of being'; this artist told me that Alí always said 'if the singer doesn't act in a way that is consistent with [the message of] his own song, then he fails'.

In interviews, Alí Primera emphasised his distance from show business and commercial music and represented his conduct as being consistent with the messages of his songs. In an interview with Mariam Núñez published posthumously in *El Nacional* on 23 April 1985, Alí proclaimed:

> I cannot convert my stance into a mercantilist one. I am not interested in making a name for myself through publicity. I am interested in the people knowing my songs, not [them knowing] Alí Primera. (quoted in Hernández 1991: 250)

Alí defended these views in the face of apparent attacks on his integrity. In an undated interview published in *Pueblo*, Alí 'denied categorically that he uses the people's pain to grow rich and ... affirmed that he distributes seventy per cent of his royalties amongst needy people ... [and] ... of the eleven records he has recorded, the profits from five were for the benefit of the PCV (*Partido Comunista de Venezuela*/Communist Party of Venezuela) and the MAS' (cited in Hernández Medina 1991: 181). In a letter he wrote and which was published in *Punto* on 13 March 1974, in response to accusations apparently made in public against him and other *Nueva Canción* artists by an individual using the pseudonym 'Señor Delpino', Alí Primera claimed:

> You maintain that our way of saying things is only motivated by an interest in earning money to enjoy villas, race horses, yachts and even a Renoir. Do you know, Señor Delpino, that the only vehicle I have ever owned in my life was a bicycle that I won ... even though I have recorded five LPs ... And do you know why? Because I do not view this type of song as a means of personal profit, nor as charity ... My conscience makes me fight with all my strength to transform this inhumane society, whose fundamental base, whose essence, is the accumulation of wealth by a few on the back of the poverty of the great majority. (Alí Primera, cited in Bigott 2005: 100)

Such words suggest that Alí had critics who accused him of seeking to make money from his songs about poverty, exploitation and oppression. Alí himself claimed that private television station owners, aware of his mass appeal, offered him twenty-five thousand *bolívares* (almost the equivalent of an average annual salary in the 1970s[16]) to sing on one of their programmes for 15 minutes (Alí Primera, cited in Hernandez Medina 1991: 184). Alí publicly rejected these financial incentives. In his interview with Edith Guzman published in *El Nacional* on 17 February 1974, Alí claimed that television was not 'compatible' with the message he wanted to project, and that though he knew he could reach large numbers of people through television, the medium would 'dilute' his message; 'I am saying that what man needs is bread, and in the end the programme convinces the public that what they need is a soft drink' (Alí Primera, cited in Hernández Medina 1991: 62). Alí refused to compromise his message by fitting it in 'between advertisements for deodorant and fizzy drinks' and submitting to the dictates of censors as to what he could say and sing on air, maintaining that:

> It is essential that I refuse offers to sing on television ... [what is important] is my presence in front of the people so that they have the chance to boo or applaud or say 'I'm with you, Alí', ... because I believe that song is con-structed in the presence of the people. (Alí Primera, quoted in Hernández Medina 1991: 184)

Alí Primera fervently and repeatedly denounced the private media during interviews and live performances. At a concert on behalf of political prisoners held in Maturín in August 1982, Alí referred to the private television channel Venevisión as the 'vanguard of the United States Central Intelligence Agency' in Venezuela, and he called for television channels to be directed by 'the Venezuelan people, in defence of their dignity, their culture, their history, their struggle, their hope'.[17] Percussionist Jesús Franquis, who provided the Afro-Venezuelan percussion for a number of Alí Primera's studio recordings, asserts that the private *Venevisión* television channel contacted Alí Primera in the 1970s and asked him to sing on television with Joan Manuel Serrat. According to Franquis, Alí refused even this offer.[18] Radio presenter, journalist and writer Lil Rodríguez states that 'Alí could have been a millionaire', but that he chose to remain faithful to his ideals even if this meant that he did not accumulate personal material wealth.[19] When I asked Alí's widow Sol Mussett whether Alí had ever been tempted to accept the large amounts of money he claimed he had been offered to appear on television, she insisted that Alí never had been attracted by such offers at all but that he always told her that to grow rich from his music would be 'hypocritical'.[20] It is not my aim here to seek to verify whether Alí was ever offered vast amounts of money to appear on television, and whether he really did refuse such offers in order to remain faithful to his principles; what is significant is that Alí maintained that he was not motivated by money, and his allies repeated and supported these claims in narratives that circulated in the leftist press and added to the perceived 'authenticity' of his music.

According to Alí's cousin Ramiro Primera, Alí started the *Cigarrón* record label partly in order to have 'more ideological freedom', and also partly in order to have more control over the profits from his record sales because he 'had differences with the record label that distributed his records'. This, according to Ramiro, was because in 1976 Alí composed and recorded a song, which was not explicitly political but which was instead about life in the *llanos* cattle plains, 'Cunaviche adentro'. This song reached number one on the radio, and Alí estimated that he had sold more than eighty thousand copies of it. According to Ramiro, 'they paid him for ten thousand copies. Alí thought that was daylight robbery', and he established his own record label in order to maintain control over the profits his recorded music made.[21]

Cantautor and journalist Gregorio Yépez, who in 1980 recorded Alí's song 'Canción Bolivariana' (Bolivarian Song) with Alí, observes that while the dissemination of *Nueva Canción* albums was always a problem, there was 'always someone who wasn't happy with censorship' and who would play Alí's songs on the radio.[22] In my interviews with *Nueva Canción cantautores* who worked with Alí, all emphasised to me the informal methods Alí employed to sell his records; he would drive around the country with records in his old car,[23] and distribute piles of his albums to his friends and family to be sold to their friends and contacts.

Despite these informal methods of distribution, Alí Alejandro Primera estimates that Alí Primera's albums were owned by 70 % of households in Caracas during Alí's lifetime.[24] An undated and anonymous newspaper article claims that though Alí's records were seldom heard on the radio, 'paradoxically, each album sells almost 100,000 copies' (cited in Castillo and Marroquí 2005: 39). Yépez claims that Alí Primera was one of the few Venezuelan artists able to support themselves and their families from the proceeds of their music. This is not an insignificant claim—in addition to his four sons with Sol, Alí had two daughters with a Swedish partner while he was living in Europe and a son with a Venezuelan partner after returning to Caracas. According to Yépez, Alí maintained all seven of these recognised children with money earned from record sales. While most Venezuelan artists at that time kept only three per cent of the profits from record sales, Alí, Yépez claims, had a 'different relationship' with the recording industry and was able to keep 50 to 60 % of the profits earned through sales of the albums he recorded on the *Cigarrón* label. According to Yépez, after supporting his own family Alí used these profits to record other *Nueva Canción cantautores* and to finance live music events, which were usually free to the public. However, there are no official sales figures for Alí's albums. Family members assert that after Alí's death, the Primera-Mussett family had debts and relatives sought to 'protect [Alí's] children' by requesting an inventory from the Promus company *Cigarrón* was affiliated was affiliated with, but they did not succeed in ascertaining official sales figures for Alí's albums.

It is beyond the scope of this book to verify the sales figures and profit margins that many claim for Alí's LPs. However, newspaper reports of Alí's high levels of dissemination and of his donation of so much of the profit from his record sales are significant; these reports constructed Alí as a popular *cantautor* whose reputation as an 'underground' artist was not tarnished by fame or by high record sales. Such narratives arguably added to the significance of Alí's songs and made it possible for him to become a well-known *cantautor*, and to reach a high level of penetration, while his songs could continue to be perceived and accepted as subversive. As Geoff Baker (2012: 14) observes in the Cuban context, 'From an underground perspective, making music and selling it is acceptable; it is making music while thinking about selling it that is not'. Alí apparently made money from his records, but he insisted that he did not make these records in order to make money. In an interview with William Guzmán published in *El Siglo*, Caracas, on 20 May 1983, Alí said:

> The fact that my records sell does not mean that I am commercial, because I have never written songs with lucrative aims. I am not at the service of money. (cited in Castillo and Marroquí 2005: 41)

Alí insisted that he took only the money that he and his family needed to survive, and that he gave away the rest. This narrative was repeated by his allies. It was thus possible for Alí to become famous and sing 'I remember the worker who told me "don't sell your song; if you sell it, you sell me. If you sell it, you sell yourself,[25]'" while simultaneously denouncing the trappings of fame and fortune; the message perceived to lie within his songs could be accepted as consistent with his own conduct in life.

ALÍ'S SEARCH FOR THE 'AUTHENTIC' SOUND OF *EL PUEBLO*

On the *Cigarrón* label, Alí recorded 13 albums in approximately 12 years. For all of the covers for these albums, Alí used the art of local painters, and in the sleeve-notes he included reproductions of his own hand-written messages about the songs' meaning, and copies of the songs' lyrics. The music is varied and based on local Afro-Venezuelan, indigenous and popular *mestizo* forms such as the *tamunangue* from Lara, the *gaita* from Zulia, the *joropo* and *llanera* from the plains and polyrhythmic forms associated with the *tambor* drum ensembles of Barlovento. Alí studied these styles informally[26] as he travelled around the country performing. Noel Márquez, member of the Afro-Venezuelan Grupo Madera and a personal friend of Alí's, told me in 2005 that Alí wanted his songs to sound 'authentic'.[27] Instrumentation includes stringed instruments (harp, guitar, mandolin, *cuatro*) and African and indigenous percussion instruments and drums (maracas, *charrasca* scrapers, *quitiplás*, *mina* and *furruco* drums of African descent).[28] Alí tied his music with the land and its workers, describing it somewhat romantically in an interview with Mariam Núñez on 24 January 1985 as:

> The music of the birds, the wind, the trees, the songs of the peasants as they sowed the land, *salves, merengues, valses,* old clarinets and violins, the *cuatro* with goat-hair strings; that's where my song comes from. (quoted in Hernández Medina 1991: 247)

Alí claimed in an interview with Gloria Martín that he had no formal music education (Martín 1998: 100), and that his inspiration came from *el pueblo*. His lyrics celebrated and defended the land, the subordinate, and leftist struggles; Afro-Americans ('Black Power'), children ('La piel de mi niña'), the victims of war throughout the world ('No basta rezar'), the environment ('El lago, el puerto y la gente'), popular heroes ('Comandante Che'), Latin American solidarity ('El sombrero azul'), love ('La sirena de este tiempo'), indigenous people ('Un Guarao') and common people ('Canción para no olvidarme'). Many of the songs have verses that Alí did not sing but which he recited as he strummed a rhythmic accompaniment on the *cuatro*. During his frequent live performances at music events throughout the country, Lilia Vera[29] comments, Alí 'sang for a minute, then just strummed his *cuatro* while he held a political meeting for twenty-five minutes, then carried on with the song'.

Diego Silva, a multiple award winning composer, researcher and musician who worked with Alí Primera in the 1970s and 1980s as a violinist and arranger of his songs, describes Alí's performances as 'meetings where he sang', and asserts that Alí had an ability to 'channel messages with his songs'. Silva characterises Alí as someone who, through his use of national music forms and his vernacular lyrics, 'touched the essence of what it is to be Venezuelan', and he remembers Alí's dedication to producing an 'authentic' and non-commercial sound in his songs; Alí once telephoned him at 11.30 in the evening and pleaded with him to go to the studio where he was recording a song dedicated to the popular Venezuelan singer, Pío Alvarado (1895–1983). The problem was that the academy trained violinist Alí had contracted could not play 'like a peasant', and Silva recalls arriving at the studio that night and Alí Primera asking him to 'play as if we were in the village' in order that the recording should resonate with ordinary Venezuelans.[30]

Musically, Alí's songs do not require exceptional skill to perform in the manner that Alí chose to have them arranged; Silva remembers that Alí always insisted that the arrangements should not be 'too sophisticated'. Lyrically, the language is frequently vernacular and conversational in tone. These qualities led some to criticise Alí's songs for their lack of aesthetic concern and to refer to them as nothing more than political 'pamphlets' (Obregón Muñoz 1996: 12). However, *cantautores* who knew and worked with Alí point out that towards the mid-1980s, Alí had begun to exhibit a greater concern with the aesthetic value of his songs and to work towards more complex arrangements with other instruments such as the cello. Nevertheless, throughout most of his musical career, Alí made no apologies for privileging the socio-political message over aesthetic form in his *Canción Necesaria*:

> I don't like using pretty words
> To perfume shit
> ('Panfleto de una sola nota' [Single Note Pamphlet], from the album *Cuando nombro la poesía*, 1979).

'CANCIÓN BOLIVARIANA' (BOLIVARIAN SONG)

Alí sought, he explained in an interview published in *Punto* on 7 July 1974, to 'articulate a class ideology in a language which ordinary people will relate to' (quoted in Hernández Medina 1991: 64). In his songs, he aimed to provide a vocabulary with which ordinary people could recognise and articulate their condition, and in recognising and articulating it be spurred, as he said an interview with Miriam Núñez published posthumously in *El Nacional* on 23 April 1985, to 'transform [society], because a people that is unconscious of its own reality, even its own strength, is incapable of mobilising and transforming anything (quoted in Hernández Medina 1991: 248). Alí claimed that his songs even reached the 'forgotten' peoples of rural Venezuela, in spite of high levels of illiteracy in these regions, because illiteracy 'isn't an obstacle to understanding my songs, ... my songs are simple, the language of the people' (ibid.). Chilean *cantautor* Eduardo Carrasco quite independently makes a claim that supports Alí's assertion; Carrasco (1982: 39) states that a distinctive feature of Venezuelan *Nueva Canción* is that unlike other Latin American countries, where the movement remained concentrated in the largest cities, in Venezuela '*Nueva Canción* immediately spread to the provinces and took off there, and remains popular [in the provinces] to this day'.

Alí frequently toured both in Venezuela and abroad where he participated in international *Nueva Canción* festivals in Mexico, Argentina and Nicaragua, and events organised in solidarity with the peoples of Central and South America. In Venezuela, Alí was instrumental in organising numerous music events. These events were aimed at raising awareness of environmental issues and human rights abuses, and also at uniting people around popular culture. For example, Alí was active in bringing about the *Canción Solidaria en Coro* music festival, which was organised to raise funds to build a *Casa de Cultura* (House of Culture) and to call for the defence of the Cerro Galicia area. Hidalgo Quero wrote that Alí 'assum[ed] his natural condition of poet', and that the *cantautor* spoke at this event of the trees which 'have served the *turpial* and all the *guacharacas* [national birds] of the mountain ... and which [allowed] José Leonardo ... [the hope] of being free and freeing his people' (cited in Hidalgo Queros 1998: 99). Alí thus linked trees and the natural environment with patriotism and revolutionary ideals. Silva emphasises how Alí, at a time when few people spoke of the environment, fervently believed that capitalism was not only the enemy of man but that it was a system that endangered the planet because of its reliance on the extraction of natural resources.[31]

Significantly, Alí drew on and reinterpreted the philosophy of Simón Bolívar; Diego Silva asserts that it was largely Alí who revived interest in the ideology of Bolívar at a time when the left widely repudiated the nineteenth-century figure. Gregorio Yépez was 13 years old when in 1980 he recorded the child's voice on Alí Primera's 'Canción Bolivariana' (Bolivarian Song), a song which takes the form of a conversation between Simón Bolívar and a modern-day child. Yépez claims that Alí was deeply committed to CUP ideals and acted upon them, and that 'Alí's magic as an artist and as a politician was that he united everyone and transcended political ideologies; he was a great unifier'. According to Yépez, Alí avoided preaching to the converted and genuinely sought to reach and affect people. For example, in Barquisimeto in the late 1970s, a radio disc jockey called Gerardo Britto presented a show called *Los venezolanos primeros* (Venezuelans First), in which considerable air time was dedicated to Venezuelan music. Though Britto was a member of COPEI, Alí became friends with him because of their shared interest in and respect for local music. Yépez recounted to me how Alí always maintained that it was 'more important' that they should reach someone like Britto and encourage him to support the revolutionary *Frente Farabundo Martí para la Liberación Nacional* (Farabundo Martí National Liberation Front, FMLN) in El Salvador, because one would anyway expect such things from the left.

In 'Canción Bolivariana' (Bolivarian Song), recorded in 1980 on the album *Abrebrecha, y mañana hablamos*, Alí reinterprets the ideology of Simón Bolívar for a twentieth-century audience. By choosing to humanise Bolívar and make him speak directly to the child, who can be seen to represent *el pueblo*, Alí proclaims in this song that Bolívar should not be a mere patriotic symbol for the elite to light candles for. In the song, Alí accuses the elite of only paying attention to Bolívar in order to make sure that he and his revolutionary ideas are 'well and truly dead'. Through the conversation between Bolívar and the child, Alí resurrects Bolívar's dream of a unified and united Latin America and proclaims that Bolívar's ideas should 'ride again'. Calling for pan-Latin American unity, Alí asserts that 'if the fight for freedom is dispersed/there will be no victory in the battle'. With a sung chorus and recited verses, 'Canción Bolivariana' is a direct call for Venezuelans to look back to revolutionary ideals of the Liberator in order to find inspiration for the future. Also within this song, in addition to its main message concerning the revival of Bolívar's ideals, Alí comments on environmental problems (Bolívar and the child meet 'underneath a tree/that was saved from the fire') and the lack of educational facilities (the child is 'of school age and without a school').

In 1983, the bicentenary of Bolívar's birth, Alí was the principal coordinator of a series of festivals that took place in five Venezuelan cities in July in homage to Simón Bolívar (Days Martínez, cited in Castillo and Marroquí 2005: 19). In an interview with Hector Hidalgo Quero published in *El Falconiano* on 16 February 1983, Alí Primera said that the festivals were supported by the *Federación Venezolana de la Cultura Popular* (Venezuelan Federation of Popular Culture), which was directed by Rafael Salazar, and that important *Nueva Canción cantautores* from across Latin America were scheduled to participate (cited in Hernandez Medina 1991: 185–6). Alí called the events *Festivales de la Canción Bolivariana* (Festivals of Bolivarian Song). The aim of these festivals, Alí said, was to 'highlight Bolivarian thought and take it to *el pueblo* by means of song, in order to recover the moral strength which today is more necessary than ever' (ibid.) (Figs. 3.2 and 3.3).

STATE PERSECUTION OF ALÍ

Alí claimed that the state viewed him as a dangerous subversive who encouraged 'non-conformity'. His evident popularity, his involvement in organising a large number of festivals and music acts, and his ability to attract large numbers to his music events meant, he said, that he was perceived to pose a particular threat to the status quo. In the 1980s, Alí's narrative in interviews and letters to the press increasingly emphasised the personal danger which he said he faced in order to sing *Canción Necesaria*. In an open letter which was published in *El Nacional* on 3 May 1982, Alí claimed that the Venezuelan state harassed him constantly, and he gave eight concrete examples of the persecution he said he was submitted to. These examples heighten Alí's 'outlaw' status and emphasise the personal danger which he said he faced because of his music:

Figs. 3.2 and 3.3   Alí Primera singing with other Latin American musicians at Festivales de la Canción Bolivariana [Festivals of Bolivarian Song] in Venezuela, 1983 (Photographs courtesy of Jesús Franquis)

1. They hand out drugs to addicts with the aim of sabotaging the mass events where we perform.
2. They telephone me in the early hours of the morning with death threats.
3. They have shot at me on two occasions with the aim of frightening or softening me (since the distance was too short for them to have missed me).
4. They have tried to cause an accident when I have been travelling in my old car on the country's roads. This has happened three times.
5. They got into my house when I was away. They broke the door locks and then tried to make this look like a mistake. If it was a mistake, I want to ask:
   (a) Why did they shoot at the lower part of the building before entering my flat?
   (b) Who was the man wearing green shorts who came into my apartment first followed by two DISIP[32] policemen? ...
6. They came back to my house, this time four armed men, and they scraped their guns against the outer door and uttered offensive words against my person (Wednesday 12-4-82, 3:30a.m.).
7. Calls to my mother in which they tell her to go out and buy mourning clothes.
8. Threats to kidnap my children, etc. (Alí Primera, cited in Bigott 2005: 132)

In an interview with Hector Hidalgo Quero published in *El Falconiano* on 16 February 1983, Alí repeated such claims:

They have just threatened me again. They cannot forgive the fact that I have not been intimidated and that I maintain a conduct which is consonant with my song. ... They are trying to destroy me, they are trying to destroy ... what it means that there is a certain relationship between my work and the dreams of young people. Now they call my neighbours to intimidate me. They continue to persecute me and try to cause me to have an accident. (quoted in Hidalgo Quero 1998: 84-5)

Alí remained publicly defiant and emphasised in his narrative that song was his 'duty' and the only way he had to support *el pueblo* (cited in Bigott 2005: 132). In an open letter which was published posthumously on 28

May 1985 in the national newspaper *El Nacional*, Alí said that though he loved life he was not afraid to die for what he believed in:

> I want to say something to those who have been threatening me and trying to kill me for so long. Breaking into and searching my house, shooting at my car windows, persecuting me on the roads, etc.: none of that will silence me. My weapon is song ... my weapon is the desire to always be useful to my country. I don't have the makings of a hero, but since I don't have the makings of a deserter either, I prefer to take the risk of using my 'weapons' to confront yours. (cited in Hernández Medina 1991: 212)

Other *Nueva Canción cantautores* and leftist intellectuals and journalists repeated and heightened Alí's narrative, denouncing the persecution to which they said Alí was subjected. Dozens of politicians, *cantautores* and union leaders signed letters decrying the state repression of Alí. For example, on 26 February 1982, the following statement was published in *El Nacional*:

> We emphatically declare that we are not prepared to tolerate the *Copeyano* government making Alí Primera into a hostage. He ... belongs to the people; he is one of the clear reference points for the people's organisation. We therefore assume his defence and express our solidarity with [Alí] who does not represent art for art's sake but culture at the service of our people's struggles. (cited in Hernández Medina 1991: 120)

The *Comité Venezolano de Solidaridad con el Pueblo de El Salvador* (Venezuelan Committee for Solidarity with the People of El Salvador), of which Alí was Secretary, wrote in *El Nacional* on 9th June 1984:

> As if it were possible to silence the voice of *el pueblo*! As if it were possible to close the mouth of the student, or to stop the strong arm of the worker, or to take away the hope of the peasant, or to steal the breath from *el pueblo* who fight for their freedom! ... The songs of Alí Primera are rooted, irreversibly, in the deepest part of the Venezuelan *pueblo*. And it is so because they [the songs] surge from their very own history, from the history of ... Bolívar ... and so many others. (cited in Bigott 2005: 141)

The narratives of Alí's allies, circulated in the leftist press, constructed Alí as the very essence of the Venezuelan people; these narratives therefore represented threats against Alí as threats against the Venezuelan people. Alí was depicted as the archetype of the student, the worker, the peasant and the common person. *Canción Necesaria* was constructed as the product of *el pueblo* and of the country's history, and as a weapon that posed a genuine threat to the prevailing political order.

CONCLUSIONS

In this chapter, I have examined the local conditions that shaped Alí Primera's political ideas and which he responded to, and how he used *Canción Necesaria* to seek to raise awareness of the racial, economic and cultural inequalities that he attributed to the impact of the oil industry in Venezuela. I have argued that Alí's own narratives, and his refusal to become too closely linked to a single political party, contributed to his songs being legitimated as representative of 'the people' and to Alí being popularly perceived as the 'backbone of popular song' in the country.[33]

Alí's output was prolific; between 1973 and the year of his death, he recorded and released an album of his own material almost every year. His narrative about his life and his motivations, which was disseminated in the press and at live performances, was referred to by writers and journalists who wrote about the significance of his songs during his lifetime. This narrative was characterised by an overall plot composed of six dominant themes through which Alí represented himself to the public and formulated knowledge of his motivations as a *cantautor*. First, Alí represented himself as *a man who knew poverty, suffering and political repression* at first hand. Second, *he rejected the mainstream media and show business* and publicly refused to compromise his message in order to gain personal material benefits. Third, he articulated a concern *to raise the consciousness of el pueblo*, to recuperate their memory and to tell their 'true' history. Fourth, he expressed a concern *to protect the land and the environment* from the destruction of capitalist progress. Fifth, he called for *the revival of Bolívar's philosophy* in order to unite and fortify *el pueblo* in their struggles against dictatorship, imperialism, economic exploitation, racism and poverty. Sixth, he made *repeated denunciations* of state attempts to silence him.

Considered to be the most prolific and the most active Venezuelan *Nueva Canción cantautor*, Alí travelled widely to perform his *Canción Necesaria* directly to his audiences. He disseminated his songs via 13 independently recorded albums, and was seen to support other *cantautores* by offering them opportunities to perform and to record. His songs drew on local music styles and vernacular and idiomatic language, and appear to have sold well and attracted large numbers in live performances. He rejected the mass media as a means of disseminating his songs and acquired a reputation for being 'authentic' and motivated by ideological rather than commercial concerns. His own narrative in interviews enhanced the 'underground' qualities of his songs; his denunciations of the censorship of his songs and of persecution from state authorities lent him what John Kane (2001) calls 'moral capital', defined as 'a source of power that derives from the way in which individuals are judged as moral beings' (cited in Street 2006: 60). Alí presented himself as a *cantautor* of integrity who practised what he preached, who identified with the rural and urban poor, who rejected wealth, and who was deeply committed to uniting people. In his narratives in interviews and letters to the press, Alí depicted himself as brave and defiant in the face of state persecution, and as a committed person who continued to compose and perform his *Canción Necesaria* in the face of threats against him. These narratives conditioned the narratives of leftist writers and journalists who wrote about Alí in the press.

On 16 February 1985, Alí was returning home after working on his thirteenth album when an oncoming vehicle collided with his. He was killed instantly. This sudden death, which came after repeated denunciations of state persecution and harassment, led to new interpretations of his life and songs in the late 1980s and early 1990s. These are the focus of the next chapter.

NOTES

1. Alí Primera, open letter to *El Nacional*, 3 May 1983. Reproduced in Castillo and Marroquí, 2005: 12.
2. The barrios (shanty-towns) of Caracas, 'like the favelas of Rio de Janeiro … are places that have been formed by exclusion, rural-urban migration, and poverty' (Fernandes 2010: 9).
3. Interview with Cordero and Guerra, Caracas, September 2008.
4. Personal communication from Suárez, July 2009.
5. Interview with Vera, Caracas, July 2005.
6. Interview with Mussett, Barquisimeto, July 2005.

7. Biographical information in this chapter is based on interviews with Alí Primera's cousin, Ramiro Primera, and nephew, Alí Alejandro Primera, conducted in Caracas in July 2005 and September 2008.
8. On 17 October 1965, four days before Alí Primera enrolled at UCV, Lovera was detained in the Plaza Las Tres Gracias, Caracas. Lovera was tortured and murdered by the DIGEPOL, and his body was thrown into the sea after being bound with chains in an attempt to prevent it from floating. On 27 October 1965, a fisherman discovered Lovera's body on the Playa de Lecherías (Bigott 2005: 67, Muskus and Vasquez 2004: 26–28). Alí Primera later wrote a song about this murder, 'Alberto Lovera hermano' (Alberto Lovera, Brother).
9. In 1971, Jara recorded 'El derecho de vivir en paz' and 'Abre tu ventana' with Los Blops.
10. The 1973 elections were won by Carlos Andrés Pérez of AD. For more on MAS see Ellner 1988.
11. Interview with Sandino Primera, Caracas, July 2005.
12. See http://www.youtube.com/watch?v=UuFEl-iRxL4 (last accessed 8 January 2016) for a video recording of Alí during the 1983 MAS election campaign.
13. Héctor Mujica (1927–2002) was a Venezuelan intellectual and journalist, founder of the School of Journalism at the UCV and candidate for the Venezuelan Communist Party in 1978.
14. Los Guaraguao's recordings may have helped to popularise Alí's songs among younger audiences. The group was particularly successful in the Dominican Republic and in Nicaragua, where, musician and arranger Diego Silva told me in an interview in 2008, the running joke in the late 1980s was 'If the Sandinistas don't win the elections, Los Guaraguao will!'
15. Interview with Cordero and Guerra, Caracas, September 2008.
16. In the 1970s, the average annual salary in Venezuela was approximately thirty thousand *bolívares* http://frrodriguez.web.wesleyan. edu/docs/Books/Venezuela_Anatomy_of_a_Collapse.pdf, p. 37 (Last accessed 8 January 2016).
17. See http://www.youtube.com/watch?v=GZP6iO2s5Vg (Last accessed 8 January 2016).
18. Interview with Franquis, Caracas, September 2008.
19. Interview with Rodríguez, Caracas, July 2005.

20. Interview with Mussett, Barquisimeto, July 2005.
21. Interview with Ramiro Primera, Caracas, September 2008.
22. Interview with Yépez, Caracas, July 2008.
23. In his letter to Sr Delpino in 1974, Alí claimed not to own a car. By the end of the 1970s, his friends told me, Alí had bought an old vehicle to enable him to tour.
24. Interview with Alí Alejandro Primera, Caracas, July 2005.
25. Lyrics from 'Canción para acordarme' (Song to Remember), from the album *Al pueblo lo que es de César*, 1981.
26. Personal friends of Alí's, and artists who worked with him, emphasised the care Alí took when composing in the musical styles of various regions of Venezuela, often travelling to those areas in order to steep himself in local musical traditions before composing a song in that style.
27. Interview with Noel Márquez, Caracas, July 2005.
28. For more on Venezuelan music styles and instruments see Brandt 1994, 2008; Olsen 1996; Sweeney and Rosenberg 2000; Aretz 1990.
29. Interview with Vera, Caracas, July 2005.
30. Interview with Silva, Caracas, September 2008.
31. Interview with Silva, Caracas, September 2008.
32. The DISIP (*Dirección Nacional de los Servicios de Inteligencia y Prevención*, 'National Directorate of Intelligence and Prevention Services') replaced the DIGEPOL in 1969.
33. Luis Suárez, personal communication, July 2009.

CHAPTER 4

Collective Memories of Alí Primera in the Late Punto Fijo Period (1985–1989)

Immediately after Alí Primera's death, newspapers carried articles in which his life and his *Canción Necesaria* were commemorated and memorialised, and their importance discussed and reconstructed. On 17 February 1985, one day after the collision in which Alí was killed, the national newspaper *Últimas Noticias* reported that Alí's death 'produced great pain amongst political, artistic and popular circles where the singer was loved and admired' (cited in Castillo and Marroquí 2005: 230). Photographs published in *Últimas Noticias* on that day show crowds of mourners in Caracas, many of whom are seen to be bearing flowers and carrying Venezuelan flags and images of Simón Bolívar. On 18 February, Alí's body was transported to the Paraguaná Peninsula for burial in the cemetery of the barrio where Alí spent much of his childhood. According to Rafael Salazar (undated, p. 15), then director of the *Federación Venezolana de la Cultura Popular* (Venezuelan Federation of Popular Culture), more than one hundred thousand people from Paraguaná and across the country followed the funeral procession. Several photographs of Alí's funeral were published in the local *Médano* and *El Falconiano* newspapers on 19 February 1985. In these photographs, crowds of mourners carry flags, guitars decorated with flowers, images of Alí, and large banners on which lyrics from his songs are painted. Under the headline 'The People Weep for the Death of Alí', *El Falconiano* refers to the funeral as 'an impressive demonstration of popular affection and warmth', reporting that the 'anguished crowds' that accompanied the body sang Alí's songs, which

© The Editors (if applicable) and the Authors 2016
H. Marsh, *Hugo Chávez, Alí Primera and Venezuela*,
DOI 10.1057/978-1-137-57968-3_4

'left a deep mark on all the dispossessed sectors not only of our country but of all Latin America' (cited in Castillo and Marroquí 2005: 229). In *Médano*, Luis Yamarte wrote:

> ...a whole *pueblo* is in mourning. But a whole *pueblo* is ready and willing to take up the flag embroidered with [Alí's] songs. If weeping is inevitable, even more inevitable is the commitment to keep [Alí's] revolutionary example alive. (cited in Castillo and Marroquí 2005: 185)

Journalists, writers and politicians demonstrated their commitment to doing just this by writing commemorative newspaper articles in which they lifted out and elevated Alí's qualities as a songwriter and a human being. These articles were conditioned by previous narratives about Alí's humble origins, his experiences of state repression and his artistic integrity, but they also added new significance to Alí's songs by constructing collective memories of the *cantautor* which represented him as a touchstone of moral values and as a martyr who had died fighting for *el pueblo*. As the Punto Fijo system entered into political and economic crisis in the late 1980s, the articulation of collective memories of Alí, and grassroots memorials and commemorations of his life and *Canción Necesaria*, acted as a means of formulating and expressing resistance to the prevailing political order. The sharing of collective memories of Alí's 'revolutionary example' came to function as a form of political opposition.

This chapter focuses on the various ways in which Alí Primera's songs were commemorated and represented in the late 1980s and early 1990s, and on the significance of *Canción Necesaria* for Venezuelans at that time. To examine collective memories of Alí Primera, which were constructed and circulated by his allies and by leftist intellectuals in the decade after his death, I adopt a 'dynamic' approach to memory (Misztal 2000: 69). This approach does not view collective memory as an 'invention' or a form of manipulation imposed by any group to serve its own interests; instead, it sees the past as providing resources for the articulation of attitudes towards the present, and present circumstances as shaping how the past is interpreted. I accept Annette Kuhn's premise (2010: 298) that 'memory is a process, an activity, a construct', with 'social and cultural, as well as personal, resonance', and her contention (ibid.) that:

> It is impossible to overstate the significance of narrative in cultural memory – in the sense not just of the (continuously negotiated) contents of

shared/collective memory-stories, but also of the activity of recounting or telling memory-stories, in both private and public contexts—in other words, of performances of memory.

I analyse 'performances' of the memory of Alí Primera and *Canción Necesaria* as articulated in narratives recounted in commemorative articles and books from the late 1980s and early 1990s, in which Alí and his music were remembered and his legacy was evaluated. I also analyse the narratives surrounding grassroots memorials and commemorative rituals, which were articulated and published in the press during those years.

I identify the values and qualities which were selected by Alí's allies, those which were left out, and the main themes that characterise collective memories articulated in texts in the late 1980s and early 1990s. I argue that collective memories of Alí Primera and his songs acted as resources through which resistance to the ailing Punto Fijo system was articulated during this time period. After 1994, Hugo Chávez made use of these resources in his own political communication; in the late 1990s and the early twenty-first century, Chávez linked his political movement with collective memories of Alí's songs and with collective memories of Alí's life and actions. The collective memories Chávez connected with had already been constructed in the late 1980s and early 1990s, outside state structures, by writers and journalists, by *cantautores*, and by grassroots communities.

COLLECTIVE MEMORIES OF ALÍ PRIMERA: THE PRINCIPAL THEMES

In the Venezuelan collective memory, Alí Primera acquired a posthumous significance that helped Venezuelans to make sense of and to create knowledge about their circumstances in the late 1980s and early 1990s. Any qualities and events that did not fit with the image of an exemplary figure appear to have been cleansed from the collective memory in commemorative articles and other texts. For example, a Venezuelan I interviewed in 2005 told me that Alí had conducted extra-marital affairs which his wife Sol knew nothing about. At the time I was unsure whether this was rumour or fact, but a further interviewee in 2008 began our interview by volunteering the information (without me raising the subject of Alí's marital fidelity or otherwise) that the *cantautor* had an illegitimate son, Alí Rafael Vásquez, who was born out of wedlock and just a few months before Alí's youngest legitimate son. Indeed, Alí Rafael Vásquez was later recognised publicly by Alí's widow and his four legitimate sons as Alí Primera's biological offspring.[1] Although *machismo* is a widespread characteristic of Latin American gender relations (Sara-Lafosse 2013: 107–114), this is not a quality that the collective memory has celebrated in Alí's conduct. On the contrary, Alí's apparent sexism and lack of sexual fidelity to his wife have been overlooked. In an interview for *Momento* dated 8 May 1985, Sol says that after marrying Alí he 'forbade' her from working, and that he was 'very, but very jealous' (cited in Castillo and Marroquí 2005: 94). However, while Alí celebrated maternity and expected his own wife to give up work in order to raise their children, a Venezuelan I interviewed in 2005 indicated that Alí had become rather impatient with a female artist who withdrew from appearing at a *Nueva Canción* festival due to her own pregnancy.

Another feature from Alí's life often overlooked in the collective memory is his failure to be elected congressman for the *Liga Socialista* in 1983. Instead of critically engaging with this defeat and posing serious questions about what might have been lacking in Alí to equip him for this political role, his disappointment has been dismissed by one writer as the result of 'the sixth consecutive time that this demagogic and lying two-party system has taken power, backed up by the majority of Venezuelans' (Hernandez Medina 1991: 206). This defeat, Alí's marital infidelity and his apparent *machismo* do not generally appear in the collective memory, which instead simplifies the past in order to construct an archetype that can stand beyond reproach.

In 1996, literary critic Hugo Obregón Múñoz published the second edition[2] of his literary analysis of Alí Primera's song lyrics, *Alí Primera o el poder de la música* (*Alí Primera, or the Power of Music*). In this study, Obregón Múñoz (1996: 40) cites the findings of two Venezuelan psychologists, Noguera and Escalona, who conducted research into the values of Venezuelan youth in the early 1990s. According to Obregón Múñoz (ibid.), these psychologists concluded that in the artistic sphere the collective memory of Venezuelan youth selected and retained:

> the work of the great *cantautor*, Alí Primera, as a prime example of the class struggle ... and as an outstanding artist of the counter-culture who was persecuted and practically exterminated [for his beliefs].

According to Obregón Múñoz (1996: 40), the endurance of Alí Primera in the collective memory is due to 'the aesthetic-ideological value of the songs', and also to 'the social and ideological conduct [Alí] maintained during his existence'. Obregón Múñoz (ibid.) argues that Alí Primera's qualities, as a songwriter and human being, are not seen objectively but are 'elevated' and 'idealised' to the status of myth, and that these idealised, or mythologised, qualities are foremost in the 'musical and spiritual consciousness of common people and Venezuelan intellectuals' in the early 1990s. Articles and interviews with family and friends published since the artist's death, Obregón Múñoz (1996: 42–43) argues, show that Alí Primera came to represent a set of positive values that acted as a sharp contrast to the corruption and lack of morality widely perceived to characterise the Punto Fijo government in the late 1980s and early 1990s.

According to Obregón Múñoz (1996: 42–43), Alí Primera came to be seen by many as extraordinary; 'kind', 'humble', 'one who loved the poor and the common people', 'charitable', 'uninterested in material goods', 'a good companion/husband/father/son', 'a man who needs to live for others', 'a Marxist who captures our national and Latin American reality and shapes it into songs', 'Bolivarian consciousness at its best'. Furthermore, Obregón Múñoz (1996: 5) argues, Alí Primera was constructed in commemorations as 'a dangerous master of rebellion ... remembered and honoured year after year ... [for his] ... leadership and ideological position, which was transparent, consistent, and exceptionally incorruptible'.

In Latin America, as historians Samuel Brunk and Ben Fallaw (2006) and Chris Frazer (2006) have shown, there is a strong tendency to memorialise deceased men and women who are perceived to have struggled on behalf of 'the people'. Historian Lyman Johnson (2004) argues that the high levels of social and economic inequality that characterise Latin America frequently lead various social, ethnic, regional and class groups to reject officially sanctioned versions of history in favour of their own. Johnson (2004: 16) argues that the rural and urban masses 'often establish their own claims on martyrs and other heroes, producing in effect their own versions of these lives, versions that emphasize qualities and actions subversive to elite political needs'.

In his examination of the circumstances in which important links may be forged between the dead and the living in Latin America, Johnson identifies four biographical factors that make a person more likely to be remembered posthumously as a popular hero. First, the hero has forged a connection with 'the people' in life. Second, the hero has been perceived as a defender of the poor and the oppressed. Third, the hero has generated both affection and hatred and has suffered persecution, torture and/or defeat. Fourth, those deemed to have died at the hands of the enemy are more likely to be perceived as martyrs and to endure as symbols in the popular imagination (Johnson 2004: 16–21). All four of these biographical factors were emphasised in collective memories of Alí Primera.

MEMORIALISING ALÍ'S CONNECTION WITH *EL PUEBLO*

In 2008, a resident of the 23 de Enero barrio of Caracas told me that Alí 'was always at the service of *el pueblo* … [Alí] was *la voz del pueblo* (the people's voice)'. According to a Venezuelan artist I interviewed in 2005, Alí was widely remembered by *el pueblo* after his 'untimely death' because of the 'correspondence between the discourse of his songs and the way he lived, his moral and artistic integrity in the face of state repression and persecution, and his identification with the impoverished masses'.

Within days of Alí's death, writers, journalists, artists and leftist political groups had started to publish articles in local and national newspapers in which they highlighted Alí's identification with *el pueblo*, and *el pueblo*'s identification with Alí and his songs. These articles were frequently accompanied by photographs of Alí, many of which were taken by percussionist Jesús Franquis during Alí's live performances, in which Alí is seen holding his fist or his *cuatro* in the air as he sings or speaks passionately to his audience (Fig. 4.1). In an article entitled 'Adiós al amigo', Luis Alvarez emphasised Alí's solidarity with other Latin American countries and represented the *cantautor* and his songs as deeply connected to *el pueblo*:

> Today you have died Alí Primera, friend, comrade. … *El pueblo* didn't understand … semiotics, but they realised that [your] words were their words and they made you their singer, their symbol. And if you never got to be their official representative, the fault was not yours. (undated, cited in Castillo and Marroquí 2005: 196)

According to Ramiro Primera, one of Alí's cousins, Alí was accepted by *el pueblo* as their singer not because the television or the radio said that Alí was *el cantor del pueblo* (the people's singer), but because *el pueblo* recognised Alí as theirs.[3] Similarly, in her 'Carta Abierta al Pueblo de Alí Primera' (Open Letter to Alí Primera's *Pueblo*), which was published in *El Mundo* on 21 February 1985, journalist and television presenter Isa

Fig. 4.1 Photographs of Alí published in posthumous press article. Tarabacoa, 18 March 1985 (Reproduced in Castillo and Marroquí 2005: 231)

Dobles remembers Alí as a person who was fully identified with ordinary people. In this letter, Dobles reminisces about how Alí 'never wanted to work for television', and she remembers him telling her "I can't do it, Isa. I know that you'd present me with dignity. But that medium [television] is degrading; it distorts, it damages the people's consciousness. I cannot be an accomplice of TV". Dobles represents Alí as 'the generous Venezuela, which extends its hand, which listens, which suffers the pain of others, which shares its bread, which gives everything out of human solidarity ... Alí is all of you' (cited in Castillo and Marroquí 2005: 208).

In these 'performances' of memory, articulated in written texts that were published in the national press, narratives about Alí's refusal to pander to the interests of the mass media are lifted out and highlighted. Alí is constructed as a person whose commitment to *el pueblo* was absolute, even if this commitment was to the detriment of his own material wellbeing. On 25 February 1985, the MAS leader José Vicente Rangel, whose election campaigns Alí had supported, reiterated this theme when he wrote in *Últimas Noticias*:

> Alí Primera was a committed artist; committed to his people, to the humble, to the poor, to the powerless. He was an artist who assumed his commitment fully, to the extent that he never wanted to be implicated commercially with the mass media or with record companies. He could have made a lot of money and considerably improved his status in life, but he believed that to do so would have been to betray himself, to give up. His commitment was with those who fought, with those in the world who raised the flag of liberty. Alí's greatest commitment was to his art ... he defended the cultural essence of the country. (cited in Castillo and Marroquí 2005: 215)

Here Vicente Rangel selects and elevates certain elements from Alí's conduct which he uses to construct a collective memory of Alí as a person who placed *el pueblo* before his own physical and material comfort. Alí's rejection of wealth was frequently selected and highlighted in other newspaper articles written by his allies. For example, in *El Nacional* on 23 February 1985, Naudy Enrique Escalona emphasised that Alí:

> ... could have achieved wealth and glory, but he disdained fame. He didn't want anything to do with lights and cameras, because he resisted commercialising his music. A protest singer who broke the mould, who will always be a seed in the soul of the Latin American people, and above all else, a man who will never die because 'those who fight for life cannot be called dead'. (cited in Castillo and Marroquí 2005: 218)

To comment on Alí, Escalona uses the *cantautor*'s own lyrics. Alí wrote 'Los que mueren por la vida no pueden llamarse muertos'[4] (Those Who Die for Life cannot be Called Dead) as an expression of grief and in homage to the murdered socialist leader, Jorge Rodríguez, and as a call to keep alive the ideas of those who died fighting for *el pueblo*. These and other lyrics composed by Alí were remembered after his death, and were used in new ways to express grief for the death of the *cantautor* and to pay homage to him. In 2005, Noel Márquez of *Grupo Madera* told me that Alí's lyrics conveyed the 'capacity to express hope',[5] even in suffering, and this made Alí 'eternally revolutionary'. Márquez asserts that Alí's song 'Tin Marín', a song based on Afro-Venezuelan forms which Alí recorded in 1980 on the *Abrebrecha* album, was originally composed in homage to the eleven members of the Afro-Venezuelan Grupo Madera who had drowned in a tragic boat accident as the group travelled to perform in Amazonas state. The song carries the message that the members of the group 'only got wet/and they're on the river bank/drying in the sun/they will soon be heard again'. According to Márquez, Alí's song became 'a symbol of the pain and indignation of the Venezuelan *pueblo*' after the death of the group's members, but also an expression of hope that the group's exploration of Afro-Venezuelan traditions would live on. After Alí's death, this 'pain and indignation' was 'more terrible'; 'Tin Marín' was thus remembered as a song that 'symbolised hope and faith, the need to carry on in the face of adversity, in the face of the worst conditions, even in the face of death', and it was remembered and collectively sung during grassroots commemorations of Alí's life in order to express and share that hope and to keep Alí's revolutionary example alive.

In 1992, Sandra Zapata published a song book with the *Euroamericana de Ediciones* publishing house which she coordinated. Zapata was motivated to publish Alí's song lyrics because of her desire to preserve and to disseminate Alí's 'message' at a time when state institutions marginalised his songs.[6] This song book contains the lyrics of 236 songs composed by Alí, and it was reprinted in 1994 and in 1997, suggesting that there was significant public demand for copies of Alí's lyrics in the 1990s.

The song book takes Alí's own words as its title: *Que mi canto no se pierda* (May my Song not be Lost). Alí wrote these words in the sleeve notes of his 1973 album, *Lo Primero de Alí Primera*. Zapata's collection starts with three pages of dedications and poems written for Alí by *cantautores* Gloria Martín, Gregorio Yépez and La Chiche Manaure, the writer Aníbal Nazoa, the radio presenter Carlos Ricardo Cisterna, and Alí's widow, Sol Mussett. These dedications represent Alí as a person whose revolutionary example lives on in his songs and in *el pueblo*. Sol Mussett dedicates the book to 'the children of the world, our children. To Eduardo [of Los Guaraguao] and 'Grupo Ahora', to the journalists, writers, poets and groups of singers who have always shown their solidarity with the *Canción Necesaria* that you left us'. Sol's dedication thus recognises journalists, writers, poets and *cantautores* as playing an important role in remembering Alí Primera through their writing and their art.

On the inside of the front cover of the song book, Sandra Zapata writes:

> The artistic work of Alí Primera is a chronicle of Latin America, written with the sensitivity of an authentic man, who gave his hand with tenderness in order to sow the paths of hope.

Similarly, a *cantautora* I interviewed in July 2005 asserts that Alí's songs told the 'unofficial history' of *el pueblo* of all Latin America. Gloria Martín (1998: 74) also expresses the idea that Alí's songs preserved 'the people's history' at a time when the Venezuelan state sought to exclude *el pueblo* and their experiences from official history—what she refers to as *Operación Olvido* (Operation Oblivion). The inside of the back cover of Zapata's songbook carries the words:

> Alí Primera is, without a doubt, the Venezuelan singer who, with a language which was distinctively his own and a personality that transcended borders, became the most universal of our *trovadores*. Alí developed a *nuevo canto*, a *canción nueva, la canción política, la canción necesaria*, or whatever you want to call it. His song is spiritual sustenance for optimism and the way forward, always based on the unity of *el pueblo*, on the legitimacy of our values.
>   A song that has as its support the Bolivarian ideal that transcends epochs, or simply, as he said:
>   'Song for victory, song for the unity of the people, song for the *patria buena*'. From this beautiful polyphony which Alí sowed universally, this song book is born, fruit of the efforts of many, song by song, battle by battle, harvesting what was always [Alí's] will:
>   'Song that is sung to the people who have always sung to us'.

Obregón Múñoz (1996: 86) observes that newspaper articles, leaflets and fliers produced in the years after Alí's death 'continually refer to [the] links the *cantautor* has with the exploited classes of Venezuela'. In these texts, according to Obregón Múñoz (1996: 86–7), Alí's relationship with common people is represented as one of 'total identification', and Alí's experiences of poverty and hardship endow him with the quality of 'belonging' to the people. Alí is represented as being in 'direct contact with the people', as standing 'in support of the people's causes', as having forged 'love for the people', as being 'identified with' the people and as a 'defender' of their interests (Obregón Múñoz 1996: 86–7). For Alí, Obregón Múñoz (1996: 87) argues, the notion of *el pueblo* is not a 'mere abstraction' but instead it is embodied in his songs:

> Through embodying the oppressed, [Alí] becomes one of them. His inner soul is rent like that of all men oppressed by the system ... [His music] invests aesthetic value in popular culture and popular values, in opposition to official culture ... Alí Primera is not a mere spectator of the suffering and exploitation of the people. (Obregón Múñoz 1996: 47)

Obregón Múñoz represents Alí's music as a link that binds him to *el pueblo* not merely as an onlooker who created songs about suffering and exploitation, but as the embodiment of *el pueblo* and their struggles against oppression. Obregón Múñoz thus selects elements from Alí's own narrative and uses these to construct *Canción Necesaria* as the very expression of *el pueblo* and as a collective resource which bestows a shared sense of identity upon those who remember and commemorate it.

MEMORIALISING ALÍ AS DEFENDER OF THE POOR AND OPPRESSED

Oswaldo Mussett, brother of Alí's widow Sol, asserts that during the late 1980s and early 1990s wherever he travelled in Venezuela he met people who knew Alí's songs and 'followed [Alí's] message', and that strangers would give him gifts to take to Alí's orphaned children because they felt that Alí had always looked after them and now they must look after Alí's family.[7] In collective memories which they articulated in various forms, Alí's allies emphasised the *cantautor*'s defence of the poor and the oppressed, and how these qualities inspired the poor and the oppressed to defend his legacy. In an undated press article (cited in Castillo and Marroquí 2005: 224), Miriam Suzzarini Baloa wrote that she and her peers were 'hypnotised' when they attended Alí's live performances:

> He impressed [us] because he was sincere. He didn't dare to act against his principles and that is why he was one of the few people who you could genuinely call revolutionary ... He gave all of his body and soul to try to help the oppressed.

Thus Alí's allies emphasised his willingness to sacrifice himself in order to defend the poor and the oppressed and their interests, while he was elevated as an exemplary revolutionary. Alí's song was represented in a further undated and anonymous newspaper article as:

> One of the few means of permanent criticism of everything that over the last fifteen years has been kept hidden [by dominant groups] ... At all times [Alí] brought attention to the most difficult situations in a country where the absolute poverty of the majority exists alongside the increasing opulence of a few. (cited in Castillo and Marroquí 2005: 227)

Obregón Múñoz (1996: 11) argues that the way Alí chose to distribute his songs locates them firmly on the side of the poor and the oppressed in the collective memory. According to Obregón Múñoz (ibid.), commercial culture has access to the mass media, but the channels via which Alí Primera chose to disseminate his songs were informal and lay outside official state institutions:

> Official culture and the groups that diffuse and preserve it have at their service the official systems of communication known as the mass media; the press, radio and TV. They have practically unlimited access to a technically sophisticated machinery which is productive of messages ... Since it has no access to this system, the counterculture uses other communicative systems which are characterised, in general, by their low levels of distribution. Often hardly tolerated, openly censored, or persecuted by governmental groups, amongst these forms of communication we have graffiti, and all non-official press, such as fliers, pamphlets, magazines, newspapers, rumours, jokes, and protest songs. (Obregón Múñoz 1996: 11)

Obregón Múñoz thus argues that it was not only the lyrics or folk music forms that endowed Alí's songs with oppositional meaning in the collective memory, and not only the well-known biographical narratives about Alí's life of hardship and poverty. The very means of diffusion were highlighted after Alí's death and represented as 'evidence' that Alí was dedicated to defending the poor.

Alí Primera was characterised by his allies as a profoundly generous man who put the needs of the poor before his own needs. In a book about Alí published in 1990, *La poesía en la voz de un cantor* (*Poetry in the Voice of a Singer*), MAS member Miguel Angel Paz[8] recounts an anecdote that constructs Alí Primera as a person who was dedicated to protecting the interests of the poor and oppressed even at his own personal expense. Paz remembers that Alí organised an event—'Songs of Solidarity in Coro'—in December 1982. The proceeds from this event, in which Lilia Vera, Los Guaraguao and other *Nueva Canción cantautores* performed, were to be used to help construct a House of Culture for the city of Coro, where the event was held. The amount of money raised was less than expected and, Paz writes, Alí did not seek to cover his own expenses 'because that was not his objective':

> With this personal experience, and knowing that this same thing happened at similar events throughout the country, I can testify that Alí's path was

none other than to invest his efforts in waking up the people to their every-day reality. (Paz 1990: 19)

Similar memories of Alí's generosity and his dedication to the poor were recounted in other written texts. For example, in a magazine produced by the *Federación Nacional de la Cultura Popular* in the late 1980s, Rafael Salazar writes that one day, while Alí was travelling with his son Sandino from Maracaibo to Paraguaná, Alí bought every caged *turpial* (Venezuela's national bird) he came across being sold by peasants on the roadside. Then, when Alí reached his mother's house near the oil refinery, he took the cages out into the countryside and told the five-year-old Sandino to open them one by one and release the birds as he sang to them (Salazar, undated: 12). In Venezuela in 2005 and 2008, this story was repeated to me by several people I spoke to about Alí. For example, Benito Márquez, brother of Noel and also a member of *Grupo Madera*[9] told me that Alí loved freedom so much that he could not tolerate to see even a bird being oppressed, and that Alí bought caged birds in order to free them. Similarly, a student I interviewed at the University of Coro in 2005 told me that Alí bought birds in order to release them on the beach so that they could be free. This student insisted that Alí's compassion for the less fortunate was so great that he could not bear to see even birds in cages. Alí's widow Sol Mussett told me in 2005 that she once became angry with Alí because they had saved enough money to purchase a washing machine. Alí went out to look at the washing machines available for purchase, but on the way to the shop he encountered a couple poorer than he and Sol were, and so he gave them the money. Alí's half-sister Mireya de Lugo told me in 2005 that as a child Alí was so compassionate that she remembers him pleading with their mother to give away some of their *arepas* (corn bread) to poorer children.

It is of course practically impossible to verify whether such events ever took place. However, Kuhn's (2010) approach to 'performances' of memory in narrative forms does not take what is remembered as 'truth' but instead as material for interpretation. What is important is not the veracity or otherwise of such remembered episodes as re-told in narratives, but instead the significance which people attribute to these shared memories. Venezuelans who remembered and repeated stories about Alí's generosity and love of freedom were also, at a symbolic level, telling stories about what they believed Alí's motivations were as a *cantautor*; to bring liberty to the oppressed and to make sacrifices on behalf of the poor.

MEMORIALISING ALÍ AS PERSECUTED VICTIM
OF THE PUNTO FIJO STATE

On the day of Alí's death on 16 February 1985, the Central Committee of the Venezuelan Communist Party called for the circumstances of Alí's death to be investigated (cited in Castillo and Marroquí 2005: 205). In *El Nacional* on 23 April 1985, Mariam Núñez suggested that Alí had been murdered by state authorities who wanted to silence a troublesome voice in order to prevent his songs from influencing the public:

> The causes and conditions of the accident are not very clear and many doubts remain owing to the continuous raids the Disip police carried out on [Alí's] residence; the persecution [of Alí] on the roads, the shots at his car windows, sabotage of the events where Alí convened *el pueblo* for any politico-cultural work, etc., etc. (cited in Hernández Medina 1991: 251)

After Alí's death, many of his allies remembered Alí's denunciations of state persecution, and they highlighted these denunciations in order to construct Alí as the voice of opposition to the state. On 7 April 1985, Mery Sananes published an article in *Últimas Noticias* in which she proclaimed that Alí's songs are 'not neutral' but that they have 'friends and enemies'; the 'friends' are *el pueblo*, and 'the enemies' are those who violate human rights, grow rich at the expense of the masses, destroy the natural environment, distort the philosophy of Simón Bolívar and make a façade out of democracy (cited in Castillo and Marroquí 2005: 188). This sentiment was repeatedly highlighted in the narratives about Alí, which were produced and disseminated by his allies in newspapers; those who immortalise Alí are represented as *el pueblo*, while those who do not remember Alí, or who remember his songs 'with hatred', represent the 'enemy of the people' and the protectors of elite political interests. On 18 May 1985, UCV professor Luis Cipriano Rodríguez argued that:

> [Alí's] song is not neutral—Alí's song has enemies, above all those who 'make a lie out of ... democracy'. It is they who hold on to power and privilege, property and culture. They are the ones basically responsible for the repression manifested in raids, in machine-gunning and persecution. (cited in Castillo and Marroquí 2005: 55)

Alí is represented in such narratives as standing in clear opposition to governing elites. Since Alí embodies *el pueblo*, Alí's enemies are represented as the enemies of *el pueblo*. The persecution and harassment of Alí by state authorities are frequently underlined in the collective memory. In addition, Alí's defiance in the face of such threats to his personal safety and his family's well-being is highlighted and assumes significance for el *pueblo* on whose behalf he is perceived to have suffered. Alí is remembered as being 'persecuted and practically exterminated' by these enemies because of his commitment to his beliefs and his defiance of state repression (Obregón Múñoz 1996: 40). In his study of Alí, Miguel Angel Paz (1990: 20) writes:

> Being a man who persistently acted in accordance with his ideals, Alí felt the most brutal persecution ... on more than one occasion he was arrested, not to mention the raids on his residence.

One year after Alí's death, on 16 February 1986, José María Gauna Morena wrote in a commemorative article published in *El Nacional*:

> Alí Primera has not died; he has disappeared physically, but his message, his songs and the principles which he courageously defended until the last moment of his life ... are firmly rooted in the hearts of the people ... [he fought] in a selfless way and with great abnegation ... without fear of the threats and dangers [he faced] from the powerful and eternal enemies of liberty and the violators of human rights. (cited in Castillo and Marroquí 2005: 80)

Such words indicate that in the collective memory Alí was remembered not only for the affection he won from the poor and the oppressed, but also for the hatred his conduct and his music were seen to generate in the dominant classes and their representatives.

MEMORIALISING ALÍ AS MARTYR

Alí's early death in a 'strange, dark traffic accident' (Hernández Medina 1991: 33) lent him an aura of martyrdom which singled him out from other *Nueva Canción cantautores* who continued to practise their music in the late 1980s. His qualities were elevated to the status of myth:

> [Alí] always defied failure ... His vast spirit allowed him, like Christ on his path towards the cross, to stand up and continue on his way. He succeeded in conquering within himself doubt and stagnation. He produced a rupture with everything that can be called pessimism ... the artist's strong character would

never have allowed him to face humiliation ... He managed to rise up and break through unfavourable milieu, [and] he achieves a metamorphosis such that we can begin to gauge the true dimension of his success. (Paz 1990: 24)

In a published lecture on the posthumous significance of Víctor Jara, Robert Pring-Mill (1990: 63) discusses the ways in which the meaning of certain *Nueva Canción* compositions can change after the sudden and early death of a committed *cantautor*. Pring-Mill (ibid.) argues that when a committed poet dies, he or she is set apart from other artists and also above them:

... partly because the dead are no longer fallible, partly because a heroic death endows them with the aura of martyrdom, and partly because their characters and their careers begin to be both simplified and ennobled as they undergo a two-stage process of transformation.

The first phase of this process, writes Pring-Mill (ibid.), takes the singer out of life and into history. The second phase, 'which frequently takes place in the popular imagination, takes them onto another plane altogether' as legends whose shining example 'remains forever with the revolutionary masses':

The role which they played in life becomes subsumed into, or sometimes replaced by, their posthumous role as inspirational figures, whose generalised symbolic importance rapidly transcends the particularities of their life histories. (Pring-Mill 1990: 63)

In this way, the memory of a committed artist is converted into a myth which becomes more important for the present than 'objective' history:

... such individuals come to stand for things which are of greater importance for those who have survived than the individuals themselves may have been—other than for their immediate relatives and friends—in life. Socially speaking their 'usefulness' is not over but merely changed, as their completed lives begin to perform a different function. (Pring-Mill 1990: 64)

Pring-Mill (1990: 65–6) argues that there are many Chilean *Nueva Canción* artists, such as Patricio Manns, whose talents equal those of Víctor Jara, but that these artists are not so widely remembered because they survived the coup. This, according to Pring-Mill (1990: 65–6), is not wholly due to prejudice or political sympathy; 'martyrdom does not merely enhance reputations but [it] alters meanings or, more strictly, adds new ones to old'. Pring-Mill argues that Víctor Jara's songs acquired new levels of meaning after Jara's death at the hands of the military during the 1973 coup against Salvador Allende; people brought new 'hearings' to the songs in the light of current circumstances, and Jara came to represent the many others who had died as a result of the coup (Pring-Mill 1990: 66).

After his death in February 1985, Alí's life was simplified and ennobled; his allies remembered him as the archetype of *el pueblo*, as a defender of the poor and oppressed, and as a person of great integrity who rejected wealth and remained defiant in the face of state attempts to silence him. Alí came to represent an example for the future, and he was likened to Jara and other committed singers whose legacies endure in Latin America. Venezuelan writer Aníbal Nazoa proclaimed:

Alí Primera will live on … [He was] an artist who never sold his song or rented his voice to the enemy … Alí Primera has disappeared, but only momentarily. He will return … [he is] preparing his next number in the company of … Paul Robeson and other great singers … — Woody Guthrie and Cisco Houston— … Violeta Parra and Víctor Jara. (cited in Castillo and Marroquí 2005: 207)

The quality of Alí's death, in 'suspicious' circumstances and following state repression and harassment, sets Alí apart from other Venezuelan *Nueva Canción cantautores* and groups. In poems published in newspapers and fliers, Alí is represented as standing with other martyrs. In a biography of Alí published independently in 1999, Andrés Castillo writes:

I do not want to place the singer [Alí] on a pedestal where nobody can reach him, but rather to show him … [in a place] where all those who want reach him can do so without … fear … [In Alí we see a form of] human transformation already undergone by men like Jesus, Che Guevara, Ghandi and so many others. (Castillo 1999: 63)

Similarly, in a UCV newspaper, engineering student Carlos Reyes places Alí in the company of other leftist heroes from Venezuela and Latin America who died fighting for their beliefs. In 'Song for Alí Primera', Reyes writes:

He [Alí] found Death, singing to Life
He found Life, with his Death …
… singing to Life
Until my last breath

With the image of my *pueblo*
I will rise up
And offer you the future.
I will rise up with the future
And bring
Argimiro, Chema, Livia, Che
Rodas Mezones
Allende, Camilo, Fabricio, Sandino,
For those who have died, opening the way!
To those who will fall, opening the path!
All together
Together with ... Bolívar
They will all be there, and You. (cited in Castillo and Marroquí 2005: 193)

In other poems, Alí's own words and lyrics are put together in new combinations. Franck Armas wrote in *Momento*:

They cannot be called dead
Those who died for life
Did your song become eternal
On the day you left?. (cited in Castillo and Marroquí 2005: 201)

Gloria Martín wrote a poem for Alí which was reminiscent of the Lord's Prayer:

... although you do not let us fall into temptation
You do not deliver us from evil either
Now we are weaned
.... The song is ours
Primera vez
Primera voz
De nuestro canto (First time/First voice/of our song).[10] (cited in Castillo and Marroquí 2005: 204)

In newspaper articles and poems like these, Alí is represented and commemorated as a person who gave everything for *el pueblo*, even his own life. The quality of Alí's death adds to the significance of his legacy; one who sacrifices himself for *el pueblo* transcends death to become eternal. On 18 March 1985, Pedro Hernandez Febres wrote in *Tarabacoa*:

Alí Primera lives and will live for ever in the heart of our people, because even if his physical presence is not with us, rivers of love and combat will run in our veins, with the energy of his song and the generosity of one who gives everything without asking for anything in return. He who gives all for *el pueblo* cannot die. (cited in Castillo and Marroquí 2005: 231)

GRASSROOTS MEMORIALS

Alí was remembered not only by writers, journalists and *cantautores*, but also by *el pueblo* in grassroots commemorations and rituals. Martín (1998: 59) writes that after 1985, Alí's birth and death were honoured year after year in informal local festivals and events, and in fliers 'whose only certainty is the face of Alí Primera' and which were circulated in the days prior to 31 October and 16 February. A community radio worker from the 23 de Enero barrio of Caracas who I interviewed in 2008 told me that she and people like her in the barrios had kept Alí's memory alive throughout the 1980s and the 1990s by singing his songs together and sharing and re-telling stories about his life. In 2005, a radio worker in Barquisimeto told me that there was not a single demonstration in the late 1980s or the early 1990s during which the public did not collectively remember and sing Alí Primera's songs.

In *Grassroots Memorials* (2011: 2), Peter Jan Margry and Cristina Sánchez-Carretero argue that popular memorialisation expresses not only grief for a deceased individual but also social discontent with the present. Grassroots memorials form foci of protest and resentment and articulate social or political disaffection. Memorabilia and commemorations are dedicated to the memory of the deceased, but they also imply a message about taking action in the present; they seek an understanding of what has happened, ask for responsibilities for the loss to be recognised, and demand changes (Margry and Sánchez-Carretero 2011: 3). Grassroots memorial initiatives, Margry and Sánchez-Carretero argue (2011: 4), can be seen as the ultimate expression of the democratic process; they come from the lowest level of organisation and are aimed at influencing social and political situations and developments. In this manner, 'atomized individuals find each other interrelated in their grief and protest without constituting actual network connections, apart from the commemorative assemblage they collectively give shape to in public space' (ibid.).

After Alí died, communities in Paraguaná and in Miranda organised petitions in order to press the local government to allow them to rename streets and barrios for Alí in order to 'keep alive the image of one who today more than ever continues to be our main singer: Alí Primera' (anonymous and undated, cited in Castillo and Marroquí 2005: 223).

The barrio where Alí spent much of his childhood, La Vela, was officially re-named 'Alí Primera' on 10 April 1985 in response to local demand.

Throughout Venezuela, communities gathered in order to discuss the establishment of local foundations dedicated to Alí Primera (Castillo and Marroquí 2005: 232). These foundations organised musical events in homage to Alí, which were supported by *cantautores* such as Gloria Martín, La Chiche Manaure, Lilia Vera, Gregorio Yépez, Los Guaraguao and Grupo Ahora (Castillo and Marroquí 2005: 234). On the first anniversary of Alí's death, a foundation named for Alí established *La Marcha de los Claveles Rojos* (The March of the Red Carnations), an annual public procession from Alí's childhood home to his grave, 'for the people to honour their singer' (quoted in Castillo and Marroquí 2005: 234).

The house where Alí spent much of his childhood in Paraguaná, and where Alí's mother Carmen Adela continued to live until her death early in the twenty-first century, came to act as a shrine or an informal 'museum' dedicated to the memory of Alí Primera; paintings and photographs of Alí were displayed in the home, as well as objects such as Alí's bootblack box, which acted as symbols of Alí's humble origins. Alongside these objects and images of Alí were displayed images of Simón Bolívar, and saints associated with Catholicism and with *Santería*, thus linking Alí to local heroes and saints (Fig. 4.2). When I visited Paraguaná in 2005, Alí's half-sister Mireya de Lugo, who lived nearby, opened up Alí's childhood home to show me inside. The house had remained uninhabited after the death of Carmen Adela, Mireya told me, but visitors regularly travelled to Paraguaná to pay their respects to Alí at his tomb and at his home. Mireya welcomed such visitors to the house, and she told me that Carmen Adela had also been happy to allow visitors into her home to view the memorabilia she kept there.

In Paraguaná, I encountered several statues and paintings of Alí in people's homes and yards (Figs. 4.3 and 4.4). The barrio inhabitants told me that these statues and images, which depict Alí with Afro hair, a beard and a guitar or a *cuatro*, were not purchased from markets or shops; they themselves had made or painted the statues and images in order to display them in their own homes. These images can be seen as grassroots memorials: they act not only as expressions of grief for the loss of Alí, but as a form of social activism. Through creating their own visual articulations of the memory of Alí, barrio inhabitants told me, they honoured and kept alive the memory, songs and ideals of a hero who, they believed, died fighting for them.

Fig. 4.2 Alí Primera's *caja de limpiabotas* [bootblack box] displayed with images of Bolívar and of Catholic and Santería figures at Carmen Adela's home in Paraguaná in July 2005 (Photograph courtesy of the author)

Figs. 4.3 and 4.4 Homemade figures of Alí, in Barrio Alí Primera, Paraguaná Peninsula, July 2005 (Photographs courtesy of the author)

COLLECTIVE MEMORIES OF ALÍ AS A FORM OF RESISTANCE TO *PUNTOFIJISMO*

In 1991, six years after Alí's death, engineering student Jaime Hernández Medina published a compilation of press articles about Alí in *Alí Primera: Huella profunda sobre esta tierra. Vida y obra* (*Alí Primera: Deep Imprint on this Land. Life and Work*). Hernández Medina (1991: 33) refers to this publication as a 'Chronological Documentary Reconstruction of [Alí's] life, work and significance'. In his prologue to the selection, dated March 1989, Hernández Medina claims that Alí Primera is 'immortalised in the loving memory of a race ... the most important Revolutionary Singer of all Latin American history' (1991: 32). Hernández Medina (1991: 6) represents Alí's songs as 'a living presence' in the late 1980s:

> We turn to [Alí's] songs because of their validity ... the arsenal he carried in his throat is not diluted by the passage of time but instead it is a living presence at each and every act that the people undertake for their liberation and their well-being.

I do not approach Hernández Medina's 'chronological documentary reconstruction' of Alí Primera's life, work and significance as fact; such texts are no more 'history' than they are 'objective', as Pring-Mill (2002: 26) argues with reference to laments for Che Guevara and Víctor Jara. The retelling of the past is always intertwined with an interpretation of the present which is designed to involve the audience in actively reshaping their common future (Pring-Mill 2002: 10–11). When dead heroes are praised, it is primarily to inspire the living in the present moment; the simplification of deceased heroes heightens their chosen 'distinguishing characteristics' so that they are transmuted into myths which become more important for the present moment than 'objective' history (ibid.).

In constructing and disseminating versions of Alí Primera's life and the significance of his songs, Alí's allies frequently aimed to use the past to interpret the present and to call for change in the future. The 'exceptionalism' thesis held Venezuela to be 'different' from the rest of Latin America and a 'model democracy' during the Punto Fijo period (López Maya and Lander 2005: 92). As Alí's allies constructed and shared collective memories of Alí's life and actions, they challenged this dominant view of Venezuela and of the successes of *Puntofijismo*. For example, in the prologue to his 'reconstruction of Alí's life, work and significance',

Hernández Medina (1991: 5) expresses an alternative view of the country's political system. Hernández Medina refers to the Punto Fijo Pact as the 'New York Pact' due to the intervention of 'North American imperialism' in its implementation and continuation in late-twentieth-century Venezuela. Rather than portraying Venezuela as a 'near perfect' democracy, Hernández Medina remembers a different version of Venezuela's recent past, arguing that *Puntofijismo* established a two party system which:

> ... exclude[d] and segregate[d] large sectors of the population and ... deepened ties between a local oligarchy and transnational capital... Demonstrations carried out by the unemployed in the main squares of Caracas ... [were] ... machine-gunned. More people were killed, tortured or disappeared for their political beliefs in the first nine years of *Puntofijismo* than in the nine years of dictatorship which preceded it. (Hernández Medina 1991: 5)

By the late 1980s, the Punto Fijo system faced serious problems of legitimacy. The apparent stability of the system had begun to unravel with the 1983 devaluation of the *bolívar* currency, and the economy entered into crisis. By the late 1980s, the distributive capability of *Puntofijismo* was proving to be inadequate, and confidence that the system would spur development had largely evaporated (Ellner and Hellinger 2005: 30). The benefits of economic growth appeared inaccessible, and poverty and exclusion ceased to be seen as temporary phenomena or as conditions that might be overcome through individual effort (Lander 2005: 27). Instead, crisis-like conditions increasingly became permanent features of society. It was no longer a matter of a minority being categorised as 'marginal' in relation to society as a whole; the living conditions of the great majority of the population had deteriorated notably (Lander 2005: 27). In what Ivez Pedrazzini and Magaly Sánchez (1992) refer to as a 'culture of urgency', the informal economy, illegality, illegitimacy, violence and mistrust of official society became commonplace (cited in Lander 2005: 27). The political dominance of AD and COPEI, and their control over state institutions, were no longer acceptable to Venezuelan society, and the Punto Fijo model these parties had created was no longer seen as legitimate (Buxton 2005: 334).

As its capacity and credibility deteriorated, the Punto Fijo state increasingly resorted to violence, corruption and electoral fraud in order to maintain authority (Buxton 2005: 334). The *Caracazo* uprisings, which broke out in Caracas and surrounding towns on 27 February 1989, were symptomatic of this profound crisis in Venezuelan political life. These uprisings, the largest in Venezuelan history, broke out in anger at the neo-liberal reforms imposed by President Carlos Andrés Pérez, who had recently been elected on an anti-neoliberal platform. The government ordered the military to suppress the insurrection; soldiers opened fire in the barrios, and over four hundred people were killed and thousands injured (Buxton 2005: 334). In the early 1990s, incidents of human rights abuses and extra-judicial killings increased and constitutional guarantees were suspended, including the inviolability of the home and the right not to be arrested without a warrant (Buxton 2005: 334).

The *Caracazo* and subsequent state repression signalled violent and widespread dissatisfaction with and repudiation of *Puntofijismo*, which left a vacuum in Venezuelan political life that AD and COPEI could no longer fill (Ellner and Hellinger 2005: 27). A *cantautora* I interviewed in July 2005 remembers that during this period, people in the barrios remembered, listened to and sang Alí Primera's songs:

> When on the 27th of January 1989 *el pueblo* came down from the hills,[11] without a single leader, they confronted Venezuelan institutionalism in the *Caracazo*. Bullets were fired and more than three thousand people died. The only person you could hear at that time [on people's cassette players] was Alí Primera, and he had died four years earlier ... anthropologist Daniel Castro Aguilar was caught up in the firing, and he wrote a chronicle in which he said that you could hear Alí's songs coming from tape recorders and being sung [during the violence].

Journalists, *cantautores* and barrio residents I interviewed in 2005 and 2008 all supported this *cantautora's* claims that Alí's songs were widely played and sung in the barrios during the *Caracazo* uprisings and throughout the late 1980s and early 1990s. For example, a resident of the 23 de Enero barrio told me in 2008:

> During the repression [of the late 1980s—early 1990s] Alí gave [us] hope to struggle and carry on ... [Alí] was very present amongst us, ... we played his songs ... we never stopped listening to Alí.

This resident told me 'when you listened to Alí you felt represented by him ... [by] the lyrics'. In his prologue to *Deep Imprint on this Land*, Hernández Medina (1991: 10) represents Alí's songs as instruments which 'get to the bottom of things' and explain 'the causes of exploitation and the miseries generated by this system which so degrades the human condition'. For example, Hernández Medina (1991: 13) quotes from 'Ruperto'; 'the police are always very efficient when it comes to the poor'. Hernández Medina (ibid.) uses these words, with reference to events that had recently taken place during the *Caracazo* uprisings of February 1989, to accuse the police of targeting and persecuting the poor. According to Hernández Medina (1991: 6), Alí's songs 'stimulate' the struggle against *Puntofijismo* in the late 1980s; a 'new chapter' in national political history is beginning, and Hernández Medina (ibid.) claims that it is Alí Primera's songs that provide 'spiritual sustenance and optimism to go forward':

> In universities, factories and secondary schools, people are joining the struggle for social change, stimulated by the *Nueva Canción* that Alí Primera created. Protests are preceded by the presence of Alí Primera, otherwise they are not protests. His message echoes ... his songs are still relevant.

CONCLUSIONS

This chapter examined collective memories of Alí Primera and his *Canción Necesaria*, and the functions that these served in the decade after his death. Obregón Múñoz (1996: 39) argues that in Venezuela the struggles of the 1960s and the 1970s, which were linked to the guerrilla movement, left 'an everlasting mark in the popular memory'. Though the state subsequently 'pacified' this movement, and 'neutralised' dissident groups, the political thought associated with the movement survived in the form of an anti-establishment discourse, which Alí Primera's songs transmitted in the late 1980s and early 1990s (ibid.).

Collective memories of Alí Primera's life and songs were conditioned by Alí's own narratives about his life, his conduct and his motivations for composing and performing *Canción Necesaria*. These collective memories provided resources that Venezuelans mobilised in order to make sense of the political and economic difficulties they were experiencing in the 1980s, and to construct and share understandings about the crisis of *Puntofijismo* in the late 1980s and early 1990s. Alí's songs, more than those of any other Venezuelan *Nueva Canción cantautor*, were in a privileged position to transmit an 'anti-establishment discourse'. These songs were capable of doing this because, in the collective memory, Alí was represented as an authentic embodiment of *el pueblo*, as a defender of the poor and the oppressed, as a person who had generated both affection and hatred in life, and as a persecuted victim of the state who never betrayed his principles and who willingly sacrificed his life defending them. These qualities are identified by Johnson (2004) as the qualities that are most likely to lead a deceased individual to be remembered as a hero in the popular imagination. During the political and economic crisis of the late 1980s and early 1990s, Alí's songs were able to direct Venezuelans' awareness to these heroic qualities and to a set of moral and political values, which were contrasted with those of the *Puntofijista* system. At a time of increasing material hardship and state repression, collective memories of Alí Primera and his songs, through their elevation of a set of values that were identified with *el pueblo* and with the defence of the poor, and through their emphasis on ideas of selflessness and moral integrity, functioned as a form of resistance to *Puntofijismo*. In 1994, the then colonel Hugo Chávez was to mobilise these collective memories in his own political communication

NOTES

1. http://cotilleo-mundano.blogspot.co.uk/2008/11/chepa-candela-en-su-columna-tendra-un.html. Last accessed 8 January 2016.
2. No date is provided for the first edition.
3. Interview with Ramiro Primera, Caracas, September 2008.
4. From the 1978 album *Canción mansa para un pueblo bravo*.
5. Interview with Noel Márquez, Caracas, July 2005.
6. Interview with Zapata, Caracas, September 2008.
7. Interview with Oswaldo Mussett, Barquisimeto, July 2005.
8. On 29 October 1992, *Médano* newspaper reported that this book was sold out (Castillo and Marroquí 2005: 104).
9. Interview with Benito Márquez, Caracas, July 2005.
10. Alí's surname, Primera, is also the Spanish for 'first' (feminine singular form).
11. As Alí Primera's song 'Casas de cartón' depicts, Caracas is surrounded by hills where the majority of the urban poor live.

CHAPTER 5

Alí Primera and Hugo Chávez in the 1990s: 'Together in Hope and Song'

In 1994, the then colonel Hugo Chávez was asked by journalist Laura Sánchez if he had a message for the people of Venezuela. Chávez replied '¡Que escuchen las canciones de Alí Primera!' (Let them listen to Alí Primera's songs!)[1]. In public appearances, interviews and political speeches, and later in his television programme *'Aló Presidente*, Chávez frequently mobilised and connected himself with collective memories of Alí and *Canción Necesaria*. Chávez was demonstrably familiar both with Alí's lyrics and with his biography; he sang Alí's songs, voiced his admiration for Alí's work and conduct and reminisced about listening to and learning from Alí's music as a young soldier.

In this chapter, I will examine how Chávez mobilised existing discourses about Alí's life, death and *Canción Necesaria*, and attached them to his own political programme in order to communicate a new ideological project and fresh set of social, economic, political and cultural priorities for Venezuela. To do this, I use critical discourse analysis, which approaches discourse as a political practice that 'establishes, sustains and changes power relations' and also 'the collective entities (classes, blocs, communities, groups) between which power relations obtain' (Fairclough 1992: 67). As such, this approach focuses on the ways discourse structures 'enact, confirm, legitimate, reproduce, or challenge relations of *power* and *dominance* in society' (Van Dijk 2001: 353, emphasis in original).

© The Editors (if applicable) and the Authors 2016
H. Marsh, *Hugo Chávez, Alí Primera and Venezuela*,
DOI 10.1057/978-1-137-57968-3_5

Discourses constructed around grassroots collective memories of Alí Primera's life and songs provided Chávez with cultural resources, which he used to create a political persona through which to challenge *Puntofijismo* in the mid-1990s. This persona helped Chávez in two ways; first, it functioned to identify Chávez with *el pueblo* and second, it functioned to represent Chávez and his political movement as a distinctive break with *Puntofijismo*.

HUGO CHÁVEZ AND THE BOLIVARIAN MOVEMENT

Born on 28 July 1954 in the village of Sabaneta, in the cattle lands of Barinas State, Hugo Chávez was the son of schoolteachers. Like much of rural Venezuela, Sabaneta had no high school, so the young Hugo was sent to live with his grandmother to complete his secondary education, and at the age of 17 he moved to Caracas to study at the Venezuelan Academy of Military Sciences. Chávez would later recall listening with rapt attention to his grandmother's stories about her grandfather's participation in the revolutionary land reformist Ezequiel Zamora's march through Barinas in 1859 (Gott 2005: 112). It may be this fascination with 'tales of Venezuelan dissidents' from the nineteenth century (Gott 2013: 21) that inspired Chávez to go on to become, in 1981, a history teacher at the Caracas military academy. Here, in a Venezuela 'dominated by white European immigrants and overlaid with a thick cultural veneer of American consumerism', Chávez sought 'to recreate pride in an alternative historical vision of a land peopled by the often-ignored descendants of Native Americans and black slaves' (ibid.). In 1982, 'dismayed by the growing decadence and corruption' of civilian politicians, Chávez formed the *Movimiento Bolivariano Revolucionario 200* (MBR-200, Bolivarian Revolutionary Movement 200) within the armed forces (ibid.). Initially, the MBR-200 was a political study group that focused on Venezuelan military history, but it became 'a subversive organisation hoping for an appropriate moment to stage a *coup d'état*' (ibid.).

Chávez first came to public attention in Venezuela in February 1992, when officers from the MBR-200 launched a coup attempt against the deeply unpopular AD government of Carlos Andrés Pérez. The coup attempt was not successful and, as one of its leaders, the then Colonel Hugo Chávez was given television air time to surrender and ask other rebels to stand down. Chávez personally assumed full responsibility for the coup's failure, announcing on television that 'por ahora' (for now) the movement's objectives had not been met. The words 'por ahora' were remembered and widely interpreted as an indication that Chávez's struggle against the ailing Punto Fijo system was only just beginning (Blake 2005: 370). President Pérez was removed from office in 1993 via impeachment proceedings relating to misuse of public funds. Hugo Chávez meanwhile, serving a prison sentence for his role in the coup attempt, became 'a symbol of many citizens' growing rejection of the prevailing political and social order' (ibid.). Though his political thought was unknown to the public at that time, Chávez was celebrated in folk songs, graffiti, poems, and even in a new version of the Lord's Prayer:

> Our Chávez who art in prison
> Hallowed be thy name
> Thy people come
> Thy will be done
> Here
> As in your army
> Give us today the lost confidence
> And never forgive the traitors
> As we ourselves will never forgive them
> Who betrayed us
> Save us from corruption
> And liberate us from the president
> Amen. (Taussig 1997: 108, cited in Michelutti 2013: 177–8)

In March 1994, the recently elected president Rafael Caldera,[2] who had pledged during his election campaign to pardon members of the military imprisoned for their involvement in the 1992 coup attempt, ordered Chávez's release from prison. Chávez was greeted as a popular hero (Blake 2005: 370). One of his first public acts upon release from prison was to pay a formal visit to the National Pantheon, a burial place in Caracas dedicated to Simón Bolívar.[3] This visit was highly symbolic; the tombs of martyred heroes, and other places associated with them, frequently act as important sites for patriotic remembrance and commitment (Johnson 2004: 6). These places are 'sanctified' because of the idea that the heroes' lives 'were given willingly on behalf of a set of beliefs, a people, or a nation' (Johnson, ibid.). Individuals perceived to have sacrificed themselves for their beliefs become powerful symbols that bond the hero to future generations, and the identification and remembrance of martyrs thus acts as a form of 'intergenerational communication' (Johnson, ibid.).

Chávez's visit to the National Pantheon in 1994 functioned as a form of 'intergenerational communication', which bonded Bolívar to Chávez and to his political movement. Chávez viewed the Punto Fijo system as 'too corrupt and too weighted against newcomers' (Gott 2000: 134), and he, therefore, sought to differentiate himself from the establishment parties and to establish a new political movement based on the thought of heroes from Venezuela's nineteenth-century history. This movement was named Bolivarianism for the Liberator Simón Bolívar (López Maya 2005: 80). Chávez's views on electoral politics began to change as his popular support grew following his release from prison (Gott 2005: 134). In April 1997, he declared his intention to stand for the presidency and he created a political organisation, the *Movimiento Quinta República* (MVR, Fifth Republic Movement[4]), in order to mount an election campaign. As Margarita López Maya (2005: 80) notes, the image of a tree with three roots was used to symbolise the ideology of Bolivarianism, with each root representing the philosophy of a political figure from the nineteenth century. The 'trinity' of nineteenth-century figures was composed of the Liberator Simón Bolívar, the pedagogue Simón Rodríguez, and Ezequiel Zamora, who fought for land reform. As Richard Gott (2005: 92) details, Chávez sought to recover some of the ideologies of these figures that could be of political value in the present, aiming to 'draw on the country's historical traditions to help lay out a pattern for the future'. The use of these national symbols was extremely important for Chávez and his Bolivarian allies:

> [they] achieved a command of the symbols and images of nationality and applied them to political propositions in a way that was novel, and that became one of the keys to their political success. (López Maya 2005: 81)

In December 1998, four and a half years after being released from prison, Chávez was elected president with 56 % of the vote, and, in February 1999, he became the first Venezuelan president who was linked with neither AD nor COPEI to take up office in over 40 years (Gott 2005: 143). Chávez proclaimed that the country's poverty and underdevelopment were a consequence of the political and policy failures of *Puntofijismo*, a political system which he viewed as 'the perversion of Bolívar's vision and a model that privileged an elite to the detriment of Venezuela's national interest and potential' (Buxton 2005: 339). In August 1999, Chávez gave a speech to an Assembly which was meeting to draft a new constitution for the country:

> Our existing laws are disastrous relics derived from every despotic regime there has ever been, both ancient and modern; let us ensure that this monstrous edifice will collapse and crumble, so that we may construct a temple to justice away from its ruins, and dictate a new Venezuelan legal code under the influence of its sacred inspiration. (Hugo Chávez, quoted in Gott 2005: 146)

These words did not originate from Chávez; Simón Bolívar had originally addressed them to the first Venezuelan Congress in 1819. By reviving and adapting Bolivarian thought to contemporary circumstances, Chávez linked himself with Bolívar and the political thought of this nineteenth-century national hero.

In their analysis of the effectiveness of Chávez's discourse, Emilia Bermúdez and Giraldo Martínez (2000: 62) note that 'Bolivarianism' was not a new concept in Venezuela when Chávez formed his Bolivarian movement. In Venezuela, at times of crisis and political fragmentation, people seeking to lead new political processes have frequently revived the 'unifying myth' or the 'cult' of Simón Bolívar (ibid.). This cult has been conceptualised as a symbolic construction which draws on ideas of 'historical legitimacy' in order to project a political identity based on the building of symbols, ideas and behaviours around the figure of Bolívar (Bermúdez, cited in Bermúdez and Martínez 2000: 62). With the Punto Fijo system in deep crisis, Chávez's discourse drew on the 'myth of Bolívar'; Chávez frequently quoted from Bolívar's thought and speeches and represented these as offering the path to the country's salvation (Bermúdez and Martínez 2000: 63). According to Bermúdez and Martínez (ibid.), this discourse linked with the popular imagination and articulated a messianic vision of salvation for the country and the hope of delivery from despair via the Bolivarian movement. Similarly, Lucia Michelutti (2013: 183) argues that in his discourse Chávez created 'a new Venezuela' by evoking a 'scared history' shaped by two principal elements; the 'defolklorization' of Venezuelan myth and history, which implied the revitalization of popular religious cults such as *Santería* and *Espiritismo* (Spiritism), and the development of a salvation political theology. Faced with the crisis the country was experiencing, in his political discourse Chávez constructed an image of himself and his political movement as the continuation of the work of Bolívar and as the salvation of the country.

CHÁVEZ AND COLLECTIVE MEMORIES OF ALÍ

While the influence of Bolívar's political thought on Chávez has been noted by several scholars, few have commented on the prominent role that Alí Primera's songs played in Hugo Chávez's political discourse. Yet Alí Primera featured frequently in Chávez's public communications, and often at important moments. After winning the presidential elections on 7 December 1998, Chávez gave a speech in which he represented Alí's influence on the Venezuelan people as being equal to that of Bolívar:

> We will have a homeland again! Thanks be to God and thanks be to the courage and bravery of the Venezuelan *pueblo*! You, the *pueblo* of Bolívar, the *pueblo* of Alí Primera, the noble *pueblo*, the liberating *pueblo* of Venezuela! (cited in Bermúdez and Martínez 2000: 64)

Chávez represented Alí Primera, along with Bolívar, as a saviour of the country, and his own political thought as being the continuation not only of Bolívar's but also of Alí's ideas. On 30 August 1992, in an interview conducted from Yare prison, Hugo Chávez explained to former MAS leader José Vicente Rangel that he based his understanding of *la patria* (the homeland) on Alí Primera's approach to the concept, as propounded in Alí's song 'La patria es el hombre' ('Man is the Homeland'):

> the men in the *Movimiento Bolivariano Revolucionario 200* are worried and pained ... Fundamentally pained by *la patria*, defined by *el cantor del pueblo venezolano* (the singer of the Venezuelan *pueblo*), Alí Primera, as man; that is to say, man is *la patria*. (Chávez, cited in Rangel 2012: 28)

Chávez's 'for now' message in February 1992 had implied that he would return to continue the struggle against *Puntofijismo*. Six months later, in his discourse Chávez represented this struggle as the continuation not only of Bolívar's struggle but of Alí's struggle too. In his 1992 interview with Rangel from Yare prison, Chávez made a direct link between his aims and those which the collective memory invested in Alí's songs and Alí's actions in life:

... however long we spend here [in prison], and however we get out from behind these bars, we will go, dear *compatriotas*, to meet you again in person, in order to continue with the struggle [*marcha*], as *el cantor del pueblo venezolano* Alí Primera used to say: gathering flowers, knocking on doors, gathering the sunshine, until we succeed. (Chávez, cited in Rangel 2012: 39)

Chávez and Collective Memories of Alí: Identification with *El Pueblo*

After his release from prison, and soon after visiting the National Pantheon to pay homage to Bolívar in March 1994, Chávez travelled to the Paraguaná Peninsula in order to visit Alí Primera's tomb (Fig. 5.1). He then paid his respects to Alí's mother, Carmen Adela, in her nearby home. In the visitors' book which Carmen Adela kept at her home, Chávez wrote

Fig. 5.1 Alí Primera's tomb in Paraguaná (Photograph courtesy of the author)

a message which linked him to Alí in brotherhood and which echoed the 'for now' phrase he had famously uttered on television two years earlier:

> This day of reunion has a special significance for me. To come to Alí Primera's house, to the nest of Carmen Adela and her dreams, is heart-warming, and the warmth that inhabits [this house] fills our blood with tremendous, supernatural strength.
>
> Alí, your song was always the people's weapon, your example and your guitar are engraved on our flag.
>
> Carmen Adela, on this day, Mothers' Day, I have felt here, with the fresh breeze of your parched Paraguaná land, the kisses of my own mother and the holy fire of the homeland.
>
> Here we will remain, together in song and hope, with Alí leading the way.
>
> For now and for ever!!
> Punto Fijo,[5] 7 May 1994
> Hugo Chávez Frías
> Comandante.[6]

Michelutti (2013: 179) notes that in his discourse, Chávez emphasized how *el pueblo*, and in particular Afro-Venezuelan and indigenous people, 'have *naturally* been part of the struggle to liberate Venezuelan people first from Spanish rule and now from the elites and the US neoliberal empire'. Michelutti (ibid.) shows that in Chuao, a village on the northern coast of Venezuela, Simón Bolívar was vividly present in the memories and narratives of local communities. Popular versions of Bolívar in Chuao are related to '*lived* local revolutionary experiences' which are 'remembered and passed down through generations by local epics and through the spirits of Afro-American cults' (Michelutti 2013: 180). These were the versions of Bolívar's significance that Chávez mobilised in his discourse.

Alí Primera's songs, and stories about Alí's exemplary life and actions, were also related to lived local revolutionary experiences; these songs, and narratives about Alí's life and actions, persisted in the collective memories of *el pueblo*. By mobilising these grassroots collective memories of Alí's life and songs, Chávez emphasised how *el pueblo* were 'naturally' part of the struggle against *Puntofijismo*. Chávez's visit to Alí's tomb and to his childhood home, and his discourse about the significance of Alí for the country and for his political movement, functioned to identify Chávez as one of *el pueblo*.

A Venezuelan I interviewed in 2005 argued that *el pueblo* had always identified with Alí, and when they saw Chávez singing Alí's songs they saw this as a sign that Chávez also identified with Alí, just as they did. Diego Silva, who worked with Alí Primera as a musician and an arranger, believes the message people took from seeing and hearing Chávez singing Alí's songs was extremely important; as Chávez travelled the country in the mid-1990s to harness support for his political movement, he sang and spoke about Alí's songs. According to Silva, the rural and urban masses interpreted Chávez's knowledge of Alí's songs as evidence that Chávez was 'theirs':

A type like Chávez had never been seen before, singing Alí's songs. Other presidents might have dressed up in the *liquiliqui* (Venezuelan national dress), but they were from the oligarchy. Alí was *el gran prohibido* [the great forbidden one], and Chávez knew his songs! Alí made an impact on *el pueblo*, and Chávez [was] one of *el pueblo*[7].

Many Venezuelans I spoke to in barrios in Caracas, Paraguaná and Barquisimeto in 2005 and in 2008 told me similar stories; they told me that before Chávez, they had not heard a politician singing 'their' songs or talking about 'their' hero, Alí, in this way. One of a group of bus-drivers I interviewed in Barquisimeto in 2005 told me:

Alí was like Robin Hood ... he belongs to *el pueblo* ... through his songs we learned what to want ... The president [Chávez] refers to Alí a lot ... he [Chávez] talks [about Alí] like we do.

Another bus-driver from this group told me that Chávez '[spoke] to the poor people through [Alí's] songs':

When I hear [Chávez] talk, I laugh. He talks like *el pueblo* ... that's something new ... other presidents bored me, but he [Chávez] seems like a real person. You don't see him like a president; he breaks protocol ... he sings ... he's *un hombre del pueblo* (a man of the people).

Chávez's knowledge of and fondness for Alí's songs identified him as an ordinary person who these bus-drivers felt they could relate to, and who they felt could understand them. Similarly, a community cultural worker in Barquisimeto told me in 2005 that Alí's music 'is identified with *el pueblo*, and Chávez is from *el pueblo*, that's why he [Chávez] identifies [with Alí's music]'; for this community worker, if a person came from *el pueblo*, it was common sense that they would feel identified with Alí, and Chávez's identification with Alí indicated that Chávez was genuinely from *el pueblo*.

CHÁVEZ AND COLLECTIVE MEMORIES OF ALÍ: A BREAK WITH THE PAST

Michelutti (2013: 179) writes that the policies and ideas associated with what the Chávez government termed *desarrollo endógeno* (development from within) were 'entrenched in indigenous frameworks' and in a language that linked alternative routes to development with 'a variety of vernacular "naturalization" discourses'. Michelutti (ibid.) argues that at the heart of this project for 'development from within' lay 'the creation of a new history and a new modernity that put at the centre of the Venezuelan nation traditionally marginalized groups such as the Afro-Venezuelans'. In this way, the 'history of the village and its historically oppressed inhabitants' became the history of Chávez (ibid.). Similarly, Zúquete (2008: 102) details how Chávez empowered his followers by making them feel that their struggle was not circumstantial but historical; they were 'participants in the long-running struggle for liberation' that 'official historiography' had ignored. Chávez called for a 'comprehensive moral and spiritual revolution' (Chávez 2006, cited in Zúquete 2008: 114) that was directed at the 'demolishment of the old values of individualism, capitalism, and selfishness' (Chávez 2007, ibid.) so that 'a new man, a new society, a new ethics' (Chávez 2003, ibid.) would emerge.

In his discourse, Chávez represented himself and his movement as creating a new start for the country based on the values and the history of the Venezuelan *pueblo*. Alí Primera's songs provided Chávez with a resource to articulate the vision of a definitive break with the Punto Fijo past; in his political communication, Chávez tapped into collective memories of Alí and Alí's songs in order to represent his government as a fresh beginning in which the Venezuelan *pueblo* would be protagonists. For example, on 5 August 1999, Chávez gave a speech at the *Palacio Federal Legislativo* (Federal Legislative Palace) in Caracas in order to present the newly drafted constitution for legal approval. In this speech, Chávez used Alí's lyrics to communicate the image of a fresh start for the Venezuelan *pueblo* who had been excluded and marginalised during the Punto Fijo government. Chávez quoted lyrics from Alí's song 'Tin Marín', composed by Alí after the drowning of eleven members of the Afro-Venezuelan Grupo Madera:

> And just as *el cantor del pueblo* used to sing in those songs, when he said 'with fire tears [turn into] nothing, they go away',[8] they evaporate. *El pueblo* are like that. In these conditions, in the situation we are in today, we have *pueblo* again. It has rained and *el pueblo*, who had disappeared a decade ago, two decades ago, or three ... we were evaporated as *pueblos*, disappeared, but a decade ago it started to rain, *el pueblo* started to appear again, and again I quote the singer Alí Primera: 'Like rain will return/to commence the sowing'. Like rain, that which evaporated will return so that the sowing can commence, those who cannot see it may be blind, but for a while now it has been raining *pueblo* in Venezuela and it has been a long while since the new sowing started. (Chávez: 1999)

Using Alí's image of rain as a metaphor for nourishment which leads to rebirth and growth, Chávez uses Alí's lyrics to construct a vision of *el pueblo* rising up from oppression to construct a new future. Alí's lyrics provide Chávez with a means to place traditionally marginalised groups at the centre of the Venezuelan nation; it is *el pueblo* who started the struggle which Chávez will continue with *el pueblo*, and it is *el pueblo* who are driving the revolution.

Alí Primera's songs provided Chávez with a means of linking to a cultural past that was perceived to be far removed from *Puntofijismo*. The songs provided cultural resources for Chávez to call on in his political communication in order to link his government's vision for alternative development routes with the history of *el pueblo* and their activism. Chávez used Alí's songs to represent to the Venezuelan public the values that the Bolivarian government placed at the centre of its vision for the country's future. In a speech that Chávez gave in Maracaibo in 2008 (uploaded to YouTube on 1 December 2008),[9] Chávez sang 'Los que mueren por la vida' (Those who Die for Life) and 'América Latina obrera' (Proletarian Latin America) in full, beating a percussion accompaniment with his hands on the table at which he was seated. In the audio-visual recording of this speech, the audience can be seen singing along with Chávez, applauding and dancing in the auditorium. After singing these songs, Chávez uses

Alí's words as a didactic tool to represent a vision for a new future based on Alí's ideas:

> Alí Primera and his song, which was *la siembra* (the sowing) of Bolivarianism. Look, I'm going to read to you ... to all the country ... what Alí Primera said here in Maracaibo in a speech on the 11th of February 1985. I'm just going to read it. (Reading from a page he holds in front of himself) ... 'Man's liberty has a relation with his culture, a relation with his health, a relation with his work, a relation with education, with his vital space, with the environment, with his surroundings ... Man's freedom has to go beyond mere individual freedom, where they want to enclose us. The man who lives only within his individual freedom is a prisoner'. (To the audience) Mind, it's Alí Primera! These are Alí Primera's words! 'The man who lives only within his individual freedom is a prisoner. A prisoner because his spiritual-ity, his solidarity, have not developed, and a man without spirit and solidarity with others is a prisoner'. Let us liberate ourselves with Alí Primera! With Alí, let us liberate our spirituality, our solidarity!

Chávez represents himself as a political leader who is inspired and guided by Alí's message; he appeals to the audience to also look to Alí to understand what genuine liberty is, and to build alternative roads to devel-opment based on their collective memories of Alí's example. In another speech uploaded to YouTube on 22 August 2008,[10] Chávez speaks to a young man, Adolfo, who, Chávez announces, was unable to finish high school 'because of the system of exclusion'. Chávez asks his audience 'what is the system of exclusion called?', and Adolfo answers 'Capitalism'. 'Capitalism', confirms Chávez. Then Chávez asks the audience:

> You remember Alí Primera, don't you? We remember him, every day we live him. But there is a poem of Alí Primera's, a song which is a poem; 'Ruperto'. Do you remember?

Chávez mobilises collective memories of Alí and highlights the endur-ing importance of these memories both for himself and for *el pueblo*. Chávez then recites 'Ruperto' without consulting written notes and with no hesitation or prompting. Chávez's recitation of 'Ruperto' from mem-ory not only conveys his knowledge of Alí's lyrics; it also converts the song into a passionate political speech. Before reaching the final verse of this recited 'performance' of Alí's song, Chávez pauses to insert his own words:

And at the end Alí, who gathers all the pain of one hundred years, of two hundred years of solitude, of *un pueblo* tired of being downtrodden. Alí says at the end...

At this point, Chávez recites the last verse of 'Ruperto',[11] before emphasising the song's anti-capitalist message by exhorting his audience:

Let us bury capitalism, the old, the odious and the savage capitalist system! If we want to save *la patria*, to save *el pueblo* and the children!

Chávez constructs a political speech from Alí's song lyrics, and in this speech represents Alí's anti-capitalist message as the salvation of the country. Chávez uses Alí's words to call for radical change and to appeal to *el pueblo* to remember their own history and their own heroes in order to 'save' *la patria*, their children and themselves. In this case, Alí's song provides Chávez with a resource to construct a discourse about *desarrollo endógeno* (development from within). This discourse, drawing on Alí's lyrics, links ideas about alternative routes to development with collective memories of the values attached to Alí's songs. Chávez constructs these songs as guides to his government's alternative path to development.

'ALÓ PRESIDENTE

Michelutti (2013: 181) argues that it was 'through television and radio that Chávez mainly enter[ed] *directly* the lives of common people'. Radio and television provided Chávez with one of his main outlets to sing and reminisce about Alí Primera and his songs. On 23 May 1999, the first episode of a predominantly unscripted talk show hosted by Chávez was broadcast in Venezuela. *'Aló Presidente* (Hello President) was a weekly talk show aired on national radio and television stations. During this programme, and especially to mark the anniversary of the birth and death of Alí, Chávez regularly made reference to Alí Primera's songs and paid homage to Alí's life and actions. Chávez also sang Alí's songs with passion and gusto and demonstrated that he knew their lyrics and melodies by heart. On the tenth anniversary of the show, an Australian writer and activist resident in Venezuela noted:

Chávez is renowned for singing on the show. The first song he sang was one by Alí Primera, who was a Venezuelan communist and musician, with lyrics that go, "Sing, sing friend, so that your voice is a bullet, so that the hands of *el pueblo* won't sing unarmed." (Pearson 2009)

I will now examine in detail Chávez's discourse in a specific episode of *'Aló Presidente* which was broadcast on 21 February 2006. In this episode of *'Aló Presidente*, broadcast shortly after the twenty-first anniversary of Alí's death, Chávez dedicated 18 minutes to Alí Primera. This exemplifies how Chávez mobilised collective memories of Alí, and reminisced about his own memories of the *cantautor*, in order to construct a political persona. First, this persona linked Chávez with a remembered vernacular history of opposition to elite political rule. Second, this persona linked the birth of the Bolivarian movement to the oppositional messages attached to Alí's songs in the collective memory.

CHÁVEZ AND ALÍ: LINKING TO A VERNACULAR HISTORY OF OPPOSITION

Chávez's discourse in this episode takes the form of an intimate reminiscence. Chávez speaks directly to the camera in a relaxed and warm manner, as if in conversation with friends in his home. He utilises the first person plural forms 'we' and 'us' to include the audience in his recollections, as if he were speaking for them too. Chávez begins by saying:

> What a lot of help Alí Primera gave us! How timely was his arrival on this land! His revolutionary song, we'll never forget it, those of us who have been revolutionary for a long time, who always have been [revolutionary].

Chávez thus forges a link between himself and his listeners; they share Alí's songs, and these songs unite them and identify them as being engaged in the same historical struggles against elite political rule. Chávez then goes on to reminisce about the first time he heard Alí Primera; as a 'little lad', he explains, he attended an event in Barinas which formed part of an election campaign. Chávez says that he cannot remember who the candidate was, but that Alí was singing at this event and he has 'never forgotten' it. At this event, Chávez recalls:

> Alí Primera sang, his songs were just beginning to be heard, those songs that you sang then in high school. 'Las casas de cartón' [sings]; 'how sad the rain sounds', and you imagined what the cardboard houses were like,

what a poem! Ruperto, his wife and his three children, herbs were his medicine, and the shaman his doctor, and one day he went to Caracas, to the local shop ... capitalism helped him, it helped him to build his shack, using empty Pepsi cola cans for walls, and empty Mobil Esso cans, and for a roof he used a Ford company billboard, 'It's easy to have a Mustang', and then you learned, you were being filled, filled with curiosity; what is this? And then we saw reality, with that song that on one occasion a boss of mine complained about, why was I singing those songs? That song, 'Proletarian Latin America', [sings] 'raise the flag in the revolution'. We used to sing those songs, we were going together to fight for a second independence. And that song about Bolívar, it touched your soul, above all the soul of the soldiers and *el pueblo*, but I from my position as a soldier, when I sang Alí Primera's 'Bolívar Bolivariano', and the child[12] said to Bolívar in the song [sings] 'You go from town to town/Waking up the people/So that they raise their heads higher/To be worthy of glory/And make history again/ Liberating the oppressed/Because if the people are asleep/They will never achieve glory'. He was prophesising, he was like a prophet and he went about like a troubadour on the roads, and he went about with his guitar, [sings] 'and I was filling my rifle with poetry and flowers', what a song! And he sang to the soul of the people, [sings] 'Come on El Salvador, there isn't a single little bird',[13] and he sang to the soldiers, [sings] 'when the soldier serves us in the homeland ... when there is no more oppression, then I will sing to peace'. He sang to the great Bolívar, he sang to everyone, he sang to [sings] '*Comandante* Che they killed you, but in us they left forever your memory', and he sang to the Cuban Revolution, [sings] 'Cuba is a paradise'. (Audience applause and cries of 'Alí lives', to which Chávez replies 'Of course!').

In this discourse, which lasts for six minutes, Chávez refers to and quotes or sings from nine of Alí's songs. Chávez represents himself not only as being familiar with Alí's songs, and as having been informed and influenced by the songs throughout his life; Chávez presents the songs as depictions of 'reality' which caused him (and his allies) to ask themselves about the conditions in which the poor masses lived. Through Alí's songs, Chávez portrays himself as having learned about the 'cardboard houses' and about the lives of urban immigrants like Ruperto, and as being filled with curiosity to find out the causes of such social and economic inequality. Chávez represents this questioning as being subversive and something which his boss 'complained' about; Alí's songs led to an awareness which, Chávez implies, was considered subversive by state authorities, but which filled him with curiosity and taught him about 'reality'.

Alí's songs thus provided Chávez with resources to mobilise alternative versions of the lives and actions of historical figures which underlined the revolutionary and anti-oligarchic qualities of these figures. By referring to the Bolívar of 'Canción Bolivariana', Chávez was able to emphasise the Liberator's subversive qualities and represent the Punto Fijo government as making only symbolic gestures (lighting candles in church) while official *Puntofijista* visits to Bolívar's tomb were really motivated by a desire to see that Bolívar's revolutionary ideas were 'well and truly dead'. Through reference to Alí Primera's songs, Chávez could attribute to the Liberator an oppositional set of values, which functioned to critique the Punto Fijo system. Alí's songs provided Chávez with a means to invoke national symbols as constructed in counter-cultural narratives, and not as represented in official *Puntofijista* discourses. Chávez represents Alí's version of Bolívar in 'Canción Bolivariana' as having 'touched the soul' of the soldiers and of *el pueblo* in particular; Chávez thus links the concept of *el pueblo* and their history with the military, who would fight on behalf of *el pueblo* and not to protect the interests of the oligarchy. By making this connection, Chávez represents Alí's songs as prophetic, suggesting that the future that Alí's songs foretold is the future that Chávez is creating through his Bolivarian government, a future which places the history of *el pueblo* at the centre.

Alí's songs provided Chávez with a means to mobilise many of the symbols of the left, such as Che Guevara and the success of the Cuban revolution, and to tie these symbols to his own government and its vision for the country. In 2005, the late *Nueva Canción cantautor* Jesús 'el Gordo' Paez told me that he believed that when Chávez quoted Alí's lyrics, or sang a fragment of one of Alí's songs, 'the people remember[ed] the [whole] song, and there [was] Alí Primera, telling the people what the president want[ed] to say'. According to Paez,[14] Alí Primera's struggles against poverty, imperialism, racism, capitalism and elite political rule were popularly seen to be resurrected in Chávez's political movement. By referring to Alí's songs, Chávez linked his government to a history of grassroots social activism.

CHÁVEZ AND ALÍ: LINKING THE BIRTH OF THE BOLIVARIAN MOVEMENT TO ALÍ'S SONGS

Alí Primera served a different function in the Chávez period; no longer standing in opposition to state interests, his songs were rendered as a fundamental basis of the origins of the Bolivarian state. Chávez links the birth of Bolivarianism to Alí Primera in his discourse in this particular episode of *'Aló Presidente*:

> I never had the good fortune to meet Alí in person, but then I went, after prison, I went to get to know Alí's roots, and there we arrived one day, and there we wept and we sang, with the old lady Adela, Alí's mother, and there with his brothers, with José Montecano ... and there I saw the *semeruco* bush that he sang of, and where he dreamed. Well one day Alí died, although he didn't die. It was one 16th of February, and I will never forget that day, because we were in Maracay. We were captains and we were in a meeting. It was a Saturday, and it was dawn when Alí died, and we were in the house of captain [inaudible], where we used to meet from time to time. And his wife was making us coffee and some breakfast because she had woken up early that day. And it was a meeting of the Bolivarian movement, and we were waiting for a group of officers; we used to meet in a semi-clandestine way. I remember that Yurima, the wife, was listening to the radio in the kitchen, while she was cooking ... 'Alí Primera's been killed, they've just said on the radio'. I will never forget, it hurt us so much; 'Are you sure?', 'It can't be!'. We put the radio on and yes, they were talking about the news, in an accident ... there in El Valle in the early hours of the morning. We, we had, we had our meeting, we were already putting together the Bolivarian line, and we finished off by singing Alí Primera's songs until dawn. The people's singer! Venezuela's applause for its singer! The singer who accompanies us in this battle of love, in this beautiful revolution, and, as he used to say, as he used to sing, [sings] 'we will gather flowers, we will knock on doors, we will sow love, we will stay with the sun, until we succeed, because we will succeed'. Alí, you will succeed, with this *pueblo*, always.

In this discourse, Chávez reminisces about his 1994 visit, after being released from prison, to Alí Primera's home. Then Chávez shares a story about a very personal memory; where he was, what he was doing, and who he was with at the moment he heard the news of Alí's death. Martin Conway (1997: 35) refers to such memories as 'flashbulb memories', which he defines as vivid memories which preserve knowledge of an event in an almost 'indiscriminate' way. Such memories, according to Conway (ibid.), are for events that hold a high level of personal importance and relevance to the individual, and they are extremely enduring.[15] Chávez's recounting of this memory in such detail, whether or not the memory is factually accurate, serves to heighten the personal significance of the experience of Alí's death for him; this 'flashbulb memory' conveys to the audience the sense that for Chávez Alí Primera's songs mattered and continue to matter a great deal. Chávez remembers his reactions of disbelief ('Are you sure?', 'It can't be!') and pain ('it hurt us so much') upon hearing the news of Alí's death, and he links these responses to the birth of the Bolivarian movement in semi-clandestinity; 'we had our meeting, we were already putting together the Bolivarian line, and we finished off by singing Alí Primera's songs until dawn'.

Thus Chávez connects the birth of the Bolivarian movement not only to the influence of Alí Primera's songs on the shaping of his political consciousness, but also to the shock of the *cantautor*'s death; Chávez links the impact of this loss to his drive to construct a movement that will work towards the realisation of the hopes and dreams that Alí expressed in his songs and that he died defending. Chávez finishes by addressing Alí directly, proclaiming 'you will succeed, with this *pueblo*', thus tying *el pueblo* to his government and uniting both around collective memories of Alí's songs. Chávez represents his government as working with *el pueblo* in order to bring to fruition the dreams which the collective memory associates with Alí's songs and which Chávez links to the birth of his political movement.

CONCLUSIONS

This chapter examined how Chávez personally connected with the legacy of Alí Primera. In speeches and interviews in the late 1990s, Chávez used collective memories of Alí's *Canción Necesaria* as a discursive tool with which to challenge and resist the dominant social and political order at that time. During a period of political crisis and widespread loss of faith in the hegemonic Punto Fijo system, Chávez mobilised shared grassroots memories of Alí and his songs to represent his movement, and after 1999 his government, as the continuation of the struggles already begun by *el pueblo*. Through mobilising memories of Alí and his songs in his political communication and via the mass media, Chávez linked with *el pueblo* and placed the marginalised masses and their history at the vanguard of a new start for the country.

Collective memories of Alí and his songs already functioned to articulate resistance to *Puntofijismo* in the late 1980s and early 1990s; Chávez did not 'invent' the oppositional values attached to Alí's *Canción Necesaria* in the collective memory. Instead, Chávez made use of these memories in his discourse in order to create a political persona that allowed him to identify with *el pueblo*, and to represent the lower class and mixed-race masses and their traditions of resistance as the fundamental basis of his government. Michelutti (2013: 185) argues that in his discourse, Chávez transformed 'desperation' into 'hope' through the making of a 'sacred political dream'. This dream drew on the cultural salience of 'the hero-*caudillos* who in Robin Hood fashion fight for a political idea and for *el pueblo*' (Michelutti 2013: 181). Alí Primera, popularly remembered, in Robin Hood fashion, to have fought for a political idea and for *el pueblo*, offered Chávez cultural resources with which to articulate his identification with *el pueblo* and their remembered history of resistance to elite political rule. In the twenty-first century, the Chávez government used cultural policy to officially represent Alí's *Canción Necesaria* as a valuable part of the country's cultural heritage and as a precursor of Bolivarianism, as I examine in the next chapter.

NOTES

1. This anecdote is recounted in the CD ROM, *Alí Primera: El cantor del pueblo* (Oscar Arango, Caracas, 2004).
2. A founding member of COPEI, Caldera had formed a new political party, Convergence, for the 1993 presidential election campaign.
3. Chávez's 1994 visit to Bolívar's tomb was broadcast on Venezuelan television http://www.youtube.com/watch?v=XwytICWp_NE (Last accessed 8 January 2016).
4. This name indicated a conscious vision of a break with the past; Venezuela had had four republics since the declaration of independence from Spain (Gott 2005: 135).
5. The use of the words 'Punto Fijo' here has no connection to the political system. Punto Fijo is the name of the small town in the Paraguaná Peninsula where Alí spent much of his childhood. The Punto Fijo Pact, signed in 1958, was named for the house of one of the pact's founders.
6. "Este día de reencuentro tiene para mí un significado especial. Venir a la casa de Alí Primera, al nido de Carmen Adela y sus sueños, es reconfortante y el calor que aquí pervive nos llena la sangre de fuerzas tremendas, espectrales.

   Alí, tu canto siempre fue arma para la lucha, tu ejemplo y tu guitarra van grabados en nuestras banderas.

   Carmen Adela, en este día de la madre, he sentido aquí, con la brisa fresca de tu Paraguaná seca, los besos de mi madre y el fuego sagrado de la patria.

Aquí estaremos, junto al canto y la esperanza, con Alí en vanguardia,

¡¡Por ahora y para siempre!!

Punto Fijo, 07 de mayo de 1994

Hugo Chávez Frías, Comandante".

7. Interview with Silva, Caracas, September 2008.
8. Here Chávez misquotes Alí; the lyrics Alí wrote and recorded are *'Fuego con llanto es vapor, vapor con viento no es na'a, se va'* ('With tears, fire [turns into] vapour/with wind, vapour [turns into] nothing, it goes away'). Chávez's slight variations arguably add to the perceived authenticity of his delivery.
9. See   http://www.youtube.com/watch?v=n1GEYdOxFOM   (Last accessed 8 January 2016).
10. http://www.youtube.com/watch?v=rulwA_EmkME (Last accessed 8 January 2016).
11. Again, Chávez misquotes Alí, using the word 'blame' instead of 'cause' in the final verse of 'Ruperto'.
12. The song's title is 'Canción Bolivariana', and in Alí's recording it is Bolívar who says these words to the child.
13. From the song 'El sombrero azul', dedicated to El Salvador, in which Ali sings 'Come on El Salvador, there isn't a single little bird that takes off and then stops flying'.
14. Interview with Paez, Caracas, July 2005.
15. Conway (1997: 38) also provides evidence that flashbulb memories differ across social groups. For example, while both Whites and African Americans sampled by Brown and Kulik (1977) report high flashbulb memory rates for the assassination of JFK, only African Americans reported high flashbulb memory rates for the assassinations of Malcom X and Martin Luther King (cited in Conway 1997: 38).

CHAPTER 6

Alí Primera and Venezuelan Cultural Policy in the Twenty-First Century

In the mid to late 1990s, as a political outsider with no links to the dominant Punto Fijo parties, the then colonel Hugo Chávez publicly identified with and expressed his admiration for Alí Primera and *Canción Necesaria*, and he harnessed already existing collective memories of Alí Primera's life, songs and death in order to construct a political persona that resonated with the masses, and to create an identity for his political movement.

Following its election in December 1998, the Chávez government expressed the need to:

> ... break the perceived 'taboos' of the dominant paradigm (marginalization of the poor, devastating effects of globalization) by creating new sources of knowledge (regular contact between the leader and the people, new universities, new forums of discussion for the Bolivarian ideology), [to be] promoted through new media channels. The weekly live program *'Aló Presidente* ... the creation of a new public channel, Vive Television, and a 'Bolivarian' news agency, along with the replacement of a private TV station with a new state-funded public channel (Teves) ... these constitute[d] new conduits through which 'suppressed knowledge' ... [could] pass ... to the Venezuelan people. (Zúquete 2008: 103)

The Chávez government used these 'new conduits' to officially promote *Canción Necesaria* and link itself with the legacy of Alí Primera, incorporating Alí's critique of Puntofijismo into its own political communication, and

© The Editors (if applicable) and the Authors 2016
H. Marsh, *Hugo Chávez, Alí Primera and Venezuela*,
DOI 10.1057/978-1-137-57968-3_6

representing Alí's songs as precursors of twenty-first-century Bolivarianism. In February 2005, on the twentieth anniversary of Alí Primera's death, the then vice president José Vicente Rangel inaugurated a state-funded exhibition of photographs, paintings and album covers in honour of Alí at the National Library in Caracas. In the speech he gave at this official event, Rangel attributed a fundamental role to Alí in the development of the Chávez government's Bolivarian thought:

> Alí Primera was ahead of his time when he revived the thought of Bolívar. Many of us today are Bolivarian because Alí Primera discovered Bolívar; what President Chávez [did was] merely to revive the legacy of Alí Primera. That is why there is no better way to define the revolutionary quality of this *proceso*[1] than through Alí Primera. Those of us who believe in social change, in a more just Venezuela, in a revolutionary Venezuela, are with this *proceso*, because we are identified with the thought of Bolívar and with the vindication [*reivindicación*] of Bolívar through the songs and the words of Alí Primera. (Rangel 2005)

This chapter looks at how the Chávez government used cultural policy to officially construct and represent Alí Primera's *Canción Necesaria* as a precursor of Bolivarianism and as a valuable part of the country's cultural heritage.

I take cultural policies to be 'systematic, regulatory guides to action [in the cultural sphere] that are adopted by organisations to achieve their goals' (Miller and Yúdice 2002: 1). Through the introduction of new cultural policies, the Chávez government aimed to invest Alí Primera's *Canción Necesaria* with value for the country and to construct Alí as a root of Bolivarianism. Without purging *Canción Necesaria* of its subversive associations, Chávez sought to institutionalise those values and harness them for the state and for the Bolivarian project. By giving official space to representations of Alí's legacy, which had already been constructed outside state institutions in the decade after Alí's death, the Chávez government sought to raise the official status of Alí's legacy and to represent itself as the continuation of Alí's struggles on behalf of *el pueblo*.

BOLIVARIAN CULTURAL POLICY: A BREAK WITH THE PAST

During the Chávez period, structural changes were implemented with the aim of providing the channels for the government to construct stronger support networks for previously devalued cultural forms. In December

1999, Venezuela's first constitution approved by popular referendum was ratified. Chapter IV of this constitution, dedicated to culture and education, was the first chapter in the Venezuelan constitution to guarantee state support and protection of cultural rights and cultural well-being.[2] Article 100 of this chapter states:

> The folk cultures comprising the national identity of Venezuela enjoy special attention, with recognition of and respect for intercultural relations under the principle of equality of cultures.

New laws were implemented to put these articles into practice. For example, with regard to music and the media, the *Ley de Resorte* (Law of Social Responsibility),[3] passed in December 2004, aimed to support and promote Venezuelan musicians by establishing quotas; 50 % of all music played on radio and television was to be Venezuelan. According to former vice minister of culture[4] Ivan Padilla, of that 50 % it was specified that half should be traditional folk music, and half music of other 'fusion' genres, such as reggae, rap or hip-hop, which was produced in Venezuela by Venezuelans. This law, Padilla explained, was intended to 'support and strengthen local [cultures]' by giving these forms greater media access.[5]

The Consejo Nacional de la Cultura (CONAC) which had been formed in 1975 (Guss 2000: 44) was replaced in February 2005 with the *Ministerio del Poder Popular para la Cultura* (Ministry of Popular Power for Culture). The new Ministry was established by the National Executive to devise and implement cultural policy; its official website stated that the office was created with the aim of initiating a process of 'profound change' leading to the complete reorganisation of the cultural sector.[6] Such changes were needed, argued former minister of culture, Farruco Sesto, because in the cultural sphere:

> We inherited a public institutionalism that was designed to satisfy the demands of a small number of families, I'd say no more than fifty thousand, who were located mainly in Caracas. (Sesto, quoted in Wisotzki 2006: 14)

Ivan Padilla also characterised previous governments' cultural policy as elitist and designed to 'benefit a wealthy minority', and asserted that the Chávez government aimed to break with past approaches to cultural policy:

Until now, the society in which we have lived has always created pedestals to glorify the few ... [but] ... in an equal society, all culture ... is as valid. ... [This is] a revolution that calls for inclusion, for us to recognise ourselves as a people.[7]

According to Padilla, the aim of Bolivarian cultural policy was two-fold; first, it aimed to widen access to cultural goods and services by, for example, allowing the public free entry to concerts at the Teresa Carreño theatre in Caracas, a venue that musician Diego Silva states was previously seen as a 'symbol of the elite'.[8] Second, according to Padilla, Bolivarian cultural policy aimed to break down elitist divisions between 'high' and 'low' culture and to strengthen local forms of culture, which previous governments had dismissed as 'popular' and shown little concern to support in any way, financial or otherwise.[9]

THE 'TRADITIONAL' GOALS OF VENEZUELAN CULTURAL POLICY

The thesis that postulated Venezuelan 'exceptionalism' in the Latin American context has historically led Venezuelan political and academic elites to represent their country as a modern nation 'following in the foot-steps of the developed nations, having left behind virtually all vestiges of the past' (Ellner and Tinker Salas 2005: 9). This 'exceptionalism' thesis had its counterpoint in the arts too:

> In contrast to the situation in other Latin American countries ... Venezuela's elites could negate the contributions of indigenous and Afro-Venezuelan groups to the country's history and culture ... For the ruling classes and intellectuals who set cultural and social policy for the country, Europe was the model. (Mayhall 2005: 130–1)

In Venezuela, cultural policy in the twentieth century was predominantly devised and implemented by and for intellectuals who sought to emulate Western classical models of 'high art' (Labonville 2007: 6) and who aimed more to 'indicate the sophistication and competence of the Venezuelan elite than to illustrate the context of the country's past' (Lombardi 1981: 253). These elite groups generally regarded national cultural forms to be 'inferior' to those of Europe. For example, in the 1920s the Venezuelan classical composer Juan Bautista Plaza complained about 'the prevalence of poor taste in music, widespread ignorance of the masterworks of Western art music, and the general laziness that made Venezuelans disinclined to learn about new kinds of music' (Labonville 2007: 74). In 1950s Venezuela, *Los Disidentes*, a group of geometric abstract artists, proclaimed that they fought against folklore and everything it stood for (Mayhall 2005: 132). The European heritage of Venezuelan cultural forms was emphasised while the contributions of indigenous and Afro-Venezuelan sectors of the population were disparaged or negated (Mayhall 2005; Wright 1990).

In Venezuela, the *joropo* or *llanera* 'melody of the plains' (Slonimsky 1946: 289) is the form of folklore that Venezuelan elites have historically been most willing to promote as the national music. This folk genre, associated with the cattle plains of the interior, has generally been represented as closely related in origin to the Spanish *fandango* (Béhague 1979: 155). Winthrop Wright (1990: 57), in his study of race and national image in Venezuela, suggests that the *llanera* genre has been privileged by Venezuelan elites because the African presence in Venezuela is concentrated predominantly along the coast of north-central Venezuela, far from the vast cattle plains of the interior, which Venezuelan elites have frequently sought to populate with European immigrants in an attempt to 'whiten the race'. *Llanera* music is thus not usually associated with the Afro-Venezuelan population (Wright 1990: 57). Wright (1990: 70) argues that Juan Vicente Gómez, who created a strong central government and ruled Venezuela by force from 1908 until his death in 1935, represented the western state of Táchira he was from as a region that had a white aristocracy and few blacks; Táchirans considered themselves 'serious, industrious, hardworking people of European origin' who contrasted their austere way of life with that of the 'darker-hued lowland Venezuelans, whom they depicted as being descendants of fun-loving and frolicking slave ancestors'.

On the whole, Venezuelan governments in the twentieth century generally displayed little interest in the cultural sphere and provided scant support, financial or otherwise, for cultural initiatives of any kind (Labonville 2007: 3–11). During the dictatorship of Juan Vicente Gómez, music historian José Antonio Calcaño notes, cultural activities in the country 'persisted by a real miracle of devotion, amid an almost total lack of support and stimulus on the part of the government' (cited in Labonville 2007: 5). In 1972, Alfredo Tarre Murzi wrote in a book about Venezuelan cultural policy:

If there is any country where culture and its development confront problems, that country is Venezuela. They are problems inherent in the past: a tradition of barbarism in which are mixed civil wars, dictators, rough *caudillos*, illiteracy, absurd administrative centralization, instinctive violence, chronic calamities, and the apathy of the Venezuelan, a being disheartened by more than a century and a half of frustrations. (quoted in Labonville 2007: 3)

In his study of Venezuelan festivals and 'the ideology of tradition', anthropologist David Guss (2000) shows that in Venezuela it was only in the 1970s that governments began to pay attention to the cultural sector. By this time, oil revenues had led to the massive importation of Western consumer goods and to the rise of the middle-class *miamero*, the wealthy Venezuelan who 'slavishly mimicked an American lifestyle', and of the couples who 'flew to New York City to shop for the weekend' (Guss 2000: 99). Historian Briceño Iragorry expressed the concerns of many Venezuelans who were beginning to fear the consequences of this new materialism in the 1970s:

We've come even further now on our unconscious journey to destroy the character of this nation. The wave of Anglo-American consumer goods has taken over our *criollo* values and replaced them with exotic symbols. (quoted in Guss 2000: 99)

The nationalisation of the steel and oil industries in 1975 and 1976 unleashed a 'groundswell of patriotic fervour' in Venezuela, which stimulated the adoption of the country's first comprehensive cultural plan under the government of Carlos Andrés Pérez (Guss 2000: 100). A key aspect of this plan was the formation of the *Consejo Nacional de la Cultura* (CONAC), 'the council empowered to coordinate cultural and artistic activities for the entire country' (ibid.). For the first time, groups and individuals actively working in the cultural sphere were given official government support (ibid: 100–1). Much of this assistance was for 'projection groups' such as Un Solo Pueblo, who were engaged primarily with the performance of traditional music and dance, but efforts were also made to establish workshops where students would be taught a variety of national folkloric forms. In 1980, the *Ley Orgánica de Educación* (Organic Education Law) was drawn up, a National Education Plan which required that Venezuelan folklore and popular traditions be taught as part of the school curriculum. However, resources for this plan never materialised, and little attempt was made to expand these programmes beyond the capital. Most of these activities remained extremely centralised or were suspended altogether with subsequent changes in government. Ultimately, these unsuccessful government attempts to respond to widespread concern about the perceived loss of traditional cultural values left a vacuum into which British American Tobacco stepped in 1981 (Guss 2000: 101).

British American Tobacco was an extremely successful business in Venezuela; in 1922, it had purchased an already existing corporation with a national reputation and adopted its name, Cigarrera Bigott. In 1981, Bigott had firm control of more than 80 % of Venezuela's tobacco market (Guss 2000: 95). However, a presidential decree that year banning all advertising of tobacco and alcohol on television presented the corporation with a new challenge. Seeking new ways to promote its brand, Bigott commissioned Venezuela's largest advertising firm, Corpa, to conduct a survey asking Venezuelan people what they would most like to see private industry sponsor. The results of this survey indicated a widespread concern to see more support for Venezuelan culture. Bigott responded by restructuring and creating the Bigott Foundation, which it dedicated to the promotion of national cultural forms. In this way, Bigott was able to reinvent itself and maintain a high profile for its brand while circumventing the television advertising ban. Via publications, workshops taught at its base in Petare, Caracas, and a successful television series about popular culture, Bigott and its tobacco leaf logo came to be associated with what it presented as Venezuela's most 'traditional' cultural values (Guss 2000: 128).

Thus before the election of Chávez, most support for cultural initiatives originated from the private sector. Such support rests on a conception of culture as a resource for the generation of profit and allows no space for any form which is critical of the dominant economic, political and social order (Miller and Yúdice 2002: 133). It constructs national cultural identity primarily to attract tourism and increase revenue and as 'an apolitical expression of a simpler folkloric age' (Guss 2000: 101).

THE GOALS OF VENEZUELAN CULTURAL POLICY IN THE CHÁVEZ PERIOD

According to Ivan Padilla, before the election of Chávez cultural services had been reserved for a privileged Caracas-based minority, while the cultural values of the majority were officially marginalised. Padilla represented previous Venezuelan governments as discriminating against what they deemed to be 'popular culture'; any support provided for such forms under the old regime, he said, amounted to merely 'throwing bread-crumbs' for the poor. Padilla argued that it was imperative that a revolutionary process should involve the official recognition and inclusion of the marginalised masses and their cultural worth throughout the country, which meant an attempt to *descaraqueñizar* culture (to de-centralise culture and to diffuse cultural goods and services beyond Caracas).[10] Oscar Acosta, former president of FUNDARTE (a state-funded cultural institute located in Caracas), asserts that previous cultural policy in Venezuela had been elitist; when Acosta inherited FUNDARTE in 2002, the institute served the cultural needs of a select minority while 'vast areas of knowledge were undervalued'. Acosta argued that Bolivarian cultural policy aimed not only to democratise access to existing cultural goods but also to officially recognise the 'immense cultural wealth' of those Venezuelans who had been historically marginalised:

> A revolution is fundamentally a cultural change … it is a change in the way we understand the world and relate to other human beings. Recognition of the culture that I create with my neighbours is what gives me identity … [and] when I affirm my cultural identity, I resist … when I express my own cultural values … I resist the spread of media-transmitted consumer culture … which seeks to erase my identity.[11]

Acosta thus argued, like Venezuelan leftists had in the 1970s (Guss 2000: 98–100), that 'cultural change' must precede social and political change. Similarly, Padilla asserts that the Chávez government's cultural policy aimed to support and strengthen the cultural expressions of '*all* Venezuelan class, social and ethnic groups in order that *all* Venezuelans should recognise that their cultural identity has value in itself and not only when and because another grants it to you'.[12]

CULTURAL HERITAGE

Cultural heritage is closely related to issues of power and identity (Marschall 2008: 347), and as such it is an aspect of cultural policy that is a 'key feature' of cultural policy statements, particularly for post-colonial countries (Throsby 2010: 9). Stuart Hall (2005: 24–5) argues that the concept of heritage is not a neutral one but a 'powerful source of meanings'; those who cannot see themselves reflected in the 'mirror' of the nation's official heritage cannot properly 'belong' to the nation. Similarly, Brian Graham and Peter Howard (2008: 3) argue that heritages are 'present-centred', for they are 'created, shaped and managed by, and in response to, the demands of the present'. Notions of what constitutes a country's heritage are open to 'constant revision and change', which is both a source and a result of social conflict, and as such these notions are deeply implicated in processes of social inclusion and exclusion (Graham and Howard 2008: 3). Heritage can, therefore, be seen as a form of knowledge, a cultural product and a political resource (Graham and Howard 2008: 5), which is 'closely allied with issues of identity and power' (Marschall 2008: 347).

The concept of heritage and what this means was redefined in Venezuela during the Chávez period; the Chávez government articulated a concern to include the subordinate masses in official representations of the country's cultural heritage in new ways. In official documents, available to download for free from its website, the Ministry of Popular Power for Culture stated that it aimed to create 'a solid cultural structure, which emerges from the people themselves', not from external actors or elite groups, and which would 'boost national identity in order to counteract imperialistic manipulation'.[13] Local cultural traditions were conceived of as resources to be protected from the negative impact of globalisation. *Misión Cultura* was launched in 2005 with the following aims, as stated in a government publication:

> We need to unleash a conscious cultural struggle that recovers and revitalises collective traditions, customs and beliefs that come to us from the past and are tied to the present as our heritage. We have to approach the writing of our own history and recover our memory ... in order to advance towards the future.[14]

In 2005, I asked a participant in the *Misión Cultura* what she aimed to achieve through the project. She replied:

> We aim to recover popular tradition, music, art, that which is characteristic of our country. ... to recover our heritage, local history, which is real history, history told by *el pueblo*. Not history told by a group that ... imposes a version of history that never was, or the history of others ... It's time to go out into the streets, collect [history] and bring it to show the people what the real history of the country is.

This participant was clear in her assertion that the government's *Misión Cultura* opened spaces for *el pueblo* to be actively involved in the construction of their own representations of their cultural values, as they themselves defined them. *El pueblo*, she said, were recovering what they saw as their 'authentic' heritage and challenging dominant versions of the country's history.

THE BOLIVARIAN APPROACH TO CULTURAL HERITAGE

In the Chávez period, the inventory of the cultural heritage took on a new focus with the aim of reinforcing the cultural identity of *el pueblo* and symbolising their participation in the new government. In June 2005, the Chávez government added articles to the 1993 *Ley de Protección y Defensa del Patrimonio Cultural* (Law of the Protection and Defence of Cultural Heritage). Hector Torres (2010), architect and president of the *Instituto de Patrimonio Cultural* (Institute of Cultural Heritage, affiliated with the Ministry of Popular Power for Culture), argued that prior to this 2005 addition to the law, heritage was defined by 'experts' whose values mirrored those of dominant groups:

> ... those who did the inventories were technical experts; it was these experts who decided what was or was not heritage, and they based these decisions on criteria that were exclusively technical.

According to Torres, the inventory of cultural heritage took on a 'different ideological focus' under the Chávez government, because it prioritised the evaluations of the communities and placed the experts at the service of these communities (Torres 2010). The nominations communities made were catalogued by experts and inventoried in *Catálogos Patrimoniales* (Heritage Catalogues), which were printed and distributed within those communities for free, as well as being published in digital format and being made available online.[15] These catalogues contain five sections; 'Objects', 'Buildings', 'Individual Creation', 'Oral traditions' and 'Collective Expression', which embrace both 'traditional' items of tangible heritage, such as classical paintings and buildings, but also intangible items not previously recognised by scholars to have any aesthetic value, such as myths, legends and stories passed from generation to generation (Torres 2010).

Former minister of culture Farruco Sesto emphasised the ways in which the new approach to cultural heritage functioned to bestow worth and recognition upon local communities. Sesto referred in a published interview to two particular communities (cited in Wisotzki 2006: 47–8). According to Sesto, one of these communities requested that the house where a local boxing champion was born be declared a heritage site, and the other community proposed that an iron bridge that crossed a nearby river be recognised as part of their heritage. In both these instances, Sesto said, scholars responded initially with disbelief, arguing that the sites were 'ordinary and common' and 'no jewels of architecture' (ibid.). However, the revised law for the protection and defence of cultural heritage created space for the official recognition of such community-led interpretations of cultural heritage, and the Institute of Cultural Heritage provided the support and structures necessary to include such 'bottom up' claims in its inventory. Sesto (ibid.) emphasised that 'the people recognise a value [in these sites], and one must pay attention to these values ... the community feels represented [by these sites ... which are] part of their history'. Sesto argued that scholars and technical experts were 'welcome', but that those who best knew what their heritage was were *el pueblo*:

> We welcome the opinions of technical experts, of specialists, of those who are educated in the areas of heritage, history and preservation, but we also ... welcome the opinions of communities who highlight which are their values, be they architectural, cultural, gastronomic, or sporting, [these are values] which must be protected and which deserve to be disseminated. This is revolutionary. (Sesto, quoted in Wisotzki 2006: 47)

The revised law for the protection and defence of cultural heritage aimed to create official spaces for community-led interpretations of cultural worth; communities were invited to make their own selections regarding what they held to be of value. This policy gave local communities the power to define their heritage and its importance for their communities in the present; it gave *el pueblo* official resources to represent their heritage on their own terms. According to community radio workers and personal friends of Alí Primera who I interviewed in Barquisimeto in July 2005, it was their community that originally nominated Alí Primera for inclusion in official representations of the country's cultural heritage. Alí, according to this community, was particularly well known and loved in Barquisimeto because he married a local woman (Sol Mussett) there in 1978, and though the couple lived in Caracas they frequently visited Sol's family in Barquisimeto. In February 2005, the month of the twentieth anniversary of Alí's death, the Venezuelan National Assembly met to discuss the nomination, and it unanimously agreed that Alí's songs should be officially declared cultural heritage (Peraza et al. 2005: 46).

ALÍ IN OFFICIAL REPRESENTATIONS OF VENEZUELAN CULTURAL HERITAGE

The National Assembly announced that 2005 was officially dedicated to the memory of Alí Primera and that official measures would be taken to diffuse his *Canción Necesaria*; state funding for compilations of his songs was approved, as well as for an exhibition of photographs, album covers, newspaper articles, letters and other paraphernalia to be inaugurated at the National Library in Caracas (Peraza et al. 2005: 46–7). The official document affirming the National Assembly's decision to recognise Alí as part of the country's cultural heritage draws on pre-existing collective memories of Alí's songs. This document refers to Alí's humble 'peasant origins' in the harsh countryside of Paraguaná, in contact with nature, fishermen, humble people, the *semeruco* fruits and 'the music of the *turpial* birds' (ibid.). The document highlights Alí's detention and the composition of 'Humanidad' in the cells of the DIGEPOL; 'with music and his guitar on his back, [Alí] experienced the arbitrary actions of the *Puntofijista* DIGEPOL, whose informers and hired assassins sent him to the dark cells of the torturers' (ibid.). From these 'humiliating cells', the official document states, Alí's 'song of dignity, his first *Canción Bolivariana*, surges forth:

> Alí Primera ... [was] the founder of *Canción Popular Necesaria* and, in his action and his revolutionary song, precursor of the Bolivarian Homeland ... Alí Primera endures and lives on in the hearts and memories of Venezuelans! ... His unexpected death does not remove him from our midst. We are present to witness his return to earth and the sowing [of his ideas] for all eternity. (cited in Peraza et al. 2005: 46–7)

In this state document, grassroots collective memories of Alí Primera and his songs are given official recognition. These collective memories, conditioned by Alí's own narratives and those of his supporters, are not cleansed of their subversive content; instead, the government harnesses these subversive qualities and connects them to its own vision for the country, declaring Alí 'precursor of the Bolivarian Homeland'. In this way, the Chávez government invests value and worth in aspects of Venezuelan culture that were and are important for *el pueblo*, but which previous governments ignored, disparaged or actively sought to repress due to the perceived capacity of those cultural forms to subvert the status quo. In the Chávez period, the state sought to recognise and raise the status of cultural forms associated with social activism and resistance to elite political rule. Carlos Lanz Rodríguez, an educational adviser to the Chávez government, stated in a government publication that:

> In the construction of a new social hegemony we must valorise and defend the 'pockets of cultural resistance' where our people have preserved elements of their identity, traditions and customs that are loaded with revolutionary fervour (Lanz Rodríguez 2004: 29)

According to Lanz Rodríguez, the Bolivarian revolution linked up with these 'pockets of cultural resistance' and recognised them as part of the social imaginary and the 'memory of the exploited and the oppressed' (2004: 30). These links were forged by putting into practice a cultural policy that, in the words of Oscar Acosta,[16] aimed to 'strengthen and raise the status of those local cultural values which are opposed to the penetration of foreign cultures and consumer values'. Acosta represented the official inclusion of Alí Primera's songs in Venezuela's cultural heritage as official recognition of 'the cultures of *el pueblo*' and of 'cultural values that stand in opposition to foreign aggression'. Alí Primera, according to Acosta, was a man 'genuinely of the people' whose work is steeped in 'native rhythms' and has a 'transcendence which goes beyond politics'. When *Puntofijista* governments were in power, Acosta argued, they could have recognised and honoured Alí, but they chose not to and instead sought to silence him.[17] Acosta thus represented the raising of the status of Alí Primera's songs and their inclusion in official representations of the country's cultural heritage as symbolic of the deconstruction of the old order and a reconfiguration of power relations in favour of the previously subordinated; previous governments suppressed Alí's voice, while the Chávez government invested it with such value that it was officially included in the country's cultural heritage.

In discussing why Alí Primera was included in the country's cultural heritage, Ivan Padilla described this official act as one that responded to *el pueblo*, who had already made Alí part of their heritage, and not as an act which was imposed by a government authority:

> The Institute of Cultural Heritage has the authority to declare what and who constitutes tangible and intangible heritage ... [but] ... those who made Alí part of their heritage are *el pueblo* ... not an authority.[18]

Padilla represented the inclusion of Alí in official representations of the country's cultural heritage as the end result of a history of grassroots activism which the government merely recognised and connected with. According to Padilla, Alí was already a part of the heritage of *el pueblo*; the government simply created an official space for this to be formalised by the state.

THE CHÁVEZ GOVERNMENT AND THE PROMOTION OF ALÍ'S LEGACY

The Ministry of Popular Power for Culture financed a number of pamphlets, books and documentaries about Alí Primera. These texts overlook Alí's marital infidelity, his apparent sexism and his failure to be elected congressman for the *Liga Socialista*. Instead, they highlight the subversive qualities of Alí's songs, Alí's rejection of material wealth, and the personal persecution that Alí and his allies had denounced. The documentaries, which were broadcast on state television and screened with free admission in cinemas under the auspices of the Ministry of Culture, follow a similar format; Alí's songs are interspersed with interviews with his friends and family, journalists and fellow musicians, who talk to an unseen interviewer about their memories of Alí. *Alí en cinco compases* (Alí in Five Bars, 2006, by Patricia Figueroa, Betsy Ceballos and Daniel Castro[19]) is representative of the manner in which these state-funded resources[20] memorialise Alí Primera. In this documentary, many of the interviewees refer to Alí as 'an example to follow'; he is likened to Jesus, Malcom X, Salvador Allende and a host of other martyrs, and termed 'a predecessor of Bolivarianism' whose political thought 'does not differ at all from [that of] Chávez'.

In state-financed publications, the Chávez government was represented as reaping the ideas sown by Alí's songs in a previous epoch, an epoch when these ideas were severely suppressed by the *Puntofijista* state. *Alí Primera: entre la rabia y la ternura* was produced by the *Asociación Cultural Canción Bolivariana Alí Primera* in Barquisimeto with the support of the state institute *Consejo Autónomo de la Cultura del Estado Lara* (CONCULTURA). There were one thousand copies printed and distributed for free. The authors of this publication, which consists of a collection of photographs of Alí Primera accompanied by biographical information and laudatory texts, were personal friends of Alí; Víctor Ramírez and brothers Porfirio and Wilmer Peraza who run *Guachirongo*, a community centre and radio station in Barquisimeto. A fourth author is the Cuban ethnomusicologist José Millet, who moved to Coro, Venezuela, to research Alí Primera's biography after the election of Hugo Chávez. Millet is the author of a further publication about Alí Primera's life, which was published in Caracas by the *Ministerio del Poder Popular del Despacho de la Presidencia* and distributed for free (it is also available to download[21]); *Alí Primera: Padre cantor del pueblo* (2008). These publications simplify and ennoble Alí's life; they recount the familiar episodes, which constitute the plot of Alí Primera's musical career, and they add to these narratives by representing Alí's songs as the inspiration for the Chávez government's Bolivarian project:

> Alí resuscitated. Extracted from the tomb where he had been placed by those who saw him for what he really was: a danger to the oppressive system. Out of the urns and from under the floorboards where they wanted to hide him ... His song is the most beautiful legacy that we enjoy today. In these songs *el pueblo* found shelter more than once, they found inspiration and weapons with which to rebel and ... they will not be enslaved again ... much less by the foreign oppressor that sucked our blood to fatten itself and its allies. [Alí's] *cuatro* will never fade, and if it does it will serve as firewood to nourish the same bonfire of liberation that the poet and singer from Paraguaná offered his life for. (Peraza et al. 2005: 14–15)

These laudatory words do not originate from professional politicians or members of the government, but instead from grassroots activists. However, by providing financial support and official spaces for such narratives, the Chávez government symbolised its support for the 'pockets of resistance' where communities had created their own spaces within which to articulate their political discontent in the Punto Fijo period. The Chávez government also provided support for cover versions of Alí's songs to be recorded by artists who worked within different genres. For example, in 2003 the Ministry of Communication and Information financed the recording of heavy metal covers of a number of Alí Primera's songs by Venezuelan rock artist Paul Gillman on his album *El despertar de la historia* (*Waking up in History*). This was perceived as an official attempt to make Alí Primera's *Canción Necesaria* accessible to wider and younger audiences; in an article published on the Axis of Logic website in 2012, Arturo Rosales and Les Blough assert that Gillman 'always maintained that Venezuelan bands should not imitate their Anglo Saxon counterparts' but that they should 'strive to establish their own style and content within a Latin American heavy metal context'. The recording of Alí's songs, according to Rosales and Blough (ibid.), represents Gillman's 'most successful effort in reaching this goal':

As a committed supporter of President Hugo Chávez and the Bolivarian Revolution, Gillman found a musical and lyrical context in which he could fully express his art in a revolutionary way in the knowledge that the CD of Alí Primera's songs, entitled 'Waking up in History', would be distributed nationwide, free of charge, with no copyright restrictions in [a] truly socialist and nonprofit way. It was a way of revolutionizing the Bolivarian revolution through rock and attract[ing] more of Venezuela's youth to appreciate the fact that rock music was a force backing the revolution itself.

Similarly Bernardo Loyola, Senior Editor for the online television network VBS.TV, states in an article published on the online news website Vice Beta in 2011 that Gillman's band Arkangel had previously been known for playing 'independent venues', for singing 'politically charged songs ("Latin American Repression," "Unemployed," "The Maggots of Power")' and for 'denouncing the corrupt governments that ruled Venezuela'. However, Loyola writes (ibid.):

> when Venezuela's leftist president, Hugo Chávez, took power in 1999, Paul, once the scourge of the political establishment, became one of its most vocal defenders. For a few years he even changed the name of his act to 'Paul Gillman and His Bolivarian Band', a nod to Chávez's 'Bolivarian revolution'.

The Chávez government financed and supported several initiatives aimed at disseminating, formalising, strengthening and institutionalising already existing grassroots commemorations of Alí and his *Canción Necesaria*, as well as creating new memorials. For example, with government funding, an official museum dedicated to Alí Primera was inaugurated on what would have been Alí Primera's sixty-sixth birthday, 31 October 2008. On the same date, the *Anfiteatro Carmen Adela* was officially opened in order to provide a space for live music concerts in Alí's childhood village.[22] Both the museum and the amphitheatre were built next to the house in Paraguaná where Alí spent much of his childhood with his siblings and his mother Carmen Adela; this was the house that Hugo Chávez visited in 1994, when it acted as an informal museum dedicated to Alí's memory. Alí's *caja de limpiabotas* (bootblack box), a symbol of his humble origins, which had been displayed next to *Santería* images in Carmen Adela's home, was put on formal display in a glass case in the museum (Fig. 6.1). When the newly built Los Teques metro service

Fig. 6.1 Alí's *caja de limpiabotas* [bootblack box] displayed formally at the state funded Casa-Museo Alí Primera, Paraguaná (Photograph taken from http://www.aporrea.org/educacion/n151166.html, last accessed 8 January 2016)

(connecting Caracas with the capital of Miranda state) started functioning in 2006, the final station in Miranda, which had formerly been known as El Tambor, was officially renamed for Alí Primera and a statue of the *cantautor* was placed on the site. In the same year, a monument to Alí was installed in Caujarao, close to the *cantautor*'s birthplace in Falcón state (Fig. 6.2). In 2011, in order to commemorate the bicentenary of Venezuela's independence, Plaza Henry Clay in Caracas was renovated at a cost of over one million *bolívares* and re-named Plaza Alí Primera.[23]

These official acts and state-funded memorials act as physical and visual manifestations of the Chávez government's formalisation of and support for grassroots commemorations of Alí Primera's life and songs. These grassroots spaces had previously expressed political discontent with the Punto Fijo state; in the Chávez era, support for the official commemoration of Alí's legacy, implemented via cultural policies, symbolised a change in the social order in favour of *el pueblo*.

Fig. 6.2 Monument to Alí in Caujarao, Falcón (Photograph taken from http://www.pueblosdevenezuela.com/Falcon/PUFA-Caujarao-MonumentoAli Primera1.jpg, last accessed 28 September 2013)

ALÍ AS PRECURSOR OF BOLIVARIANISM

The very fact that Alí did *not* succeed in being elected congressman for the *Liga Socialista* renders his political thought free from attachment to a single political party and, therefore, available to be used to support a wide range of leftist, anti-imperialist, anti-capitalist and anti-racist views. Moreover, the very breadth of the platform outlined for the *Comité por la Unidad del Pueblo* (CUP), which Alí coordinated and actively supported, encompasses such a diverse array of general leftist principles that it can be adapted to other leftist ideologies with ease. Thus the broad leftist scope of Alí's political thought renders it malleable, and indeed facilitated its construction as a precursor of Bolivarianism.

In his inauguration of the 2005 exhibition dedicated to Alí at the National Library in Caracas, the then vice president José Vicente Rangel represented not Chávez but Alí Primera as the one who had originally discovered and revived Bolívar's thought. According to Rangel (2005), there was 'no better way to define the revolutionary quality of this *proceso* than through Alí Primera'. Alí Primera, said Rangel (2005), was 'the past ... the present ... and at the same time the future'. This official promotion of *Canción Necesaria* invested the songs' subversive and oppositional qualities with value for the past, present and future; Alí's songs were represented as the basis of the Chávez government's political thought and Alí, by being referred to as 'ahead of his time' (Rangel 2005), was officially constructed as a precursor of the Chávez government's Bolivarian *proceso*.

The Chávez government invested Alí Primera's songs with prophetic qualities. Alí's songs were represented as 'foretelling' what the Bolivarian government aimed to achieve, and they were constructed as the epitome of the government's political thought. Alí's *Canción Necesaria*, which under the *Puntofijista* system had circulated outside state institutions and acquired oppositional and subversive connotations, constituted a cultural resource for the Chávez government to officially express its opposition to elite political rule and its support for *el pueblo* and their struggles. Ivan Padilla describes Alí Primera as a 'predecessor of Bolivarianism'. According to Padilla, though Alí died before the *Caracazo* of 1989 and before the emergence of Hugo Chávez on the political scene in 1992, and was, therefore, unable to comment on these events, Alí 'prefigured' the Chávez government's political thought. Padilla explained his rationale in the following way:

We cannot take historical phenomena out of their context. We say Jesus and Bolívar were socialists, but this is wrong. They cannot have been socialists because 'socialism' did not exist as an idea [during their lives]. But some things they did and said could be what somebody today identifying them-selves as socialist could do or say ... Alí wrote from the perspective of the exploited, for the exploited and on behalf of a class dream ... Alí rebelled against the reality he knew but he had no idea of what could happen [in the future] ... It might seem eclectic to someone from outside to take a lyric here, a bit of Bolívar there ... [but] I believe all revolutionary struggles have converged into this movement. When I was in the guerrilla movement, I believed that only through the armed struggle would we be free. But now I'm convinced that *el proceso* we're living through [is the right way forward], because it brings together Christ, Bolívar ... we're bringing [everything] together into one vertex ... and Alí's song contributed to this ... Alí gave us strength in his song and in his person ... We don't know if Alí would be with the revolution if he were alive ... Would [Alí] have sold out? It would be presumptuous to say so. But his song is revolutionary, and it prefigures what we are living through now, [which is] progress towards socialism.[24]

Oscar Acosta also represented Alí Primera as a forerunner of Bolivarianism, and he claimed that Alí would recognise his political thought in that of the government. Acosta told me 'Alí's lyrics express very well what this government is doing', and he said that this was 'proof that what's happening now is what Alí wanted'. By representing the Chávez government's actions and policies as 'what Alí wanted' and what Alí expressed in his lyrics, Acosta constructs Alí's songs as a basis of the government's *proceso*.[25] The idea that Alí's songs live on in the Chávez government's actions echoes Rangel's words at the 2005 exhibition:

Alí's death shows that it is possible to live on ... I am sure that we would all want [Alí] to be here ... accompanying, as I am sure he would, this *proceso* of the Venezuelan *pueblo* ... but nevertheless [Alí] is reborn every day.

Representatives of the Chávez government thus attributed a funda-mental role to Alí Primera in the development of twenty-first-century Bolivarian thought. In linking the Bolivarian *proceso* with Alí's songs, state officials constructed Alí as a precursor of Bolivarian thought, and the Chávez government as the continuation of Alí's ideas. Government representatives thus implied, or claimed directly, that if Alí Primera were alive he would recognise his political ideas as being the basis of the Chávez government's *proceso*, and that Alí would therefore 'accompany' and support the Chávez government in the twenty-first century.

BOLIVARIAN CULTURAL POLICY: A COMPARATIVE APPROACH

Historically in Latin America, ruling groups have 'scarcely constructed elite cultures', leaving outside the majority of the countries' indigenous, black and mixed-race populations (García Canclini 1992: 17). It is these marginalised and subordinated populations that revolutionary leftist governments in the region have sought to recognise, to represent and to gain legitimacy with, and cultural policies have provided a means to do this. In his study of the politics of culture in Nicaragua, David Whisnant (1995: 189) argues that revolutionary transformation brings with it a collective sense that 'old pains, fears and frustrations have been conquered and banished, that structures have been changed fundamentally, and that the future is full of new hopes, energies, and possibilities'. Since human beings, Whisnant argues (1995: 190), have a 'limited tolerance for total discontinuity', processes of radical transformation must also generate efforts to reconnect with a familiar past, which is frequently defined in cultural terms (Whisnant 1995: 190). However, the culture of the immediate past is likely to appear inseparable from the oppressive political and social order being replaced; the past with which a connection is sought, therefore, needs to be remote enough to predate the 'perversions and distortions of the old regime' (Whisnant 1995: 190).

If it does not predate the old regime, this cultural past needs to have been despised, marginalised or suppressed by that regime in order to be distinguished from it. Ethnomusicologist T. M. Scruggs (1998: 53) points out that periods of dramatic political and economic change cause 'symbols of national unity, social identity and ethnic solidarity' to be questioned, 'their meaning(s) recast and their import heightened' as the government seeks to legitimise itself. At such times, Scruggs argues (1998: 53), the cultural practices of subaltern groups can 'achieve an abrupt increase in symbolic power, a change in status which state cultural initiatives may both promote and utilize' in order to represent 'a significant break with the preceding period'.

Leftist revolutionary cultural policy such as that implemented in Cuba after 1959 and during the Sandinista government of 1979–1990 is designed to give expression to that which was previously suppressed; it aims to use cultural initiatives 'as part of a broader program of social transformation', seeking to develop a 'collective consciousness' of the 'dignity and self-worth' of the cultural practices of the masses to whom the government addresses its discourse (Mulcahy 2008: 17). In Cuba after 1959 and in Sandinista Nicaragua (1979–1990), the new cultural policy began with unprecedented funding being allocated to cultural initiatives and the establishment of new institutions, such as the *Instituto Cubano de Arte e Industria Cinematográficas* (ICAIC), the *Casa de las Américas* and the *Consejo Nacional de Cultura* in Cuba, and a new Ministry of Culture and *Centros de Cultura Popular* (Centres for Popular Culture) in Nicaragua (Miller and Yúdice 2002: 134–6). One aim of these institutions was to 'democratize culture', making previously 'elitist' forms of culture more accessible and affordable to the masses (Miller 2008: 687).

A further aim of these state institutions was to support and promote the cultural practices of people who had previously been marginalised or suppressed. Previously suppressed cultural forms were presented by leftist intellectuals and government representatives as 'authentic' national forms that had been hidden or virtually extinguished by the sheer quantity of foreign cultural forms imported from the advanced capitalist countries, primarily the USA. There is a strong tendency for leftist governments in Latin America and the Caribbean to present their political programmes as contrary not only to the economic interests of the USA but also as contrary to that country's cultural influence (McPherson 2003: 68; Dore 1985: 414). Therefore, cultural policies intended to protect and strengthen local cultural practices can provide an important means for new regimes to begin to deconstruct the previous order and its economic and cultural links with the USA. In Cuba, national identity before the 1959 revolution was perceived by supporters of the revolutionary government to be 'pegged to US influence' (McPherson 2003: 39), while in Nicaragua prior to the 1979 Sandinista Revolution, Sandinista vice president (1985–90) Sergio Ramírez argued (Scruggs 1998: 54), Miami was seen as the elite's 'spiritual Mecca':

> Miami became the cultural capital of Nicaragua and the cultural values and cultural expressions of middle-class North Americans were upheld as the zenith of artistic achievement. (Dore 1985: 416)

Scruggs (1998: 54) argues that in Nicaragua pre-revolutionary 'infatuation' with imported cultural forms granted the Sandinista government's official support for the cultural forms of indigenous and lower-class sectors of society 'an inherent connotation of asserting the nation's cultural and political independence' and 'rendered expressive forms identifiably Nicaraguan as potentially politically charged nationalist responses to foreign domination'. As Sergio Ramírez put it, the aim was to create a culture deriving from a 'nationalist and anti-imperialist position' (Dore 1985: 413):

> Once we lifted the Yankee stone which weighed Nicaragua down everything that was fundamental and authentic had to surface again, dances, songs, popular art and the country's true history. And we discover a history that is based on a continuous struggle against foreign intervention. (Ramírez, cited in Rowe and Schelling 1991: 176–7)

In Nicaragua, however, such policies raised challenging questions about *whose* definitions of 'the authentic' and 'the national' were accepted and officially supported. The Ministry of Culture, for example, sought to restore and revive certain folkloric forms of ceramic production, which it represented as the product of Indian techniques from the pre-colonial epoch (Field 1995: 797). The women who made the ceramics were 'infuriated' by this official history; they had never been consulted by anyone in the Ministry of Culture about their craft and insisted that what they produced had 'nothing to do with indigenous civilizations but had been invented by their female ancestors a few generations ago' (Field 1995: 797). Sandinista cultural policy, which defined the 'authentic' and 'traditional' from above, 'failed to create a constituency' among artisans, many of whom perceived that official discourse 'ranked them as subaltern ethnics' (Field 1995: 797). Similarly, the Sandinista government's promotion of *marimba* music caused tensions as regionally based performers 'resisted the representations of "the people's culture" that a Managua-based group of culture workers produced' (Borland 2002: 77). Scruggs (1998: 70) shows how Sandinista attempts to empower Indian musical traditions meant that these traditions were ascribed worth on the terms of the dominant *mestizo* world. Cultural political action imposed from above in Sandinista Nicaragua demonstrated that 'modes of social relations that are not acknowledged and challenged will be reproduced despite the best intentions' (Scruggs 1998: 70).

In Nicaragua, the Ministry of Culture tended to define arbitrarily 'the indigenous, the authentic, the marketable', and its top-down bureaucracy meant that many artisans experienced cultural policy as a guide to action as interpreted by urban, educated middle-class functionaries in the construction of which they themselves played no part (Field 1995: 795). In Cuba, though culture has been a 'key element' in attempts to implement an alternative model of modernity, each decade since the revolution has seen instances of repression and censorship. The *quinquenio gris* (grey period) of 1971–1976 was a particularly difficult time for Cuban artists and intellectuals, many of whom, Robin Moore (2006: 149) writes, experienced public condemnation of their work, blacklisting, or time served in prison or in 'voluntary' labour camps.

Nevertheless, it is important to bear in mind that Cuban cultural policy has not remained static. Geoff Baker (2011b: 3) argues that critics of Cuba who 'see censorship everywhere' in the twenty-first century fail to appreciate that Cuban cultural policy today consists of a 'contradictory mix of support and restriction' rather than a totalitarian ban on all that appears critical of the government. In the Cuban context, Baker (2011a: 11) argues, censorship is 'a very blunt, monolithic term for a rather more nuanced reality' which in more recent years has concerned 'multiple layers of state bureaucracy between the top levels of the government and underground artists' (ibid: 17). It is also important to consider that since 1959 the Cuban state has provided the economic and social conditions that allow artists to devote time to their art and experience an 'existential freedom that many in the capitalist world would envy' (Baker 2011a: 18).

During times of revolutionary transition in Cuba and Nicaragua, the cultural forms of subaltern groups, historically maligned by the state, acquired new status. However, in Nicaragua there was a tendency for cultural policy to be imposed in a 'top-down' fashion, and, therefore, to be experienced at grassroots levels as disconnected from the people the policy aimed to recognise. In Cuba, during the first two decades of Castro's government, state officials found it difficult to tolerate 'plurality and ambiguity' in the cultural sector, and censorship was often imposed (Rowe and Schelling 1991: 182).

In Venezuela during the Chávez period, the government implemented new cultural policies which, like the cultural policies of revolutionary Cuba and Sandinista Nicaragua, were aimed at raising the status of previously marginalised groups. In the Venezuelan case, however, the Chávez government launched projects and created spaces, such as *Misión Cultura* and the Heritage Catalogues, in which local communities were given the resources and support to represent themselves on their own terms, and to define their own cultural heritage as they saw it. Unlike the Nicaraguan case, cultural policy in the Chávez period can be viewed to rest on 'bottom-up' interpretations of the country's cultural worth, rather than on the 'top-down' interpretations of educated middle-class functionaries.

During my fieldwork in Venezuela in 2005 and 2008, I found numerous examples of oppositional music CDs and publications being sold openly in shops and in the streets, such as *Chávez de papel*, written by various authors and published by Editorial Actum in 2003. This book, to quote from the back cover, 'brings together several articles written by intellectuals [and] professionals ... to reject the false "Bolivarian" revolution which has damaged the country so much'. Unlike Cuba during the 'grey period' of the 1970s, the Chávez government did not censor such oppositional expressions. Indeed, in 2005 and 2008 I attended meetings of the opposition during which I witnessed well known satirists, cartoonists and singers using their art to express their resistance to the Chávez government. For example, I attended a meeting of the opposition held at the UCV in July 2005 in which cartoonist Luis Zapata and political satirist Laureano Márquez spoke against Chávez. *Cantautora* Soledad Bravo, a vociferous opponent of Chávez, was scheduled to appear, but she sent her apologies, saying that the heavy rain that day made it impossible for her to travel to the venue. Furthermore, posters and fliers advertising this oppositional meeting, and the names of the people who would be speaking, were posted in prominent places in Caracas, and the oppositional artists spoke and performed to the audience without any apparent fear of state reprisals. Moreover, there is little credible evidence to support the opposition's claims that the Chávez government imposed censorship on the private media, which have continually acted as one of the principal voices of opposition in Venezuela since the election of Chávez (Gottberg 2010, 2011; McCaughan 2004: 101–8).

CONCLUSIONS

In this chapter, I have examined how the Chávez government used cultural policy to raise the status of Alí Primera and his *Canción Necesaria*; Alí's songs were included in official representations of the country's cultural heritage, and were represented as a fundamental basis of Bolivarianism. By investing *Canción Necesaria* with value for the country, and by constructing Alí's legacy as a root of Bolivarianism, the Chávez government also, at a symbolic level, invested *el pueblo* and their collective memories of Alí Primera and his work within the *Nueva Canción* movement with value for the country, and it constructed their history of grassroots social activism as the forerunner of Bolivarianism. The Chávez government linked with the 'pockets of resistance' within which *el pueblo* remembered and articulated their opposition to elite political rule through commemorating and memorialising *Canción Necesaria*, and it used cultural policy to give official status to these links and to symbolise the central role of *el pueblo* and their collective memories in the construction of a new social order.

In 2008, I asked the then vice-minister of culture Ivan Padilla if he thought any other *cantautor* could represent what Alí represented for the government. Padilla told me that he did not believe that any other Venezuelan *cantautor* could, because Alí had 'survived' a difficult childhood, a media ban, state repression, and had never given up fighting on behalf of *el pueblo*. When I asked Padilla to tell me what he believed Alí contributed to *el proceso*, Padilla answered:

> [Alí] never abandoned his class (*nunca se desclasó*) ... he travelled all over the country and defended the struggles of *el pueblo* ... Alí was an emblem of the search for liberty ... he brought people together. In Alí people find a reference point. Even if they are not in agreement with each other, in Alí they have something in common.

Padilla thus suggests that Alí's songs were useful resources for the government's political communication not only because of the songs' leftist political content and the goals of the *Nueva Canción* movement from which the songs emerged, not only for Alí's identification with the poor and oppressed, and not only for Alí's artistic integrity and his perceived martyrdom. Alí's *Canción Necesaria* was also important for the Chávez government, Padilla observes, because Alí and his songs were widely recognised and recognisable cultural resources in which people found 'a reference point' which they knew others shared. Even if they were not in agreement with each other about how to achieve it, Padilla asserted, people recognised that Alí Primera symbolised 'the search for liberty'.

During the Chávez period, the government associated itself with the songs of Alí Primera and implemented new cultural policies with the aim of recognising and fortifying the cultural status of the subordinate in order to symbolically invest *el pueblo* with higher social status and value for the country. Alí Primera's legacy of *Canción Necesaria* was recognised by the government as constituting an important part of the cultural history of *el pueblo*, and in its political communication and via cultural policies the government connected with these songs in order to connect with that history. Moreover, the Chávez government constructed *Canción Necesaria* as a forerunner of Bolivarianism, and, therefore represented itself as bringing to fruition the goals of the *Nueva Canción* movement as articulated by Alí Primera in his compositions.

Venezuelans recognised the connection between Alí's *Canción Necesaria* and the government. Even if they were not in agreement with each other about the effectiveness of the government's policies and the legitimacy of the government's construction of Alí's songs as forerunners of *el proceso*, people recognised that the Chávez government identified with Alí's songs. People responded to this connection in various ways; while some embraced it, others resisted it. State incorporation of Alí's *Canción Necesaria* in the Chávez period gave rise to conflicting interpretations of Alí's value and his legacy; while *Chavistas* tended to see the government's inclusion of Alí's *Canción Necesaria* as a recognition of their history and their interests, some *anti-Chavistas* accused the government of inventing Alí's significance for its own benefit. These contradictory views led Alí's songs to acquire new political functions. In Chap. 7, I analyse examples of the conflicting uses of Alí's *Canción Necesaria* in the Chávez period and explore what these can reveal about the contradictions which the institutionalisation of leftist popular music legacies may give rise to at a time of leftist political transition.

NOTES

1. Chávez supporters often refer to the government's programme as *el proceso* ('the process').
2. The constitution in English can be accessed at http://www.venezuel-aemb.or.kr/english/ConstitutionoftheBolivarianingles.pdf (Last accessed 8 January 2016).
3. http://www.leyresorte.gob.ve/wp-content/uploads/2012/07/Ley_de_Responsabilidad_Social__en_Radio_Television_y_Medios_Electronicos2.pdf (Last accessed 8 January 2016).
4. In Spanish the full title is of the position held by Padilla was 'Viceministro de Cultura para el Desarrollo Humano', or Vice minister of Culture for Human Development.
5. Interview with Padilla, Caracas, September 2008.

6. http://www.ministeriodelacultura.gob.ve/index.php?option=com_ content&task=blogcategory&id=16&Itemid=45 (Last accessed 6 December 2010).
7. Interview with Padilla, Caracas, September 2008.
8. Interview with Silva, Caracas, September 2008.
9. It is beyond the scope of this book to detail all aspects of Bolivarian cultural policy. However, significant initiatives include the *La Villa del Cine* (launched in June 2006 to promote the Venezuelan film industry), ALBA Cultural (approved in February 2008 to promote cultural exchange and unification among ALBA-TCP [*Alianza Bolivariana para los Pueblos de Nuestra América – Tratado de Comercio de los Pueblos*] member nations, and teleSUR (launched in July 2005 as an alternative source of information to the dominant CNN and Univisión networks). See Villazana, 2013. Also of note are the *Librerías del Sur* (Bookshops of the South), which were established, vice-minister of culture Ivan Padilla told me in 2008, to 'open a door to reading' for sectors of the population who had not previously had affordable access to books. Padilla told me that whereas publishing houses had before functioned to 'satisfy an elite', the new *El perro y la raña* (The Dog and the Frog) publishing house was intended to provide cheap books intended, according to Padilla, not to instil a line of thought but to provide 'an incentive for reading' and to 'put people in contact with reading and with the thought of the world'.
10. Interview with Padilla, Caracas, September 2008.
11. Interview with Acosta, Caracas, September 2008.
12. Interview with Padilla, Caracas, September 2008.
13. See p. 9, http://www.minci.gob.ve/libros_folletos/6/p--19/tp-- 27/libros_folletos.html (Last accessed 26 November 2010).
14. See p. 2 of government publication *Misión Cultura*, Caracas 2005. Available online: http://www.minci.gob.ve/libros_folletos/6/p--19/ tp--27/libros_folletos.html (Last accessed 12 December 2010).
15. See http://www.ipc.gob.ve/ for Catalogues of Heritage (Last accessed 24 September 2013).
16. Interview with Acosta, Caracas, July 2008.
17. Interview with Acosta, Caracas, September 2008.
18. Interview with Padilla, Caracas, September 2008.
19. The documentary is available to view on YouTube http://www.youtube.com/watch?v=P6IvntyIiTc (Last accessed 8 January 2016).

20. Other state-funded documentaries about Alí include *Alí Primera: Herido de vida* (Directed by Luis Rodríguez: 2005) and *Alí Primera: La siembra de un cantor* (Directed by Alejandro Medina: 2005).
21. http://www.presidencia.gob.ve/doc/publicaciones/perfiles/ali_primera_padre_cantor_del_pueblo.pdf (Last accessed 24 September 2013).
22. http://www.fondas.gob.ve/index.php/noticias/reportajes-especiales/2490-casa-museo-ali-primera-un-pedacito-del-cantor-del-pueblo-en-falcon (Last accessed 28 June 2013).
23. http://www.ciudadccs.info/?p=191421 (Last accessed 28 September 2013).
24. Interview with Padilla, Caracas, September 2008.
25. Interview with Acosta, Caracas, September 2008.

CHAPTER 7

Alí Primera's *Canción Necesaria* and *Chavismo*

The institutionalisation of *Canción Necesaria* gave rise to conflicting interpretations of Alí Primera's life and legacy as Venezuelans were compelled to respond not only to Alí's songs, but also to the government's association with those songs. Many Venezuelans embraced, negotiated or contested the state's promotion of Alí and his legacy, and in doing so they revealed, at a symbolic level, much about their judgements regarding the value of Bolivarianism. Charles Hardy, a freelance writer from the USA who has lived in a Caracas barrio for three decades, observed during the early years of the Chávez government:

> [Chávez's] ideas are not pleasant to many ears. Much of what he says is a reflection of the words in the songs of Alí Primera, songs that the president sometimes sings during his Sunday program, *'Aló Presidente* ... the kind of words that workers can appreciate as they drag themselves home at night with a little food for the family after a hard day at work. They are not the words that a factory owner would like to have played over the company intercom. Chávez singing them automatically evokes different responses in his listeners: love from some ... hate from others. (Hardy: undated)

In their study of the political uses of popular songs in US election campaigns, Benjamin Schoening and Eric Kasper (2012: 186–7) note that popular musicians are frequently concerned about their political reputations among their fans. This concern leads some artists to denounce presi-

H. Marsh, *Hugo Chávez, Alí Primera and Venezuela*, DOI 10.1057/978-1-137-57968-3_7

dential candidates whose election campaigns make use of their music in order to appeal to large numbers of people. Schoening and Kasper (ibid.) cite the example of George W. Bush and his campaign's attempt to use a song by Tom Petty, who did not hold the same political views as Bush. In February 2000, the Bush campaign dropped Petty's song after the artist threatened a lawsuit because, Petty's publishing company complained in a letter to Bush, 'Any use made by you or your campaign creates, either intentionally or unintentionally, the impression that you and your campaign have been endorsed by Tom Petty, which is not true' (cited in Schoening and Kasper, ibid.).

Since Alí Primera died in 1985, it is not possible to know whether he would have endorsed Chávez's election campaigns, and it is not possible to know how Alí would have responded to the Chávez government's uses of his songs. Yet while Alí himself was not alive to witness Chávez's election campaigns or to comment on the Chávez government's representation of his songs as precursors of Bolivarianism, Venezuelans actively responded to and engaged with the new associations these songs acquired in the Chávez period. Some Venezuelans accepted and embraced the official promotion of Alí's songs, and others resisted and contested this official promotion, claiming that Alí Primera would never have supported the Chávez government.

This chapter explores conflicting public uses of Alí Primera's *Canción Necesaria* in the Chávez period, and what these reveal about the contradictions that the institutionalisation of popular music legacies can give rise to. Drawing on semi-structured interviews I conducted in Venezuela in 2005 and 2008 with self-identified supporters and opponents of the government, I acknowledge that my interviews, while providing rich material for analysis, may also be affected by people feeling prone to tell me what they thought I wanted to hear about Alí. In fact, many people I interviewed spoke so highly of Alí's character and his music that I was concerned that they were doing this for my benefit, and that I may have unwittingly introduced a level of bias. I, therefore, also draw on data that I did not elicit in order to examine the extent to which such 'naturally occurring' phenomena support material that I generated in face-to-face interactions with Venezuelans. I analyse content posted in social media websites, and draw on my own observations as a participant observer in Venezuela in order to explore how the Chávez government's official identification with Alí Primera's songs caused these songs to acquire new functions in the twenty-first century.

Alí's *Canción Necesaria* came to act as a resource that both supporters *and* opponents of the Chávez government made use of in order to express their feelings about what they understood their place to be in the new social and political order, and what they perceived to be the successes and failures of *el proceso*. In the late Punto Fijo period, the Venezuelan public collectively remembered and used Alí Primera's songs to express resistance to the state. By linking itself with *Canción Necesaria*, the Chávez government sought to harness and institutionalise these oppositional qualities in the early twenty-first century. The incorporation of Alí's legacy into official structures during the Chávez period gave rise to conflicting evaluations of the significance of *Canción Necesaria*; *Chavistas* tended to use Alí's songs to express support for the government, and *anti-Chavistas* tended either to ignore or distance themselves from the songs, or to harness the songs' oppositional qualities in order to express resistance to the Bolivarian *proceso* itself. State support for *Canción Necesaria* thus resulted in the songs acquiring new uses; they came to act as resources with which Venezuelans located, defined and re-defined themselves (as *Chavistas* or *anti-Chavistas*) within a changed social and political order.

PUBLIC REACTIONS TO STATE USES OF ALÍ PRIMERA'S LEGACY

In the Chávez period, Venezuelans could not listen to Alí Primera's music in the same way as they had done before. State support for Alí Primera and his legacy linked Alí and his *Canción Necesaria* with the government, and officially represented Alí and his music as precursors of Bolivarianism and as a fundamental basis of the Chávez government's political thought. This official construction changed the ways Venezuelans responded to Alí and his *Canción Necesaria*; the Venezuelan public now reacted not only to Alí's songs and to the collective memory of Alí's life and death, but also to the Chávez government's links with the songs and the figure of Alí.

During my interviews with musicians who had worked with Alí Primera in the 1970s and early 1980s, I often found that my respondents, with no prompting from me, started to talk about Hugo Chávez and his government when I had asked them about Alí Primera. They linked Alí Primera and Hugo Chávez; the *cantautor* reminded them of the president. For example, Jesús Cordero of Los Guaraguao, in remembering Alí, was prompted to make a comparison with Chávez; 'Alí's words were very direct, like our president's. He [Chávez] talks and everyone understands. Alí had the same way'.[1] Journalist, disc jockey and musician Gregorio Yépez, while talking about Alí Primera's live performances, switched from Alí's vernacular discourse and how it resonated with *el pueblo* to Chávez's mannerisms and way of speaking, and he drew a clear connection between the two:

> Alí used to make a lot of speeches. He talked a lot, with a very clear and national ideological thread and in a language that was very close to *el pueblo* but at the same time loaded with poetry, that everyday poetry of *el pueblo*. In some way, I think president Chávez copies Alí's way of speaking. The president refers to a lot of the things that Alí used to say. For me those things aren't new. What is new is that it used to be underground ... Chávez copies Alí's way of talking, of gesticulating; he uses the people's images, vulgar language, characteristics of the people. Chávez discovered an important tool of communication with the people, and he uses it like a politician should; a good president should do this.[2]

State promotion of Alí Primera's legacy in the Chávez period rendered Alí Primera and his songs official symbols of the Bolivarian *proceso*. To use Antoni Kapcia's (2000: 27) term, there had been many 'high priests' of the Alí myth in the Punto Fijo period, people within civilian society who were invested with the legitimacy to re-tell Alí's life-story and re-interpret the significance of *Canción Necesaria* to construct an ideology of resistance and opposition to the state. The difference now was that a 'high priest' of Alí's myth was *in control* of the state and its resources. This led Venezuelans to use Alí's music and to refer to his significance in new ways. While many Venezuelans accepted Chávez as being in a legitimate position to interpret the myth of Alí for everyone else, others laid their own competing claims to Alí and his songs and rejected those of the government. Alí's songs, and narratives about his life, became cultural resources with which people redefined and relocated themselves within a changed social and political order.

The Deceased Individual as Cultural and Political Resource

In their work, Katherine Verdery (1999), Sarah Paige Baty (1995) and Antoni Kapcia (2000) argue that significant deceased individuals (people who were seen as important cultural or political figures during their lifetimes) can have important posthumous cultural and political lives. Such deceased individuals can act as resources people use to help create meaning in the present; they can exemplify the qualities a society values, and they can act as surfaces onto which the public projects contemporary concerns. Even when people agree that the deceased individual is important, they may construct this importance in different ways and defend their interpretations of the deceased individual's significance while they resist the interpretations of competing groups. In this way, deceased individuals can create spaces for debates that concern the values people think are important for the present and the future.

'NEW WORLDS OF MEANING'

During times of major social and political transformation, Verdery (1999: 34) argues, people may find that new forms of action are more productive than the ones they are used to, or that 'ideals they could only aspire to before are now realizable'. According to Verdery (ibid.), major social and political transformation involves 'the redefinition of virtually everything, including morality, social relations, and basic meanings. It means a reordering of people's entire meaningful worlds'. Verdery (1999: 27–8) contends that during such times, deceased individuals can function as 'symbolic vehicles' that help people to create new worlds of meaning and to understand their place in the new order. The dead cannot talk and disclaim any values attributed to them by various groups, and this means that:

> Words can be put into their mouths—often quite ambiguous words—or their own actual words can be ambiguated by quoting them out of context. It is thus easier to rewrite history with dead people than with other kinds of symbols that are speechless. (Verdery 1999: 29)

Thus although a dead person has a single name and a single body, thereby presenting the 'illusion' of having only one significance, he or she may mean many different things to different groups; all that is shared is 'everyone's *recognition* of this dead person as somehow important' (Verdery 1999: 29). It is precisely because certain deceased individuals allow identification from several possible vantage points that they can function as powerful political symbols in the creation of newly meaningful worlds. As such, deceased individuals can become powerful political symbols, but also sites of political conflict as different groups struggle to assert and defend their own interpretations of the symbolic significance of the dead person's life and death (Verdery 1999: 31).

THE 'REPRESENTATIVE CHARACTER'

Baty (1995: 88) develops her concept of the 'representative character' from the work of Ralph Waldo Emerson, who aspired to 'write the lives' of people who had accomplished great achievements, taking them to be 'representative of the possibilities of human achievement' and exemplary role models. Baty (1995: 9) writes that her use of the term 'representative character' is also related to that of Bellah et al., who define the representative character as:

> A kind of symbol. It is a way by which we can bring together in one concentrated image the way people in a given social environment organize and give meaning and direction to their lives. In fact, a representative character is more than a collection of individual traits and personalities. It is rather a public image that helps define, for a given group of people, just what kinds of personality traits it is good and legitimate to develop. A representative character provides an ideal, a point of reference and a focus, that gives living expression to a vision of life. (Bellah et al, cited in Baty 1995: 9)

For Baty (1995: 10), the representative character may embody a diverse array of values, and changes in society may alter the meaning of specific representative characters over time, leading particular lives to be read as more or less successful expressions of a community's values, aspirations and achievements. The representative character is, therefore, not frozen in history but acts as a 'surface on which struggles over meanings can be waged' (Baty 1995: 59).

In Baty's (1995: 31) view, the construction of various versions of a representative character's life and death is crucial for the creation of a community within which people recognise their shared interests and values and contest those of competing groups. The mass media facilitate the circulation of various versions of a representative character's life and death, allowing significant deceased individuals to act as powerful figures in the virtual realm; people refer to these figures in conversation and writing as a way of discussing a range of cultural and political issues and of defining themselves in relation to other people (Baty 1995: 47). In retelling stories about representative characters, Baty (1995: 42) argues, communities offer examples of men and women who have embodied and exemplified the meaning of the community

THE DECEASED INDIVIDUAL AS MYTH

Kapcia (2000: 11) argues that one pre-requisite for revolution is an available body of 'alternative' values, embodied in folk tradition, popular culture or specific manifestos, to act as an 'ideological reservoir'. Without an ideological reservoir on which to draw, discontent 'can easily become incoherent protest', since revolution must be based on a 'blueprint' of some sort; there must exist in the minds of enough participants and active supporters a viable, credible and legitimate alternative to the existing system (ibid.). Kapcia (2000: 24) argues that the 'blueprint' or 'ideological reservoir' that is necessary for revolution to be successful and sustained relies on myth, which he defines as:

> ... the cohesive set of values seen to be expressed in an accepted symbol or figure, which is perceived by a given collectivity ... to articulate the 'essence' of all, or a significant component part, of its accepted ideology, and to articulate it in simple, symbolic or human—and therefore comprehensible—form. (Kapcia 2000: 25)

Kapcia argues that in Cuba, certain deceased individuals acquired a mythical status, which allowed their legacies to be used as powerful tools of persuasion in the construction of a national ideology of *Cubanía rebelde* (rebel Cubanness). Myth, writes Kapcia (2000: 25–56), is 'necessarily expressed in personal (human) form, either in a real, a fictitious or a legendary person' such as an agreed national hero, a historic liberator, a patron saint or a Robin Hood-type figure, or in an event (real or imagined) involving 'specific and defined human beings'. The myth requires 'a caste of interpreters who are, by definition, accepted by those for whom they interpret'; these 'high priests' of myth are 'seen to be the best placed to interpret the myth legitimately for the rest of the group' (Kapcia 2000: 27). Myth requires a 'story-line', which can be interpreted and re-interpreted in order to remain 'as a living, adaptable and meaningful guide to real collective action' (Kapcia 2000: 28).

Kapcia (2000: 164–7, 189–93) examines in detail the evolving role of the myths of José Martí and Che Guevara in the construction of *Cubanía rebelde* in the twentieth century. Kapcia (2000: 166–7) argues that the imprecision of Martí's political writings about the *monstruo* (monster) represented by the USA, and about *Nuestra América* (our America), was a help rather than a hindrance in the mythification of his figure; for subsequent generations, the story-line of Martí's life and heroic death in 1895 acted as an 'ideological reservoir' from which to draw 'Cuban solutions for Cuban problems', and Martí was located in history as a precursor of the revolution. Similarly, Che Guevara's idea of the 'new man', Kapcia (2000: 192) argues, was but 'a set of intellectual propositions and emotional postures' before his death in 1967; after this, the story-line of Che 'the fallen hero and archetypal guerrilla, who had abandoned the relative comfort and security of a government post to risk death ... fighting to liberate his fellow Latin Americans', led to the construction of Che as the mythical embodiment of the 'new man' all revolutionary Cubans were to strive to emulate.

Kapcia points out that the myths of Martí and Che have performed different functions for different groups and communities at different times. The Martí myth continues to act as a point of historical reference and a source of legitimacy for the revolution within Cuba, but it is also claimed by Cuban émigrés in Miami for whom it serves quite distinctive counter-revolutionary purposes (Kapcia 2000: 177). Cubans adhering to the myth of Che Guevara also use his myth for often 'contradictory' reasons:

> In the first place, many have been attracted by a figure who represents a permanently young face of the system, someone from a 'heroic' age who tragically ... died young in pursuit of his ideals ... [he seems] untainted by the marks of failure, ageing and disillusion that his surviving ex-comrades inevitably bear. By clinging to *Che*, the young can therefore be 'revolutionary' and still distance themselves from the present leadership. (Kapcia 2000: 212)

Myths, for Kapcia, provide story-lines that are told and re-told, and which over time acquire new functions as their significance is re-interpreted. Myths act as 'ideological reservoirs', but the material they provide can be used to support numerous competing views as different groups claim the right to be the 'authentic' interpreters of those myths.

In Venezuela, as Zúquete (2008: 107) details, Chávez made 'steady use of myths, rituals, and symbols to sustain both the community and its commitment to the [Bolivarian] mission'. Such activity was central in the establishment of:

> ... a form of popular participation that many people perceive as more 'authentic' and 'real' than previous modes, while creating at the same time messianic expectations about the leader and, consequently, playing an essential role in the development of a charismatic dynamic between the leader and the community. (Zúquete 2008: 107)

The charismatic leader taps into 'the reservoir of relevant myths in his [or her] culture', and 'knows how to draw upon those myths that are linked to its sacred figures, to its historical and legendary heroes, and to its historical ordeals and triumphs' (Willner 1984, cited in Zúquete 2008: 107). This functions to collapse the past into the present so that historical struggles (against colonialism, for example) are experienced as eternal sources of strength for people in the present (Zúquete 2008: 108). By invoking a mythologised historical narrative of 'pure patriots' against 'corrupt enemies', Chávez was able to make historical figures, such as Simón Bolívar, Ezequiel Zamora and Simón Rodríguez, function not as 'ossified monuments to the past'; instead, through Chávez their 'exemplary lives [became] the driving force of the Bolivarian revolution' (Zúquete 2008: 107–8). Through Chávez, such figures were endowed with 'powers of redemption over the ills that afflict society' (ibid.: 109). By officially honouring and exulting the sacrifices of nineteenth-century heroes, and introducing changes to national symbols and rituals (for example, renaming the country the Bolivarian republic of Venezuela [National Assembly, 1999]; adding a machete and bow and arrow to the national seal to represent the indigenous people and the labour of the workers [National Assembly, 2006]; changing the Columbus Day holiday to a commemoration of the Day of Indigenous resistance [2002]), Chávez aimed to represent a new Venezuela in a way that would resonate profoundly with the masses:

> These changes to official national symbols are derided by Chávez's critics as superfluous. A commentator wrote that this 'exaggerated focus on symbols' only served to divert attention from the 'real problems' afflicting Venezuela … Yet in the self-understanding of the missionary community, these are not cosmetic changes; they serve to objectify the popular will and testify that the leader's sacred narrative (as opposed to the narrative promulgated by the elites) is a genuine attempt to integrate the people. (Zúquete 2008: 111)

In the Chávez period, I contend, Alí and his *Canción Necesaria* provided rich cultural resources for the government to construct a 'living history' intended to connect historical struggles with those of the present, and to objectify the popular will and act as tangible proof that Chávez's declared intention to integrate and value *el pueblo* was genuine. First, *Canción Necesaria* created new 'worlds of meaning' by acting as resources, which people drew on to create new understandings about their place in a society that was no longer governed by the familiar *Puntofijista* political parties.

Second, Alí, the deceased individual, functioned as a 'representative character' whose life, work and death provided an example and an ideal for society (and even for the government) to aspire to and to be measured against. Finally, *Canción Necesaria* and Alí's life-story offered an 'ideological reservoir' and a myth that acted as a reference point for Venezuelans, but people asserted various competing claims to be best placed to interpret this myth legitimately for the country during the Chávez period.

ALÍ PRIMERA AND THE CREATION OF NEW 'WORLDS OF MEANING'

In December 1998, Hugo Chávez became the first Venezuelan president with no ties to the Punto Fijo establishment parties to be elected in over 40 years. With the definitive end of the Punto Fijo system of government, Venezuelans could not rely on their previous knowledge of the state, how they should engage with it, and how state institutions impacted upon their lives; they needed to reconsider their understanding of their government and how it operated, and to redefine their relationship to the state and their place in society.

During this time of social and political change, Alí Primera and his music had posthumous significance in the creation of new 'worlds of meaning', particularly for previously marginalised barrio residents and leftist students and intellectuals. The Chávez government's association with Alí Primera and his *Canción Necesaria* raised the official status both of Alí the deceased individual and of Alí's songs. This change in status symbolised a change in the status of *el pueblo* and the voice of the left with which Alí and his songs were identified; cultural policies invested value in Alí Primera and his songs, which at a symbolic level officially rendered *el pueblo* and the voice of the left of value for the country. Venezuelan writer José Roberto Duque expressed this idea when he said that he believed that Hugo Chávez 'formalised' the homage that *el pueblo* were already paying to Alí Primera. According to Duque, this official act transmitted the message to barrio inhabitants that 'the people in charge now are ours'.[3]

In the Chávez period, Alí and his songs became a symbol of a change in the social and political order in favour of the poor and the marginalised; the songs were used by barrio residents to assert a new sense of agency, to say 'the people in charge now are ours'. Alí's songs were no longer officially repressed but instead were officially represented as forerunners of *el proceso* and as a fundamental basis of Bolivarianism. This official recognition led Alí's songs, and stories about Alí's life and death, to act as resources which barrio residents and leftist writers and musicians used to formulate knowledge about their new place in society and their raised status in twenty-first-century Venezuela.

In interviews I conducted in Venezuela in 2005 and 2008, leftist writers and musicians and barrio residents predominantly referred to the change in the official status of Alí Primera and his songs as symbolic of social and political transformations which they viewed as raising their status in society; they viewed the official support for Alí's legacy as evidence that *el pueblo* were of value, and that their needs mattered to the government. The official visibility of Alí Primera's legacy came to represent the visibility of *el pueblo* and the left within the new political order. For example, radio presenter, journalist and writer Lil Rodríguez asserts that official support for Alí Primera's legacy had 'raised the self-esteem' of the poor, and that the official status attributed to Alí Primera and his legacy in the Chávez period meant that 'we recognise ourselves ... in this *proceso*'.[4] A *Cantautora* I interviewed in July 2005 believes that the Chávez government's support for Alí Primera and his songs meant that barrio residents, who this *cantautora* believed had been officially 'forgotten' prior to the election of Chávez, could 'see their images and hear their voices' in the government's discourse about Alí. This *cantautora* argued that this may appear very trivial for the middle classes, but that for the poor and excluded 'this is a revolution, because they are included'. According to this *cantautora*, Alí's songs came to symbolise this new sense of inclusion for the poor.

In 2005 and 2008, I conducted interviews with barrio residents in Barquisimeto, in Coro, and in the 23 de Enero and the El Valle neighbourhoods of Caracas in order to examine how they spoke about Alí Primera and his songs and about the Chávez government's uses of Alí's music. Chávez's promotion of Alí Primera's songs legitimised the government in the eyes of barrio inhabitants I interviewed. For example, one community radio worker in Barquisimeto told me in 2005 'People are happy with this government embracing Alí. It gives us more confidence that this *proceso* is ours'. Two ex-guerrillas I interviewed in Barquisimeto told me that they believed Chávez liked Alí's songs because these songs described 'the construction of a new order' which would favour the poor and which Chávez sought to bring to fruition democratically.

Barrio residents I interviewed saw the Chávez government's official recognition of Alí Primera's songs as an acknowledgement of their struggles, of their worth as human beings and of their value as contributors to a new order and a new society. A community radio worker in 23 de Enero explained to me in 2008 how she saw the government's promotion of Alí Primera's songs:

> ... *el pueblo* have a sense of belonging now ... we have a government we feel identified with ... We never stopped listening to Alí. We were the ones who kept Alí alive, we talked about him, distributed fliers, and commemorated him. Other governments didn't name Alí part of the cultural heritage because Alí didn't represent their neo-liberal project. Alí was always against all that. This government made him cultural heritage because Alí represents the dream of the left that we're all building—the peaceful socialist revolution. This is the responsibility of all of us, not Chávez alone ... he can't do it without us. Alí belongs to *el pueblo*, and it's *el pueblo* who are now [central to] this *proceso*.

This radio worker viewed her community's work in keeping the memory of Alí alive before the election of Chávez as part of the same struggle against neo-liberalism that the Chávez government was continuing. She felt that her work and that of *el pueblo* was essential to Chávez; she and *el pueblo* put Chávez where he was, and Chávez's support for Alí symbolised his support for *el pueblo*, whom he needed. For this interviewee, Chávez's association with the songs of Alí Primera symbolised his association with *el pueblo* and his willingness to listen to them, and to recognise and connect with their struggles in order to build an alternative society based on new priorities. Official support for Alí Primera's songs led these songs to symbolise the official recognition of *el pueblo* and their history of social activism; the new official space that the songs inhabited in the Chávez period acted as a manifestation of the new official spaces that *el pueblo* occupied within a new social and political order. University students I interviewed in Coro saw a direct link between the messages of the songs of Alí Primera and the political, economic and social aims of the Chávez government; Alí and his songs symbolised the Bolivarian *proceso*, which they embraced. In 2005, a member of a student movement affiliated with the University of Coro and named for Alí Primera, told me:

> Chávez always names Alí, he always sings a song of Alí's, because the project on which all this [Bolivarianism] is based ... it is based on the essence of *el pueblo*. The Bolivarian project owes a lot to Alí's ideas; Alí gives us the will to carry on, Alí is alive in our hearts, and whoever learns about Alí is a follower of Chávez.

This student believed that there was a close correspondence between the political ideas contained in Alí Primera's songs and the political ideas on which the Chávez government based its policies. For him, to accept the message of Alí's songs was to accept the Bolivarian government; both represented the same social and political aims and values. Similarly, another member of the same student movement told me in 2005 that she believed that Chávez was 'putting into practice ... what Alí said in his songs'; the government's *misiones*⁵ were 'Alí Primera's children', because these programmes aimed to bring about what Alí called for in his songs. For this student, Chávez listened to these songs, absorbed their ideas, and created official mechanisms to put these ideas into practice. A cultural worker in Barquisimeto told me in 2005 that while his community met to discuss the new constitution that the population voted for and ratified in referenda in 1999, they listened to Alí Primera's songs for inspiration. This cultural worker told me that the Chávez government had provided the official space for the country's constitution to be created and approved by ordinary people, and *el pueblo* drew directly on the songs of Alí Primera in order to do this. For this cultural worker, Alí's songs acted as resources that provided guides to action both for *el pueblo* and for the government. Similarly, a group of bus-drivers I interviewed in Barquisimeto in 2005 said that they believed that Chávez was guided by Alí Primera. One of these bus-drivers told me:

> For Chávez, Alí is a great guide. [Chávez] learns from Alí. In 1999, when he was elected president, in the Plaza Bolívar [in Caracas] Chávez's first words were 'My homeland is pregnant. Who will help her to give birth so that she will be beautiful?' These are Alí Primera's words.⁶ Chávez said Alí's words when he took up power. Alí had the idea of creating socialism *a la Venezolana*. Great men never stop living. On the contrary, every day they are more alive. Alí is living, he's being reborn in this revolution, thanks to *el pueblo*.

This bus-driver saw Alí as the originator of a Venezuelan form of socialism, which Chávez adopted for his government. Like other interviewees, the bus-driver saw *el pueblo* as being essential to *el proceso*; it was *el pueblo* who had preserved Alí's thought and songs, and *el pueblo* who had started the struggle that culminated in the election of Chávez.

When they spoke about Alí Primera, Chávez supporters in the barrios frequently emphasised the *Puntofijista* persecution of Alí and the prohibition of his songs under previous governments. They contrasted this official suppression with the Chávez government's support for Alí Primera and his songs, and interpreted this change in state attitudes towards Alí as evidence of a change in state attitudes not only towards *el pueblo* and their needs but also towards wealthy elites and US influence in the country. One student at the University of Coro told me in 2005 that he believed that:

> ... twenty years after [Alí's] death, this *proceso* is stimulated by Alí's songs. Chávez includes sectors that other governments excluded; other governments were controlled by the USA, but Chávez put an end to that.

For this student, the Chávez government's support for Alí's songs made manifest the inclusion of people who, like Alí, had been repressed and marginalised under the Punto Fijo system, and it symbolised new priorities which placed *el pueblo* above wealthy elites and US interests. One participant in *misión cultura* and a resident of El Valle barrio of Caracas, told me in 2005 that for her Alí's songs and figure 'supported' Chávez and made her feel closer to the government:

> [Alí's] message supports [Chávez]. The very language [of the songs], which is straightforward and reaches people, supports Chávez. *El pueblo* identify with Alí. When you identify with something, you make it yours and it's very easy to have it in your home and carry it with you. The government discovered this, which is a good thing because it just adds a little bit more to what [the government] already has.

For this participant, *el pueblo* had made Alí theirs because his songs touched them and made sense to them. The Chávez government's connection with Alí Primera's songs, which belonged to *el pueblo*, added to the legitimacy of the government as a representative of *el pueblo*. This participant linked Alí's message and the Chávez government's *proceso* with the grassroots struggles of the late 1980s to which she attributed the demise of the Punto Fijo system and the rise of Bolivarianism:

> [Alí] spoke about people's needs ... about imperialism, Yankees, the oligarchy ... he was always calling people to start the revolution ... and just look! [Revolution] is what happened here on the 27th of February [1989, the date of the *Caracazo*].

Alí as prophet and instigator of the Bolivarian process was a theme emphasised by other barrio residents I interviewed. For Chávez supporters I spoke to in the barrios where I conducted my fieldwork, Bolivarianism symbolised the meaningful end result of Alí Primera's perceived martyrdom; Alí's songs were used to represent the Chávez government as the inevitable result of the struggles of Alí and of *el pueblo*. A further participant in *misión cultura* who I interviewed in 2005 told me:

> Alí Primera is heard a lot more than he was before, with this [Bolivarian] *proceso* he's heard a lot more. His music is at every political rally, in all the barrios, in many communities. Alí Primera is an extremely important person and now you hear him more than ever, his image has grown. Why? Because the leaders of this revolution have put Alí Primera in the place he deserves. Because what [Alí] called for in his songs is extremely important. We are living it now, just imagine, so many years after [Alí's] death, he remains valid. People have taken him as an example to really understand what this *proceso* is all about.

The Chávez government's inclusion of Alí Primera in official representations of the country's cultural heritage was seen by Chávez supporters I interviewed as symbolic of the inclusion of *el pueblo* in the new social and political order. Writer José Roberto Duque asserted that with the official status attached to Alí Primera's legacy by the Chávez government, the poor could see themselves reflected in official representations of the country's heritage. This, Duque argued, was not possible under the Punto Fijo system; the official recognition of Alí required revolutionary change such as that introduced by the Chávez government. The fact that Alí was included in the cultural heritage, Duque reasoned, acted as evidence that revolutionary change had happened in Venezuela, because, argued Duque, if this were not the case then Alí would still be officially excluded.[7] Similarly, when in 2008 I asked José Guerra of Los Guaraguao why he believed Alí had been included in the country's cultural heritage, he replied:

> That had already happened, [Alí] was always our heritage, it just wasn't official. With Chávez, the first thing that came in like a hurricane was Alí's song, immediately. Only a revolution [could] release Alí's songs.[8]

For Guerra, Alí was already seen by popular sectors as part of their heritage, and like Duque he argued that this could only be possible if a revolution had taken place. For Guerra, the increase in Alí's official value was evidence of revolutionary change taking place in the country. When I asked the late Jesús 'el Gordo' Paez in 2005 how he viewed the Chávez government's promotion of Alí's songs, Paez told me that 'at a grassroots level, Alí was always there', but that this was not visible before Chávez assumed presidency because Alí's *Canción Necesaria* 'was silenced'. According to Paez, after the *Caracazo* uprisings state authorities were likely to imprison members of the public who they discovered owned any albums of Alí's songs. Paez contrasted Chávez's support for Alí's songs with *Puntofijista* persecution not only of Alí but of the people who listened to Alí's songs; by raising the official status of Alí's songs, Paez argued, Chávez dignified and made visible the very people the Punto Fijo state had sought to repress.[9] For the poor and the marginalised sectors Chávez directed his discourse to, Alí Primera and his songs, which people could identify with from various vantage points, acted as resources to create new 'worlds of meaning' within which their status and their value for the country were redefined.

ALÍ PRIMERA AS 'REPRESENTATIVE CHARACTER'

According to a Venezuelan artist I interviewed in 2005:

> All societies need symbols. Alí has become a symbol of the [Bolivarian] transformation. In the ideal of his life and his song, [Alí] matches the discourse of what we call *el proceso*.

Alí Primera can be seen as what Baty (1995) calls a 'representative character'. In the Chávez period, Alí and his songs came to act as a symbol, which brought together ideas about what Venezuelans, particularly supporters of the Chávez government, considered to be the qualities to which not only they but also the government should aspire. Barrio residents I interviewed referred to Alí Primera as a 'reference point' and 'an example for us all'. In online forums, Alí was frequently held up as a model of Bolivarian values and an exemplary human being. On 29 October 2006, César González 'El Culi' wrote:

> To speak of Alí is not to speak [only] of a *cantautor*. When one speaks of Alí Primera, one speaks of a poet, a troubadour, a friend, a brother, a fighter for dignity, for life, for love, for a better world in which we can all feel and be equal. Therefore, to speak of the *padre cantor* ... is to speak of *la venezolanidad* (Venezuelanness), of the Bolivarian ideal, of the revolutionary sense of *un pueblo*.

These words, representing Alí Primera as 'the Bolivarian ideal', were uploaded to Aporrea.org, an independent, interactive and privately funded website founded in May 2002 (Hellinger 2011: 222). Aporrea.org was established in response to the mainstream media's open support for the coup which ousted Hugo Chávez for 48 hours in April 2002 (ibid.). Aporrea states that it seeks 'to divulge socio-economic news and opinion, identifying with the process of revolutionary and democratic transformation in Venezuela' as 'a popular alternative news agency, [and] open digital bulletin board interactive with the movement of people and workers' (Hellinger 2011: 222). The stated aim[10] of Aporrea.org is to counteract the anti-Chávez bias of the private media in Venezuela by providing a forum for the exchange of information and opinions generated from within the 'popular movement' (Hellinger 2011: 222). However, Aporrea maintains its independence and 'provides a forum for some very harsh criticism, all the more biting in that it comes from within' (ibid.).

Aporrea offers 'a forum for contributors, a blog, and news taken mostly from publications sympathetic with the government' (Hellinger 2011: 225). The principal contributors to the site fall into two groups. The first group consists of grassroots leaders who distinguish themselves from the professional political class that occupies bureaucratic posts and elected positions. Many of these people work in the *misiones*, popular radio stations, grassroots committees, radical union movements, and women's circles (Hellinger 2011: 225–6). The second group consists of professional politicians, government officials and traditional intellectuals who have aligned themselves with Bolivarianism, if not with Chávez himself (Hellinger 2011: 226). According to Hellinger (2011: 225), the first group can be seen as what Antonio Gramsci called organic intellectuals' who 'arise directly out of the masses, but remain in contact with them'.

Hellinger (2011: 241) writes that the organic intellectuals of Aporrea assume they are giving voice to popular attitudes and aspirations, but that it is difficult to evaluate the degree of correspondence between the views of these organic intellectuals and the people for whom they claim to speak. With regard to Alí Primera and his songs, I found a high degree of correspondence between the views of contributors to Aporrea and the views of barrio residents I interviewed. A search for Alí Primera on Aporrea in May 2013 produced approximately 10,600 results. A detailed thematic analysis of 50 of these articles, posted between 2002 and 2012, revealed a concern with the same principal themes which barrio inhabitants articulated in interviews. First, the Chávez government's official recognition of Alí Primera's songs was perceived as an official recognition of *el pueblo* and their struggles. Second, the state persecution of Alí Primera and the suppression of his songs under Punto Fijo governments were emphasised in order to contrast the old order with the present. Third, Alí Primera's songs were perceived as prophetic and as proposing ideas that were being made concrete through the actions and policies of the Chávez government. Fourth, the Bolivarian *proceso* was perceived to draw on the ideas contained in the songs of Alí Primera, which were presented as a 'root' of the revolution. Fifth, Alí Primera was represented as endorsing the Chávez government via the repeated claim that if he were alive Alí Primera would be a *chavista* and even Minister of Culture. Finally, any attempts by the opposition to claim Alí Primera's songs as representative of their political views were denounced and discredited.

In addition to the above themes, on Aporrea Alí Primera and his songs were used as a yardstick and a means of calling Chávez to account in areas where he was perceived to be failing. Alí Primera was constructed as a 'representative character' and as a symbol of what Chávez needed to achieve. For example, an article posted in February 2007 by Ramón García took the form of a letter to Hugo Chávez:

> I'm sure that Alí Primera would not be offended with what I'm telling you, Hugo; don't you realise that Alí continues to sing not because he likes to, but because it is necessary? ... he would be happy to be able to go away completely Hugo, but while his songs are still relevant, he will keep on singing, because his revolutionary soul would never be able to let him rest until he sees his dream of justice, that he insisted on transmitting in his song, has been built. I ask you, Hugo, let's help Alí Primera to rest. How? I'm going to help you with some ideas.

García lists a number of social and political problems, which he calls for Chávez to address, including poverty, corruption, and the lack of justice for the torture and political assassination of communist leader Alberto Lovera, which took place in 1965, during the first decade of the Punto Fijo period. García uses Alí Primera's lyrics to call on Chávez to achieve these goals; there should no longer be *techos de cartón* (cardboard houses), García says, and Chávez needs to be sure that those who accompany him to the National Pantheon on the anniversary of the death of Bolívar are not doing so only 'to make sure that the Liberator is dead ... well and truly dead'.[11] García attributes the high profile of Alí's songs in the Chávez period to the continued existence of social and political problems, arguing that Alí 'would be happy to be able to go away completely' if the 'dream of justice' which he sang of were fulfilled.

García uses Alí's songs to call Chávez to account, telling Chávez 'you are intelligent and, above intelligence, you have that pure heart that is needed to interpret and feel the songs of Alí Primera correctly'. For García, Alí Primera's songs, which are a common link between García and Hugo Chávez, act as a resource to engage in a personalised form of communication with the president. García uses Alí's 'example' and his songs to express what he believes *el pueblo* want from their government, and to urge Chávez to act to build the society that Alí's songs represent in order that the songs' criticisms should no longer be valid. In this way, Alí's 'exemplary' life and his songs become resources for the evaluation of the Chávez government's policies; Alí and his songs are used to criticise areas of government policy which do not match Alí's example, and to urge the government to act in areas that Alí, and by extension *el pueblo*, hold to be important for the country. Alí is held up as a 'representative character' through whom the Chávez government is evaluated and judged, and, in some areas, found lacking.

In a similar manner, a community radio worker I interviewed in 2005 in Barquisimeto used Alí Primera as a 'representative character' to question some aspects of the Chávez government's actions. This radio worker told me that there remained many unresolved social and political problems in his community; unemployment was 'still a big problem' and though there was now access to free health care and education and significant improvement in the quality of life for people in the barrios, there were problems with corruption, which prevented the *proceso* from becoming 'more profound'. According to this interviewee, Alí Primera expressed 'a new way of thinking' and 'a different way of looking at history' in his words and songs, and Chávez 'seized [this] for the revolution'. For this radio worker, Chávez was doing 'the right things' and 'using Alí's lyrics' to guide *el proceso*. The problem as my informant saw it was with 'the people below [Chávez]', some of whom 'used their power to threaten to remove grants'. According to this radio worker, these *escuálidos* (squalid ones)[12] who formed the local government could not reach 'Alí's stature'. A student at the University of Coro also told me in 2005 that unlike Chávez, some local governors 'used Alí just to appear revolutionary'. According to this student, though these governors used pictures of Alí and played Alí's songs during their campaigns, they did not really listen to Alí's music.

Therefore, *Canción Necesaria* could represent the Bolivarian *proceso* while the songs simultaneously critiqued local governors who did not appear to aspire to Alí's example.

Alí Primera acted as a 'representative character' whose life and songs provided a shared pool of resources, which Venezuelans used to construct knowledge about what they should demand from the Chávez government, and which aspects of the government they should denounce. On 12 February 2011, the *Colectivo Socialista Alí Primera* (Alí Primera Socialist Collective) published an article on Aporrea announcing that on 20 February the annual *Marcha de los Claveles Rojos* (March of the Red Carnations) would take place in Paraguaná to commemorate the twenty-sixth anniversary of Alí's death. This article stated:

> Those of us who consider ourselves to be revolutionaries should always have Alí's legacy as our guide; [Alí's] conduct, thought and political action, Bolivarian, anti-imperialist, Marxist, Socialist ... emphasised his humanity, his solidarity, his honesty, his detachment from all material and bureaucratic ambition, in spite of being a natural leader. He was harassed and threatened in the times of the ADECO-COPEYANO [Punto Fijo] hegemony. Alí Primera always walked with his hands and his heart open to the *pueblo*, who were hungry for hope in a time of capitalist abundance. It is important to emphasise that with this 'March of the Red Carnations' it will be twenty-six consecutive years that *el pueblo* have been paying tribute to the singer ... with red carnations, with songs and slogans, against reformism, against corruption, inefficiency and hidden bureaucracy, and with a single voice, we say 'Together with Alí we are bound for the popular victory of *Comandante* Chávez in the year 2012'.[13]

In these words, Alí Primera is depicted as a 'representative character' who embodies an array of humane, social and political qualities which are of value for the country. He is represented as the epitome of the Bolivarian ideal, and as 'a guide' for revolutionaries. He is used simultaneously as a tool with which to criticise some aspects of the Bolivarian government (reformism, corruption, inefficiency and hidden bureaucracy) and as a resource to harness support for the 'popular victory' of Hugo Chávez in the 2012 presidential election.

In the Chávez period, *Chavistas* used Alí's songs to actively engage with the actions of the government and to articulate what they wanted from the state. Alí was depicted as a 'representative character' against whom the actions of members of the Chávez government were measured. This personalised form of address, via the figure and songs of Alí, supports Sujatha Fernandes' (2010: 107–8) finding that barrio residents viewed Chávez as someone who listened to their stories, was mindful of their concerns, but who was a human being who made mistakes and needed the guidance and protection of *el pueblo*. For Chávez supporters, Alí's songs represented *el pueblo* and their demands; although the Chávez government was perceived to be failing in some respects, they believed that Chávez was struggling to achieve Alí Primera's goals on their behalf. University students from Mérida performing with their band in the Festival del Fuego in Santiago de Cuba explained this to me in an interview in 2005:

> [Alí] is a resource for *el pueblo*. ... What Alí criticised, the president takes on board. The president responds to Alí's anguish because it is the anguish of *el pueblo*. Alí made a powerful criticism of capitalism and exploitation [which Chávez listens to].

Alí was thus upheld as the pinnacle of human achievement, and his songs and stories about his life were used to evaluate and critique specific aspects of the Chávez government and to talk about what people should want and expect from their government.

ALÍ PRIMERA AND COMPETING 'HIGH PRIESTS' OF MYTH

In February 2005, the National Assembly unanimously agreed to include Alí Primera's *Canción Necesaria* in official representations of Venezuela's cultural heritage. However, this unanimous decision was not reached without disagreement concerning which groups Alí's legacy represented. On 15 February 2005, the *Agencia Bolivariana de Noticias* (ABN, Bolivarian News Agency) reported[14] that during the National Assembly's meeting, Ismael García of the leftist *Por la Democracia Social* (PODEMOS, For Social Democracy) party referred to Alí as 'a visionary who sang to the oppressed and whose ideal is present in the Bolivarian Revolution'. However, according to the ABN report, Juan José Caldera of the conservative *Convergencia* party raised objections because the Assembly's official documents used the term *Canción Bolivariana* (Bolivarian Song). Although Caldera considered the homage to Alí Primera to be 'very just', ABN reports that Caldera argued that Alí belonged to 'all Venezuelans' and not only the Bolivarian movement. According to ABN, the then president of the Assembly, Nicolás Maduro, countered that Alí himself had coined the terms *Canción Bolivariana* and *Canción Necesaria* to refer to his music. ABN reports that the discussion took a 'political turn' which was only 'calmed' when members of parliament were asked if they were in agreement with Alí being officially named heritage, and all present affirmed that they were.

Even though the members of the National Assembly agreed that Alí Primera should be recognised officially as part of the country's cultural heritage, they apparently did not agree about what this meant. In addition to creating new 'worlds of meaning' at a time of political transformation, and acting as a 'representative character' and a symbol of what people valued, Alí Primera and his songs provided an 'ideological reservoir' which offered resources for the expression of political conflict in Venezuela during the Chávez period. Both *Chavistas* and *anti-Chavistas* sought to legitimate competing claims to Alí's myth, and both *Chavistas* and *anti-Chavistas* expressed anger at what they perceived to be the 'incorrect' interpretations of Alí's life and music.

ALÍ PRIMERA AS CONTESTED SPACE

Verdery (1999), Baty (1995) and Kapcia (2000) emphasise that significant deceased individuals are not 'frozen' in history; their significance can be constructed in competing ways, and people can identify with them from a number of conflicting vantage points as various aspects of the deceased individual's life are highlighted or suppressed. Changes in society may lead people to re-evaluate the perceived successes and failures of the deceased individual, and since they are unable to express their own views, the dead may be made to act as spokespeople for a range of different groups. Although the importance of the 'representative character' may be recognised by a diverse range of groups, such figures can reflect political conflict as different groups seek to legitimate their claims to the social and political value of the dead person. Thus although the recognisable dead may act as reference points and bring people together around a single name, the significance of the dead person's life and death may be construed in a variety of competing ways.

A student I interviewed at the University of Coro in 2005 referred to Alí Primera as 'a fundamental pillar in political discussion'. During my fieldwork, I found that Alí Primera and his songs were used to assert, defend and contest an array of opposing political ideas in the Chávez period. Chávez's association with Alí Primera's songs created a political persona for the president, and represented Chávez as one of *el pueblo*. Voices within the opposition viewed this in a negative light; Chávez's identification with Alí's songs was for some evidence of Chávez's low class and cultural ignorance, and, they felt, rendered him unfit to represent their values. For example, one *anti-Chavista* who I interviewed in Caracas in 2005 told me that she could not tolerate Chávez, who was 'not fit to be president'. She argued that Alí Primera was a drunkard whose fatal car accident was caused by drink-driving, and that the people who liked Alí Primera's songs were from low social classes while she was of European heritage and preferred to listen to rock or classical music. According to this interviewee, the fact that Hugo Chávez liked Alí Primera's songs was of little surprise and served as an indication that the president too was from a vulgar background and of low social status:

> ... you have to grow up with [folklore] to get used to it ... Our president is very folkloric ... [Now] the country is going backwards. It's because of his culture, the tiny bit that he has. ... He wants us all to live like he used to live.

This criticism of Hugo Chávez was presented in cultural and economic terms; my interviewee argued that a president should be *un señor* (a gentleman) who has eaten hot food all his life and speaks English, and not someone who only started wearing shoes at the age of eight, as she claimed Chávez did. The people who liked Alí Primera, according to this interviewee, had 'a different concept; it's to do with the atmosphere you grow up in'. These people were 'lazy' and wanted 'everything for free'. This interviewee did not see Chávez's association with the songs of Hugo Chávez as an opportunistic manoeuvre, but as evidence of a lack of culture which, in her eyes, rendered him unsuitable to act as president. Such views reflect the elitist cultural values associated with Venezuela's traditional ruling classes, who sought to 'civilise' the country through importing classical European cultural values, and who saw folklore as 'primitive' and pre-modern.

The interviewee rejected Alí Primera's songs as being of value to her, and she viewed the Chávez government's support for these songs as a sign of Chávez's 'primitive' cultural taste, his unsuitability to govern the country and evidence that he was taking the country backwards. A former guerrilla and an opponent of the Chávez government who I interviewed in 2005 told me that Alí Primera was 'a nice enough man', but that a government should aim to raise the taste of the masses by promoting high art, not popular forms of culture. By promoting Alí and his songs, this interviewee argued, the government was 'pandering to the masses' but making no real difference to their lives.

At meetings of the opposition, which I attended in Caracas in 2005, Alí Primera was not mentioned[15] and his songs were not played or sung. Although I did not witness the opposition playing or speaking of Alí Primera's music at their meetings during my fieldwork, Chávez supporters claimed that the mainstream media had sought to use Alí's songs to undermine the government. For example, on 18 February 2008, Venezuelan blogger Yosmary de Rausseo wrote that at a concert held in homage to Alí Primera *cantautora* Lilia Vera declared to the audience:

> We singers are not going to allow the image and the songs, the social attitude and the political ideology that our brother Alí Primera sowed in us, to be stolen from us. [The private television channel] Globovisión is using Alí Primera's songs to spread their lies [and] their fallacies to the world.

In these words, Vera represents the private media's apparent attempt to feature Alí's music in its programming as an attempt to 'steal' Alí from the *Chavistas*, and she claims Alí for the government's supporters. On 15 June 2011, Aporrea published a statement, signed by several artists and groups, which denounced a specific attempt by Globovisión to use Alí Primera's songs to attack one of the Chávez government's *misiones*:

> In a short programme entitled '*Misión* Promise', the Globovisión channel, advocate of fascism and dehumanising of the Venezuelan mind and spirit, in an attempt to discredit the new *Misión* Venezuelan Home, used the dignified song 'Cardboard Houses' by the revolutionary father of song, Alí Primera, in order to sow hatred upon the social achievements of a *pueblo* that they refuse to recognise … This task of manipulating Revolutionary Song comes from those who have always looked for ways to stop the hopes and liberating dreams of *el pueblo*, from those who look to drown the Socialist revolution that *el pueblo* fought for. [This task] of mobilising and bringing together the historic force of Alí Primera, is totally UNACCEPTABLE.[16]

Chávez supporters I spoke to also reacted vehemently against what they described as the private media's attempts to use Alí's music to undermine the government and its supporters. For example, musicians from Los Guaraguao told me in 2008 that oppositional media outlets had sought

to use Alí Primera's songs to promote an *anti-Chavista* agenda, but that
'few are taken in, Alí cannot be used against a government that is doing
what he [Alí] proposed'. A resident of El Valle in Caracas and a participant
in *misión cultura*, told me in 2005 that she believed that if Alí Primera
were alive he would support the Chávez government and not endorse the
opposition in any way:

> I am [sure] that [Alí] would be with the revolution. There are many people,
> mainly from the opposition ... who don't think this is so, but I don't believe
> Alí would be on the other side. Because he always stayed with the neediest,
> right? And at this moment, with this *proceso* which is for *el pueblo* and of *el
> pueblo*, I think that of course [Alí] would be with the revolution. And I think
> that the flag of the revolution is Hugo Chávez and Alí Primera, they are the
> great leaders, the most important; Chávez and Primera.

This interviewee reasoned that those who opposed Chávez also opposed
el pueblo and the poor, and they could not therefore legitimately claim
Alí's songs to express their views. Similarly, a community radio worker
told me in 2008 that she believed that if Alí Primera's songs could genuinely represent the opposition, the opposition would have wanted to claim
them many years earlier during the Punto Fijo years. The perception that
the opposition had never shown an interest in Alí's songs before Chávez
officially recognised them indicated to her that the songs could not represent the opposition's view. This radio worker told me:

> If the opposition feel identified with Alí, why did they never show it before?
> You never saw anybody on the right protesting against the shooting of us;
> the people who cried for RCTV[17] ... never cried when we were shot [during
> the *Caracazo*]. If they really identify with Alí, great! That would really mean
> they identify with the revolutionary *proceso* ... Alí is the voice of *el pueblo*,
> and he was for a long time before Chávez.

This interviewee told me that she believed that the opposition had
never even listened to Alí Primera's songs, and that any attempts to identify these songs with the opposition's political aims in the Chávez period
were 'insincere' and 'manipulative', aimed only at the undermining of
the Chávez government and its supporters, *el pueblo*. For her, the songs
represented the *Chavista* point of view, because to listen to Alí's songs
was to listen to *el pueblo*. Similarly, a student from Mérida told me in
2005:

[Chávez's] election campaign was based on Alí's music. It wasn't out of opportunism. The president listens to Alí with the same love that *el pueblo* listen to Alí. He did not use Alí's music as a tool to gain votes, but Alí expressed what he felt. When the president put Alí in his rightful place, it wasn't to win votes or to use him; the President loves him. The opposition has also tried to use Alí's music and make him theirs, but this attempt back-fired and had the opposite effect. When the private media tried to use Alí's music and therefore confuse people, *el pueblo* reacted against it. Chávez has put Alí up there because he [Chávez] belongs to *el pueblo*.

For this student, any attempts by the private media to feature Alí Primera's songs in television programmes constituted a form of sabotage aimed at undermining the Chávez government's support by confusing the audience. This was perceived to be because the private media were expressive of the voice of the opposition, and the voice of the opposi-tion could make no legitimate claim to Alí. Barrio residents I interviewed frequently emphasised Alí's rejection of the private media and of com-mercial music. They linked this with ideas about Alí's 'authenticity' and his artistic integrity, values which they believed were important for them and for the government. For example, in 2008 a community radio worker told me; 'Alí was not on television, but he was in the streets, the squares; the police arrested him and beat him ... [even now] you don't hear him on private radio'. In 2005, a community radio worker I interviewed also emphasised to me how Alí Primera's songs were 'never on television' and Alí was 'always independent'. For barrio residents I interviewed, it was 'inappropriate' to use Alí's music in the private media. Barrio residents I interviewed reacted against the perceived purposes of featuring Alí's songs on private television channels; they denounced what they understood to be attempts to undermine them through placing Alí's music in a commer-cial context and, at a symbolic level, linking him with oppositional values.

The perceived connection between Alí's rejection of the private media and his artistic integrity and authenticity was highlighted and invested with value by barrio residents I spoke to who criticised the musical choices of Alí's four sons from his marriage to Sol Mussett. In the 1990s, the Primera-Mussett brothers, all of whom were then children or teenagers, became famous for performing salsa-pop music on commercial record labels. The music of the two middle sons, Servando and Florentino, fea-tured in *telenovelas* made by the private Venevisión television channel.[18] In the early years of the Chávez government, the Primera-Mussett broth-ers publicly denounced the state's uses of their father's music.[19] Chávez supporters perceived this as a personal betrayal and as the result of the opposition's 'dirty' tactics. On 1 December 2002, this idea was expressed in a post published on Aporrea under the pseudonym 'Anaconda y A.I.':

> After reading that the Primera brothers 'repudiate the use of their father's songs for state propaganda and they do not support a regime which has destroyed society', I was very saddened to see that these poor lads not only suffered the loss of their father. They lost the opportunity to develop and to learn to think for themselves. They have been kidnapped by a regime of drugs, fame, and a false sense of triumph. Our poor *cantautor*, because he defied the mortal enemy, not only did they assassinate him, but they also kidnapped his sons.[20]

In this article, the opposition is represented as attacking the 'integrity' of Alí Primera and the 'authenticity' of his songs by turning his sons against what Alí symbolised. The opposition's claim to Alí Primera, via Alí's sons, is denounced and resisted. Similarly, a community radio worker in Barquisimeto told me in 2005 that he believed that the Primera-Mussett brothers acted 'as if their father's music was out of fashion'. This radio worker made sense of the Primera-Mussett brothers' salsa-pop style and their perceived opposition to the Chávez government by claiming that the brothers were 'stoned' on drugs. This interviewee, like many barrio residents I spoke to, could not accept music associated with Alí Primera and with the *Nueva Canción* movement being used by the private media or to oppose Chávez. For example, the former *Nueva Canción cantautora* Soledad Bravo became a public and a vociferous opponent of the government in the Chávez period.[21] This radio employee rationalised Bravo's opposition to the Chávez government by claiming that she had never been an 'authentic' *Nueva Canción cantautora* and that she had only 'used the poor people's music all along to make money for herself'. Bravo's early *Nueva Canción* recordings were thus reassessed and redefined in the Chávez period; for some supporters of the Chávez government, Bravo's opposition to Chávez in the twenty-first century rendered her early 1970s recordings 'commercial' and 'inauthentic'. It angered my informant to hear music which was meaningful for him, *Nueva Canción*, in the mouths of artists who declared that they were opposed to the Chávez government; such 'inappropriate' uses of the music of *el pueblo* led him to revise his opinions about Bravo's intentions in the past, and to undermine the moral behaviour and the personal integrity of the Primera-Mussett brothers in the present.

As Simon Frith (2004) argues, the apparent judgement of music as 'bad' may rest not so much on the sound of the music in itself, but instead it may originate from a sense of betrayal that a particular artist has chosen to perform that music. Indeed, the quality of the Primera-Mussett brothers' salsa-pop music was recognised in Miami and in other Latin American and Caribbean countries where people carried no expectations of the Primera family name; for example, the album *Servando y Florentino* (2006), co-written with Yasmil Marrufo and released by *Universal Music Latino* in partnership with *Venevisión*, was nominated for a Grammy award for Best Pop Album by a Duo or Group with Vocals. Yet in Venezuela, according to Alí Alejandro Primera, the brothers were widely rejected, and this was not because of the music they performed, but because of who they were. According to Alí Alejandro, the opposition took advantage of the public rejection of the Primera-Mussett brothers' salsa-pop; 'the ultra-left mixed with the right to take advantage of [the Primera-Mussett brothers'] fame' and their comments about Chávez, and to present an image of 'a family divided' over the Chávez government. In this way, Alí Alejandro believed, the opposition used his family to undermine the integrity of Alí Primera's life and music and, by extension, the basis of Bolivarianism.[22]

The Primera-Mussett brothers admit that they had indeed initially denounced and been angered by Chávez's singing of their father's songs. As Sandino, the oldest of the Primera-Mussett brothers, asserts:

> In this house, we kept our distance from the government. Chávez wanted to talk to us about Alí. We care about the poor, but [we didn't want to talk to Chávez].[23]

However, by 2005 the brothers had begun to distance themselves from their earlier oppositional stance. Florentino reflects:

> I was an opponent of Chávez for a long time … but now I've changed, not out of resignation but because I can see that Chávez is going in a new direction, a Latin American direction. Alí was used by this *proceso*, but used in a good way.[24]

The Primera-Mussett brothers expressed frustration with public expectations that they would follow in their father's footsteps and act as political guides who would lead people 'to the future'. According to Juan Simón, the youngest of the brothers:

There are some people who think they have their hands on our shoulders, and that we can lead them to the future, and it's not true. Some people sometimes expect from us something that we cannot give them. That's frustrating for everyone involved.[25]

Similarly, Sandino believed that the Primera surname created expectations of his music:

It was very hard. When I composed and recorded my first CD, everybody was saying 'your dad's music is like that [*Nueva Canción*], your music is garbage, just Latin-pop ballads' ... Nobody trusted my music ... It's really hard to have this surname.[26]

Sandino felt that people's apparent judgement of his music was not based on a judgement of the aesthetic or technical qualities of his compositions, but on those people's pre-conceived ideas about the type of music that a member of the Primera family should write and perform and the uses to which this music should be put. Sandino and Juan Simón both felt that people wanted to 'use' their music in some way, because of the associations that their surname bore. According to Sandino, he and his brothers had not wanted other people to claim 'ownership' of their father's music, which they said belonged to all Venezuelans. Sandino said that 'if anyone plays one of my father's CDs, people will shout '*¡Chavista!*'. Florentino said that it 'hurt' him to see so many people using his father's music to manipulate the public:

[People] fix on songs that are in their interests, both in the official sector and in the opposition. The opposition uses my dad's songs. Many people who oppose Chávez tell me 'I love your dad, but I won't listen to [his music] because Chávez has seized it'. This is dividing people, it's misinterpreting the songs, it's using them badly. When the hills flooded,[27] the opposition used 'Cardboard Houses', as if to say Chávez had caused them [the slums].[28]

The brothers felt that their father's songs were being used by many competing groups, both in favour of and opposed to the Chávez government, to assert their political claims and to undermine those of others. According to Florentino, there were people who told him that they liked Alí Primera's songs, but that they could no longer listen to them because of their association with the Chávez government. Similarly, Sandino said that anybody playing his father's music was automatically labelled

Chavista. These claims exemplify Frith's (2004: 20) argument that 'the apparent judgment of music is a judgment of something else altogether'; it is a judgment of the social institutions or the social behaviour for which the music 'simply acts as a sign'. Frith argues that people are sometimes angered by music which, in other circumstances, they may enjoy listening to; it is not the music alone that people react to, but the perceived uses of that music and the perceived motivations underlying its performance in a particular context by a particular person or group.[29] The Primera-Mussett brothers felt that they experienced these apparent musical judgements on two levels. First, they believed that their music was dismissed in Venezuela by people who might otherwise enjoy it, and that this was not because of the sound itself but because of who they were and what people believed music produced by a Primera should be like. Second, they believed that when Alí Primera's music began to act as a 'sign' of *Chavismo,* some Venezuelans who might have enjoyed this music previously gave up listening to it because they did not wish to be identified as *Chavistas.*

Venezuelans I interviewed during my fieldwork also suggested that some fans of Alí Primera's music gave up listening to Alí's songs in the Chávez period because of the new associations which these songs had acquired through the government's cultural policies and political communication. For example, a Venezuelan I interviewed in Caracas in 2008 claimed that he and his wife had both loved Alí Primera's music and gone to hear Alí performing live when they were university students. However, this interviewee told me that his wife was opposed to the Chávez government and as a result she was now unable to reconcile her previous pleasure in Alí Primera's songs with her current distaste for the government. According to my interviewee, his wife had subsequently denied that she ever liked Alí Primera's songs and that she had ever enjoyed listening to them. This interviewee believed that his wife had not changed her taste in music, but instead that her feelings about the other people who liked Alí's music affected her willingness to admit that she enjoyed Alí's music. In other words, she changed her apparent judgement of Alí's music in order not to appear to be identified with the *Chavistas.*

COMPETING INTERPRETATIONS OF THE MYTH OF ALÍ AND *CANCIÓN NECESARIA*: A CASE STUDY FROM YOUTUBE

In the Chávez period, although some *anti-Chavistas* claimed that they no longer listened to Alí Primera's music, others used Alí's songs to express their resistance to the government. Using netnographic methodologies, YouTube provides a fruitful forum to analyse the ways in which opponents and supporters of the government defended their competing claims to Alí's music and, at a symbolic level, their claims about Bolivarianism. A YouTube search for Alí Primera on 18 September 2013 produced over 68 thousand results. Some of these results had stimulated tens or even hundreds of thousands of views and comments as people debated the meanings of the songs and reacted to the Chávez government's uses of them. While Alí Primera's songs officially represented the 'illusion' of symbolising one thing—the Chávez government's Bolivarian project—the songs in fact meant different things to different people, and Venezuelans actively sought to persuade other people of the legitimacy of their own interpretations of the music. As they did so, at a symbolic level people used Alí's music to assert and contest ideas and opinions about the Chávez government.

I will focus here on the predominant themes articulated in comments posted in response to the framing of Alí Primera's song 'Ahora que el petróleo es nuestro' (Now that the Oil is ours) as oppositional. Uploaded by a user called 'Chuparin80' on 7 June 2007, by 18 September 2013 the video had been viewed 203,558 times, received 148 likes and 105 dislikes, and elicited 529 comments. It is not possible to know who the people who posted these comments are, or which type of background they come from. According to Internet World Stats for 2006, approximately three million of Venezuela's twenty-six million were Internet users in the early twenty-first century (Hellinger 2011: 224). This amounts to an Internet penetration of 11.8 per cent, but Hellinger (ibid.) argues that this estimate, which is based on Nielson ratings and the International Telecommunications Union, may be much lower than actual Internet usage since computer access in Venezuela is widely shared in apartments and neighbourhoods and numerous low-cost Internet cafés can be found throughout the country. I acknowledge that data collected from YouTube users present problems of representativeness, and it remains unclear whether the people posting comments reside in wealthy neighbourhoods, or whether they access the Internet in cafés in poor barrios. However, the purpose of my analysis here is not to determine the socio-economic background of Chávez supporters or opponents, but to examine how supporters and opponents of Chávez reacted to government uses of Alí Primera's songs. Comments posted on YouTube provide valuable data about these reactions.

The song, 'Now that the Oil is ours', and video are uploaded under the heading 'Alí Primera sings to Hugo Chávez'. Chuparin80 makes explicit the intention to use the song, composed some three decades earlier, to criticise the Chávez's government's handling of the country's oil wealth, writing:

> Song dedicated to the work of Hugo Chávez. Poverty continues to increase while MILLIONS OF DOLLARS of oil have been wasted on corruption, luxuries, propaganda, weapons and gifts for armed delinquents in other countries.[30]

This framing of the song as oppositional to the state generated debate in the form of comments defending a variety of arguments about the Chávez government's perceived successes and failures. In their arguments about what the song means, the people posting comments on YouTube at the same time argue about what the Chávez government represents. The song functions as a resource through which YouTube commentators define themselves as supporters or opponents of the Chávez government. The comments supporting the opposition, posted in response to Chuparin80's video, fall into five principal categories: (1) it is asserted that Alí Primera would not support the Chávez government if he were alive, but would be composing songs to denounce the government's failures; (2) the Chávez government is seen to be betraying the ideals that Alí Primera's songs are perceived to contain, and Bolivarianism is represented as the perversion of Alí's ideology; (3) attempts are made to discredit supporters' uses of the song to defend the government, and Chávez's allies are accused of using the songs as propaganda; (4) the past is disputed, and Alí's reported persecution under Punto Fijo governments and the previous level of popularity of his songs are questioned; (5) Alí Primera's music is used to resist the Chávez government, and the song's denunciations of the elites' squandering of oil wealth while the people go hungry become denunciations not directed at *Puntofijismo* but at Hugo Chávez himself.

A brief examination of some of the comments posted in response to Chuparin80's framing of 'Now that the Oil is ours' as oppositional will illustrate how Alí's song becomes a resource with which to debate Bolivarianism. In many of the comments, claims are made about whether or not Alí Primera would support the Chávez government if he were alive:

> … this is a lack of respect for the memory of Alí who I'm sure, if he were alive, would not be against Chávez. Look for another song or create one to express your discontent, but don't do such an indecorous thing[31]

> If Alí were alive he'd have written a hundred songs insulting Chávez[32]

> Do you think that Alí supported crazy people? ... How he'd be slamming Chávez with his songs if he could see the abandoned hospitals, the beggars in the streets and the neo-socialists ... in their hummers and their mansions, with their trips abroad ... You have no idea who Alí Primera was[33]

In such comments, competing communities of *Chavistas* and *anti-Chavistas* claim Alí Primera's song as their own and seek to use it to endorse their viewpoint; both supporters and opponents of the Chávez government want the song to express their view of Hugo Chávez. It is of course impossible to know what Alí Primera would have thought of the government of Hugo Chávez had he not been killed in a car accident in 1985. In making such claims about what Alí Primera would have thought of Chávez if he had been alive, Venezuelans use Alí and his song to disclose and assert what are in fact their own political views in the present moment. Through their claims to know what Alí would have thought of Chávez, Venezuelans place their own opinions in the mouth of the *cantautor* and project their own concerns onto his music. Alí's song is made to represent a variety of competing views about the perceived successes and failures of the Chávez government. Some argue that the ideals contained in Alí Primera's song were being betrayed by the Chávez government:

> Alí must be turning in his grave, seeing how Chávez has ruined all possibility of a real change in our society, destroying everything that half works and giving away our resources to other countries to buy their international votes. In these times it's worth listening to Alí Primera's song, 'Now that the Oil is ours'. Chávez, nobody can say you're selling off the country[34] because in reality you're giving it away!![35]
>
> If the people's singer were alive he'd have been utterly disappointed in this farcical government which calls itself Socialism of the twenty-first century. Above all by those in government who are now the new rich wearing designer clothes and watches.[36]

Through arguing that Alí would be 'turning in his grave' and 'disappointed' in the Chávez government, these comments do not serve to urge Chávez to act to reach Alí's exemplary ideal. Instead, Alí's song serves as a resource to call on Venezuelans to reject the Chávez government and its perceived squandering of the country's oil wealth; the song's perceived oppositional qualities are directed *at* the Chávez government. The song, originally composed by Alí to call on the Punto Fijo government to use the country's oil wealth to benefit the poor, is used some thirty years later to denounce the Chávez government's perceived mishandling of the country's resources in the twenty-first century. In these comments, it is not the music itself which is resisted; instead, what is resisted is the link between the Chávez government and the music. Chávez opponents claiming Alí's song as their own seek to make the song symbolise not *Chavismo* but *resistance* to the Chávez government.

While asserting their interpretations of the song, Venezuelans seek to discredit understandings that contradict their own. Some defend *Chavismo* by claiming that a song composed some three decades earlier with reference to a Punto Fijo government cannot be used to oppose a twenty-first-century government:

> What shit, they are to be pitied, those in the Venezuelan opposition who take the lyrics and the music of the great Venezuelan singer … to question the Venezuelan President … they are really to be pitied … that song was written before Chávez came to power ANIMAL SCUM OF LIFE…!!![37]
>
> Hey Chuparin80 you counterrevolutionary, Alí Primera died twenty-two years ago, this manipulated video clip has nothing to do with the present Bolivarian government.[38]

Others acknowledge that the song was not written about the Chávez government, but nevertheless they defend the use of the song to criticise *el proceso* and its perceived failings:

> This song was a protest against the democratic government in the period 1970–1980. If you pay attention to the lyrics and you know a little bit about Venezuela today (after eleven years with Chávez) you'll see that in reality everything is the same, or perhaps worse, and that Chávez has incited hatred, division, racism and has changed attitudes towards success and merit with the exaltation of mediocrity and genuflexion[39]
>
> This song is a good one to dedicate to the president. What imbeciles are those who listen to the great Alí Primera and use him as propaganda for the socialism that they preach … you idiots, stop being so ignorant and really open your eyes[40]

These comments illustrate how both supporters and opponents of the Chávez government struggle to legitimate their own claims to Alí's music for their own purposes, and to represent themselves as the 'authentic' interpreters of the myth of Alí Primera and the 'ideological reservoir' symbolised by *Canción Necesaria*. However, in some comments, apparent opponents of Chávez display no desire to claim Alí Primera's song as representative of their views; they question official discourses and grassroots narratives about the *Puntofijista* suppression of Alí Primera's songs, claiming that the *cantautor* himself was of little worth, and asserting that Alí was virtually unknown before the election of Chávez:

> Alí Primera was practically unknown in Venezuela. I lived all of that time in Venezuela until he died, so nobody can contradict me. Alí censored? Please!!! What radio station in the 1970s and 1980s was going to play that rubbish music. At that time they didn't even play Spanish rock, they only played American music. Do you think 'Soda Stereo'[41] were censored too? Wake up![42]
>
> What rubbish music. Not even his own sons followed his absurd ideology; I think that alone says enough. Alí Primera was never anybody, only the four communists there were in Venezuela at that time knew who he was. If his songs didn't talk about communism he'd be forgotten now in the dustbin of history, like so many others much better than him.[43]

In these comments, Alí's music provides a resource for people to contest the past and, by extension, to seek to undermine and discredit the basis on which Chávez supporters justify their claims to Alí's value for the country in the present. By seeking to legitimate their claims about Alí's *insignificance*, these commentators use Alí to resist and critique the Chávez government for which Alí's music acts as a sign.

It is interesting to note that one commentator (iroking13) reveals a concern that any 'defence' of Alí will identify a person as *Chavista*. Iroking13 disputes the claim that Alí Primera was little known, writing 'Alí Primera followed by four communists? Please, Alí Primera marked an epoch, not only in Venezuela but in Latin America ... When I was nine years old I used to listen to Alí Primera, and my family wasn't communist'. In response, commentators claim that 'the only place you ever saw Alí Primera was painted on the walls of the UCV', and that 'when Venezuela ends up like Cuba, you'll be wiping your bottom on Alí's records and everything else that's got anything to do with Communism'. Iroking13 replies:

> Haven't you understood that I'm not a *Chavista*, we're in the same fight? Alí was unjustly hogged by the *Chavistas*, Alí's 'communism' was something else, nothing to do with this shit. That's why I'm defending him[44]

This response suggests that iroking13 suspects that any claim that Alí Primera 'marked an epoch', and that a person's family used to listen to

Alí's music, is likely to identify one as a *Chavista*. Iroking13, who is 'not *Chavista*', affirms support for 'the same fight' against the Chávez government, but rather than dismiss Alí Primera as 'rubbish', iroking13 argues that Alí was 'unjustly hogged by the *Chavistas*' and that it is the *Chavistas* one must struggle to defend Alí from.

Conclusions

In this chapter, I examined both elicited and non-elicited examples of conflicting interpretations of Alí Primera's *Canción Necesaria* legacy in the Chávez period, and argued that state institutionalisation of Alí's songs gave rise to competing and contradictory evaluations of the significance of those songs, and of Alí's life and death. I contended that in the Chávez period, Venezuelans were compelled to respond to the government's association with *Canción Necesaria*, and that in doing so they revealed much about their judgements regarding the value of *Chavismo*.

In the Chávez period, state support for Alí Primera's songs linked these songs to the government, and Venezuelans reacted to this link in various ways. No longer officially repressed and marginalised by the state, the songs were officially included in representations of the country's cultural heritage, and they were constructed as precursors of Bolivarianism. This changed the ways the Venezuelan public reacted to Alí Primera and his music. First, Alí Primera and his songs provided resources with which people, particularly the poor and the marginalised, constructed fresh 'worlds of meaning' in order to create knowledge about their new status in Venezuelan society. Second, Alí Primera acted as a 'representative character' who embodied the qualities that many Venezuelans considered to be important for the country, whether or not these Venezuelans believed that Chávez and his government possessed those qualities. Third, Venezuelans could not listen to Alí's songs in the same way because the songs now symbolised Bolivarianism; competing groups sought to assert, contest and negotiate the legitimacy of the government's status as 'high priest' of the Alí Primera myth. Alí Primera's life and songs, an 'ideological reservoir', thus came to function as a symbolic political language through which Venezuelans were able to identify and define themselves in relation to the Bolivarian process. In the Chávez period, to engage in state involvement in Alí's *Canción Necesaria* legacy, to defend, negotiate or to contest this link, was a form of political activism in and of itself.

NOTES

1. Interview with Cordero, Caracas, September 2008.
2. Interview with Yépez, Caracas, September 2008.
3. Interview with Duque, Caracas, September 2008.
4. Interview with Rodríguez, Caracas, July 2005.
5. The *misiones* are programmes introduced under the Chávez government to deal rapidly and directly with a wide range of social, economic and cultural problems. See Hawkins and Rosas 2011.
6. From the song 'La patria es el hombre' (Man is the Homeland).
7. Interview with Duque, Caracas, September 2008.
8. Interview with Guerra, Caracas, September 2008.
9. Interview with Paez, Caracas, July 2005.
10. http://www.aporrea.org/nosotros (Last accessed 8 January 2016).
11. Lyrics from 'Canción Bolivariana', from the 1980 album *Abrebrecha, y mañana hablamos*
12. *Escuálido* is a common derogatory term which Chávez supporters use to refer to the opposition in Venezuela.
13. http://www.aporrea.org/actualidad/n174771.html (Last accessed 8 January 2016).
14. http://www.aporrea.org/tiburon/n56304.html (Last accessed 28 June 2013).
15. Interestingly, at one opposition meeting I attended at the UCV in July 2005, 'Yo vengo a ofrecer mi corazón' (I Come to Offer my Heart), a song composed by the Argentine leftist rock *cantautor* Fito Paez, and performed by the leftist Argentine singer Merecedes Sosa, was played in the background before the meeting started. Towards the end of the meeting, a poem by the Chilean Communist poet Pablo Neruda, 'Pido castigo' (I ask for Punishment) was recited and used to critique the Chávez government.
16. http://www.aporrea.org/medios/n182991.html (Last accessed 30 January 2016).
17. *Radio Caracas Televisión Internacional* (RCTV *Internacional*) is a Venezuelan cable television network which was implicated in inciting the 2002 coup attempt against Chávez (McCaughan 2004: 101–8; Stoneman 2008). In 2007, RCTV's terrestrial broadcast licence expired and the government did not renew it. Though

RCTV continued to broadcast online, the opposition protested against the Chávez government's decision not to renew the network's terrestrial broadcast license, seeing this as a curtailment of the freedom of speech.

18. Servando and Florentino and their music, co-written with and produced by Ricardo Montaner, featured in *De Sol a Sol* (1996) and *Yo Sin Ti* (1997), in addition to four films made in the 1990s.

19. The Primera-Mussett brothers later publicly announced and demonstrated their support for the Chávez government, which I discuss further in this chapter.

20. http://www.aporrea.org/actualidad/a1147.html (Last accessed 30 January 2016).

21. See for example http://archivo.abc.com.py/2003-01-03/articulos/27602/soledad-bravo-critica-al-presidente-chavez and http://www.opinionynoticias.com/entrevistas/79-cultura/1015-soledad-bravo- (Last accessed 20 September 2013).

22. Interview with Alí Alejandro Primera, Caracas, July 2005.

23. Interview with Sandino Primera, Caracas, July 2005.

24. Interview with Florentino Primera, Caracas, July 2005.

25. Interview with Juan Simón Primera, Caracas, July 2005.

26. Interview with Sandino Primera, Caracas, July 2005.

27. In December 1999, towards the end of Chávez's first year in office, torrential rains caused massive destruction of property and loss of life in Vargas State. Many of the homes destroyed and the people killed were of poor barrios.

28. Interview with Florentino Primera, Caracas, July 2005.

29. Significantly, as this book was nearing completion in January 2016, fans of the recently deceased David Bowie organised a petition to 'Stop Kanye West from being allowed to record covers of David Bowies [sic] music', arguing 'David Bowie was one of the single most important musicians of the 20th and 21st century, it would be a sacrilege to let it be ruined by Kanye West'. (https://you.38degrees.org.uk/petitions/stop-kenye-west-recording-covers-of-david-bowies-music, last accessed 25 January 2016).

30. http://www.youtube.com/watch?v=3exhvD51Tqk (Last accessed 8 January 2016).

31. For ease of reading, I have used Standard English grammar, spelling and punctuation in my translations of these comments and include the original Spanish in footnotes. 'estoy seguro que si ali

primera estuviera vivo no estaría en contra de chavez. busca una canción, o crea una, en la que expreses tu descontento pero no hagas esto tan indecoroso'.

32. Si Alí estuviese vivo, tendría 100 canciones insultando a Chavez.

33. tu crees que Alí apoyaba a locos ... como estaria azotando a Chavez con sus canciones al ver los hospitales abandonados, los pordioseros en las calles y a los neosocialoistas ... en sus hummers, mansiones y viajes al exterior ... Tú no tienes ni idea de quien fue Ali Primera.

34. The Spanish *vendepatrias* is usually translated as 'traitor', but it literally means 'one who sells the homeland'.

35. Ali debe estar retorciéndose en su tumba viendo cómo Chávez ha arruinado toda la posibilidad de un verdadero cambio en nuestra sociedad, destruyendo todo lo que medio sirve y regalando nuestros recursos a otros Paises para comprar sus votos internacionales. En estos tiempos vale la pena escuchar la canción de Alí Primera 'Ahora que el petroleo es nuestro'. Chavez, nadie puede decir que seas un vendepatria porque en realidad la estas regalando!!!

36. Si el cantor del pueblo estuviera vivo se hubiera decepcionado completamente de esta farsa que se hace llamar Socialismo del siglo XXI. Sobre todo por los que estan en el gobierno que ahora son nuevos ricos usando ropa y relojes de marca....

37. k mierda dan pena los de lo oposicion vnzola tomar la letra y musika y memoria de este gran cantante venezolano.. para cuestionar al Presidente venezolano....que pena dan de verdad.... esta cancion fue echa ants de k chavez tomara el poder ANIMAL ESCORIA DE LA VIDA..!!!!

38. Oye contrarrevolucionario chuparin80, Ali primera murio hace 22 años, este videoclip manipulado no tiene nada que ver con el actual gobierno Bolivariano xdespertarx

39. Esta cancion protestaba contra el gobierno democratico de la epoca 70–80. Si ponen atencion a la letra y conocen un poco la Venezuela actual (despues de 11 años con Chavez), veran que en realidad todo sigue igual, o tal vez peor pues, Chavez fomento el odio, la division, el racismo y cambió la actitud hacia el logro y el merito, por la exaltacion a la mediocridad y la genuflexion....

40. esta cansion si esta buena para dedicarsela al presidente.q pajuos los q escuchan al gran ali primera y lo usan como propaganda para el

ique socialismo q predican.....gafos dejen de ser tan ignorantes iy abran los ojos de verdad.

41. Argentinean rock Group that composed and sang rock music in Spanish.

42. Ali Primera no era practicamente conocido en Vzla, yo vivi toooda la epoca de Ali En Vzla hasta cuando murio, asi que nadie me puede hacer cuento. Ali Sensurado? por favor!!! que radio en los 70 y 80 va a pasar esta porqueria de musica. En esa epoca no pasaban ni Rock en espanol, solo ponian musica americana. Acaso 'Soda Stereo' tambien estaban sensudados? Despierta!

43. Que porqueria de musica. Ni sus propios hijos sigueron su absurda idiologia (sic), creo que solo eso ya dice bastante. Ali Primera nunca fue nadie, solo lo conocían los 4 coministas que habian en Vzla en aquel entonces. Si sus canciones no hablaran de comunismo estaria ahora olvidado en el basusreo de la historia, como tantos otros muchisimo mejores que el.

44. Acaso no has comprendido que no soy Chavista, estamos en la misma lucha? Ali fue acaparado por los chavistas injustamente, el 'comunismo' de Ali era otra cosa, nada que ver con esta mierda? por eso lo defiendo.

CHAPTER 8

Latin American New Song: An Enduring Legacy

'*Alí Primera es el alma nacional*' ('Alí Primera is the national soul'), answered President Hugo Chávez when, after an official speech he gave in London in May 2006, I had the opportunity to ask him what Alí Primera represented for Venezuela. To explore the significance of Alí Primera's *Canción Necesaria* for Chávez in the twenty-first century, in this book I started by examining how the *Nueva Canción* movement within which Alí Primera operated was invested with political meaning in Latin America in the 1960s–1980s. Influenced by the Cuban revolution and the leftist struggles of the 1960s, Latin American *Nueva Canción cantautores* approached the composition, performance and dissemination of music and song in new ways. Rejecting the label 'protest song', they sought not only to denounce injustices but also to convey hopes for a better future and to represent and value the daily reality of marginalised peoples in their countries. In their songs they primarily used historically repressed native musical forms and socially engaged lyrics to express their dream of a unified continent, free from US imperialist intervention, in which the cultural worth of the urban and rural masses would be recognised and greater social and economic equality would be achieved. They sought to create a non-commercial popular music, based on local traditions and realities, which would counteract foreign cultural influence and function as an 'authentic' representation of ordinary people's daily struggles and experiences in their countries.

© The Editors (if applicable) and the Authors 2016
H. Marsh, *Hugo Chávez, Alí Primera and Venezuela*,
DOI 10.1057/978-1-137-57968-3_8

207

The music became part of the social struggles it was tied to; it was not only symbolic of those struggles, but the very act of engaging with the songs constituted a form of political expression. The making and sharing of music was itself perceived as 'participative social action' (Fairley 2013: 124). Tied to the social and political struggles of the 1960s and 1970s, *Nueva Canción* united a generation of young urban *cantautores* and their audiences in a loose network, which crossed and transcended party political lines. Although at the end of the twentieth century *Nueva Canción* may have appeared to have lost its relevance, the active and dynamic uses of the enduring legacy of Alí Primera's songs in the Chávez period supports Jan Fairley's claims (2013) for the influence and longevity of the movement. The fact that the movement was not tied exclusively to one political party, that it was not restricted to 'protest song', that it encompassed a broad and diverse array of music styles and genres that symbolically linked regions and countries throughout Latin America and the Caribbean, and that musicians brought together through the movement maintained close ties with the audiences they sought to represent and were not perceived to profit financially from their performances and recordings, all combined to endow *Nueva Canción* with an enduring social and political significance beyond the time frame of its original emergence in the 1960s and 1970s.

Alí Primera was shaped by the *Nueva Canción* movement, which he adapted to local circumstances. In his songs, he articulated a leftist critique of local Venezuelan conditions; the social, cultural, economic and environmental impact of the oil industry, the prevalence of racist patterns of thought and cultural worth, the 'pacification' programme of the Punto Fijo system, and the prevailing cultural and political influence of the USA. Refusing to become too closely identified with any single political party, in his *Canción Necesaria* he expressed a broadly anti-imperialist, anti-capitalist line of political thought, aimed at uniting the left, which was easily adaptable to the ideologies of a wide spectrum of political parties and organisations. His music was based on an ample range of national traditions, thus appealing to large and diverse sectors of the population, and his lyrics drew on local customs, myths and symbols. In particular, he revived and reinterpreted the thought of the Liberator, Simón Bolívar, in order to comment on the perceived failures of the prevailing political and social Punto Fijo order he lived under.

In addition to his music, Alí's communication with his audiences was based on his self-representation, in numerous interviews with the leftist press, as an artist whose *Canción Necesaria* was born of personal experience of hardship, suffering and repression at the hands of the Punto Fijo state. Alí constructed himself in his narratives as a *cantautor* who identified with and spoke for the poor and oppressed, who rejected fame and fortune, and who defied state attempts to intimidate him in order to continue to fight for his ideals through the composition and performance of his songs. These narratives added to Alí's perceived qualities as a cultural and political spokesperson for *el pueblo*, and helped to legitimate him as a committed artist of great moral integrity in the eyes of his audiences.

Alí's own narratives influenced the ways in which his supporters interpreted and spoke about his music in Venezuela in the decade after his death; journalists and writers repeated and re-circulated the *cantautor*'s stories about his humble origins, his refusal to profit personally from his music, and his persecution at the hands of state authorities. Certain biographical elements were selected and highlighted in commemorative articles; his connection with *el pueblo*, his dedication to the poor and the oppressed, his personal suffering on account of this dedication and commitment, and his perceived martyrdom. Other less flattering qualities and failed endeavours, such as his marital infidelity, his illegitimate child while married to Sol and his failure to be elected as a congressman for the *Liga Socialista* (Socialist League) in December 1983, were suppressed and erased from the collective memory in an apparent attempt to not detract from the construction of an exemplary, selfless and irreproachable popular hero in the collective memory.

The 'dynamic' approach conceives of collective memory as an ongoing process of negotiation in which people selectively use the past to interpret current reality, and the past endures and shapes perceptions of the present. In the decade after his death, Alí remained a dynamic force in the collective memory; at a time of dramatically increasing poverty and political repression, the collective memory selectively elevated and lifted out the features from Alí's life that were useful for the creation and articulation of knowledge about the present. Current needs influenced how the past was remembered and represented, and shaped the construction of the memory of a flawless figure whose moral and artistic integrity served to highlight the perceived corruption and greed of present political leaders. At the same time, the broad leftist and oppositional associations of Alí's songs endured in the collective memory and shaped the ways in which people experienced the economic and political crisis of *Puntofijismo*; Alí's

Canción Necesaria provided a vocabulary that people remembered and used in order to make sense of and express opposition to the prevailing political order.

Venezuelans dynamically selected elements from the past to bring to bear on their interpretation of the present; Alí's biography exemplified an oppositional set of moral and political values, embodied in *Canción Necesaria*, with which to construct grassroots communities of resistance encompassing and uniting a broad and diverse party-political spectrum. Grassroots commemorative practices and the memorialisation of Alí's life and songs created spaces that functioned as a form of social activism in the decade after his death. Alí's legacy came to constitute a unique realm for Venezuelans; at a time of political and economic crisis, and during the political repression of the *Caracazo*, Alí's songs were re-signified and re-interpreted in order to create and circulate knowledge and understandings of the present and to articulate oppositional values in aesthetic form.

Chávez did not 'invent' *ex novo* the political significance of Alí in the mid-1990s; in speeches, interviews and political rallies, he connected with and added to pre-existing public narratives about Alí's life and songs and what these represented. Chávez made use of Alí Primera's legacy of *Canción Necesaria*, and stories about Alí's life, to create a political persona with which to construct himself and his political movement as representative of all Venezuela's impoverished, marginalised and oppressed masses, regardless of previous party political affiliation, and as a break with the Punto Fijo past.

In the twenty-first century, the Chávez government used cultural policy to formalise grassroots commemorative practices and memorials, and to construct Alí Primera's songs as precursors of Bolivarianism and as part of the cultural heritage. This was intended to give Alí's *Canción Necesaria* new significance as a symbol of the readjustment of hegemony in favour of the poor and the marginalised. Government support for Alí's legacy in the Chávez period was intended to convey to the public in a direct way that the Chávez government situated itself within local revolutionary paradigms, and that it placed *el pueblo* and their interests and values at the heart of the nation.

State involvement with the legacy of Alí Primera added new meanings to *Canción Necesaria* in the Chávez period. As a result, when Venezuelans heard *Canción Necesaria* or were reminded of Alí Primera's life, they reacted not only to the sound of the music or to the biographical details highlighted in the collective memory, but also to the government's *uses* of that music and those collectively remembered biographical qualities. It was not the sound of *Canción Necesaria* which had changed, but the social and political milieu within which that music now circulated. Official support for Alí's songs meant that Venezuelans could not listen to *Canción Necesaria*, or talk about Alí, in the same way as they had done during the Punto Fijo period. To use Simon Frith's phrase (2004: 20), the music acted as a 'sign' for the Chávez government, and hearing that music prompted Venezuelans to 'hear' the voice of Chávez within it and, therefore, to react not only to *Canción Necesaria* but also to *Chavismo*.

In the Chávez period, Chávez supporters in the barrios predominantly saw Alí's music as a symbol of their historical suppression and marginalisation and of their political and social struggles under *Puntofijismo*. They emphasised their memories of the state persecution and repression which both they and Alí had suffered under the Punto Fijo system. For many, state support for Alí's legacy in the twenty-first century represented official recognition of their history and their contributions to the nation as political activists; it acted as a symbol of the government's identification with the poor and their values and concerns, and of their inclusion, participation and elevated status within a new social and political order.

Opponents frequently ignored Alí in interviews and at oppositional meetings which I attended, while other opponents I interviewed recognised a similarity between the political thought and values of Chávez and those of Alí, but considered these values to be detrimental for the country. Yet other opponents, particularly in on-line forums, contested the official representation of Alí as a precursor of Bolivarianism and harnessed the oppositional qualities of Alí's songs in order to express resistance to the Chávez government. The debates in these on-line forums illustrate how Alí Primera's broadly leftist, anti-imperialist, anti-racist and anti-capitalist discourse, embodied in *Canción Necesaria*, held the power to shape not only the discourse of *Chavismo* but also the discourse of the opposition in the Chávez period; through being given official space by the Chávez government, Alí's legacy provided material for the political right (and the extreme left) to construct oppositional discourses by asserting alternative interpretations of Alí's life and music and contesting those of the government.

In the Chávez period, Venezuelans asserted an array of competing interpretations of Alí's moral, political and artistic worth; both *Chavistas* and *anti-Chavistas* affirmed, negotiated and resisted the 'authenticity' of the past as represented by Chávez and his supporters. Venezuelans from across the political spectrum debated the impact and meaning of Alí's legacy for the present, and argued about the perceived distortions of the past propounded by groups with which they were not in political agreement. Both *Chavistas* and *anti-Chavistas* upheld their claims to be the 'authentic' interpreters of the legacy of Alí and the meaning of *Canción Necesaria*.

These competing debates illustrate the paradoxes and contradictions that state co-optation of leftist popular musical legacies may give rise to at a time of leftist political transition; state promotion of Alí's legacy was neither universally accepted nor universally rejected but instead was actively engaged with by Venezuelans, whose various competing interpretations of Alí's worth and meaning constituted a symbolic political language through which *Chavismo* was defended, criticised and contested. Discourses about the meaning and value of Alí's legacy of *Canción Necesaria* became symbolic discourses about the meaning and value of *Chavismo*.

Alí Primera's *Canción Necesaria* had an important social and political impact in Venezuela in the 1970s and the 1980s, but its impact was not confined to this period. Alí's music legacy, collectively remembered, continued to play a significant part in leftist struggles against the Punto Fijo system in the 1990s, and in the twenty-first century this music played an important role in the Chávez government's cultural politics. Alí Primera's *Canción Necesaria* enabled Chávez to construct a political persona that resonated profoundly with the oppressed and marginalised masses; popular music connected Chávez with his supporters in a powerful way and, arguably, it contributed greatly to his first electoral success in 1998 and to the subsequent electoral successes of his government.

The power and enduring influence of popular music legacies derive not uniquely from musicians' intentions, nor from social movement actors reviving and mapping meaning onto popular music traditions in order to highlight political causes. Instead, the power and influence of music legacies lie in their capacity to be constantly re-interpreted in order to make meaning in the present; music legacies are actively and simultaneously engaged with by competing groups, for different purposes and with different goals, in a dynamic process involving a complex interplay of past associations and present needs.

Political and cultural values are not inherent in music itself but are instead actively ascribed and attached to music in complex ways, which are in turn shaped by biographical, institutional, economic and political factors. These values are continually negotiated and re-negotiated over time to create meaning in the world; music audiences dynamically engage with others' constructions of musical worth, both those promoted by the state and those advanced by competing social groups, in order to legitimate, oppose or negotiate those constructions. The critique of music, therefore, becomes a form of social and political critique. In many ways, Alí Primera's *Canción Necesaria*, and the ways in which it was collectively remembered at grassroots levels, actively shaped and influenced the political communication of Hugo Chávez when he stood in opposition to the state. In the twenty-first century, the Chávez government used the state's resources and cultural policy to promote Alí Primera's *Canción Necesaria* legacy and incorporate it into the national cultural heritage as a precursor of Bolivarianism. I have argued that this was neither an emancipating rupture of hegemony emerging spontaneously from below, nor an imposition of social control enforced from above. The Chávez government associated itself with Alí Primera's legacy of *Canción Necesaria* in order to connect with and raise the status of the masses, but this was a complex, dynamic and paradoxical process, which produced competing power struggles over *who* was best placed to legitimately interpret the music 'correctly'. State incorporation of Alí's legacy endowed the songs with new significance as a space in which political alternatives for the twenty-first century were not only imagined and shared, but also defended, challenged and resisted by Venezuelans actively locating themselves and redefining their relation to the state within a new social and political order.

In Venezuela, Alí Primera's *Canción Necesaria* has been drawn into repeated use in different ways over the decades. On 5 March 2013, the then Venezuelan Vice President Nicolás Maduro officially announced that President Hugo Chávez Frías had died, after battling for almost two years with cancer, at 4.25 pm that afternoon. In his announcement, Maduro urged Venezuelans to be strong and not lose hope. And he did this by inviting the nation to turn, once again, to Alí Primera and his songs:

> Let us take [with us] our songs of homage and honour to our heroes, let us take the songs of Alí Primera; 'Those who die for the sake of life cannot be called dead, and from this moment it is forbidden to cry for them'. Let us rise with the songs of Alí and the spirit of Hugo Chávez, the greatest forces of this land, in order to face whatever difficulties we may have to face ...[1]

How Alí Primera's songs will be understood and used in Venezuela in the post-Chávez period, it remains to be seen.

NOTE

1. My translation here is consistent with the transcript provided by rtve.es – see the first link below. However, a different interpretation arises if 'las fuerzas' are taken to be the object of the verb 'levantar', in which case the message would read 'Let us raise the greatest forces of this land with the songs of Alí and the spirit of Hugo Chávez, in order to face whatever difficulties we may have to face' – which, having listened to the speech given by Maduro (see second link below), I feel is more faithful to the original Spanish.

   rtve.es transcript: Que llevemos nuestros cantos de homenaje y de honor a nuestros héroes, que llevemos el canto de Alí Primera 'Los que mueren por la vida no pueden llamarse muertos y a partir de este momento es prohibido llorarlos'. ¡Levantemos con el canto de Alí y el espíritu de Hugo Chávez, las fuerzas más grandes de esta patria, para afrontar las dificultades que nos toque afrontar ...

   http://traducompol.com/wp-content/uploads/2013/03/Transcripción-Discurso-Nicolás-Maduro_anuncio-muerte-Hugo-Chávez.jpg (Last accessed 1 April 2013).

   http://multimedia.telesurtv.net/media/telesur.video.web/telesur-web/#!es/video/vicepresidente-maduro-anuncia-fallecimiento-de-hugo-chavez (Last accessed 1 April 2013).

Discography

1969 *Vamos gente de mi tierra.*	Partido Comunista de Venezuela
1969 *Canciones de protesta*	Juventud Comunista de Venezuela
1972 *De una vez (Canciones del Tercer Mundo – Para Un Solo Mundo)*	Verlag Plane (East Germany)
1972 *Alí Primera: Venezuela*	Verlag Plane (East Germany)
1974 *Lo primero de Alí Primera*	Cigarrón – Promus (Venezuela)
1974 *Alí Primera, Volumen 2*	Cigarrón – Promus (Venezuela)
1975 *Adiós en dolor mayor*	Cigarrón – Promus (Venezuela)
1975 *La patria es el hombre*	Cigarrón – Promus (Venezuela)
1976 *Canción para los valientes*	Cigarrón – Promus (Venezuela)
1978 *Cuando nombro la poesía*	Cigarrón – Promus (Venezuela)
1978 *Canción mansa para un pueblo bravo*	Cigarrón – Promus (Venezuela)
1979 *Abrebrecha, y mañana hablamos*	Cigarrón – Promus (Venezuela)
1981 *Al pueblo lo que es de César*	Cigarrón – Promus (Venezuela)
1983 *Con el sol a medio cielo*	Cigarrón – Promus (Venezuela)
1984 *Entre la rabia y la ternura*	Cigarrón – Promus (Venezuela)
1985 *Por si no lo sabía* (posthumous)	Cigarrón – Velvet – Sonográfica (Venezuela)
1986 *Alí ¡En vivo!* (posthumous)	Cigarrón – Promus (Venezuela)

Source for Venezuelan albums: CD ROM *Alí Primera: El cantor del pueblo* (Oscar Arango, Caracas, 2004).

East German albums: author's own collection.

© The Editors (if applicable) and the Authors 2016
H. Marsh, *Hugo Chávez, Alí Primera and Venezuela*,
DOI 10.1057/978-1-137-57968-3

215

REFERENCES

Antequera, J. (2008). Palabra, canto y poesía. Orígenes de la nueva canción latino-americana: oralidad y difusión poética. Fondo Editorial Ipasme. Caracas.

Arango, O. (2004). *Alí Primera: El cantor del pueblo*. Caracas: CD-ROM.

Aretz, I. (1990). *Música de los aborígenes de Venezuela*. Caracas: FUNDEF-CONAC.

Arzola Castellanos, A. (2005). *La desaparición forzada en Venezuela 1960–1969*. Tropykos: Caracas.

Austerlitz, P. (1997). *Merengue: Dominican music and dominican identity*. Philadelphia: Temple University Press.

Azzi, M. (2002). The tango, peronism, and Astor Piazzolla during the 1940s and '50s'. In W. Clark (Ed.), *From Tejano to Tango*. New York: Routledge.

Baker, G. (2011a). *Buena Vista in the Club: Rap, reggaetón, and revolution in Havana* ((Refiguring American Music)). Durham: Duke University Press.

Baker, G. (2011b). Cuba rebelión: Underground music in Havana. *Latin American Music Review, 32*(1), 1–38.

Baker, G. (2012). Mala Bizta Sochal Klu: Underground, alternative and commercial in Havana Hip Hop. *Popular Music, 31*(1), 1–24.

Baty, S. (1995). *American Monroe: The making of a body politic*. California/London: University of California Press.

Béhague, G. (1979). *Music of Latin America: An introduction*. Englewood Cliffs: Prentice-Hall, Inc.

Béhague, G. (1994). *Music and black ethnicity: The Caribbean and South America*. New Brunswick: Transaction Publishers.

Benmayor, R. (1981). La Nueva Trova: New Cuban song. *Latin American Music Review, 2*(1), 11–44.

© The Editors (if applicable) and the Authors 2016
H. Marsh, *Hugo Chávez, Alí Primera and Venezuela*,
DOI 10.1057/978-1-137-57968-3

Bermúdez, E. and Martínez, G. (2000). Hugo Chávez: la articulación de un sentido para la acción colectiva. 54/*Espacio Abierto* Volume 9, Issue 1. http://www.redalyc.org/pdf/122/12290104.pdf. Accessed 4 Sept 2013.

Bianchi, S., & Bocaz, L. (1978). Discusión sobre la música chilena. *Araucaria, 2,* 111–73.

Bigott, L. (2005). *Alí Primera: No sólo de vida vive el hombre.* Caracas: Editorial El Tapial.

Blake, C. (2005). *Politics in Latin America.* Boston/New York: Houghton Mifflin Company.

Borland, K. (2002). Marimba: Dance of the revolutionaries, Dance of the folk. *Radical History Review, 84,* 77–107.

Brandt, M. (1994). African drumming from rural communities around Caracas and its impact on venezuelan music and ethnic identity. In G. Béhague (Ed.), *Music and black ethnicity: The Caribbean and South America.* New Brunswick/London: Transaction Publishers.

Brandt, M. (2008). Venezuela. In D. Olsen & D. Sheehy (Eds.), *The Garland handbook of Latin American music.* New York: Routledge.

Brister, J. (1980). Letter from Santiago. *Index on Censorship, 9*(1), 55–60.

Brown, R., & Kulik, J. (1977). Flashbulb memories. *Cognition, 5*(1), 73–99.

Brunk, S., & Fallaw, B. (Eds.). (2006). *Heroes and hero cults in Latin America.* Austin: University of Texas Press.

Buxton, J. (2005). Venezuela's contemporary political crisis in historical context. *Bulletin of Latin American Research, 24*(3), 328–347.

Buxton, J. (2011). Venezuela's Bolivarian democracy. In D. Smilde & D. Hellinger (Eds.), *Venezuela's Bolivarian democracy: Participation, politics, and culture under Chávez.* Durham: Duke University Press.

Cabezas, M. (1977). The Chilean New Song. *Index on Censorship, 6*(4), 30–36.

Cañas, D. (2007). El perfume de la Nueva Canción. Valoración del canto de Gloria Martín. In Presente y pasado: Revista de la historia. Año 12. No. 23. pp. 45–67.

Cannon, B. (2008). Class/Race polarisation in Venezuela and the electoral success of Hugo Chávez: A break with the past or the song remains the same? *Third World Quarterly, 29*(4), 731–748.

Carrasco, E. (1982). The Nueva Canción in Latin America. *International Social Science Journal, 34*(4), 599–623.

Castillo, A. (1999). *El sonido de una huella.* Caracas: Talleres de Gráficas Mateprint.

Castillo, A., & Marroquí, G. (2005). *Alí Primera a quemarropa.* Caracas: Ministerio de Educación Superior.

Castro, D. (1998). Carlos Gardel and the Argentine Tango. In W. Washabaugh (Ed.), *The passion of music and dance.* Oxford: Berg.

Chávez, H. (1999). Speech given at the Palacio Federal Legislativo. Available at: http://eficem.an.gob.ve/documentos/TomoI_HugoChavezDiscursos DelComandanteSupremoAnteLaAsambleaNacional_1999-2001.pdf. Accessed 15 Sept 2013.

Chávez, H. (2003). *El golpe fasdsta contra Venezuela*. La Habana: Ediciones Plaza.

Chávez, H. (2006, September 3). *Áló Presidente* no. 261. Academia Militar de Venezuela, Fuerte Tiuna.

Chávez, H. (2007, January 8). Palabras del presidente reelecto Hugo Chavez Frias, durante acto de juramentacion en el Teatro Teresa Carrefio. *ABN-Agencia Bolivariana de Noticias.*

Conway, M. (1997). The inventory of experience: Memory and identity. In J. Pennebaker, D. Paez, & B. Rimé (Eds.), *Collective memory of political events: Social psychological perspectives.* Mahwah: Lawrence Erlbaum Associates.

Cushman, T. (1991). Rich rastas and communist rockers: A comparative study of the origin, diffusion and defusion of revolutionary musical codes. *Journal of Popular Culture, 25*(3), 17–58.

Davies, N. (1995). *The Incas.* Boulder: University Press of Colorado.

Denisoff, R., & Peterson, R. (Eds.). (1972). *The sounds of social change.* Chicago: Rand-McNally.

Díaz Pérez, C. (1994). *Sobre la guitarra, la voz: Una historia de la nueva trova cubana.* Havana: Editorial letras Cubanas.

Dore, E. (1985). Culture. In T. Walker (Ed.), *Nicaragua: The first five years.* New York: Praeger.

Dorfman, A. & Matterlart, A. (1984). How to read Donald Duck: Imperialist ideology in disney comics (Trans: and with an introduction by Kunzle, D.) New York: International General.

Ellner, S. (1988). *Venezuela's movement toward socialism: From Guerrilla defeat to innovative politics.* Durham/London: Duke University Press.

Ellner, S. (2005). Introduction: The search for explanations. In S. Ellner & D. Hellinger (Eds.), *Venezuelan politics in the Chávez Era: Class, polarization and conflict.* London: Lynne Rienner Publishers.

Ellner, S., & Hellinger, D. (Eds.). (2005). *Venezuelan politics in the Chávez Era: Class, polarization and conflict.* London: Lynne Rienner Publishers.

Ellner, S., & Salas, T. (2005). Introduction: The Venezuelan exceptionalism thesis: Separating myth from reality. *Latin American Perspectives, 32*(2), 5–19.

Eyerman, R., & Jamison, A. (1998). *Music and social movements: Mobilizing traditions in the twentieth century.* Cambridge: Cambridge University Press.

Fairclough, N. (1992). *Discourse and social change.* Cambridge: Polity Press.

Fairley, J. (1984). La Nueva Canción Latinoamericana. *Bulletin of Latin American Research, 3*(2), 107–115.

Fairley, J. (1989). Analysing performance: Narrative and ideology in concerts by ¡Karaxú!. *Popular Music, 8*(1).

Fairley, J. (2000). An uncompromising song. In S. Broughton & M. Ellington (Eds.), *World music: The rough guide* (Vol. 2). London: Rough Guides.

Fairley, J. (2013). There is no revolution without song: New Song in Latin America. In B. Norton & B. Kutschke (Eds.), *Music and protest in 1968.* New York: Cambridge University Press.

Fernandes, S. (2010). *Who can stop the drums?: Urban social movements in Chávez's Venezuela*. Durham/London: Duke University Press.

Field, L. (1995). Constructing local identities in a revolutionary nation: The cultural politics of the Artisan class in Nicaragua, 1970–90. *American Ethnologist, 22*(4), 786–806.

Frazer, C. (2006). *Bandit nation*. Lincoln/London: University of Nebraska Press.

Freire, P. (1970). *Pedagogy of the oppressed*. New York: Continuum.

Frith, S. (2004). What is bad music? In C. Washburne & M. Derno (Eds.), *Bad music: The music we love to hate*. New York: Routledge.

Galeano, E. (1973). The open veins of Latin America: Five centuries of the pillage of a continent. (trans: Belfrage, C.). New York and London: Monthly Review Press.

Gámez Torres, N. (2013). "Rap is War": Los Aldeanos and the politics of music subversion in contemporary Cuba. *Transcultural Music Review, 17*, 1–23.

García, R. (2007). El Día que Dejemos Ir al Camarada Alí Primera, Hugo. http://www.aporrea.org/oposicion/a30174.html%20. Accessed 30 Jan 2016.

García Canclini, N. (1992). Culture and power: The state of research. In P. Scannell, P. Schlesinger, & C. Sparks (Eds.), *Culture and power: A media, culture and society reader*. London: Sage.

Gilbert, G. (1998). *The Latin American city*. London: LAB.

González, C. (2006). Con Las Espuelas Puestas. Alí Primera, Chávez. Venezuela. http://www.aporrea.org/actualidad/a26648.html. Accessed 30 Jan 2016.

Gott, R. (2000). *In the shadow of the liberator: Hugo Chávez and the transformation of Venezuela*. London: Verso Books.

Gott, R. (2005). *Hugo Chávez and the Bolivarian revolution*. London/New York: Verso.

Gott, R. (2007). Latin America as a white settler society. *Bulletin of Latin American Research, 26*(2), 269–289.

Gott, R. (2013). Man against the world. *New Statesman*. 25–31 January. pp. 20–23

Gottberg, L. (2010). Mob outrages: Reflections on the media construction of the masses in Venezuela (April 2000–January 2003). *Journal of Latin American Cultural Studies, 13*(1), 115–135.

Gottberg, L. (2011). The color of mobs: Racial politics, ethnopopulism, and representation in the Chávez Era. In D. Smilde & D. Hellinger (Eds.), *Venezuela's Bolivarian democracy: Participation, politics, and culture under Chávez*. Durham: Duke University Press.

Graham, B., & Howard, P. (2008). *The Ashgate research companion to heritage and identity*. Aldershot: Ashgate.

Green, D. (1997). *Faces of Latin America*. London: LAB.

Guerrero Pérez, J. (2005). *La canción protesta latinoamericana y la Teología de la Liberación: Estudio de un género musical y análisis de vínculo sociopolítico y religioso (1968–2000)*. Monte Ávila Editores Latinoamericana: Centro de Estudios Latinoamericanos Rómulo Gallegos. Caracas.

Guss, D. (2000). *The festive state: Race, ethnicity, and nationalism as cultural performance.* Berkeley: University of California Press.

Gutiérrez, G. (1974). A theology of liberation: History, politics and salvation. (trans: Sister Caridad Inda and Eagleson, J.). London: S.C.M. Press.

Hall, S. (2005). Whose heritage? Un-settling 'the Heritage', Re-imagining the Post-Nation. In J. Littler & R. Naidoo (Eds.), *The politics of heritage and legacies of 'Race'.* London/New York: Routledge.

Hampton, W. (1986). Guerrilla Minstrels. Knoxville: University of Tennessee Press.

Hardy, Charles. (Undated). A love (and Hate) story, part 3. www.vheadline.com/printer_news.asp?id=6956. Accessed 25 Apr 2005.

Hawkins, K., Rosas, G., & Johnson, M. (2011). The misiones of the Chávez government. In D. Smilde & D. Hellinger (Eds.), *Venezuela's Bolivarian democracy: Participation, politics, and culture under Chávez.* Durham: Duke University Press.

Hay, J. (2013). Interview with Armand Matterlart. Communication and critical/cultural Studies. pp. 1–16. http://www.academia.edu/2976917/Interview_with_Armand_Mattelart. Accessed 25 Aug 2013.

Hellinger, D. (2011). Defying the iron law of oligarchy II: Debating democracy online in Venezuela. In D. Smilde & D. Hellinger (Eds.), *Venezuela's Bolivarian democracy: Participation, politics, and culture under Chávez.* Durham: Duke University Press.

Hernández Medina, J. (1991). *Alí Primera: Huella profunda sobre esta tierra. Vida y obra.* Editorial Escritos S.A.: Universidad de Zulia.

Herrera Salas, J. (2007). The political economy of racism in Venezuela. In S. Ellner & M. Tinker Salas (Eds.), *Venezuela: Hugo Chávez and the decline of an exceptional democracy.* Lanham: Rowman and Littlefield.

Hesmondhalgh, D. (2013). *Why music matters.* Chichester/Malden: John Wiley & Sons Ltd/ Wiley-Blackwell.

Hidalgo Quero, H. (1998). *Alí Primera: herido de vida.* IUTAG: Coro, Falcón.

Hobsbawm, E., & Ranger, T. (1983). *The invention of tradition.* Cambridge: Cambridge University Press.

Jara, J. (1998). *Victor: An unfinished song.* London: Bloomsbury.

Johnson, L. (Ed.). (2004). *Death, dismemberment, and memory in Latin America.* Albuquerque: University of New Mexico Press.

Kane, J. (2001). *The politics of moral capital.* Cambridge: Cambridge University Press.

Kapcia, A. (2000). *Cuba: Island of dreams.* New York: Berg.

Kozinets, R., Dolbec, P., & Earley, A. (2014). Netnographic analysis: Understanding culture through social media data. In U. Flick (Ed.), *The sage handbook of qualitative data analysis.* Los Angeles: Sage.

Kronenberg, C. (2011). Che and the Pre-eminence of culture in revolutionary Cuba: The pursuit of a spontaneous, inseparable integrity. *Cultural Politics, 7*(2), 189–218.

Kuhn, A. (2000). A journey through memory. In S. Radstone (Ed.), *Memory and methodology*. Oxford/New York: Berg.

Kuhn, A. (2010). Memory texts and memory work: Performances of memory in and with visual media. *Memory Studies, 3*(4), 298–313.

Labonville, M. (2007). *Juan Bautista Plaza and Musical Nationalism in Venezuela*. Bloomington: Indiana University Press.

Lander, E. (2005). Venezuelan social conflict in a global context. *Latin American Perspectives, 32*(2), 20–38.

Lanz Rodriguez, C. (2004). La revolución es cultural o reproducirá la dominación. http://www.minci.gob.ve/libros_folletos/6/p--19/tp--27/libros_folletos.html. Accessed 26 Nov 2010.

Lawler, S. (2002). Narrative in social research. In T. May (Ed.), *Qualitative research in action*. London: Sage.

Livingstone, G. (2009). *America's backyard: The United States and Latin America from the Monroe Doctrine to the war on terror*. London/New York: Zed Books.

Lombardi, J. (1981). *Venezuela: The search for order, the dream of progress*. Oxford University Press: New York/Oxford.

López Maya, M. (2005). Hugo Chávez Frías: His movement and his presidency. In S. Ellner & D. Hellinger (Eds.), *Venezuelan politics in the Chávez Era: Class, polarization and conflict*. London: Lynne Rienner Publishers.

López Maya, M. and Lander, L. (2005). Popular protest in Venezuela: Novelties and continuities. *Latin American Perspectives. 32*(2), 92–108.

López Maya, M., & Lander, L. (2011). Participatory democracy in Venezuela: Origins, ideas, and implementation. In D. Smilde & D. Hellinger (Eds.), *Venezuela's Bolivarian democracy: Participation, politics, and culture under Chávez*. Durham: Duke University Press.

Loyola, B. (2011). Bolivarian Headbangin. http://www.vice.com/read/bolivarian-headbangin-v18n9?Contentpage=-1. Accessed 30 Jan 2016.

Manuel, P. (1988). *Popular musics of the Non-Western world*. New York: Oxford University Press.

Margry, P., & Sánchez-Carretero, C. (Eds.). (2011). *Grassroots memorials: The politics of memorializing traumatic death*. New York/Oxford: Berghahn Books.

Márquez, A. (1983). When ponchos are subversive. *Index on Censorship*. Part 1. pp. 8–10.

Marschall, S. (2008). The heritage of post-Colonial societies. In B. Graham & P. Howard (Eds.), *The Ashgate research companion to heritage and identity*. Aldershot: Ashgate.

Martín, G. (1998). *El perfume de una época*. Alfadil: Caracas.

Mayhall, M. (2005). Modernist but not exceptional. *Latin American Perspectives, 32*(2), 124–146.

McCaughan, M. (2004). *The battle of Venezuela*. London: Latin American Bureau.

McPherson, A. (2003). *Yankee No! Anti-Americanism in US-Latin American relations*. Cambridge, MA: Harvard University Press.

Michelutti, L. (2013). Post-secularity and political hope in 21st century socialism. In T. Muhr (Ed.), *Counter-globalization and socialism in the 21st century: The bolivarian alliance for the peoples of our America*. London/New York: Routledge.

Miller, N. (2008). A revolutionary modernity: The cultural policy of the Cuban revolution. *The Journal of Latin American Studies, 40*, 675–696.

Miller, T., & Yúdice, G. (2002). *Cultural policy*. London: Sage.

Misztal, B. (2000). Theories of social remembering. OUP; Maidenhead and Philadelphia.

Moore, R. (2006). *Music and revolution: Cultural change and socialist Cuba*. Berkeley: University of California Press.

Moreno, A. (1986). Violeta Parra and *La nueva canción chilena*. *Studies in Latin American Popular Culture, 5*, 108–126.

Morris, N. (1986). Canto porque es necesario cantar: The new song movement in Chile, 1973–1983. *Latin American Research Review, XXI*(1), 117–136.

Mulcahy, K. (2008). Identity and cultural policy. Conference paper published online. http://iccpr2008.yeditepe.edu.tr/papers/Mulcahykevin.doc. Accessed 15 Oct 2009.

Muskus, Z., & Vasquez, J. (2004). *Los personajes en las canciones de Alí Primera*. Trujillo: Fondo Editorial Arturo Cardozo.

Nandorfy, M. (2003). The right to live in peace: Freedom and social justice in the songs of Violeta Parra and Víctor Jara. In D. Fischlin & A. Heble (Eds.), *Rebel musics: Human rights, Resistant sounds and the politics of music making*. New York: Black Rose Books.

Obregón Múñoz, H. (1996). Ali Primera o el poder de la música. Universidad Pedagógica Experimental Libertador/Maracay: Centro de Investigaciones Lingüísticas y Literarias.

Olsen, D. A. (1980). Symbol and function in South American Indian music. In E. May (Ed.), *Musics of many cultures: An introduction*. Berkeley/Los Angeles: University of California Press.

Olsen, D. A. (1996). *Music of the Warao of Venezuela*. Gainesville: University Press of Florida.

Party, D. (2010). Beyond protest song: Popular music in Pinochet's Chile (1973–1990). In R. Illiano & M. Sala (Eds.), *Music and dictatorship in Europe and Latin America*. Turnhout: Brepols Publishers.

Paz, M. A. (1990). *La poesía en la voz de un cantor*. Venezuela: Coordinación del Estado Falcón.

Pearson, T. (2009). Venezuela Celebrates 10 Years of "Hello President" Show with 4 Day Long Program. http://venezuelanalysis.com/news/4479. Accessed 6 Sept 2013.

Pedrazzini, I., & Sánchez, M. (1992). *Malandros, bandas y niños de la calle: Cultura de urgencia en la metrópolis latinoamericana*. Valencia: Hermanos Vadell Editores.

Peraza, Porfirio; Millet, José; Peraza, Wilmer; Ramírez, Víctor (2005). *Alí Primera: entre la rabia y la ternura.* Lara: CONCULTURA.

Plesch, M. (2013). Demonizing and redeeming the gaucho: Social conflict, xenophobia and the invention of Argentine national music. *Patterns of Prejudice,* 47(4–5), 337–358.

Pratt, R. (1990). *Rhythm and resistance: Explorations in the political uses of popular music.* New York: Praeger.

Pring-Mill, R. (1979). The nature and functions of Spanish American POESIA DE COMPROMISO. *Bulletin of the Society for Latin American Studies, 31,* 4–21.

Pring-Mill, R. (1987). The roles of revolutionary song – a Nicaraguan assessment. *Popular Music, 6*(2), 179–189.

Pring-Mill, R. (1990). *Gracias a la vida: The power and poetry of song.* London: University of London: Dept. of Hispanic Studies.

Pring-Mill, R. (2002). Spanish American committed song: The growth of the 'Pring-Mill collection'. In J. Fairley & D. Horn (Eds.), *I Sing the difference: Identity and commitment in Latin American song.* Liverpool: Institute of Popular Music.

Quintero-Rivera, A. (1994). The Camouflaged drum: Melodization of rhythms and maroonage ethnicity in Caribbean peasant music. In G. Béhague (Ed.), *Music and black ethnicity: The Caribbean and South America.* New Brunswick: Transaction Publishers.

Raby, D. (2006). *Democracy and revolution: Latin America and socialism today.* London: Pluto Press.

Radstone, S. (Ed.). (2000). *Memory and methodology.* Oxford/New York: Berg.

Rangel, J. (2005). Inaugural speech delivered at the opening of the exhibition Alí Primera Forjador de la Buena Patria. http://www.voltairenet.org/article123899.html. Accessed 9 Sept 2013.

Rangel, J. (2012). De Yare a Miraflores el mismo subversivo: Entrevistas al comandante Hugo Chávez Frías (1992–2012). Ediciones Correo del Orinoco. http://www.minci.gob.ve/wp-content/uploads/downloads/2013/03/WEBDEYAREAMIRAFLORES140313terceraSG1.pdf. Accessed 5 Sept 2013.

Rausseo, de Y. (2008). Un Merecido Homenaje en Voz de Mujer. http://www.aporrea.org/ddhh/n109314.html. Accessed 30 Jan 2016.

Reyes Matta, F. (1988). The new song and its confrontation in Latin America. In C. Nelson & L. Grossberg (Eds.), *Marxism and the interpretation of culture* (pp. 447–460). Urbana: University of Illinois Press.

Reygadas, L. (2006). Latin America: Persistent inequality and recent transformations. In E. Hershberg & F. Rosen (Eds.), *Latin America after neoliberalism. Turning the tide in the 21st century?* (pp. 120–143). New York: The New Press.

Rios, F. (2008). *La Flûte Indienne*: The early history of Andean Folkloric-popular music in France and its impact on *Nueva Canción. Latin American Music Review,* 29(2), 145–89.

Romero, R. (2001). *Debating the past: Music, memory, and identity in the Andes.* New York: Oxford University Press.

Rosales, A. and Blough, L. (2012). Paul Gillman wins MTV world poll as the Best Male metal voice of all time. http://axisoflogic.com/artman/publish/Article_64586.shtml. Accessed 30 Jan 2016.

Rowe, W., & Schelling, V. (1991). *Memory and modernity: Popular culture in Latin America.* London/New York: Verso.

Salazar, R. (Undated). *Música y Folklore de Venezuela: El cantor del pueblo.* Federación Nacional de la Cultura Popular.

Sara-Lafosse, V. (2013). Machismo in Latin America and the Caribbean. In N. Stromquist (Ed.), *Women in the third world: An encyclopedia of contemporary issues.* New York: Routledge.

Saunders, T. (2008). *The Cuban remix: Rethinking culture and political participation in contemporary Cuba.* PhD thesis submitted to the University of Michigan.

Schoening, B., & Kasper, E. (2012). *Don't stop thinking about the music: The politics of songs and musicians in presidential campaigns.* Plymouth: Lexington Books.

Scruggs, T. M. (1998). Nicaraguan state cultural initiative and The unseen made manifest. *Yearbook for Traditional Music, 30,* 53–73.

Scruggs, T.M. (2002a). Socially conscious music forming the social conscience: Nicaraguan Música testimonial and the creation of a revolutionary moment. In W. Clark (Ed.), *From Tejano to Tango.* New York and London: Routledge.

Scruggs, T. M. (2002b). Musical style and revolutionary context in Sandinista Nicaragua. In J. Fairley & D. Horn (Eds.), *I Sing the difference: Identity and commitment in Latin American song.* Liverpool: IPM.

Scruggs, T. M. (2004). Music, memory, and the politics of Erasure in Nicaragua. In D. Walkowitz & L. Knauer (Eds.), *Narrating the nation: Memory and the Impact of Political Transformation in Public Spaces.* Durham/London: Duke University Press.

Seeger, A. (2008). Social structure, musicians, and behavior. In D. Olsen & D. Sheehy (Eds.), *The garland handbook of Latin American music.* New York/London: Routledge.

Shaw, L. (1998). Coisas Nossas: Samba and identity in the Vargas Era (1930–1945). *Portuguese Studies, 14,* 152–169.

Shaw, L. (2005). The Nueva Trova: Frank Delgado and the survival of a critical voice. In M. Font (Ed.), Cuba today: Continuity and change since the Período Especial. Bildner Centre for Western Hemisphere Studies.

Shaw, L. (2008). Los Novísimos and cultural institutions. In M. Font (Ed.), Changing Cuba/changing world. Bildner Center for Western Hemisphere Studies.

Slonimsky, N. (1946). *Music of Latin America.* London/Toronto/Bombay/Sydney: Harrap.

Smilde, D. (2011). Introduction: Participation, politics and culture – Emerging fragments of Venezuela's Bolivarian democracy. In D. Smilde & D. Hellinger (Eds.), *Venezuela's Bolivarian democracy: Participation, politics, and culture under Chávez*. Durham: Duke University Press.

Smith, D. (2010). *A corpus-Driven discourse analysis of transcripts of Hugo Chávez's television programme 'Alo Presidente*. PhD thesis submitted to the University of Birmingham

Stoneman, R. (2008). *Chávez: The revolution will not be televised : A case study of politics and the media*. London/New York: Wallflower Press.

Street, J. (2006). The pop star as politician: from Belafonte to Bono, from creativity to conscience. In I. Peddie (Ed.), *The resisting muse: Popular music and social protest*. Aldershot: Ashgate.

Sweeney, P., & Rosenberg, D. (2000). Venezuela: Salsa con Gasolina. In S. Broughton & M. Ellington (Eds.), *World music: The rough guide* (Vol. 2). London: Rough Guides.

Syliva, R., & Danopoulos, C. (2010). The Chávez phenomenon: Political change in Venezuela. *Third World Quarterly, 24*(1), 63–76.

Taffet, J. (1997). My Guitar is not for the rich: The new Chilean Song movement and the politics of culture. *Journal of American Culture, 20*(2), 91–103.

Tandt, C., & Young, R. (2004). Tradition and transformation in Latin American music. In J. King (Ed.), *The Cambridge companion to modern Latin American culture*. Cambridge: CUP.

Taussig, M. (1997). *The magic of the state*. New York: Routledge.

Throsby, D. (2010). *The economics of cultural policy*. Cambridge: Cambridge University Press.

Tinker Salas, M. (2009). *The enduring legacy: Oil, culture and society in Venezuela*. Durham: Duke University Press.

Torres, H. (2010). Identificar el patrimonio es un elemento clave para conservarlo Correo del Orinoco, 10 September 2010 http://www.correodelorinoco.gob.ve/comunicacion-cultura/hector-torres-identificar-patrimonio-es-un-elemento-clave-para-conservarlo/. Accessed 12 Dec 2010.

Torres, R. (1980). *Perfil de la creación musical en la nueva canción chilena desde sus orígenes hasta 1973*. Santiago: CENECA.

Torres, R. (2002). Singing the difference: Violeta Parra and Chilean song. In J. Fairley & D. Horn (Eds.), *I sing the difference: Identity and commitment in Latin American song*. Liverpool: Institute of Popular Music, University of Liverpool.

Turino, T. (2003). Nationalism and Latin American music: Selected case studies and theoretical considerations. *Latin American Music Review, 24*(2), 169–209.

van Dijk, T. A. (2001). Critical discourse analysis. In D. Schiffrin, D. Tannen, & H. E. Hamilton (Eds.), *The handbook of discourse analysis*. Malden: Blackwell.

Velasco, A. (2011). We are still rebels: The challenge of popular history in Bolivarian Venezuela. In D. Smilde & D. Hellinger (Eds.), *Venezuela's*

Bolivarian democracy: Participation, politics, and culture under Chávez. Durham: Duke University Press.

Verdery, K. (1999). *The political lives of dead bodies: Reburial and post-socialist change.* New York: Columbia University Press.

Vianna, H. (1999). *The mystery of samba: Popular music and national identity in Brazil.* Chapel Hill: University of North Carolina Press.

Villazana, L. (2013). The politics of the audiovisual cultural revolution in Latin America and the Caribbean. In T. Muhr (Ed.), *Counter-globalization and socialism in the 21st century: The Bolivarian alliance for the peoples of our America.* London/New York: Routledge.

Wade, P. (2000). *Music, race and nation: Música tropical in Colombia.* Chicago: University Of Chicago Press.

Webber, J., & Carr, B. (Eds.). (2013). *The new Latin American left: Cracks in the empire.* Lanham: Rowman and Littlefield Publications.

Weisbrot, M. and Ruttenberg, T. (2010). Television in Venezuela: Who dominates the media?. http://venezuelanalysis.com/analysis/5860. Accessed 29 Jan 2016.

Whisnant, D. (1995). *Rascally signs in sacred places: The politics of culture in Nicaragua.* Chapel Hill: University of North Carolina Press.

Wickham-Crowley, T. (2001). Winners, losers and Also-rans: Toward a comparative sociology of Latin American Guerrilla movements. In S. Eckstein (Ed.), *Power and popular protest: Latin American social movements.* Berkeley/London: University of California Press.

Wilbur, D., & Zhang, J. (2014). From a false messiah to just another Latin American dictator: Analysis of U.S. mainstream news media's coverage of Hugo Chavez's Death. *International Journal of Communication, 8,* 558–579.

Willner, A. R. (1984). *The spellbinders: Charismatic political leadership.* New Haven: Yale University Press.

Wilpert, G. (2013). Venezuela: An electoral road to twenty-first century socialism? In J. Webber & B. Carr (Eds.), *The new Latin American left: Cracks in the empire.* Lanham: Rowman and Littlefield Publications.

Wisotzki, R. (2006). *El pueblo es la cultura: Conversación con Farruco Sesto, Ministro de la Cultura.* Caracas: Fundación Editorial el perro y la rana.

Wright, W. (1990). *Café con Leche: Race, class and national image in Venezuela.* Austin: University of Texas Press.

Zapata, S. (1992). *Alí Primera: Que mi canto no se pierda.* Caracas: Euroamericana de Ediciones.

Zolov, E. (1999). *Refried Elvis: The rise of the Mexican counterculture.* Berkeley: University of California Press.

Zúquete, J. (2008). The missionary politics of Hugo Chávez. *Latin American Politics and Society., 50*(1), 91–121.

INDEX

Liga Socialista (Socialist League), 68, 94, 150, 155
martyr, 92, 105–9, 150
live performance, 72, 76, 87, 96, 101, 170
Movimiento al Socialismo (Movement towards Socialism, MAS), 66
'outlaw' status, 73, 83
persecution of, 48, 83–7, 104, 105, 150, 179, 182, 184, 198
poverty, narratives about, 56, 75, 100, 102, 132
precursor of Bolivarianism, 2, 161, 169, 178, 181, 194, 197, 198, 202, 210, 211, 213
prophet, 132, 155, 181
rejection of mass media, 192
rejection of oil industry, 36–7
rejection of material wealth, 150
resistance to *Puntofijismo*, 112–16, 134
Romania, 63
state persecution, 48, 83–7
study in Europe, 63
Universidad Central de Venezuela (Central University of Venezuela, UCV), 57
YouTube discussion fora, 128, 197
Primera, Alí Alejandro, 77, 89n7, 194
Primera, Florentino, 192, 194, 195, 204n19
Primera, Juan Simón, 194, 195
Primera, Ramiro, 77, 89n7, 96
Primera, Sandino, 67, 103, 194, 195
Prisioneros, Los, 40
private media, 23n15, 76, 161, 183, 190, 192, 193
Proceso, El, 138, 155, 156, 162, 163, 169, 170, 176–82, 184–6, 191, 194, 200
'Protest song', 13, 27, 33, 36, 48, 60, 61, 102, 207, 208

prosperity (illusion of), 50
Puebla, Carlos, 56
Pueblo (newspaper), 27, 92, 127, 133, 134, 156, 186, 190
Punto (newspaper), 61, 62, 64, 66, 67, 72, 73, 75, 81

Q
Quilapayún, 35
quinquenio gris, Cuba, 160

R
racism, 12, 51, 87, 132, 200
Radio Caracas Televisión Internacional (RCTV), 191, 203n18
Ramírez, Sergio, 150, 158, 159
ranchera, Mexico, 28
Rangel, José Vicente, 66, 67, 97, 98, 122, 123, 138, 155, 156
recognition, 19, 21, 41, 68, 139, 144, 147–9, 163, 171, 177, 178, 181, 183, 184, 211
representative character, 172, 176, 182, 184–6, 188, 202
Robeson, Paul, 107
Rodríguez, Jorge, 98
Rodríguez, Lanz, 149
Rodríguez, Lil, 76, 177
Rodríguez, Luis Cipriano, 14
Rodríguez, Osvaldo, 28
Rodríguez, Silvio, 33, 34
Rodríguez, Simón, 6, 120, 175
'Ruperto', 62, 63, 115, 128, 129, 131, 136n11

S
Salazar, Rafael, 83, 91, 103
Salvador, El, 55, 82, 86, 131
samba, 9

CPI Antony Rowe
Chippenham, UK
2017-01-26 13:00